The
Manitou Bell

The Manitou Bell

Kenn Amdahl

Clearwater Publishing Company, Inc.

845 Dorris Street

Eugene, OR 97404

The Manitou BelL

Copyright Kenn Amdahl 2023

All rights reserved

ISBN 978-1-7372524-1-2

Printed in the United States of America

First printing Spring, 2023

Acknowledgments

Thanks to my family and friends who endured years of my whining while this book resisted being birthed. Extra thanks to those who had to read some or all of it over the years in various stages of disrepair. Special thanks to those who read the whole thing more than once and provided gentle suggestions. I probably should have heeded more of those. This select club includes Cheryl Amdahl, Paul Amdahl, Scott Amdahl, Joey Amdahl; and author-friends Regan Eberhart, Liz Hill, and Stan Swanson.

Thanks to Gabriella and Bella for the magic of getting to play with a toddler.

Most of the photos at the end of the book are very old, beyond copyright dates. I mostly snagged them off the Internet and don't know who to credit. If you have rights to one of these photos and are unhappy I used it, just let me know and I'll remove it from all subsequent printings.

Photo of "Stars over Bear Lake" on the cover by Mikaela Ruland, used with her permission. I used a small portion of this wonderful photo. You can see the whole thing (including the stars reflected in the lake) at the website of Colorado National Park Trips (https://www.mycoloradoparks.com/photos/rocky-mountain-sunrise-sunset-night-photography/.)

Photo of a young Frank Herbert Whiting in Alaska. Thanks to:

Sandra Johnston / Library Asst. II
Alaska State Library Historical Collections
PO Box 110571
Juneau, AK   99811-0571

Timothy Murphy. Photo— Artist's conception in oil in Town of Fulton History Local History Sec. IX History Room. Middleburg Library, Mohawk Valley Library System, NY

Photo of Jim Baker— Wyoming History association: https://www.wyohistory.org/encyclopedia/jim-baker-frontier-scout

Photo of Westminster University, later called Bellevue College, then Pillar of Fire. Westminster, Colorado.— Westminster Historical Society, Westminster, Colorado

Frank Herbert Whiting house, Westminster, Colorado photo from 1890s — Used by permission of the Westminster Historical Society and the Whiting family.

picture of a goat with one brown ear:
https://www.centreaudiovocal.com/

Blog post about Ethyl Smyth written by Christopher Wiley
https://blog.oup.com/2014/05/facts-dame-ethel

Interview with Ethyl Smyth (link from above blog post)
http://www.bbc.co.uk/archive/suffragettes/8314.shtml

Jeff Smith (Jefferson "Soapy" Smith's grandson), author of *Alias Soapy Smith*. Used with his permission

Photo of George Cherrie, Teddy Roosevelt, and crew at the end of the River of Doubt trip. Found because of Candice Millard's delightful book, "River of Doubt"

Photo of Frank Herbert Whiting as an older man, thanks to:

Sandra Johnston / Library Asst. II
Alaska State Library Historical Collections
PO Box 110571
Juneau, AK 99811-0571

I took the photos of my dogs and our house in the 1950s. The picture of the house from the north in the 1950s was in a box of my old family photos. Maybe I took it, but it might have been my sister Ruth, later Ruth Halsted, now deceased.

The Dark Horse

In the cool, in the cool of the evening wind
With the stars—all the stars— gaily sparkling
Then we ride, yes we ride,
Through the fields and trees
On a horse who ignores all the ghosts he sees.

All the trees—shadow trees— flashing past our eyes
Are alive—quite alive—and their songs are wise
As they dance, leap and dance, most seductively
But our horse keeps his course through their revelry.

Is it far, very far, 'til we reach the town?
No my dear, it is near, up that hill then down
Close your eyes, sleepy eyes, yes of course you may
For our horse, mighty horse, surely knows the way.

—Kenn Amdahl

"The past never really leaves us. It is the sound of a distant bell, forever diminishing, but never completely silent."

The old house a few miles north of Denver in the 1950s.
View from the north

Chapter 1

Charles tiptoed down the hall carrying his sneakers. In the dark, it was difficult to avoid stepping on the spots where the tired old floorboards squeaked. Pausing in front of his parents' bedroom, his hand rested on the doorjamb to maintain his bearings. They weren't in there; his mother left early to visit his father in the hospital before work.

Holding his breath, he crept past Raymond's bedroom. His older brother snored loudly and Charles smiled in the darkness.

The stairs were easier. If a person stepped only on the far left and far right where the wood hadn't been worn down by seventy years of use, they wouldn't squeak at all. A bookshelf lined the left wall, full of dusty old books that came with the house. His fingertips touched them fondly for a moment. A book fell over with a loud thud and Charles froze. That would be the Latin textbook from 1890. In his capacity as an eleven-year-old scientist, the mysterious Latin words appealed to Charles. Scientific names were always in Latin. Beyond that, in fairy tales the magic words were also Latin. In his role as budding magician, he had copied several of the cool ones from the book in hopes he'd discover a magic one. He touched the shirt pocket where he kept them.

That Latin text was always the one that fell over, as if some invisible hand pushed it. Books that fell by themselves —plus the groaning of an old house settling and complaining in the wind— convinced all his friends that the house was haunted. But not Charles. He believed in science, and he wanted to believe in magic. But there is no such thing as ghosts.

Once downstairs, he quietly unlocked the front door, walked through the porch, and sat down on the steps leading to the ground. He talked softly to his dogs while he put on his shoes.

"Sorry, Fritz," he whispered. "I'm off on a scientific expedition this morning to collect specimens for the museum. You too, Keisha." His Shepherd/Husky dogs stood against the wooden fence to their pen, wagging and smiling with enthusiasm. "I know you want to, but if that jackrabbit is around again, you'd be off chasing it and I'd never get you back. Maybe next time." The dogs pushed their noses against his hand, competing for attention. "Did you know that jackrabbits have been known to attack rattlesnakes? They're so quick they bite it then jump away from the strikes. You guys are tough, but there's no reason to go looking for trouble." He scratched their ears, then headed for a patch of sunflowers blooming sixty feet from the house, an area that always harbored interesting bugs. Armed with a digging stick like any good scientist, his expedition party of one crawled into the patch of sunflowers. Thick stalks and big leaves loomed high above him like a primordial jungle and framed patches of robin's-egg-blue Colorado sky. Yellow flowers the size of softballs twisted to face the eastern sky as it lightened, ready to warm their faces in the morning sunlight.

He began his excavation of the site the way any professional field biologist would, by scraping at the hard dirt with his stick looking for bugs and worms. One interesting rock that might be petrified wood got set aside for future study. Several pill bugs and grasshoppers were noted. Then the stick struck something hard; probably a dinosaur bone or Etruscan lamp or maybe a new species of turtle that burrowed into dry dirt. Scraping away more dirt revealed a metal object, bluish-green in color and obviously old. Surely a fossil to be cataloged and reported back to headquarters. He began digging with increased enthusiasm.

To his immense surprise, the stick unearthed an old bell, about the size of a pear. It was weathered and corroded, with no clapper inside it. From the bluish patina he guessed it had some copper in it. He tapped it with his fingernail but it only made a dull thud.

The metal felt cool in his hand as he rubbed the larger clumps of dirt off it. Why was an old bell buried in the middle of a patch of wild sunflowers? Had someone lost it? Was it valuable? Could science unravel the clues and explain it? He picked up a small, white stick, about the size of a finger. Probably a finger-bone from whoever owned the bell before, he thought. Yes, almost certainly an old bleached bone. Maybe a wizard's bone. He struck the bell but it sounded dead as a stone.

He sat back to think. The sun rose hot in the sky, his brother would have already left for summer school. Charles was completely alone, just like he preferred when solving a puzzle

Maybe this was something that would respond to magic. With a burst of excitement, he remembered one of the words on his list.

"Surgit!" he said boldly. "Wake up! Surgit!"

The bell did not change in any way. When he tapped it, it clunked. He scraped more clay from it and, using only two fingers, held the bell by its tiny handle. This time when he struck it a clear musical note hovered in the air like a hummingbird, distinct and pure. Whether the transformation was caused by science or magic or dumb luck, Charles shivered with sudden glee as the sound faded to silence. He struck the bell a bit harder, very scientifically, to determine if the sound would sustain even longer. "Surgit!" he said again, just in case.

On this sleepy morning the slowly diminishing tone was music; that single note a little symphony with themes and harmonies woven from a simple decrescendo.

He sat cross-legged holding the bell at eye level, entranced by its effortless tone when a dark image fluttered into his vision just beyond the bell. A huge black dragonfly with wings as long as his thumb flew in place for a moment, a statue in the air, then settled on the leaf of a sunflower plant two feet from his face. Charles could see the many facets on its two big eyes. It's watching me, he thought. Veins wove a webbed pattern on its transparent, iridescent wings; sunlight gleamed on the black armor of its back.

The dragonfly was listening to the bell! Charles was sure of it. When the bell's bright tone faded completely, he struck it one more time, a bit softer now to avoid frightening the strange audience.

Nature produces no sound a dragonfly might mistake for a bell. Nothing that means food, or safety or warmth or companionship. Like Charles, the bug was listening to something beyond its experience, a pure, beautiful tone with no practical benefit. Unless it had landed there by sheer coincidence, he thought, chastising himself. A scientist does not jump to quick assumptions. Not even a very young scientist. Not if they're serious, like him.

Then a second dragonfly landed. It perched as still and quiet as a monk at prayer, and listened to the dying musical tone. Like the first insect, it clutched a sunflower-leaf pew with all its tiny clawed hands and watched the boy. The air around them was charged with a primitive, cross-species bonding, the communion of congregants who speak different languages yet are moved by the same pipe organ.

Sudden movements frighten wild things, so Charles reached toward the dragonfly imperceptibly slowly, his index finger curved invitingly. "I'm not going to hurt you," he whispered. "Come on, little buddy. Why don't you step onto my finger?" Amazingly, the insect did not fly away, although it flapped its cellophane wings apprehensively a few times. When Charles' finger touched the leaf, the dragonlfy cautiously stepped aboard. Its tiny claws clutched his skin like surprisingly strong little fingers. Charles lifted his hand closer to his face. Kid and bug stared nervously at each other. It was a hypnotic sensation. Maybe some sort of science could explain the experience but Charles couldn't think of any. No, what it felt like was magic.

The sound of a dry weed crunching only a few feet away startled him away from music and magic. Charles froze in place; the two dragonflies helicoptered away. Someone was out there. His private sunflower forest concealed him but also prevented him from seeing the intruder. His heart began thumping loudly in his chest and his mind raced. Maybe it was an animal; if so, the crunch of the weeds indicated it was large. Could a bear have wandered down from the mountains, twenty miles away, and found its way here? More likely a cow from some farm. Should he stand up and yell? Chase it away?

He kept perfectly still, listening. Had he imagined the sound? He often watched predators: aggressive fish in his aquarium, his cat Lucy stalking a sparrow, and the little lizards he kept as pets. His horned toad Bumps often sat motionless for a long time, staring at a bug that was too smart to move. Eventually, the bug twitched and the lizard struck, quicker than sight. In an instant, Bumps would be chewing on the impatient ant or cricket.

Moving slowly and carefully, Charles crept on hands and knees toward the edge of the sunflower patch.

At first he saw only the four legs of a large animal and thought "elk," despite knowing elk rarely venture down from the mountains. Pushing aside a leaf, he saw it was actually a gray horse with large brown spots on its hind quarters. The horse stood still as a photograph.

Sitting motionless upon the horse was a woman dressed in strange old clothing, an outfit a crazy person might wear on Halloween. Her costume made it hard to guess her age. A band of black paint covered her eyes like a mask, and her cheeks were streaked with horizontal white lines. Thin red lines meandered aimlessly down her forehead and cheeks as if she were bleeding. Long black hair flowed wildly down her back with huge feathers protruding at crazy angles. She wore a soft tan leather outfit like the Indians Charles saw on TV westerns; a black cape covered her shoulders and back. A necklace of white bones and claws covered most of her chest. On top of that, several small dead birds were tied together to dangle from her neck like another necklace. Their stench wafted down to Charles and he nearly gagged. When she moved, the bird carcasses jiggled like jewelry creating the sad and creepy illusion of life.

Her eyes frightened Charles the most; they didn't have irises or pupils or any color at all. The entire surface of her eyeballs was a milky white, as if covered by some membrane. Clearly she was blind but she did not seem confused. She raised her face to the sun like a sunflower and nodded slowly. Charles's horned toad loved radiant heat on its face, too, he thought. She inhaled deeply, as if she'd been confined indoors for a long time and relished tasting fresh air again. Lowering her face and turning until she was almost facing Charles directly, she stared in his general direction, cocking her head slightly to one side, listening. He knew she couldn't see him, but he shuddered at her blind attention.

"I am Sapania," she said loudly. "Bride to the porcupine man and weaver of the buffalo-sinew rope. I live with the Arapaho family near the Creek of Boulders. I have ridden a buzzard to the sky and back." She paused, then nodded as if he'd replied. "You have my bell," she said. "Give it to me."

Her voice was younger and softer than he expected, but she remained completely terrifying. Charles' mind raced. She knew he was there, she knew he'd found the bell; there wasn't much point in pretending. And yet, with no other options, he decided to try.

"What bell?" he answered innocently. It wasn't a lie, it was just a question. Sapania's head pivoted toward him and she nudged the horse with her knees. The beast took a few steps in his general direction. She continued speaking.

"It was the white priest-man's bell. He gave it to me."

She couldn't know about the bell, it had obviously been buried for a long time. She must have heard him ring it and was making up a story. A crazy, disjointed story. The weeds would not conceal him for long if she rode any closer. He needed to do something.

"Could you describe your bell?" he asked. His voice trembled in a high register. He should have tried to lower his voice, make himself sound bigger and stronger but it was too late for that now. It was a mistake to have said anything at all. She was tracking him by the sound of his voice. He needed a plan.

The hint of a smile danced across Sapania's face as she reached one hand down to her waist, moving as slowly as a snake stalking a mouse. She pulled out a knife, rusty but with glints of bright metal. It was as long as Charles's forearm.

"Fear glows around you like the sun on a thunder cloud." Sapania's voice was strong and persuasive, like a preacher on TV or a magician proclaiming loud incantations. It had a rhythmic, seductive quality. You wanted to believe what she said, even if the words didn't make sense. "Lightning flashes from your weakness, but you have nothing to fear. Simply do as I ask. You think I do not see? You try to hide in silence like the baby deer, but you cannot hide. The clouds will pass away from my eyes and I will see you clearly. You have one chance to live. Give me the bell."

The horse took another leisurely step toward Charles. Sapania swiveled her head from side to side, sniffing loudly as if she could locate her prey by smell. A meadowlark whistled in the distance. The woman raised the blade up to her shoulder, poised to throw it like a dart. The fact that she was blind was no comfort. If she threw that thing in his general direction there was a chance she'd hit him by random dumb luck. He kept quiet.

"I waited until priest man's breathing stopped— that was my gift to him. Then I pulled my arrows from his back and took the bell that hung around his neck. I rescued his horse as a kindness. Sadly, it had lost its caretaker. I call her Flatpipe."

Charles' eyes grew wide. This woman was insane and obviously dangerous. He needed to get out of there. The woman continued.

"The bell was his gift to me. Fair deal. Then the Trickster-coyote stole it from me while I slept. Coyote disguised as the magical card player in Denver City clothes. Today I woke and heard it again. I looked through the hole in the turnip and saw the treetops, so far below they looked like grass. At first I was confused, I admit that, but the bell called to me, the wind told me the way and I have returned. Do not try to hide it from me!"

The horse did not walk directly toward Charles, but into the weeds a few feet to his left. The woman didn't know exactly where he was, at least not yet. She leaned her head back and spoke loudly, as if praying to the clouds.

"I speak to the moon!" Sapania shouted. "The snake and the raven sing with me! Beneath the stars, we devour the soft and slow! I shall ring the bell. Only me."

Moving stealthily, Charles picked up a rock about the size of a baseball. Sedimentary, he thought, noticing the layers. Maybe shale... he stopped himself. This was not the time to classify stones. He threw the rock as hard and high as he could off to the left. It crashed into some dry weeds and Sapania spun her head in that direction. The crash and rattle of the weeds was followed immediately by an explosion of wild activity where the stone landed. The stone had nearly struck a jackrabbit and now the frightened hare leapt from its hiding place in a flurry of tan fur and churning legs. It ran in leaping bounds faster than Charles's eyes could follow and he could not believe the lucky diversion. The woman swung around to focus on this new commotion. A jackrabbit's leaping zig-zag style makes it nearly impossible for even a good hunter to hit with a rifle. Once bounding away, they are safe from most human predators.

But not from this strange woman. With reptilian quickness, her arm straightened and the knife flew from her hand as if shot from a gun and struck the rabbit with a thunking sound in mid-leap. The impact flipped the animal three feet into the air, squealing and screaming, tumbling helplessly. When it landed, it kicked up dust as it squirmed desperately, whimpering like a child. It tried to crawl away with the knife protruding from its side. With one side of its body paralyzed, it only managed to move in a clumsy, bloody circle.

Sapania nudged the horse with her knees and it sauntered over to the franticly dying rabbit. She grabbed the horse's mane with one hand and leaned over, her legs grasping round its belly like an octopus hugging its victim. The horse didn't pause its slow walk while she snagged the rabbit in her free hand and pulled herself back up. She retrieved the knife from the rabbit's shoulder and shoved the animal, still squirming and squealing, into a brown cloth bag. The sight of the bag twitching and jerking on the horse was as horrifying as watching it being impaled but Charles could not pull his eyes away. The bag with the rabbit looked like some alien creature, wormlike and featureless, struggling against a foreign gravity or a deadly atmosphere, writhing in agony with no hope of surviving.

Sapania ignored it. She raised the knife, still wet with blood, to her face and smelled it the way a child might inhale vapor rising from a fresh, hot apple pie. She nodded with satisfaction, then carefully licked the blood from the knife until no trace remained.

"The bell belongs near my heart, as the trout belongs in sparkling water," she said loudly. She was no longer looking toward Charles; maybe she'd lost track of his location. "It was a gift. Do you understand gifts?" She tried to goad Charles into responding so she could locate him again. Charles resisted the impulse to leap up and race away. He would not make the jackrabbit's mistake. If he remained perfectly still and quiet, maybe she couldn't find him.

"I like the priest-man's jewelry," she said, her tone suddenly friendly, even flirtatious. "A pretty toy should be with a pretty lady. Give it to me and you may live. That's a fair deal." She paused. Charles didn't move. It didn't sound like a very fair deal to him.

Sapania shrugged and waited. Charles held his breath.

A dog barked on the other side of the old white house and the woman snapped her head around at the sound. Charles recognized the voice of his dog Fritz. His pet must have heard the woman and was warning the family of intruders.

Sapania cocked her head to one side, focusing on the sound. "Dog!" she said. "Dog is my favorite dinner! I'll come back for my bell—and for you, young and foolish child. You can't hide forever, for you are a butterfly and subject to the wind." Keisha, the other dog, joined in the barking. The horse walked toward the house. "Don't worry," Sapania yelled over her shoulder. "You won't have to wait long to return my pretty jewelry. Not so long as the priest did."

The dogs continued to bark as she rode toward them. Charles was too terrified to move, so he desperately tried to communicate with the dogs telepathically, like Merlin would. He concentrated as hard as he could. "Stop barking," he whispered. "Sit down and stay! Sit still and be quiet! Sit! Sit!" But his hardest concentration and grandest spell barely affected a fly at close distance or influenced a flipped coin. This was hopeless. The dogs couldn't hear him, of course, and he couldn't yell or run to them without running past the woman. There wasn't anything to do against a grown woman on a horse who could spear a rabbit she didn't even see.

As the barking continued, his panic grew, as well as his disgust at his own cowardice. Then he had a thought— if he ran around the other side of the house, maybe he could beat her to the dogs' pen. He could open the gate and let the dogs loose. If they were running free maybe they had a chance. And if he was there too, maybe three moving targets would distract her. He stood up, swallowed hard. "Sit, guys! Sit and stop barking!" he said out loud and started to run toward the house, toward his beloved dogs.

Then, suddenly the barking stopped.

Chapter 2

In the year 1553, as the noon sun beat down on a dry rolling prairie, four men dismounted from their horses to plot a strategy. They did not notice a group of five children hiding behind a pile of boulders. The children, all dressed in simple clothing of rabbit furs stitched together with tough yucca fibers, had wandered away from their tribe's camp searching for sweet cactus. At the sudden sight of the strange men in smooth clothing and hard hats they whispered and pointed with excitement. They hadn't believed the stories that such men existed.

"Their skin is so white!" a boy named Tayan whispered. "Are they gods?"

"The one in the black robe has much darker skin," the smallest little girl, Kimi, replied. "It is darker than mine. Oh, look at his jewelry!"

A shiny metal crucifix dangled on a leather strap around his neck. He also wore a much cruder necklace below that one, a leather strip strung with several small round bells, each one not much bigger than a desert beetle. In the center of that necklace, just below the cross, hung a slightly larger metal bell, about the size of a tarantula. All the bells had a dusty blue-green tint. When the man moved, the small bells jingled faintly.

"That looks like fresh grass over there." He said and pointed. "You should go get a few mouthfuls while you can." He slapped his gray horse gently on its rump. The horse seemed to understand and ambled off toward the tiny patch of green.

"If you're done whispering to your lover, Esteban, we need to come up with a plan. The Viceroy will not be pleased at our losses."

Esteban smiled. "A hundred conquistadors lost to the sea and the sickness? No, he will not be pleased. But he doesn't know about it yet."

"And nearly that many slaves as well," the third man chimed in.

"The slaves we can replace easily enough," Esteban said, dismissing the idea with a wave of his hand. "The indigenous ones here are no match for our horses and iron blades."

The first man smiled. "Perhaps we should start with our own Moorish slave," he joked. "It's not been so long since you held that title."

The joke did not amuse Esteban. He put both hands on the bluish bell on his chest. "Of course you must do what you think best." He took a step toward the other man, his eyes blazing and his jaw clenched. "Is that what you think best?

A shadow of fear crossed the other man's face and he stepped backward. "A jest!" he proclaimed loudly. "I only jest. You are no longer a slave! You are the new priest of us all, the new priest of this entire miserable land! We have seen your miracles. Surely God speaks through you and we all listen."

"Yes, I thought that was your opinion," said Esteban. He touched one of the smaller round bells and it tinkled softly. "These are copper," he said. "If we can find their mine, the Viceroy will reward us richly. Lost soldiers mean nothing to him, not compared to great wealth."

The children behind the rock could not understand any of these words, but they sensed danger. The oldest, an eight-year-old girl with long black hair and flashing eyes spoke quietly.

"We need to warn the adults," she said. "I will run out by these strangers and lead them to the left. While they are distracted, you all will run back to the right, back to the camp."

"But Sapania, you can't outrun men on their great animals. They will capture you and kill you!"

"Not if I run very fast. I'll lead them to the gully over that ridge. Once I'm inside it, their animals won't be able to climb down the steep sides."

"That's crazy!"

"Everyone stand up and get ready," Sapania said. No one resisted the authority of her young voice. "Tayan, you stand here to my left." Tayan was nearly as old as Sapania but did as he was told. "You're very fast, Tayan, we all know that. Do you see the men?"

He leaned a bit to the left and peered around the rocks. "Yes, they're right over…"

Suddenly Sapania pushed him hard in the back. Tayan stumbled forward toward the men and fell on his hands and knees. He was no longer hidden behind the rocks. The men saw him immediately and pointed.

"Run, Tayan," Sapania hissed. "Run to the gully!"

Tayan was confused. His hands were skinned and bleeding from landing on the hard ground. He looked back toward the other children, his eyes wide with terror and anger at the betrayal.

"Now, Tayan! Run!" Sapania said.

Tayan started running as fast as he could toward the ridge and the gully behind it.

Esteban shouted. "There's our first slave! The Viceroy will be pleased! Do not let him escape!"

The children looked at Sapania in astonishment. "What have you done, Sapania? You have sacrificed Tayan to these white fiends!"

Sapania smiled. "I did not do that," she said calmly. "You pushed him out there. I saw it with these eyes. The elders will not be pleased with you."

"That's a lie!"

"The elders don't believe me capable of lying, you know that. But it really doesn't matter now, does it?" Sapania said, watching Tayan run toward the hill. "The elders will believe it was an accident, that Tayan was careless. Or they will believe you pushed him. I will try to protect you, of course. Otherwise your punishment would be very harsh. Now we must get back to the camp. Tell them whatever you want. It's up to you."

The soldiers quickly mounted their horses and pursued the boy. As they did, the children ran the other direction toward the camp.

Esteban seemed in no hurry. His horse still grazed several feet away. Sapania stayed behind as well, hidden by the rocks, watching the priest.

Tayan disappeared over the crest of the ridge with the soldiers close behind him. Esteban held up the blue-green bell and rang it once. His horse looked up and trotted to him. Esteban climbed on its back, pointed to the soldiers in the distance and closed his eyes.

Then, to Sapania's utter astonishment, both horse and rider disappeared. They simply vanished. Sapania stared at the dirt where the priest and his horse had been. Hoof-prints led to that spot, but none led away. Faint wisps of dust stirred by the horse drifted slowly to the ground.

She looked up to the ridge and frowned. The priest and his horse were walking calmly over the crest, right behind the others. Her face brightened, "He moved from here to there and from then to now," she said out loud. "I will bring our fierce men back to rescue Tayan. And I shall have the magic bell for myself."

Chapter 3

Charles stopped running and froze in place, surprised that his dogs had stop barking. Then his stomach clenched in a hard ball at the realization of what had happened.

"Oh no!" he said out loud. "She killed my dogs!" He forgot about being quiet, forgot about running around the other side of the house, forgot about being afraid. He just ran straight toward the house. I should have reacted quicker, he thought. Those dogs were my best friends and my indecision killed them! If that evil woman was still there, I'd… I'd… I'd at least throw stones at her. Even better, I'd throw stones at her horse and maybe it would spook and panic, carrying her far away while I ran inside and locked the door. Why didn't I think of this earlier, before she found my dogs? Why was I such a coward? He stopped long enough to pick up four rocks each about the size of an egg.

But when he came around the corner of the house, she wasn't there and neither was the horse. Too late, he thought in despair. He looked in every direction, then walked over to the gate to the dogs' area. Fearing what he would see, he looked over the fence.

The dogs were sitting in the dirt very calmly, big dog-smiles on their faces. When they saw him, their tails began to wag, stirring up dust.

"Come here," Charles said and they bounded over and jumped up on the gate so he could scratch their heads. "Good boy, Fritz," he said. "Good girl, Keisha. You heard me, didn't you? I don't know how, but you heard me." He had never been so happy to see anyone, dog or human.

Then he stopped. Had he imagined the entire thing? Was he really crazy like his brother claimed? He wanted to open the gate and get in beside the dogs. He also wanted to scramble up the five wooden steps to the screened-in front porch, unlock the big door to the house and lock himself inside. He rubbed each dog's fur and let them lick his face.

"You coming inside?" Charles jumped back at the sound of his brother's voice. Raymond stood just inside the porch door and laughed at the reaction he'd caused. Charles tried to regain his composure. Raymond opened the porch door and stepped out onto the top step. "Man, you get lost just standing in one place!" Then he looked more carefully at his brother and got more serious.

"What's wrong with you?" Raymond asked. There was real concern in his voice. "You look like you saw a ghost."

Charles looked around several times but no one was there. Months earlier, he had vowed he'd never tell Raymond about any of the weird things he saw but he was so startled he forgot.

"I saw an Arapaho woman on a pony." The words just blurted out of his mouth. "She killed a jackrabbit with her knife…"

Relieved that his brother was back to outrageous fantasies, Raymond laughed out loud.

"I don't know if you're trying to be funny or if you decided you'd really like to try sleeping with snakes."

"It was… she was…" He stopped himself. He knew he sounded crazy. He continued in a quiet voice and tried to sound perfectly calm. "Sometimes they seem so real," he said.

"You know what I think?" Raymond asked helpfully. "I think it's the TV shows you watch. Roy Rogers, Hopalong Cassidy, the Lone Ranger, the Cisco Kid, Red Ryder. You see all these cowboys and Indians shooting at each other and then your brain just keeps the story going."

"Yeah, that's probably right." Charles bit his lower lip to remind himself to stop talking. Sapania wasn't like most of the Apaches and Sioux he saw on TV. Tonto was kind and smart. Cochise was brave and honorable. But Sapania had the cold eyes of a snake and she wanted to kill his dogs.

Raymond stood at the top of the porch-steps leaning against the door. "Don't you remember that movie I told you about? They'll send you to a sanitarium like the one in the movie."

"Yeah, you told me about it a hundred times," Charles said, but that didn't stop his brother.

"They made patients sleep in a pit full of snakes," Raymond said, making his voice eerie and mysterious. "Because that's what they're afraid of and some doctor thought it would cure them. Then they shocked them with huge jolts of electricity. They threw them into tubs of ice water and wouldn't let them out until their skin turned blue. You go there, doctors will prod and poke you with needles. They've probably got lots of other treatments that weren't even in the movie."

Charles knew his brother exaggerated just to frighten him, but he wasn't sure how much. Maybe he imagined things just like Charles did. But maybe not.

"It's not just snakes," Raymond continued in his most professional voice. "They figure out what really scares you and then they force you to do it over and over again. That's supposed to cure you. It sounded very scientific."

"How would they know what would be scary to someone?"

Raymond smiled. "They got ways. All those questions Mrs. Klein ask you? That's what therapists do. She's looking for clues about what treatment you'll get. Might be the snake pit, might be spiders, maybe heights. You don't even have to say it out loud. They got ways of putting the clues together just from how you look when they ask."

"I'm not crazy. Magic is just science they haven't figured out yet. Sometimes I can make things happen," Charles said. Once again, as soon as he said the words he regretted it. Nobody wins an argument they start with "I'm not crazy." But mention of the horrible sanitarium startled him and it was too late, so he plowed forward. "You know, just by thinking."

"Like what? What magic tricks have you actually ever done?"

"Once, I made a fly land on the couch. Sometimes I can make a red stop light turn green. Things like that."

Raymond laughed. "Flies land, red lights turn green sooner or later. There's no magic to that, just patience. You coming inside?" Raymond asked again.

"In a minute," Charles said. "I want to pet the dogs for a minute. Save some peanut butter for me."

"Now you really are dreaming," Raymond said and let the door slam behind him.

Charles returned to petting the dogs as they leaned against the gate. They wanted him to come into their pen and wrestle. That sounded great to him, too.

"There's something else I've got to do first. You guys be quiet," Charles told them. He was tired of being frightened. Tired of being bullied. His caution almost cost his dogs their lives. Never again. It was ridiculous to feel bullied by something that could not be real. He picked up the four rocks he'd dropped to the ground by the gate, swallowed hard, took one more look around, then walked back down to the sunflower patch and found the bell again. "That's it," he said, holding it up to inspect it again. "I don't know why she wants this. But she's not going to get it."

The bell at least was real, but maybe he'd imagined all the rest. No one could protect him from the dream of a witch he'd conjured from dragonfly wings and sunflower pollen. There was nothing to gain by telling his family.

Charles carried the bell into the house, upstairs to his bedroom. At some point it could join his collection of insects and rocks and other interesting specimens. Uncle Kruck would appreciate it, but he didn't want anyone to strike it if there was even a remote chance it could summon the blind woman who threw knives. If its sound had some weird power, bizarre as that idea was, muffling it might also stifle its influence on imaginary warriors and dragonflies. On the other hand, his mother would be home in a few minutes and he wanted to show it to her. Then he got an idea.

He found a piece of bubble gum he'd been saving for a special occasion. The pink rectangle was hard as cardboard; it took several minutes of chewing to soften it. When it was malleable enough, he rolled it between his hands, creating a long pink worm which he pressed inside the bell, from the edge down to the base. He squeezed it flat until it barely made a bump. He tapped the rim of the bell with a fingernail. It only made a dull thunking sound. The idea had worked, but that pink line of gum gave away the whole trick.

He took a pinch of dirt from the cardboard box where his horned toad lived and pressed it onto the pink line of gum. The gum disappeared behind a thin layer of dirt. Now mute, the thing he held was no longer a bell; it was a fossil in a a museum, dirty and useless, interesting only as a historical artifact. Perfect, he thought.

Voices drifted up from the living room. "Showtime," he said and carried the bell downstairs. Raymond was joking with two of his delinquent friends.

"What dumb thing did you do this time?" Raymond asked, staring at his younger brother. "You look even sicker than usual."

"I didn't do anything. I was pretending to be an archaeologist and I found an old bell. I think it was a missionary's."

"I doubt that," Raymond said, grinning at his friends. "Charles imagines things. There's a pretty good chance he's crazy." He turned back to Charles. "Let's see it."

Charles handed him the bell and held his breath. Raymond turned it over in his hands.

"It's sort of shaped like a bell, but that doesn't mean it is one," he said. He tapped the edge with his fingernail just like Charles had done and it made the same dull sound it had earlier. "Not much of a bell sound. I bet it's part of some old car or tractor or something." He held it up to his face and inspected it more closely. "It's really dirty," he said, wrinkling up his face as if it smelled bad. "Smells like old chewing gum."

"Then maybe you should clean it," Charles said. The last thing in the world he wanted was for Raymond to clean the bell, find the bubble gum, scrape it off and ring it. But sometimes the best way to prevent a brother from doing something is to tell him to do it.

"I'm not cleaning your stupid radiator cap! And you should wash your hands. It probably has germs." Raymond handed it back to Charles.

"Well, then you should wash your hands too," Charles said as he took it.

"I'm older," he said. "I've got more immunity."

"You're three years older."

"Three years is a lot of immunity."

Charles set the bell on the mantle above the fireplace. His experiment had worked. The bell had been de-fanged and was safe to show to his mom.

In about an hour his mother got home from work. She was a nurse and had to wear a white uniform every day. She brushed her brown hair back from her forehead and shook her head as if mosquitoes were buzzing around her. She did that every day when she got home from work. Charles never asked what she was shaking off.

"Hi, Charles," she said. Her voice sounded tired. "How was your day? You look pale. Are you feeling all right?"

"I found an old bell. It's on the mantle."

She walked over to the fireplace, took off her glasses, carefully cleaned them with a handkerchief, then looked at the new treasure.

"I bet it was lovely when it was new," she said diplomatically. "I don't want to pick it up while I'm wearing my uniform. It would look good in your museum."

"OK," he said and carried it up to his bedroom.

It's not lying if you simply omit some details, he told himself. The only detail he'd omitted, really, was the part about the scary woman riding up and killing the jackrabbit with her knife. Anyway, she had to be a hallucination. Even if she existed, she was probably in New Mexico by now.

"Maybe I dreamed the woman," he told himself "But the dragonflies liked the bell. I didn't make up that part. It's probably a lucky bell."

There was a small flat tab on top of the bell with a hole in it. Charles got an old shoelace out of a box full of "things that might come in handy some day." He pushed the shoelace through the hole, tied the two ends together and hung the bell around his neck like a necklace. Raymond would mock him for wearing it, but then Raymond would mock him if he wore a million-dollar diamond. His parents would look at each other with concern in their eyes but wouldn't say anything. After a day or two, no one would even notice it.

Wearing the old bell proudly, he went downstairs to eat dinner with his mother and Raymond. Just to be safe, he did not clean the bubble gum that prevented it from ringing. Without its voice, it couldn't summon evil spirits even if it wanted to.

That night, he kept the bell beside his pillow. If lucky charms exist, this bell must certainly be one.

Charles slept well despite all the sounds the house made. Old houses creak and groan when they settle. When the white house on the hill was first built in the 1880s, cowboys rode horses, steam locomotives roared across the prairie, and wolves howled at the moon. Now, seventy years later in the 1950s, wolves and cowboys were gone but a breeze whistling softly through an open window could still conjure frightening images of ghosts and old trains. A creaking floorboard might be a witch escaping her coffin in the attic. Sometimes real coyotes sang in the night, or a hooting owl added its eerie music to the still-sparsely-populated area a few miles north of Denver. After a while, people who live in old houses just accept irregularities. Sitting atop a hill, the view of Denver to the south and the Rocky Mountains to the west seemed more than fair compensation.

Charles went downstairs to find some breakfast.

"So, have you discovered any more Mayan radiator caps?" Raymond came breezing into the kitchen. He stood a foot taller than Charles, with short brown hair and brown eyes. No matter what he wore, he always looked neat and organized. Girls in his class thought he was cute; they said he looked like Elvis and he liked that. Charles never understood what they saw in him. "Or have you given up on archaeology?"

"Not given up," Charles said. "Retired. I sold that last artifact for so much money I won't ever have to work again. Of course, I'll need a butler if you'd like a job."

"Yeah, that sounds like something I'd do. You know, in your dreams. You're up to something, aren't you?"

"Me?" Charles said. "Nah, I've just been busy reading. And I had to clean my guppy tank. They got an infection and I had to treat the water with fish penicillin. You have to treat the water every day for ten days. I don't think I lost a single fish."

"You got a prescription for fish penicillin?"

"You don't need one. All the pet stores sell it."

"That sounds really boring," Raymond said.

"I thought you'd think that."

"I could tell Mom and Dad you need the stimulation of some good daycare," Raymond suggested helpfully. "Learn some hymns, put beads on a leather keychain." He knew that Charles hated the church daycare center. Sometimes, when noisy transients camped below the hill their parents wouldn't let Charles stay home alone and they took him there. "Or maybe you'd like to take a nap with some snakes. Get in practice for your new bedroom." He laughed.

Charles could not always tell when his brother was teasing but his stomach tightened at the thought of either the daycare or the sanitarium.

"My buddies and me are going to the movies," Raymond said. "Maybe your new home with the snake pit will be in it. Should be back by the time Mom get home." Then he was out the door.

Charles needed to ignore his emotions and summon logic the way Merlin might summon a hawk.

The woman had appeared right after he struck the bell; maybe the sound triggered his hallucination and if he repeated the experiment he'd learn to control his reactions. Just like in the movie that he scrupulously avoided. He took a deep breath and decided to clean the bell and ring it again. His body shook at the idea, but he fought down the anxiety. Better to experiment on myself than to let strange doctors with foreign accents do it, he thought.

He carried the bell into the bathroom, dampened an old sock with fingernail polish remover and rubbed the bell until there was no trace of dirt or gum. Before he struck it again, he looked at himself in the mirror.

"Are you sure you know what you're doing?" he said. His reflection looked frightened and confused but didn't answer. His T-shirt was inside out but he didn't care. "Goodbye," he said to the mirror. "At least for now."

He went outside and sat on the top step leading to the porch door. The air smelled fresh, like the sagebrush that grew wild a few feet away. When he finally tapped the bell, it made the same sweet note it made before but no dragonflies or strange women appeared. Hr flipped a coin, trying to persuade it to land heads-up with his mind, but it came up tails. He smiled. Everything was back to normal. Maybe just confronting his fears had dissipated them.

He went inside and poured himself a bowl of Wheaties to celebrate being alive and lucky. His hand shook and he spilled some milk on the table. Calm down, he told himself. It's over, she's gone, you're safe.

A huge fly lumbered around the kitchen like a bumblebee. On a whim, he tried to use magic on it. "OK, buddy," he said to the fly. "Land on the refrigerator. Right over there. Land on the refrigerator." Charles put his hands by the sides of his head like antennae to focus his magical powers.

The fly buzzed out the door and headed into the living room. Charles laughed at his little game. He tried magic nearly every day and kept careful notes, but it rarely worked. Maybe there were contributing factors that remained a mystery. After all, if you dumped all the ingredients for a chocolate cake into a bowl, you didn't get a cake. You had to know all the steps and do them in the right order. Your mixing-bowl of gloppy cake ingredients didn't prove that cakes don't exist.

Carrying a bowl of Wheaties and wearing the bell around his neck, he went up to his bedroom, passing the bookshelves built into the wall beside the stairs. The shelves were full of very old books that Charles tried to read. They contained no incantations, but gradually their old-fashioned language, with all its big words and quaint phrases, began to feel comfortable. They interested no one else; they were his alone.

Maybe today he'd join Penrod and his funny adventures from the 1890s. Every step creaked as he walked up the steps.

He sat on the bottom bed of his bunk bed, balanced the book on his knees, and ate his cereal. The book was so old Thomas Edison might have read it. He smiled at the thought. With no breeze whistling through a window for once, the house was perfectly silent. He sank into his reading and the book completely enthralled him.

A sound snapped him alert. It wasn't a loud sound or threatening, but in the quiet house, after watching for danger for so long and then completely relaxing, it struck him alert like ice water splashed onto his face. It came from downstairs: the creak a floorboard makes when someone steps on it.

Old houses make random noises; breezes play their windows like flutes and their chimneys like oboes. After a while, people subconsciously identify and quickly dismiss most of the sounds. This sound was the bottom step, down in the living room, creaking one time as if someone stepped on it. Charles listened for a moment, just to be cautious, then started reading again.

Then the second stair creaked. He looked up from the book again. The budding scientist went through the possibilities, beginning with the most logical: Was Raymond home early? Did his mother have a day off? Then he turned to the absurd possibilities: Could it be a burglar? Had that woman on the pony gotten into the house? He stared at the open bedroom door and the hallway beyond it, which was the only way to get downstairs. Someone coming up the stairs could easily block his escape.

When the third step creaked, he put down the book and sat up straight. A moment later the next step creaked. Whoever was coming up those stairs was moving very slowly, stealthily. Charles wanted to yell, "Who's there?" but he didn't. If it was a burglar, it would be smarter to hide, not tell them he was here. He considered crawling under the bed or hiding in his closet.

Or maybe I'm hallucinating again, he thought. This was exactly the kind of episode he'd vowed to confront. He should have felt excited, but he hadn't realized how scary confrontation felt. He forced himself to stay on the bed, sitting up, staring at the door.

The next stair creaked, and then the next. Finally, he heard the top step creak. The next sound was slightly different: whoever it was, they were coming slowly—inhumanly slowly— down the hall toward his bedroom. If they went into his brother's room or his parent's room before they got to his door, he would run right past them and down the stairs. He got ready to leap to his feet. If they tried to catch him, he'd swerve and spin and duck beneath their clutches. He planned it all, like a movie running quickly through his mind.

The footsteps kept coming down the hall. They did not go into the other bedrooms. Charles's door was open; in a moment he'd be able to see whoever was in the hall. He swallowed hard and remained still.

The floor right outside his door creaked but there was nobody there. For a moment he just stared. This made no sense. His brain raced trying to think of some explanation. There's no such thing as ghosts. But why would he hallucinate creaking sounds without some terrible ghost or demon to go with them?

The next creak came from just inside his room; he watched the floor move a tiny bit. Someone was walking slowly into his bedroom, but they were invisible.

The young scientist knew that was impossible, but he didn't care. He jumped up and ran out the door, right through whatever was standing there. He ran down the hall and down the stairs. He stopped in the living room and listened. The house was silent again. No one was following him. He forced himself to stand still.

"There's no such thing as ghosts," he whispered. "There's got to be an explanation." He was sure that magic permeated the world, just as science did, but only gullible, superstitious people jump to magical conclusions before they consulted science and logic.

Still, until he figured it out, he preferred to be outdoors.

As he turned to go out, he noticed something. A fat black fly was perched on top of the refrigerator. That detail seemed important, but he could't tell why. He stared at it for a minute, then quickly left.

Chapter 4

Charles walked fifty yards down the hill to figure out the mystery.

The hill had never been plowed or developed; it remained natural prairie, unchanged for hundreds of years, dotted with cactus, tumbleweeds sagebrush, and yucca. He sat in the weeds not far from the abandoned dirt road that served as his family's driveway. No one ever used this north side and tough bindweed vines spread across the compacted clay.

After the green souls of last year's dead tumbleweeds absconded from their stickers-and-stem skeletons, most broke from their roots to bounce and roll miles away, like prickly beach balls spreading seeds. A few remained. Sometimes a breeze reanimated them into apparitions to gleefully whack and startle a daydreaming young scientist. Among these dead skeletons, this summer's green tumbleweed plants clung to their roots between tufts of scrappy blueish-green buffalo grass.

Random wind gusts had rolled a dozen dead tumbleweeds together into a loose pile four feet tall, creating a natural mound with a cave just large enough for an eleven-year-old explorer. It was Charles's private laboratory, or sometimes a spaceship, made of ghost plants. The nest of brittle weeds concealed him from the outside world. He wasn't really hiding, he told himself. There was nothing to hide from. He just wanted a comfortable place to sit and think, and he felt comfortable surrounded by weeds. Simple as that. He tried to think like a scientist.

He sat perfectly still, as he had practiced. Animals notice movement but a motionless human fades into the background. The tactic works well for young scientists, too. A horned toad, snake, beetle, or spider might crawl out of hiding after tranquility has rendered the observer invisible. And when a person remains still, the landscape focusses around him and living things emerge from the background. After he'd settled, Charles could see the lazy buzzing flight of flies and grasshoppers, the quick dash and disappear of a mouse or chipmunk. Scientists understand the value of stillness in nature.

Charles thought magic might be like that, too. It's usually quiet and invisible. Even when it moves— when something completely magical happens— people look up for an instant, startled. They stare, but if nothing else happens they figure it was their imagination and forget about it.

He wondered how many rabbits have looked up for a second when a tiger's tail flicked, then decided they were safe and went back to nibbling the clover? He wondered how many humans have watched magic flick its tail beside them and never known?

The creaking stairs weren't magic or ghosts. It took Charles an hour to figure it out, but he did. Maybe floorboards dry and warp a little over the years. As it warps, the board pulls away from the underlying beam it's nailed to, just a tiny bit. Floors creak when a footstep pushes the nail back into its hole; the squeak is the nail sliding against the wood. After a while, the warped board relaxes back to where it started, pulling the nail with it. It squeaks coming out, just like it did going in. It probably happens every time you step on an old floor: it creaks, then a few minutes later the wood relaxes and it creaks again. Nobody notices because there's usually so much other noise. When Charles walked up the stairs with his Wheaties, every step creaked. A few minutes later, each board relaxed in the exact same order, only this time the house was so quiet he noticed it.

Charles felt proud that he'd figured it out, but was also a little disappointed that it wasn't a ghost. He loved science, but wanted the world to be bigger than mere science.

He started to leave his little weed cave but stopped when he saw a man at the bottom of the hill. The man walked deliberately up the rutted, weedy road, taking precise steps the way a drunk might, trying to disguise his inebriation. Or an old man pretending to be young, hoping to conceal his uncertain gait. Or a crazy person determined to look perfectly normal. Charles ducked back into the little tumbleweed cave.

Trying to be scientific, Charles observed the man carefully. The stranger looked like someone the police would want to question.

Notice details, he told himself. Yes, officer, Charles thought. The stranger was tall and thin, dressed in a dusty tan leather shirt and pants.

Both shirt and pants had leather fringes like the buckskin outfit some TV cowboys wore. A long, dark coat (probably wool, officer, because it looked heavy) covered most of his shirt and reached down halfway to his knees. That seemed odd because it was so warm out. Let's see: soft, flexible shoes, like moccasins. A shabby hat with a big round brim, stained and ripped. A long rifle leaned against his shoulder . His wild hair reached down to his shoulders. That's right sir, a rifle, yes I'm sure.

Hair color, son? the officer in his mind asked. Charles looked more closely. Mostly curly blond hair mixed with gray and red, sir. A short gray beard, unevenly trimmed, a long face that was weathered and as wrinkled as cooked bacon.

Details, Charles thought The stranger's eyes darted back and forth suspiciously. Remember the scar on his cheek. That one side of his face sagged, that the thumb on his right hand was missing. He looked old and confused, except for his eyes. His eyes were a prowling mountain lion's, quick and alert as if looking for something vulnerable and tasty. Charles shivered.

As the stranger got nearer, Charles held his breath. The man stopped and sat cross-legged in the middle of the road, looking out at the view. He pulled a wooden smoking pipe from his pocket, filled its bowl with tobacco, tamped it down with his left thumb and lit it with a wooden match. He shook the match to put out the flame then sucked on the pipe and exhaled a cloud of blue-gray smoke. He nodded and looked pleased, as if it had been a long time since he'd tasted smoke. He's probably been in prison, Charles thought. Maybe recently released. He could be a murderer looking for a new victim, contemplating some gristly crime to celebrate his freedom. Yes, that's what he looks like, Charles decided.

The man reached under the left arm of his coat and pulled out a big handgun. Charles covered his mouth with one hand and tried not to gasp. The man examined the weapon for a minute, holding it up to the light, turning it over in his hands. Then he returned it to the holster hidden under his arm. When he moved the coat, Charles saw a long hunting knife and a hatchet on his belt. The hypothesis that he was a murderer seemed completely reasonable. His intense, darting eyes gave Charles a new thought: maybe this murderer hadn't been released; he'd escaped. And now he needed a place to hide from the police. Ideally, a place where he could take a hostage.

The probable murderer wore a bulky necklace made of huge claws, each one as long as a man's finger, slick and white, curved and very sharp. Someone had dismembered a huge predator and strung those deadly weapons together like pearls.

The insane murderer stared out toward the distant horizon. Maybe I'm imagining him, Charles thought hopefully,

The pipe made a quiet whistling sound when the man sucked on it; the sweet smell of its smoke reached Charles a few times and he fought back a sneeze. Finally, the man tapped the pipe on the sole of his moccasin, emptying ashes onto the dirt. He stood and surveyed the view: mountains in the distance, native prairie on each side of the dirt road.

Then he seemed to snap to attention. He cocked his head to one side, listening. Slowly he lifted the rifle to his shoulder and turned toward Charles.

Can he smell my presence like a wolf, Charles wondered? Did I make some sound? He wanted to run up the hill but his body did not respond to his commands. Besides, Charles thought desperately, this imaginary man could not possibly see him hidden in the weeds.

And yet the man aimed the rifle right at the boy. Charles closed his eyes. There was a bang, much louder than the gunshots he'd heard on TV. I'm dead, Charles thought, but he felt no pain. He opened his eyes. The man was walking directly toward him, the gun now aimed harmlessly at the ground. The dry weeds crunched with every step. Wisps of blue smoke twirled from the end of his rifle. But the man stopped before he got to Charles and and picked up a brown rattlesnake four feet long. He'd shot it in the head. Its body twitched a few times as the man held it at arms length to examine it.

"Your business end ain't doing no more business," the man said to the dead snake. His voice was deep but old and dry. He pulled a long knife from his belt and cut what was left of the shattered head off and threw it far into the weeds. "Still dangerous though," he said. "Best to leave it for the magpies."

Charles kept perfectly still. The man kept speaking to the dead snake.

"Now this rattle," he said. "Flying Fawn thinks they're lucky." He cut off the rattles and set them on the ground. "Might be lucky for someone, but I ain't in the market for luck." He held the rest of the carcass out again and brushed some weed leaf off it. "All I want is the meat," he said. "Good woodsrunner don't need nothing but bullets and salt when he heads out scoutin'. There's always food to shoot."

He threw the bloody snake over his shoulder as if it were a scarf and walked back up to the dirt road. He started trudging slowly back down the way he'd come. As he reached the bottom of the hill, Charles crept out from his hiding place and stood tall to see over the tumbleweeds.

But the man was simply gone. Charles frowned. That made no sense. He was an old man and moved slowly; how could he have hidden himself so quickly? Charles knew that hillside like he knew his own bedroom. Maybe his parents would have an explanation.

He stopped himself. His parents wouldn't think about explanations. They wouldn't like it that he'd seen a rattlesnake. If they heard that a strange man with a rifle had walked halfway up the hill while their son was home alone, they'd make him go back to the daycare center. On the other hand, his parents would be furious if he kept it a secret and they found out.

Unless I dreamed the whole thing, he thought. He perked up a bit at the idea. It made a lot of sense. Sapania wore a strange necklace and had a long knife, too— maybe this was a variation of the same dream.

Charles heard his brother in the distance on the other side of the hill, laughing and shouting with his friends. There wasn't much time to decide what to do. OK, Houdini, he finally told himself. That's how you did it. You fell asleep in the weeds and dreamed the whole thing. No need to tell anyone about a dream.

He walked over to the spot where the man had stood. He picked up the snake's rattles, carefully with two fingers because they still felt dangerous, and shook them gently. It sounded exactly like a rattlesnake. He put them into his shirt pocket. He walked carefully back up the hill to his house, being careful not to rattle.

Maybe he'd seen the rattles on the ground sometime earlier and not consciously realized it. No need to tell anyone about a dream.

Chapter 5

"So, Charles, have you had a good week?" Mrs. Klein asked. She was a thin, bird-like woman who wore brown, conservative clothes. She rarely displayed any emotion, but her eyes were quick and she noticed the smallest reactions in her patients.

"Sure," he answered. "About like every week during summer vacation. Piano lessons, reading books, playing with my dogs. But no school."

She made a little humming sound and wrote something in her notebook. "That's good, Charles. Did anything unusual happen?" She was careful not to emphasize the word 'unusual' but he knew her real question was, "Have you been hallucinating again? Hearing voices? Seeing ghosts?"

He thought about the woman and the jackrabbit and the sound of a child crying in the walls of his bedroom late at night. Oh yeah, and a man wearing a bear-claw necklace shot a rattlesnake and the rattles are in my shirt pocket. But those were things a crazy person would say.

"I found an old bell," he said.

"Interesting. What can you tell me about it?"

"I was digging in the sunflowers," Charles said, suddenly more confident. This was something that happened, that he knew was real. If he could use up the whole hour talking about the bell and his dogs she wouldn't trick him into talking about things he couldn't prove.

"Why were you digging?"

That stopped him for a moment. He couldn't explain that he was on an archaeological expedition looking for Egyptian mummies in Colorado. Or maybe searching for new species of dinosaur that somehow survived ice ages and still live just below the surface of the prairie.

"I was digging for worms and bugs. I have a pet horned toad and he likes to eat bugs and worms."

"Interesting. Tell me about the bell."

"It's very old, bigger than a golf ball but smaller than a tennis ball. It's metal, but it turned a blue-green color from being buried so long. That probably means it's got copper in it. I think it belonged to a missionary who died near my house."

"Why do you think that?"

Charles could feel his face turning red. Mrs. Klein stared at him for a minute, then made another note in her book.

"Maybe I saw a picture of a missionary wearing a bell like this on a chain around his neck. I read a lot of books. I even read encyclopedias. I could have seen it in one of those."

"Did anyone else see the bell?" It was obvious what she was thinking.

"Yes. I showed it to my mother and my brother. Mom doesn't think it looks nice enough to put on the fireplace mantle."

"What did your brother say?"

"He thinks it's not an old bell at all."

"What does he think it is?"

"He thinks it's maybe a radiator cap from some old Model T or something. But I hit it with a stick and it's obviously a bell."

"Your brother didn't think it sounded like a bell?"

"I didn't...he didn't hear it. He just thought it looked like old junk and laughed. He's probably right. But to me it looked like a bell."

"You've certainly got a wonderful imagination," she said. "Have you imagined anything else this week?"

"Imagined? Like in a game?"

"Yes, a game or a daydream."

Charles tried not to think about Sapania or the jackrabbit.

"There was a mouse in the wall of my bedroom." That much was true—something in the wall sounded like a mouse scratching. Until it sounded like a child crying.

"Did you imagine it? Or was it real."

"The scratching was real. I just imagined it was probably a mouse. I tried to picture it like Mickey Mouse, with big ears and a funny laugh. But it could have been a bug or something. I only pretended it was a mouse."

"There's no need to be embarrassed because you have a good imagination," Mrs. Klein said reassuringly. "That's an important prerequisite for many noble careers. Business men and office managers need good imaginations, for example. You might have a wonderful life ahead of you as an office manager." She made a note and glanced at the clock on the wall. "I see we're out of time. I look forward to seeing you next week." She stood up.

Charles left her office in a hurry, feeling he had been released from captivity. He didn't know what an office manager did, or why the job might require a good imagination, but it did not sound nearly as interesting as raising guppies and horned toads.

Chapter 6

It's only a dream, Charles told himself. He couldn't always tell for sure, but tonight he was in a place and time so strange that even asleep he knew it could not be real.

He was inside a small dark tent made of animal skins. A few twigs piled in the center made a pitiful fire; its flickering tongues lit the scene dimly. The air smelled like wet dog fur and woodsmoke. Across from him was Sapania, the woman who had killed the rabbit. Dressed in a simple buckskin outfit without paint of her face or menacing claws dangling around her neck, in the dim light she was no longer terrifying.

She looked in Charles's direction and spoke but she wasn't speaking to him. A young girl sat between them facing the woman. All Charles could see of her was long black hair flowing straight down her back like a liquid.

"My child," the woman said in an urgent whisper "You have the magic within you, just as I do, just as my own mother did. Yours has not yet blossomed but when it does, you must hide it from the men for as long as you can."

"I'm not afraid of the men," the girl said.

"Then you are foolish. Every girl should be afraid of the men. But the girls with magic..." she paused. "It's worse for them."

"I thought you said we were leaving here."

"Yes. Tomorrow, I shall take you far away, to safety. They have no interest in you yet. If they try to stop us I will protect you as well as I can. But even my magic is no match for their brutality. You shall be a woman of the moon just as I am."

"I don't know what that means."

The woman smiled. "You will summon the wind and the fire with your words. The buffalo will sing with you. Men will fear you." She paused. "It's the most you can hope for from them."

"I've learned all the words you taught me. And I shoot the arrow better than any of the boys."

33

"Yes, you have been an excellent student. You already speak like an elder sage. Now I will teach you the meaning of the words. The secret meanings. And I will teach you the magical songs that my mother taught me."

"How long will it take?" the girl asked.

Her mother thought for a moment.

"In two summers you will be a woman. Maybe less. By then you'll be ready to use the gift of your ancestors."

There were footsteps outside the tent. The woman's eyes grew wide,

"It's too soon!" she whispered, "I'm not ready. Listen, my daughter. I must hide. Tell them I've gone to the creek for water. When they leave, we shall escape tonight."

The girl did not react

"Do you hear me, my daughter? Sapania! It is important!" The woman quickly hid beneath a pile of buffalo skins. The tent flap opened and a man stood in the flickering light. He was large and powerful and held a half-full whiskey bottle in one fist. He surveyed the interior of the tent slowly.

Charles was startled, not just by the imposing man but by what the woman had said. The woman he thought was Sapania was actually her mother. The girl in front of him was Sapania, only much younger than the woman who threatened his dogs and killed the rabbit. It's only a dream, he told himself again. Neither the man nor the girl noticed him crouching at the edge of the firelight.

"Where is your mother?" The man spoke loudly and slurred his words.

Charles tried to scoot sideways into an even darker part of the tent. Sapania heard him and turned to look. But although she glanced directly at him, her face gave no hint that she saw him. She did not look anxious or afraid. Just very calm.

Maybe I'm invisible, Charles thought. He looked down at his hand, but it was not there. In fact, he could not see his legs either, or any other part of his body. A surge of terror filled him briefly at this odd phenomenon, but just as quickly he saw the advantage. If he couldn't see himself, these dangerous people couldn't see him either. Reassured, he moved cautiously and silently to one side so he could see Sapania's face better. Then he realized that, if he suddenly became visible again, he would be completely exposed.

"I said where is your mother!" the man shouted, then took a long drink from the bottle. He wiped his lips with the back of his hand.

"She said she was going to the creek for water."

"Your lies will be very painful for you," the man hissed and stepped toward her.

Sapania shrugged. "She said she was going to the creek for water." This time, she emphasized the word 'said' and stared at the buffalo skins her mother hid beneath. The man followed her eyes to the hiding place. In two strides he loomed over it. In one powerful motion he jerked the skins to one side and grabbed the frightened woman quivering beneath it by her arm.

"Remember what I told you, Sapania!" her mother shouted as the man dragged her out of the tent. A few seconds later, the man said something Charles could not understand, Sapania's mother screamed, "No! No!" And then there was only the sound of her limp body being dragged away.

"Goodbye, mother," Sapania said without emotion.

Charles stared at the tent flap, then looked at the girl who remained sitting cross legged on the dirt. He was sure she couldn't see him at all. But if he made a sound, perhaps she would hear, so he remained silent.

Sapania was about his age, with smooth dark skin and eyes so dark he couldn't tell if they were brown or black. She was thin and wiry.

Something moved on the dirt near the tent flap and Sapania and Charles turned in unison to look. Incongruously, a brown-speckled chicken stepped into the tent, looking confused. It squawked and tested its wings a few times, then pecked at the dirt floor.

Did Native Americans keep chickens, Charles wondered? Or was this another fabrication of his sleeping imagination? He remained still.

Sapania very slowly pulled a little leather pouch from somewhere in the shadows and worked it between her fingers. The kernels of dried corn within it made a soft percussive sound as they moved against each other.

The chicken jerked upright in sudden attention at the familiar sound of grain. But it was wary. It took a step toward the girl, then retreated again with a flustered squawk. Sapania kept rolling the pouch slowly between her fingers. She took a single grain out of the pouch and tossed it near the bird. It raced two steps to the corn and devoured it hungrily. A moment later, Sapania tossed another kernel, this time a bit closer to herself. Again, the bird attacked it instantly. Sapania waited while the bird argued with itself, cocking its head to one side, fluffing its wings and pacing nervously.

By the time she tossed a third kernel the chicken was frantic with anticipation. This time the corn landed much closer to Sapania. When the bird raced to get it, Sapania reacted just as quickly. Her arm shot out as fast as a lizard's tongue and she grabbed the bird by its neck. Holding its legs with her other hand, she held the terrified bird on her lap. It flapped and squirmed and grunted. Sapania ignored its struggles.

"My mother says I should sing to the birds and to the sky. Music has the power, she says. Would you like me to sing to you little feather ball?" She began to hum a slow sad song, a song she'd heard her mother sing a thousand times.

Charles could not understand the words of the song, but for some reason he felt very apprehensive. He did not move.

As she sang, Sapania gradually squeezed the bird's neck. The sounds it made became muffled and its wings flapped furiously, its eyes blinked rapidly in terror. After a few moments, it stopped moving.

Sapania looked disappointed

"Not yet!" she said. "That was too quick!" She relaxed her fist around the bird's neck and began working its limp wings together then apart as if to resuscitate it. It worked. After a moment one of its legs jerked, then the other. Sapania held its legs together patiently as it revived itself. The bird flapped its wings frantically and complained but its voice was very weak. Finally it seemed completely alert again, although the sounds it made remained muffled and pained,

"That's better," Sapania said, "Now let's try that again, but this time much slower." She began to sing again as her hand closed around its neck very slowly, almost imperceptibly. As if to remind herself to be gradual,

36

she sang the song much slower too. When the bird seemed ready to lose consciousness, she relaxed her grip just a bit and it gasped for a few seconds before she squeezed again.

"Yes," she said softly and a faint smile crossed her face. "That's right. Death must be enjoyed."

Chapter 7

About midnight, Charles woke to a skittering sound in his room. Moonlight streaming through the window painted a rectangle of light on the floor, softly lighting the rest of the bedroom. Charles smiled. "Settle down, Bumps" he whispered. Horned toads are fierce little prairie dragons about the size of a fist, completely harmless to anyone who's not an ant or grub worm. When his pet scratched at the walls of its cardboard box, the sound was like a drummer using brushes on a snare drum.

The familiar sound that had once kept him awake all night had become comforting, but it still woke him like an alarm clock.

He climbed down from the top bunk to calm his pet. Against the dark silence, the lizard's relentless digging at the cardboard sounded like an Edgar Allen Poe story; a beating heart from a body buried beneath the floor, or the insane scratching of a man bricked up alive behind the wall. Those were not the stories Charles wanted to recall in the middle of the night. He wanted Penrod, or the funny butler Jeeves.

When his reptile calmed, Charles walked over to the window. The distant lights of Denver glowed brightly. A billion stars twinkled above the hulking mountains, black giants silhouetted against the slightly lighter sky. The moon was nearly full, a huge orange globe, a glowing ornament. It was a very peaceful scene.

His family bought the old house in 1951 before Charles was old enough for school. It was a two-story white box, the lower story built of stone blocks, the upper half of shake-covered wood. It stood like a block of dry ice on top of a hill, lonely but defiant, listening to its own memories. It had been built a few years after the Civil War when its neighbors were coyotes and antelopes. It was still surrounded by the same scrappy weed patches that buffalo herds had wandered through.

Sometimes those weeds hid danger. Secretive coyotes roamed at dawn and dusk, cowardly but eager to take advantage of any opportunity. Poisonous black widow spiders lurked in cool shadows, with glistening long legs as disturbing as a witch's clawed fingers and a red hour-glass badge on their bellies. Trap-door spiders—hairy brown tarantula lookalikes the size of a child's hand— hid like trolls in miniature caves in the dirt. But tonight, any danger was hidden beneath the surface of a gentle sea of moonlit weeds.

Fifty feet from the house, a movement caught Charles's eye.

Two men stood talking quietly to each other as if they were on a corner in some big city, not miles from the nearest street light. One was tall and stood stiffly. The shorter man was more energetic and gestured frequently. Both wore long dark coats and old-fashioned round derby hats like some carolers wear at Christmas.

Charles opened the window to listen through the screen, but could only hear bits of their conversation.

The short one leaned over and picked up an animal about the size of a collie. It squirmed violently and the man stumbled a little. As he turned, the moon lit them. The man held a small goat with fluffy white fur, big floppy ears, and a neat little beard of hair beneath its chin. One of its ears was dark brown. The goat made frightened bleating sounds like a baby whimpering.

The tall man pulled a long knife from his belt and stepped toward the goat, holding the knife in front of him. Charles eyes widened as he realized the man was going to cut the animal's throat and kill it, right there in his yard.

The other man stopped him for a moment. "Wait, Slim," he said. "Maybe we shouldn't kill it yet. We could take it back to Alaska."

"Too risky," the tall one said. "Anything could happen. Use your brain, Reverend." He moved in again.

There wasn't time for Charles to do anything. By the time he woke his mother it would be too late. Should he yell at the men through the window? The idea of attracting their attention terrified him, especially with his father in the hospital. But what else could he do?

In that split second, his only idea was a silly one. He could pretend he was a powerful magician, on the ridiculous chance that he secretly was. At least there was no risk in that plan. He pointed at the men as if his finger was a wand and whispered very firmly, "No! I don't want you to do that!"

Obviously, they couldn't hear him from this distance, but he wasn't trying to communicate with sound anyway. He was trying to aim his magical brain waves at them.

To Charle's immense surprise, the man with the knife stopped dead still. He looked around, confused.

Charles pointed again. "No! You will not do that!" he whispered.

The man's head jerked around and he looked directly up at Charles. He pointed straight at Charles's window with the hand holding the knife, as if it was also an imaginary wand. The other man looked up too and froze in place. They had long pale faces and dark mustaches. The simple old hats made them look more sinister. Forcing himself to stay by the window, Charles pointed at them again and whispered, as forcefully as he could, "Release the animal and leave!"

Just then, the goat managed to wriggle free and run on spindly legs into the tall weeds. A cloud passed across the moon and the scene became less distinct— only vague, dark shadows. When the moon emerged, the shadows faded away. Charles stared at the spot where the men had been. There was no one there. His dogs hadn't barked as they would have at real intruders.

The next thing he knew, Charles was waking up on the top bunk and the sun was shining. His horned toad wasn't scratching its box. Just another dream, Charles thought. Still, he dressed quickly and went outside. A few weed stalks were broken in the area where he thought he'd seen the men, but that didn't prove anything. A small tuft of white fur stuck on one of the prickly weeds was equally inconclusive. It could have been there for a year and he'd just never noticed it.

Charles put it into his shirt pocket and walked back inside. Some people share their dreams while others keep them secret. Either way, sometimes secrets develop a life of their own; they turn on you in unexpected and frightening ways. Be careful of the harmless creatures you invite into your most private rooms.

Chapter 8

The house had a screened-in porch that faced south, toward Denver. The porch was raised off the ground four feet; the crawl space beneath it was a rough place with a dirt floor, ideal for storing old tires, tools, and broken lawnmowers. It was exactly the correct dimensions for an eleven-year-old boy and two large dogs. Using bales of straw, Charles's father built a little dog house under there just big enough for two huskies to snuggle in protected from snow and wind. The family referred to "under the porch" as if it were a room, like a "kitchen" or "pantry." The yard near the porch was enclosed with chain link fencing giving the dogs their own safe domain.

Charles loved to sit under the porch inhaling the rich organic smells of straw and dog. It felt like the safest place in the world. No human could sneak up on his large dogs, with their keen hearing and sense of smell, plus the world of dusty old tires and broken tools contained no hint of the supernatural. Sometimes he'd take a book under there and get lost in a distant time or place. Near the back, it was too dark for reading but close to the opening the lighting was perfect.

Leaning against the straw-bale dog house, Charles was reading an even older book than usual: "Ivanhoe," published in 1819. The house's previous owners had left it behind to become part of the random library that Charles sampled. Fritz napped with his massive head on Charles's lap and the boy used the dog's head as a book holder.

One section of Ivanhoe seemed funny. Charles forgot he was in Colorado, forgot he was sitting beneath an old porch and he laughed out loud. Fritz opened one eye lazily, adjusted his head to be more comfortable, and fell asleep again.

"What's funny?"

A child's voice came from the shadows. It startled Charles and he stood suddenly, banging his head on a wooden joist.

"Who's there? Who said that ?" Charles dropped the book and tried to sound intimidating as he took a step backward. "I said who are you? What are you doing here?" His voice was high and thin and his hands shook.

"You were laughing," the voice said, ignoring his questions.

Near the back, in the dimmest corner, Charles could barely discern the outline of a small boy. His hair was dark and his face was pale, but that's all Charles could tell for sure. The sacred kiva had been invaded; the soft voice was as alarmingly out of place as a shiny black spider slowly crawling up his arm would be. His mind leapt to the Arapaho woman. "Where is she?" he yelled.

"Who?" the boy answered.

"The woman on the horse. Is she your mother?"

"Have you seen my mother?" The boy sounded excited. "Is she back? Can you take me to her?"

"What are you doing here?"

"I live here. And so does my mother. But she's not here now."

"Where is she?"

"My family went to Alaska. But they'll be back soon. I'm waiting for them. I thought you knew where she was." He sounded disappointed.

No one had ever invaded the space beneath the porch. There were only a few possibilities.

"Is your family camping near here? Are you traveling with… with the hoboes?" The men who sometimes camped beneath the hill on their travels rarely had children with them but if someone did, it would be easy for one to wander away.

"I don't know what a hobo is. I don't think we're camping."

"So, do you live in one of the new suburban houses down there?" Charles pointed vaguely. New people had started to move into the area and Charles did not know most of them.

"I don't know what suburban means."

"It means... never mind." A kid could live in one of the new developments within walking distance and not know the word. There was one more possibility. "Do you live in a sanitarium? A kind of hospital?"

"I was very sick. I always felt hot and I slept a lot. But I think I'm better now."

Charles thought that sounded like the most likely answer. The little boy probably had delusions just like Charles did and his parents locked him up in a special kind of facility for his own good. Now he'd escaped and somehow managed to find Charles's house and climb in with his dogs.

"Why are you waiting here?" Charles waved at the area beneath the porch. As he stared into the dark corner where the boy sat, his eyes gradually grew accustomed. The boy was obviously alone.

"I like it here. I like your dogs."

The boy in the shadows didn't seem dangerous. But how did he get past Charles's dogs? Maybe a monster or a wizard could fool them, but it was a child's voice, not a monster's. "You're being silly," Charles told himself. Some kids are just good with animals and this little boy seemed harmless enough. Besides, Charles knew what it felt like to have bigger kids bully him. There was no reason not to be kind. And you can't be afraid of everything, Charles reminded himself. You have to be calm. Don't react too strongly, listen to logic.

"What's funny?" the boy in the shadows repeated.

It was a simple question, so Charles answered it.

"These knights are being silly," he said.

"Knights like King Arthur?"

The little boy sat in the corner between a pile of rope and some old tires, staring out of the dark like an owl from a hollow tree. Fritz wagged his tail drowsily in his sleep. Out in the sunlight, Kesha playfully chased a grasshopper. Both dogs ignored the strange kid as if he were a member of the family.

"Yeah," Charles said. "Just like King Arthur only this book is about Ivanhoe. You don't think of knights being funny but sometimes these guys are. My name is Charles. What's your name?"

"My name?" He sounded confused. Maybe he wasn't very smart, which would explain how he got lost and thought Charles's house was his house. Charles had heard that sometimes people who aren't very smart get along well with animals. That could explain a lot.

" My name is Martin," He said the words slowly and carefully.

"I'm pleased to meet you," Charles said.

"I'm pleased to meet you as well," Martin said.

Charles wanted to ask why he didn't go with his family but stopped himself. If he was delusional he would have some story that made complete sense within the delusion. The dogs didn't seem at all disturbed by the little intruder, and dogs have excellent instincts about people. Charles relaxed a little. If the boy was lost and slow, Charles should try to help him get home. The idea of helping this intruder rather than running from him startled Charles, but it did something else, too. It dispelled much of his fear.

"We should get you back to your parents," Charles said. "What are there names?"

"I like King Arthur," Martin said. He sounded sad. "Merlin is my favorite." He paused for a very long time.

Some kids are shy, Charles thought. Maybe if the little guy relaxed a little he'd provide useful information about where he lived.

"Merlin is my favorite too," Charles said. He sat back down and leaned against the bale of straw. "In one story he set up the stones of Stonehenge by using music. He called them the Dancing Stones. But that's not in this book." Now Charles could see the boy more clearly. "Where are your shoes?"

"I only wear shoes to church."

"Don't you get stickers?" Charles's own feet had thick callouses, but he still wore shoes most of the time.

"No. The bottom of my feet are tough. I like the way dirt feels between my toes. Most of the ground is hard but when my father digs it up for a garden it's soft. You have to walk between the rows so you don't hurt a plant." He paused. "I like the squash plants because they have big leaves and they grow so fast."

"I have tough feet too," Charles said. He couldn't think of anything else to continue the conversation. Finally he said, "I like dragonflies."

"Do they listen to you?" the boy asked.

"What?" the question startled Charles.

"Sometimes they listen to me," Martin said. "Do they listen to you?"

"Yeah," Charles said. "Sometimes."

Charles knew he should call the police, or at least call his mother at work. On the other hand, his brother Raymond would be home soon. Raymond liked to be the big shot, he could figure out what to do. All Charles had to do was prevent the boy from wandering off before Raymond took over. But he wasn't sure how.

Finally Martin spoke again. "My mother reads to me. But not in a long time," he said. There was a long pause.

"Would you like me to read to you?" Charles said. Martin didn't respond and Charles thought maybe the boy had fallen asleep.

Then, his voice almost a whisper, Martin simply said, "Yes."

Charles turned back a couple of pages to read him the funny part aloud. It made Charles smile all over again. Martin didn't laugh. When they came to the end of the funny part Charles stopped and closed the book.

"Yes," Martin said softly. "It was quite funny." He said it so seriously Charles almost made a joke but didn't. "I lost Pan," Martin continued. "He must have gotten out of his leash. Have you seen him?"

"No. And by the way, why didn't my dogs bark…" Charles started to ask but didn't finish. Fritz suddenly lifted his head and looked out into the sunlight, instantly alert. Outside, Kesha looked up too. Fritz started wagging his tail slowly, thumping up dust with every beat. Then he rushed to the fence and jumped up against it. With his front two paws on top of the fence, he could just poke his nose over the top. Kesha jumped up beside him. Both their tails wagged enthusiastically.

"My brother must be coming home," Charles said. He scrambled out into the sunshine and looked over the fence. Raymond and some of his friends were at the bottom of the hill, just starting to walk up it. They were too far away for Charles to hear their conversation. "Dogs can hear things four times as distant as humans," Charles said over his shoulder. "And their sense of smell is 10,000 times better than a human's." He turned back to his new friend.

"Why don't you come inside with us, Martin," he said. "I bet we could find some snacks. Maybe Raymond has seen your dog."

But Martin didn't respond.

"Martin?" Charles said. He crawled back under the porch and went over to the pile of rope. Martin was gone. "Martin?" he shouted, but there was no answer.

"Oh well," Charles said to himself. Maybe Raymond would know who the kid was. There weren't many houses in the area and none of their neighbors were rich enough to vacation in Alaska. As Charles started to crawl back outside he noticed an unusual smell, familiar but of place. He inhaled deeply trying to identify it. It reminded him of Christmas.

It was the scent of vanilla. A lovely but incongruous smell near the piles of rusty cans, tangled rope, and bales of straw. Maybe Martin had dropped something that carried that smell. He inhaled again, but the scent was gone. Can people imagine smells? Can they dream them? What experiment could you devise to test that idea?

Suddenly the whole episode felt very strange and Charles shivered. He should figure this kid out himself before he told anyone else. If Martin was a mere figment of his own disturbed imagination, telling people would only worry them. Like the scary man who'd walked up the hill, or the rattlesnake, or the woman on the horse, or the men he dreamed about with the goat…this was another little secret to keep private for a while. Just until he understood. They could all be imaginary.

But if the lost boy was real, Charles was the only person who knew where he hid. He was the only person who could protect him from the dangers of the world or reunite him with his family.

He opened the gate and stepped out of the dog pen.

46

"Hi, Raymond," he said. "How was summer school?"

"School is school," his brother answered. "It's a pain. In a couple of years, you'll see. It gets harder. Have you been reading to the dogs again?"

"Yeah," Charles said. "They think Ivanhoe is funny."

"You're weird," Raymond said and marched up the steps into the porch and then into the house with his friends snickering as they followed behind him.

Charles looked back into the dog pen. "Yeah," he said to himself. "Maybe I am."

Chapter 9

The tip of a knife pressed against Sapania'a neck but she refused to cry out. The man stood behind her, his strong arms wrapped around her like a python and the smell of the his sweat made her want to retch. Even in the dark, she recognized the smell and knew who her captor was. Blue Cloud taunted her with crude grunting sounds, like an animal, squeezing her tightly to him, relishing her helplessness. The girl gauged her chances of pulling free, but the blade was poised expertly above the big blood vessel, the one she used to bleed deer and buffalo when she killed them in the hunt. Even if she pulled away, she would be dead within a few breaths. She had seen it many times.

It might be worth it, she calculated. She had her own knife hidden beneath her clothes and she knew how to use it. The world would be better if Blue Cloud's bones returned to the prairie dust. But the sun had not yet lightened the sky; there might be other men, too many men, and then she would die for nothing but their sport.

"Your uncle says you have the magic, Sapania," Blue Cloud hissed in her ear. "And yet you do not make the skies rain. If you would allow your tribe to die, then your magic is worthless and so are you."

"I've said it before, in Council and before the old women! I do not know the magic to make the skies rain!"

"Your mother did and so do you!"

"My mother died before she could teach me. As you well know." She paused, remembering Blue Cloud's brutality that night. It would not be wise to dwell on that memory. "But my father wanted me to become a warrior first."

"And that skill you have mastered. I have watched you sleep with the bell you claimed from the white priest-man. You fought like a man against the white men, I give you that. You might have protected your mother better than that scrap of hide you called father. He was worthless too."

"He would not have killed a rival in their sleep." She implied the obvious point that Blue Cloud employed the same cowardly tactic to capture the man's daughter tonight, while she slept.

"That's an old story that no one's interested in hearing. We speak now of rain and fresh meat."

"I don't know how to bring the rains."

"Then you shall die."

"Wait!" a man's voice cried out from the dim shadows. It was Sapania's uncle, Two Deers. "What Sapania says is true. It was her mother, my sister, who knew the songs of rain. I heard them a thousand times."

"Then you should sing them yourself and bring the rain," Blue Cloud said angrily.

"I've tried. The songs alone won't work. They must be sung by a witch."

"You just want her alive so you can continue to enjoy her other skills at night in your tent."

"As any man would," Two Deers said with a little laugh. "Perhaps we can come to an understanding? A sharing ?"

"You're in no position to bargain," Blue Cloud said, spitting into the dirt. "But you have given me an idea. You will teach her the songs. If the rain comes, I will let you both live. If not, you both will feel my blade. Until then, the girl sleeps in my tent."

"She is only fifteen," her uncle said, suddenly fearful for his own life. He had not anticipated personal jeopardy and now he panicked. Plus, he was deeply disappointed at the idea of losing his nightly companion. "Sometimes the magic does not appear until they're older."

Blue Cloud maintained pressure on the knife with one hand while his other hand explored the girl's body, squeezing and testing. This time when he grunted the primitive sound expressed appreciation and a new sort of interest. Sapania stood very still. Her uncle had taught her one thing well: girls who resist men will feel pain and their bruises don't heal for a very long time.

"She feels old enough to me," Blue Cloud said. "You have seven days. On the eighth, the prairie will be watered by rain or by blood." He paused, thinking. "But perhaps you will try to leave." His voice brightened as he thought of a new incentive. "The three aunts who raised her. If there is no rain, or she tries to escape, those dusty old women will pay the price too. But this one..." his hand explored her body through the leather vest. "She may live a while longer. If she pleases me."

Suddenly, he pushed her away violently and she fell on the hard ground. He motioned for his men to come closer. A dozen men materialized from the darkness. "We can't trust them here," he said. "Tie their hands behind their backs. And a noose around their necks to lead them by. If she's like her mother, she has tricks."

Blue Cloud rode his horse and his two captors followed on foot. If they faltered or slowed, he tugged on the ropes, jerking them forward. His men rode behind them, snickering and making crude jokes. Blue Cloud led them to a hill a few miles from camp. It was hot and barren, with nothing to recommend it but its own desolation. Below them, they could see the greener valley of cottonwood trees and sagebrush that would become, in a hundred years or so, Boulder, Colorado. Beyond that, to the west, the purple Rocky Mountains stood in majestic contrast to the startlingly blue sky.

This hilltop was stark, dry prairie, part of a near-desert that stretched to the east for hundreds of miles. No matter what direction his captors tried to escape, Blue Cloud could watch them for miles and chase them casually from horseback before launching arrows at their backs. He made a little lean-to of a blanket and sticks to shade himself and leaned back on his elbows.

"Untie them," he told his men. "Then set up camps below the hill and toward the sunrise as well. If they try to escape..." He shrugged. "Well, then do with them what you please. And bring me the bodies when you have finished with them."

He tossed his two captors a single skin of water. "Don't waste it," he said. He thought for a moment. "Take their moccasins," he said. His men obeyed and he tied their shoes to a leather harness on his horse. He whistled a series of short notes and his horse followed the command and wandered away to search the dead soil for dried grass. It would return to its master only when it heard a different, specific pattern of notes.

"The sun rises high in the sky," Blue Cloud said. "Go learn the songs and find your magic. But you…" he pointed to Sapania who still cowered on the ground. "You will be at my tent before it sets tonight. Or I will roast your aunts over my cook fire. Do you understand?"

She nodded slowly.

Blue Cloud lay down in his spot of shade and closed his eyes. His men moved off to serve as lookouts. Sapania and her uncle stood alone.

"He will not be kind and gentle with you," Two Deers said. "Not like I have been."

Kind and gentle? Sapania thought. You nearly killed me four times. Or perhaps it was five.

But, in a grim voice, all she said was, "Teach me the songs."

Chapter 10

Charles did not like to walk past the Pillar of Fire alone. His own house felt comfortably old and spooky, at least during the day, but this place was just creepy. Charles knew it well and usually avoided it.

A half mile east of his house atop the same long hill, the huge building designed to look like a castle loomed. It was made of big red sandstone blocks, with a bell tower that reached six hundred feet into the air. Visible from ten miles away, people used it as a landmark. It was built in the late 1800s as Westminster College. The college failed from the beginning, so the castle and some smaller buildings sat vacant for years. Sometime before Charles was born, a secretive religious group bought it for its own private school, but Charles never saw any students there.

A few old people lived there, but they kept to themselves. The women all wore black dresses with white collars, like nuns. The men dressed like farmers, in old boots, coveralls and heavy shirts. Sometimes, the lonely atmosphere attracted strange transients who had nothing to do with religion or education.

Walking through the old college grounds was the quickest way to Charles's weekly piano lesson at Mrs. Langford's house. Every Tuesday at four during the summer, he dutifully hiked over to her house and stared at notes on a page for an hour while she tried to translate their gibberish into things his fingers should do on the piano keys. It was utterly futile, but his parents liked knowing he was well-supervised and safe at least once a week.

But Charles never felt safe walking there. The bushes, corners, and doorways of the old college created many dark hiding places. Nervous people with careful eyes sometimes lurked in the shadows. A burly teenager might lean in a doorway, smoking a cigarette in a vaguely menacing way.

Charles hurried to his lesson. A man sat on the steps of one of the smaller buildings. He wore faded jeans, no shoes, and an old blue shirt that was frayed at the cuffs. The shirt's buttons weren't matched with the correct holes so one side hung lower. He ran a nervous hand back through shaggy brown hair as if combing it back, then scratched at the dark stubble on his sunken cheeks. His eyes were bright as a robin's and open too wide.

He gestured broadly, deep in animated conversation, but no one was near him.

"It's a complication," he said loudly. "Not a problem. Only a problem if you look back."

Charles detoured a bit from the sidewalk to give him a wide berth.

"It's no use arguing!" the man said. "Not with logic! There isn't any logic! It's a painting that doesn't dry. Go talk to somebody else!"

He looked at Charles, but the boy stared straight ahead and kept walking.

"Him!" the man said, pointing at Charles. "Go talk to him! Both of you! All of you!"

Charles increased his pace. The man stood up and started walking toward him with precise steps, as if evenly-spaced steps were a competition.

"They do things to you," the man said urgently, his voice barely a whisper. His eyes darted left and right. "Evil things. You can't sleep—they won't let you sleep. They talk at you from every side. They confuse you. You need to help me escape."

"I can't help you," Charles said, keeping his distance.

"They say I'm making it all up." The man's eyes widened, then closed down to mere slits. "They say everything is fine. They give you drugs to make you sleep." He laughed, a harsh dry cackle. "But sometimes I don't swallow." He frowned and shook his head sadly. "But they can tell."

"I have to go," Charles said.

The man stared at the boy and his face brightened.

"You hear them too, don't you," he said. "You're just like me. Tell them I'm not crazy. And I'll tell them you aren't. They'll have to understand if there's two of us!"

The man was obviously deranged, but one thing was clear: He imagined things and so they locked him away, just like Raymond said. That much must be true, at least. People who see things no one else can see get locked up in a place that resembles a torture chamber.

"I'm just a kid," Charles told him. "I can't help you."

The man cocked his head to one side and stared at Charles with curiosity.

"You're a child?" he asked.

"Yes, sir."

"Are you sure?"

"Yes. I have to go."

"Are you sure?" he asked again as Charles walked quickly away.

"Are you crazy?" the man asked loudly. "You've got the look. I've seen that look before." He stopped, and tilted his head to one side to peer at the boy. Now he sounded like a professor reading an old poem: "There's a jangling in my brain like bells banging into each other in a storm…" He pointed directly at Charles.

"Are you dangerous?" the man said. "Do you kill people? It's OK, it's OK, it's OK. But sometimes you can't. Can you hear me?"

"Yes, sir, I hear you," Charles said without stopping. He knew he could outrun the man if he had to, as long as he kept a little distance. "I just need to get to my piano lesson so I can't stop and talk."

"Piano,"the mane said carefully. "I know piano. Wrong to burn up the piano. That's the lesson. Don't burn it. You and me are just the same."

"Yes, sir. But I don't want to be late. You have a nice day."

The man kept walking slowly toward Charles with both arms extended in front of him, reaching like a zombie to grab him, but Charles easily dodged him by walking briskly, moving off the sidewalk onto the grass, then back. All his senses were alert. A beetle scurried across the sidewalk, like a car racing to beat a train to a crossing. The grass smelled like it had just been mowed. He glanced over his shoulder. A door to a building behind him opened and two heavy-set women dressed in black and white came out.

"Mr. Peters!" they yelled and started running. They ran clumsily in their heavy black shoes. In a moment they reached Mr. Peters. With one holding each of his elbows, they gently turned him back toward the building. He swiveled his head to look at Charles over his shoulder.

"You've got the look," he yelled. "You can't escape. They always find you. They won't let you leave."

The women steered Mr. Peters carefully toward the building, speaking soothingly in quiet voices, admonishing him gently for being outside. He seemed much calmer. Just as they reached the steps, he turned back toward Charles again and smiled, a huge, warm smile. His demons had left him for a moment and he seemed completely normal. Just a friendly old man.

"I hope you come to visit again," he said warmly. "We're just the same."

Chapter 11

Having survived his one adventure for the afternoon, Charles relaxed a little and his thoughts returned to his earlier quandary: How could he locate Martin's family and reunite them if he didn't tell anyone about the quiet little boy?

His eyes scanned the sidewalk from habit and his mind wandered. More bugs than usual crawled out of the grass and onto the concrete. Maybe a big brood had hatched. Maybe the call of mating season had gone out to the bug network. Coleoptera, he thought: beetles of some variety. There are too many species of beetles for any one person to know. Maybe they'd been hibernating beneath the grass and the warm weather finally woke them up...

"Where do you think you're going?" The deep voice stopped Charles in his tracks. A teenage boy, several years older and a foot taller than Charles, had been lurking in a doorway and now suddenly stepped out, blocking his path. The teenager's body smelled like stagnant sweat and his breath reeked of cigarettes and beer. He wore a black leather jacket with a Harley Davidson insignia and old jeans with a big grease stain. From the sneer on his face, he was pleased with himself for surprising a younger boy. His hair was black, long, and scraggly, pulled straight back from his forehead. Charles was so startled he simply answered the question.

"Piano lesson," he said.

"I don't think so," the teenaged gangster said. "You're trespassing." He took one last drag from the stub of a cigarette and threw it onto the grass. He blew smoke right in Charles' face. The smoke smelled like a trash fire.

"The church doesn't care," Charles said, coughing.

"Well, I care," the teenager said. "This is my corner. You want past, you gotta pay me."

"I don't have any money. I'll be gone in one minute."

"You got a watch, " the teenager said pointing. "Give it to me."

"I'm not giving you my watch."

"Then I'm gonna have to make an example out of you." He stepped even closer and grabbed Charles's wrist like a vice. There was no way the younger boy could pull free. On the other hand, neither of them could remove the watch until he released his grip.

"OK, OK," Charles said, thinking fast. "But if I come back with some money, you have to promise to give it back. How much do you charge for walking past you.?"

"How much you got back home?"

"About nine bucks."

"All right," he said. "I'll just hold your watch 'til you come back with nine bucks." He released Charle's wrist.

Charles slid the watch down over his hands. "You gotta be careful with it," he said. "It was a present from my uncle Kruck."

"I'll be careful," the teenager said with a smirk "But you better be back here pretty soon. I know where you live." He held his hand out, palm up, for the watch.

Charles reached over, but he didn't drop the watch. Instead, he pulled his hand back, ducked beneath the outstretched arm and started running as fast as he could toward his house. The teenager recovered quickly from his surprise and chased after Charles. The bigger boy could have caught him in a straight-line footrace, but Charles was a jackrabbit. He dodged and swerved.

Charles ran toward a tan brick two-story building. There was a big field of dead weeds beside it that were two or three feet tall. If he could make it that far, he could crawl into the weeds and hide.

The older kid was surprisingly slow, perhaps because of his cigarette habit and Charles easily beat him to the tan building. With a comfortable lead, Charles grinned as he turned the corner to run behind the building.

As soon as he turned the corner, two more teenagers stepped in front of him, blocking his path. They both wore black leather jackets just like the first one. It had been a trap.

Charles tried to run around them, but they were too quick. One grabbed his shirt and pushed him to the ground. Charles tried to roll away but the other one jumped on top, and used his knees to pin Charles's elbows tight against the dirt. The guy who'd been chasing him came around the corner, breathing hard,

"That kid stole my watch!" he shouted.

"That's a total fabrication!" Charles said. Using big words often irritates people, but sometimes he forgot.

"You're trying to make fun of us, ain't you?"

"I didn't steal your watch and you know it!"

"Looks like you're still holding it. And lying about it too!"

"I've got him," said the guy who sat on him. "Come and get your watch back!"

"It's not your watch!" Charles said. One guy sat on his legs, another on his chest pinning his arms down. He tried to wiggle free, but it was hopeless. They were too big and too strong. The first guy grinned.

"I think I'll just do that," he said. He reached down and pulled Charles's watch away, then slid it onto his own wrist.

"It's a little tight," he said. "Maybe I'll sell it and get me a new one."

"I wonder if he's got any cash," the kid on Charles's chest said. "You better check his pockets."

"Ragamuffins!" Charles shouted as they started looking through his pockets. "Ragamuffins and scalawags! Detestable brigands!"

"Kid don't even talk English," one of them said, laughing.

One of them kicked Charles hard in the side. The old leather boot had a sharp, hard point.

"Ow!" Charles groaned. He twisted his body at the pain and the bell around his neck flopped against the belt buckle of the kid sitting on him with a quiet ping.

"Shut up," the teenager said and kicked again. It felt like the boot broke his rib, but Charles didn't call out. He knew bullies. That kick was a first experimental step in being cruel. If it was fun, an evil crescendo of violence would follow. Victims that cried out were more fun.

Charles twisted and tried to pull his hands loose but there was too much weight on him. If there was ever a time for magic, this was it. Charles pictured a bee buzzing around his attacker's face, but no bee appeared. He pictured a car's horn honking and distracting his tormentors, then a dog barking, but the air remained still and silent. Clearly, magic would not help him. He could only remain alert while they searched his pockets and wait for an opportunity to escape.

Once he resigned himself to chance, his body relaxed and he began to feel distant and removed from the scene, as if watching from high above. He was a bird circling in the clear blue sky, catching an updraft to surf upon. He watched a single cloud move slowly as if gliding from one tree top to the next.

The teenagers taunted and jeered, pinching him, pretending to kick him or jab him with a stick, while they rifled through his pockets. Charles refused to cry. He focused on a tall tree at the edge of the grass, an evergreen of some sort, maybe a blue spruce. A speck of white in one of the upper branches caught his eye and he watched it. It was an enormous owl, grayish white and regally still. In spite of the situation, Charles noticed the irony of the coincidence: he'd read about Merlin's owl named Archimedes, and now an owl appeared in his own life, at the least likely time, in the middle of the day. He imagined what the scene on the ground looked like from the top of the tree.

One bully pulled a quarter out of Charles's jeans pocket and acted like he found pirate treasure. "Ho ho!" he shouted. The kid with the watch was laughing and dancing around like a fashion model showing off his new timepiece. His scraggly black hair reminded Charles of a soggy rodent from a swamp.

That gave him a crazy, desperate idea, an idea that could not possibly work.

Charles imagined he was that owl, looking down on the group. He pictured the scene from that lofty vantage point, especially the kid who had stolen his watch. Through owl eyes, he stared at the top of the kid's head, at the wild tangle of black hair.

"It's a rodent," Charles said softly. "It's a big juicy rat. A fat, tasty meal dancing around like it's injured." Owls normally hunt at night but this was an opportunity no predator could ignore. An easy meal. A fat juicy rat.

The kid on Charles's chest moved to reach a shirt pocket and his knee jabbed into Charles' ribs.

"Ouch!" he yelled. "Rat! Fat juicy rat!" The bullies just laughed and one kept trying to wedge a big hand into a small shirt pocket.

Charles looked back toward the sky just as the owl spread its wings and stepped into the air. I shouldn't have yelled, Charles thought. Now, even his dumbest idea was sailing away. But the bird's flight was lovely and Charles kept watching it. Silent as a cloud it swooped downward in a graceful curve, accelerating until it was moving faster than Charles could focus. No one else looked up, no one watched as that owl aimed like a missile for the tangled mass of black hair that looked like a struggling rat. The silent bird raised its wings, each as long as one of Charles's arms, straight up like a high diver, and its speed increased.

When the owl slammed into the teenager's head, with talons big as human hands spread wide, the impact made a loud thunking sound, like someone hitting a watermelon to see if it's ripe. The talons closed around the back of the kid's head and gripped it with the cold fierceness of a skilled predator.

The teenaged thief stumbled forward, jarred by the impact. He screamed in pain and surprise and started thrashing his arms around tying to free himself from the angry mystery on his head. Blood drooled down his forehead. The owl's wings slapped against his face a few times quickly as the bird regained its balance, then they stroked slowly and powerfully downward as if to fly off with its huge strange prey, but the teenager was far too heavy. The owl held fast, confused but determined, flapping its massive wings. The kid thrashed around erratically, flailing his arms in wild panic.

The two guys holding Charles down stood up and stared at their friend dancing around and screaming. They yelled and waved their arms, hoping to scare the bird away. With their attention diverted, Charles got up. He was eager to escape but hesitated just for an instant, transfixed by the bizarre scene.

A tall thin man walked around the corner of the building. He wore a sloppy round cowboy hat, leather clothes, and moccasins, and he carried a long, old rifle in one hand. Charles thought he looked familiar.

The man looked at each of the boys individually for a second or two as he surveyed the situation, then scowled. His face was fierce and intense, he squinted his eyes to narrow slits. He slowly raised his rifle and aimed it at the boy with the owl on his head, then moved it to aim at each of them briefly. All of them froze. Even the owl seemed distracted for a moment.

In a very deep, calm voice, he said, "Looks like we got us a big rendezvous here. Put me down for the sharp-shootin' contest. Just need to choose me a target."

Chapter 12

By the dawn of the seventh day, fifteen-year-old Sapania looked like an old woman. She crawled out of Blue Cloud's tent clutching a tattered deer hide around her for warmth. There was no longer any point to modesty. Beyond that, all her clothing had been confiscated a week ago to make escape less convenient, and for other reasons. Blue Cloud had found her copper knife immediately and taken it as well, with a big grin on his face. "You will have no need of this," he said. "If there is butchering to be done, you will not be the one holding the knife."

For the last week, Two Deers had tried to teach her the songs of her mother, songs he had largely forgotten. He did not have a musical ear or voice. She sang them to the sky, she sang them to the wind, but the rain did not come. She spent the nights in Blue Cloud's tent. Her body was covered with bruises and wounds. She had scarcely eaten food or drunk water for days. Her tongue had grown thick and black and felt disconnected from her, a wooden stick in her mouth.

In the dim light before the sun rose, she saw her uncle Two Deer trying to sneak away. She watched as he crept along, avoiding cactus, staying hunched over to make a smaller profile. He made no sound. She didn't care what happened to him. Maybe he'd escape, maybe not. After today, nothing would matter.

An arrow thudded into the dirt beside Two Deer, and he froze.

"The next one strikes your leg," Blue Cloud said from behind Sapania. She had not heard him rise, but it did not surprise her. "Bring my arrow back to me and continue your lessons. As long as you're already awake."

Two Deer sulked back and handed the arrow to his captor. "Her mother always played the buffalo-skin drum when she sang. Maybe that was important."

"We have no drum," Sapania said.

"You have a bell," Blue Cloud said. "It's as good as a drum." He whistled four short notes. His horse looked up and walked up the hillside. Blue Cloud had tied the bell on it along with the moccasins. He removed

62

it, handed it to Two Deer, then whistled for his horse to return to its grazing area.

"Her throat is too dry to sing," Two Deer said. "And mine is too dry to teach."

"You're stalling," Blue Cloud said.

"Would you have the rain or would you have your pride?"

"I would have both," Blue Cloud said, but he let each of them take a swig from his water skin.

Two Deer rang the priest's bell and Sapania sang the magic songs, weakly and without enthusiasm. Nothing happened. They tried another song, and then another but there was no magic.

"Maybe you're not doing it right," Sapania said, pointing at the bell. "Let me try it."

"So you think you know my sister's methods better than I do?" He sneered, "You who only knew her when you were a small child?"

"I could do no worse than you," Sapania said. Reluctantly he handed her the bell. She rang it and sang song after song until the sun dipped low in the western sky.

Blue Cloud roused himself from his nap and walked over to them, "The sun will set soon," he said. "And your time will be done."

"Maybe the magic comes only in moonlight," Sapania said in desperation. "We have not tried that."

"Do you think you fool me? You wish only to survive a bit longer"

"Yes, of course. But think about it: When have you witnessed magic? Can you remember a time? The moon presided over a solemn scene, didn't it? A fire lit the circle of faces around it. The music swelled with words that touched something beyond the stars. Magic is a quiet animal of the forest and river, it hides from the harsh light of cities. And yet you act like the new pale ones who argue in committees. Give me a small fire, give me the moonlight. Give me the tools my mother might have used, and her mother before her."

"No," Blue Cloud said. "I have given you your seven days. There is no magic."

Her uncle, Two Deer spoke quietly. "What have you got to lose?" he said.

Blue Cloud stared at the haggard man for a moment, then he looked at the setting sun. The clouds over the mountains turned pink and crimson. He suddenly remembered a time long ago, when his father—a man as cold and hard as granite— took him along on an antelope hunt. There had been a fire of cottonwood twigs and sagebrush. The moon cast pale shadows, a star shot across the sky. It was the one time his father said something kind to him.

"Very well," he said. "A small fire and moonlight. If you are very lucky, your song will bring the rain."

By the time they had collected twigs and started a cook fire the sun had set and the sky was fading to black. The moon peeked over the eastern horizon. The two men sat across the fire from each other while Sapania stood and rang the bell, softly and slowly. The three humans were flickering shadows on an ancient hilltop. The song was lovely but sad and she sang as if she believed the words. Something changed within her, if only for a moment. The men closed their eyes, listening, transfixed by the music. But Sapania felt more than the power of the music, the magic of a dark night. At first she didn't understand.

Out of the darkness, a horse approached with soft footsteps and a slow gait. The men didn't notice because they were focused on the song, and her young voice, and the quiet bell. They stared at the fire and did not see things in the darkness beyond it. The horse came right up to Sapania. She put one hand on it just as Blue Cloud looked up.

"No!" he screamed, standing up and reaching for his bow. "You have tricked me! Whose horse is that!"

"It has chosen me," she said.

"No one tricks Blue Cloud!" he yelled and notched an arrow in his bow and aimed it at her. "You die, and so will the accomplice who brought you the horse. And then your aunts shall die as well!"

He drew back the arrow and released it. It flew through the air. From this distance it could not miss.

When she saw him aim and pull back the bow string, she drew what she believed was surely her last breath and wished a small wish: that she stood two paces to the left. She felt the horse beside her shudder and watched the arrow fly past her. Her wish had somehow been granted; both she and the horse had somehow moved a few feet to the side. She looked at the horse in disbelief. "How did you…?"

Blue Cloud shouted in outrage and notched another arrow. He took two steps toward her, cursing loudly as he released the arrow. His face was beet-red with rage.

"Again!" she yelled at the horse. Once more the arrow flew past her harmlessly.

Blue Cloud stared at his bow in disbelief. He notched one more arrow and pulled the string back to his cheek.

Sapania didn't understand what was happening any better than he did. Suddenly, like a twig catching fire, she had a thought. The horse had the power, not the bell! The bell only summoned the animal. She whispered to the horse.

"If I were behind him I could end this forever." She held firmly to the horse's mane as it stood beside her. "Behind him! Now! Now!"

The bow string slapped Blue Cloud's wrist loudly as he hastily released the arrow. His grip was steady, his aim was true and he stared at Sapania directly in front of him. The arrow flew straight, but its target was no longer there. The arrow sailed through the vacant air, past the fire and into the darkness beyond. He dropped his arms to his sides, stunned. The woman and horse had simply disappeared.

Sapania was equally surprised. She now stood directly behind the man, with her hand still upon the horse. He had not noticed her yet. She could see herself standing in the path of the arrow, with the horse beside her, as a ghostly reflection of herself. Her image was whispering urgently to the horse, "Now! Now!" exactly as she had done a few seconds earlier. She watched Blue Cloud release the string, heard it slap against his wrist, and saw the arrow shoot toward her image. But now she stood so close to the man that he could grab her the instant he realized she was there.

The image of herself and the horse faded to invisibility as the arrow flew through it. She looked around, frantic for a tool. Blue Cloud's long metal blade glimmered in the moonlight on the ground beside him. She had watched him retrieve it from a dead man in the white priest's party. Now, she retrieved it.

"I believe this belongs to you," she said. He spun around to face her and as he did, she stabbed the knife deep into his side. His eyes widened at the pain and the shock of her sudden attack. He opened his mouth to speak and the bow fell from his hand.

"No," she said. "You have said enough. How does it feel to have me inside you for a change?" She twisted the blade and his eyes opened even wider. He stood for a few seconds more, then his knees gave out and he collapsed to the ground. She pulled the knife from his dying body. "This is mine now," she said. "And the bow and arrow." She took another long drink from the water skin, gathered the few things in the lean-to that looked useful and climbed onto the horse.

Her uncle Two Deer ran to her side. "So, the magic has come to you. Where shall we go?"

She looked at him with disdain,

"We? There is no we. You may go wherever you want, if you can escape his guards. You'll have to explain why you killed him, of course."

"But you killed him, not me."

She shrugged. "Perhaps you can convince them that a little girl overpowered their strong warrior. But you might have a better chance just taking his horse and making a run for it."

"No one else has ever been able to ride that beast!"

"The priest-man's friends rode it before that thing…" she pointed at the dead man on the ground "took it from them. So maybe you can too. But this horse…" she patted its neck. "This one has chosen me. I will call it Flatpipe, my magical companion, and it shall take me far away to a place whose name I do not know. A place where you cannot follow and neither can Blue Cloud's men."

She closed her eyes and raised her face to the starry night "I see a group of old women cooking round a fire. I smell warm meat and baked dandelion roots."

"But they will kill me!"

"Yes, that is a shame. I would have preferred to do it myself. But I may need a distraction for my own escape, and that will be a fitting use for you. If we're both gone they will come looking. Either way, if you don't get out of my way I'll gladly help you join your friend there." She used the bloody knife to point to Blue Cloud's body. Reflected firelight flickered in his open, staring eyes. Two Deer stepped away from her and her horse. She nudged it with her knees and it began to walk slowly away from the camp, past the fire, through the moon-lit prairie. As she rode, she tapped the priest's bell gently with the blade of the knife and sang the song she had been singing when the horse appeared. It felt as if the stars were listening.

"A place they cannot follow," she thought. "A warm, safe place. A place with food and water."

Suddenly she felt exhausted. She could no longer sit upright on the horse and she slumped forward. As she lost consciousness she felt herself slipping, falling off the horse. She landed on the hard dirt without even the strength to break her fall with her hands.

Cold drops of rain splattered on her cheek and forehead.

Chapter 13

"I just need to choose my first target," the man repeated, waving his rifle at each of the boys in turn.

Suddenly Charles realized that his was the man who had walked up the hill, smoked a pipe, and shot the rattler. But now he didn't look nearly so old or tired. His face did not sag, he was not missing a thumb. Even his clothes seemed less worn and dusty. His bright blue eyes blazed as he squinted. His aim settled on Charles, the rifle pointed straight at the boy's head. Suddenly, the man looked surprised.

"I know you!" he said. "You're the clay-bank hog who stole a month's take of beaver pelts from my cabin! Now you're gonna pay!"

"No sir," Charles answered quickly. "You have me confused with someone else!"

The man lowered his rifle a bit and stared. After a moment he nodded and relaxed. "You might be right. You're the chickabiddy with the campfire, ain't you?"

That sounded better than being the guy who stole the man's beaver pelts. "Yes sir, that was me," he said

"Don't much matter," the man said. "It's over. Call off your friend." He spoke very slowly.

"My friend?"

"The owl," he said. "It's done its job. I'll take over. Tell it to release the boy."

Charles didn't know exactly how he'd summoned the bird, let alone how to un-summon it. But it seemed wise to pretend a little longer. He stood beside the kid who had his watch. The bird had stopped trying to fly away but had not released its grip on the teenager's head. When it stretched its wings out, it looked as big as the young thug. The bully, terrified, stood perfectly still. His eyes were as wide as the owl's.

"I'd like my watch back now," Charles said calmly.

"Yes! Yes! Take it! Here!" He pulled the watch off his wrist and tossed it to Charles. The owl flapped its wings twice then swiveled its head left, then right. Its brown eyes were huge and intensely alert. It had no interest in releasing its prey; it had forgotten what it clutched but its claws gripped instinctively.

"Thank you," Charles said, sliding the watch on. "And thank you, my friend," he said to the owl.

He waved his hand in front of the owl grandly, hoping it looked like some important gesture a magician might make. "Thank you, " he said again very softly. Blood soaked the thief's hair and dried in rivulets on his face but this wasn't the time to think about that. The owl gradually calmed down. It pulled its wings close to its body and slowly extracted its talons from the boy's head. Its head pivoted around, huge brown eyes looking at each of the humans. Its wide round eyes made it look surprised. When it finally seemed ready to fly off, Charles waved his hand again, as magically as he could, and said, "You may go now."

As if responding to the instruction, the bird spread its wings horizontally and jumped off the teenager's head, gliding just a few feet above the lawn for fifty feet or more. Then it flapped its wings slowly and rose into the sky. Its flight was eerily silent.

That was lucky timing, Charles thought.

The man leaned his rifle against the building and inhaled deeply. He exhaled slowly, then inhaled deeply again.

"We still got the business of the fightin'," he said. "Three against one, that ain't a fight. It's an ambush. But three against me and a little kid, by gonny, that's just a good Friday night in Central City. What do you say, boys? You want to play your hand? I promise I won't kill any of you. Not on purpose, anyway."

The teenagers stepped backward away from the tall man in the strange clothes. The man took a step toward them and shook his head.

"Now, by gonny, if we don't finish the fight you boys won't proper learn your lesson," he said. "And I'll feel there warren't much point in even puttin' my moccasins on today."

The teenagers took another step backward. Charles had never heard the expression "by gonny" and wondered if the man was foreign. That's probably not the most important question at this precise moment, he told himself. He's clearly insane, regardless of his origin. Two crazy people in one day, all at the same location. Could the Pillar of Fire secretly be where the snake-pit asylum was? If so, did Raymond know it?

The man took another step toward the boys and shook his head.

"I already give you the better hand, three against two. Maybe three against one and a half. I say let's bloody up some grass and get it over with. It ain't a rendezvous without a tussle or two."

The boys were backing up a lot faster now.

"I see," the man said. "I guess I'll let it go this time. But by gonny, you boys are sorely a disappointment. Sorely a disappointment." The teenagers started running away.

"I look forward to finishing this up," the man shouted after them. "Very next time you try to ambush my young scout here. Think you can remember that?"

The teenagers disappeared down the road.

"Yeah," Charles said. "I think they can remember it."

"Sorely a disappointment," the man said one more time. He seemed lost in thought for a moment before he spoke again. What he said next didn't seem to have anything to do with what had just happened.

"Movement," he said. "That's what got to me. I'd ferry them across the river, most of 'em off on some adventure. I made a fair living at it. Then I'd watch them ride away and I'd still be in the same place. It finally got to me: muddy water pushing sticks and leaves down the river, birds flyin' past, the clouds crawling across the sky. Everything moving. But mostly people disappearing in the distance and me right where I started in the morning." He paused. "Felt like being dead," he said. "So I finally packed up a horse and went back into the woods. Back where I belong. Moving."

Then he shrugged, retrieved his rifle and started walking away. Charles felt relieved. If he did nothing at all, the man would walk away and Charles

70

would be safe. For his whole life he had wanted to feel safe, and doing nothing was usually the tactic he chose. But something had happened here, something had changed.

"Wait a minute," Charles said. The man stopped and turned back. Charles was shaking and confused but he owed the man something. The terrifying stranger had tried to help. Charles needed to overcome his first reaction.

"Thank you," he said.

"It weren't nothing," the man said. "You and your manitou had things pretty much under control."

"I don't know the word manitou," Charles said.

The stranger looked surprised, then shrugged. "It's an animal that lives in both worlds. Shoshones like Marina…" he stopped. "It's a Shoshone word. Whites don't have much need to know it."

"Well, thank you anyway," Charles forced himself to walked closer and held out his hand for a hand shake. "My name is Charles," he said.

The man stared at the boy's hand, as if he didn't quite understand the concept of shaking hands. Finally he took Charles's hand. His skin was rough with calluses and his grip was very strong.

"Pleased to meet you, Charles." Those deep, bright blue eyes stared right through Charles and the boy felt a chill. This was a very serious man. Different from the soft men who sang with his father in the church choir. Those men seemed like bread dough rising on the counter, pleasant and unthreatening. This guy had been through the oven and had a crust. He'd been cooked hard and was brittle as toast. He did nothing threatening, but danger rippled down his arm like electricity that Charles felt in his handshake.

"My name," he said, then he frowned a little as if was trying to remember some difficult word.

"My name…" he repeated. Maybe he's in trouble with the police, Charles thought and he's trying to make up a fake name. Suddenly the man's face brightened.

"My name's Jim Baker," he said and nodded slowly. "That's right, Jim Baker. Folks call me Honest Uncle Jim."

"Pleased to meet you, Mr. Baker," Charles said. Just as quickly as it had brightened, the man's face clouded over again and returned to an impassive mask, distant and vague.

"Mr. Baker's what the judge calls me after a misunderstanding," he said. "You and me been in battle together. You just call me Jim. Or Uncle Jim if you want. That "honest" part always seemed like newspaper talk to me."

"OK, Uncle Jim," Charles said. Never had it seemed so strange to call someone 'uncle.' "It was lucky for me you showed up."

"Lucky?" Jim Baker stared off into the distance. "Ain't much luck in the world. It was a dark night and I seen your campfire."

"My campfire?" Charles said. Even if Jim Baker had saved his life, Charles knew he'd just become friends with a crazy man. He tried to study the man without staring. His odd clothes were a clue— the cautious way he held his face—his slow speech— his suspicious darting eyes. His missing thumb that had miraculously regrown; his scarred, sagging face that had somehow healed. This man could not possibly be what he appeared to be. Charles took a step backward, trying to hide his sudden terror.

The man watched him carefully.

"You're a smart boy," he said softly. Either he could read Charles' face or read his mind. Neither idea was reassuring. "But you look like you seen a ghost."

"I guess the whole incident upset me more than I realized. With those guys stealing my watch and all. There's no such thing as ghosts."

"Don't know if I believe in ghosts or not," Jim Baker said. For a moment he seemed alert and talkative as he remembered some incident from his past. "Emanuel sure thought he seen Colter's ghost rise from the ground, naked as a jay bird and bloated as a dead snake, skin hanging off him. We was trapping on Jefferson Fork. When that thing come toward him, Emanuel pulled foot in a hurry." He paused. "Scared the buttermilk out of him, for sure. But then Emanuel could sleep leaning up against a tree, so we all figured he was dreaming when he was supposed to be keeping watch. Just the same, we broke camp and moved on."

"That does sound scary," Charles said. "Better safe than sorry."

Baker became more thoughtful again. "It ain't quite right to say I seen your campfire. That confused you. It was like a campfire," he said. He paused again, trying to explain. Maybe he was naturally quiet most of the time so when he did talk, he chose his words methodically. In prison, for example, he might not have spoken much…

"I been a scout all my whole life," he said. "With Bridger and Carson and the Army. I can track a white fox through a blizzard. But there's been nothing to track, no trail to follow. Everything's been confused and sort of sleepy. Like I was sick with the fever and having dreams. Then I seen your campfire, up on the hill. Didn't mean to startle you then, hiding in the weeds. You sat there just as still as a Shoshone tracker or a buffalo scout and I admire that. Mostly a scout has to shut up and pay attention," he said. "Them ain't common skills these days." He paused. "Then today, you lit that campfire again. You and your owl. Reminded me of Flying Fawn. She could talk to the birds too. Called it 'Orenda,' a spirit power, a kind of gift."

"OK, then. Well, I better get home before my parents start to worry."

Jim Baker nodded. "There's some strange men in these parts," he said. "Might be smart for you to carry a sidearm."

"I'll consider that," Charles said. "Wouldn't want to meet up with any strange men."

Charles started walking home. After three or four steps he turned back. Maybe he'd been rude.

"Thanks again," he said.

But Jim Baker had already left and Charles was talking to empty air.

As Charles walked home, with the afternoon light fading and the clouds above the mountains turning pink in the distance. Maybe Jim Baker had been a good, reasonable man before something happened to him, an accident maybe, and his brain got confused. But why was Charles encountering so many crazy people all of a sudden?

When he got home, Charles petted his dogs' heads as they jumped up on the fence, then he went inside, lay down on the bottom bunk in his room and opened a book. Within minutes, he heard his mother come in downstairs. She climbed the stairs and looked into his room.

"How was the piano lesson?" she asked with a smile. She knew music lessons were not his favorite activities.

"I'm pretty sure I'm going to be Beethoven," Charles answered.

She laughed.

"That's too bad," she said. "I was hoping for Mozart."

"It's good to dream big," he grinned.

Then she walked back downstairs to make dinner.

Chapter 14

"Why do you wear a white man's ornament?" the old woman asked Sapania. The woman pointed a bony finger at the old bell and continued to wrap the girl's feet in soft cloth soaked with medicinal herbs. Sapania opened her eyes and winced at the pain but said nothing. She did not know where she was, or who might have captured her. The old woman spoke softly, "Do you prefer the whites to your own kind?"

Sapania sat up and spat in the dirt. The effort hurt her entire body and she lay back down. She and the woman were alone in a cold, dark tipi. A tiny fire nibbled at a few damp twigs and provided weak, smoky light. The scent of wood smoke was familiar and comforting; the cool dirt floor was softer than the prairie she'd slept on for the last week, and the woman did not seem threatening. The woman's face was soft old leather, and she looked friendly enough. Still, Sapania was cautious. She would not say too much. "The bell became mine when I killed the white man. It makes a pleasant sound."

"It could be beaten into a blade," the old woman said with a grandmotherly smile. She did not react to the confession of murder. "Then at least it would be useful."

"It has been useful to me in other ways. And I already have a blade."

"Yes, we found that beside you. There was fresh blood on it. Perhaps you had been hunting?"

"A blade may be useful in many ways. For cooking, for hunting, for carving. But I am very tired. I don't remember how I used the knife."

The old woman nodded. "I am called Singing Bird." She smiled but did not look directly into Sapania's eyes. "When I was a baby, I cried loud and often. An elder sage who was a friend of my mother's said, 'Every bird loves its own voice.' And so I was named Singing Bird."

She waited and finally Sapania answered. "I am called Sapania. I don't know why."

Singing Bird nodded. "The bell has been useful? Is it magic?"

"Who knows? I am too young to understand magic."

"Yes, of course. Too young for bloody blades, too young for magic. You have much to look forward to when you're older, Sapania." The hint of a smile played across the woman's face, as if in response to her own secret joke. After a pause, she continued softly.

"I've heard of bells that can summon a manitou. Perhaps when you're older your bell will do this for you."

"A manitou? I do not know the word."

"A spirit animal. Sometimes not an animal. A thing with magical power. Old stories say that some bells can speak to them. But it doesn't matter. You have come a long way and even after your great sleep, I can tell you remain tired." Singing Bird waved her hand toward Sapania's torn clothes, her cuts and bruises, her bloody feet. "Did the white men do... all this to you?"

"No. That was all done by 'my own kind.' My uncle, my chief."

"Will they be angry if they find you? Are you safe?"

"They will not find me. And they won't hurt another girl. Their skin has been stretched into funeral drums and dried into dust."

"You mean you...?"

"What would you say if I did?"

Singing Bird thought for a moment. "A good gardener must pull the bindweed that chokes her potatoes and turnips. But she's wise to destroy the evidence, in case the bindweed has friends."

Sapania considered the woman's words. Perhaps there had been a garden within her, long ago, when she was a child. But all the green softness had been burned away. To remember the garden she would have to remember the conflagration, and that she would not do. "Do you weed your own garden?" Sapania asked.

Singing Bird smiled. "If I had, I would not brag. I would tell no one. But good gardeners should stick together. And I see the mark of the bindweed upon you. We will not speak of it again."

Sapania looked at the woman.

"I think the old stories are right," she said. "The bell was my friend. My song reached the clouds. The blade knew its job and laughed with delight…"

The old woman put a finger on her lips to stop her from continuing.

"You must rest. I will prepare a soup to restore your strength. And we shall find you better clothes. The hunt has been good this year. We have many soft deer hides, cured and softened. When you awake…"

Suddenly Sapania was alert. "Did you say the hunt has been good this year? Is that what you said?"

"Oh yes. We have hides and dried meat and many sacks of yampa-root stored. Was it not a plentiful year where you live?"

"No," Sapania said quietly. "It was not a good year for us."

"Then we are glad you have joined us."

But Sapania was already asleep.

Two more women entered the tent and sat beside her. They all stared at Sapania who slept soundly.

"We heard her words, but they might be lies. She could be a spy," one said. "White man's ornaments and a white man's blade—we should tell Little Raven."

"In good time," Singing Bird said. "This girl has had enough trouble with men. We will wait until she's stronger."

"He will be angry if we hide her from him."

"I am the oldest and therefore it is my decision!"

"You may be the oldest but you do not have the only voice. We will all be punished if he finds out."

"I said no! Let the girl sleep and regain her strength. She looks so peaceful. So…harmless."

"Yes, she is pretty as a flower, I agree with that." The woman sighed. "Very well, I will say nothing. At least not for a while."

"Something that looks so sweet could not be dangerous," Singing Bird said. The others nodded in agreement.

Chapter 15

After dinner, Charles sat on the front porch staring at the lights of Denver twinkling and glowing in the distance. To the right, the mountains formed a jagged rock wall that stretched north to Wyoming and south to Colorado Springs and beyond that to New Mexico. Even from twenty miles away, they looked like sleeping dinosaurs, huge and impossible to ignore, silhouetted against the darkening sky. This view was the unchanging wallpaper of his life.

The sky drained its color toward the horizon and Charles thought about magic. The moon rose in the east, gently illuminating the ground as if by candlelight. A coyote howled, not too far away and the eerie sound sent a shiver down his spine.

Charles had finally noticed a pattern to his experiments with magic. The few successful attempts involved three things: first, he focused all his attention on the goal. Second, he had some sort of emotional involvement, whether fear or anger or whatever. Then he got interrupted and distracted just before it worked. It didn't make sense, but that was his data. It was like aiming a bow and arrow carefully, holding it poised and still, then closing your eyes before you actually let the arrow fly. If magic works like that, it's no wonder so few practice it, let alone teach it.

He decided to test the hypothesis. An old tennis ball, frayed and faded from years of dog love, sat on the floor of the porch, exactly in the corner. He imagined it rolling a few inches to the left. He ordered it to move; he begged it to move. He put everything else out of his mind. The ball sat as still as a mountain. But how could he invest the experiment with emotion?

Just then Fritz barked. Not an angry, threatening bark, just one quiet syllable of exclamation. Charles had been so intent on the tennis ball the sound startled him. He peered through the porch screen and was sure he saw something move in the shadows, beyond the dog run. Perhaps the coyote? It stepped out into the moonlight and stared up at him.

It was a small white goat, with one dark ear, probably the one he'd seen from his window. The goat and Charles stared at each other.

It was a startling sight, but Charles was disappointed it wasn't a coyote. It would have been fun so see something wild and dangerous from the safety of the screened-in porch. The goat turned and sauntered silently back into the shadows.

"I guess I'm better at goats and owls than I am at tennis balls," he said, looking down. The tennis ball was about four inches to the left of the corner.

He was stunned.

"Perhaps my magic is crepuscular," he said out loud. He smiled at the big word, a word that would brand him as weird if he used it at school. "If you're listening Raymond, it means 'a creature of the dusk or dawn.' Creatures like bats and raccoons..." He stopped.

"And coyotes," he said with a start. No young goat or sheep stood a chance on the half-wild plains north of Denver. If that goat wasn't a ghost now, it would be soon. He should rescue it.

He hesitated. A boy his size was no match for a hungry coyote. Plus, the evening was still warm enough that rattlesnakes could be lounging in the dim light, invisible until you stepped on them. It would be foolish to venture out there. He shivered.

But the young goat was even more helpless. It could not have wandered far, and the coyote's howl hadn't seemed very close. If he could find the goat quickly, he could bring it to the house, lock it in the porch. His parents would help him find its owner tomorrow.

He grabbed the baseball bat that leaned in the corner and went outside into the wild semi-desert that surrounded his house, carefully avoiding the painful daggers of cactus and yucca. In the dim starlight, spherical tumbleweed plants huddled like stiff wire bushes or alien shadows, ready to circle and attack at any minute. He held the baseball bat above his shoulder like a batter awaiting a pitch, ready to defend against the sharp teeth of a wild canine lunging from the darkness.

From somewhere ahead in the darkness a child's voice yelled "Go away! Leave him alone!"

Charles walked quicker toward the voice. It was Martin, the boy who'd been hiding beneath the porch. The young white goat was beside him. In front of them, a coyote the size of a collie bared its teeth and lunged toward them. Martin waved his arms and yelled, the goat whimpered behind him. The coyote snapped its jaws and jumped back. The canine circled, hoping to lunge at the goat from behind. Martin pivoted to continue facing the coyote, trying to protect the goat with his own body. The snarl of pointed teeth looked like a grin on a scary Halloween mask and Charles took a step backward.

"Martin!" Charles yelled. He was terrified but he was the only person who could help. He clutched the bat tight and ran toward them.

"It's trying to get Pan!" Martin said, looking up quickly, panic and fear on his face. The coyote glanced indifferently at Charles then jumped toward the goat again. Charles reached them and swung the bat at the coyote's head as hard as he could. The creature easily dodged and skipped back a prudent step, then circled again like a nimble dancer. Charles swung at it again; once more it danced away.

"Pity that club is not a rifle," Martin said.

"Yeah," Charles said. "But he's so quick I probably couldn't hit him with a rifle, either."

"Pity it is not a shotgun then," Martin said.

That gave Charles an idea. They kept turning in place, keeping the goat behind them, with the coyote orbiting them like a planet. While they pivoted, Charles scraped at the dirt they were standing on with his foot.

"Coyotes are cowards," Charles said. "But it won't be afraid of us until it feels the sting of our wrath."

"We can't even touch him with your club," Martin said. "How will he feel our wrath?"

"Like this," Charles said. He leaned down and picked up a big handful of loose gravel he'd scraped free with his shoe. Then he took a step toward the beast. Its ears lifted and its expression changed.

"That's right," Charles said. "You've become the prey. I've got a handful of red-hot shotgun shot right here. You just jump toward me one more time so there's no chance I'll miss."

The coyote snarled again, took a tentative step forward, then danced backward and kept circling. It feinted like a boxer, jumping forward and back, shifting side to side, waiting for an opening.

"Two can play that game," Charles said. He took a step backward and pretended to stumble a little. In less than a second, the animal rushed toward him, mouth wide open to bite. Charles threw the handful of gravel directly into its face. Pebbles hit its eyes, its nose and its quick pink tongue. It stopped in its tracks and yelped in pain and surprise, as if Charles really had hit it with a shotgun blast. It kept yelping as it turned and raced away into the darkness. Charles waited a minute to be sure it was really gone, then turned back to Martin.

"I can't believe that worked," he said.

"You're very brave," Martin said.

"No one's ever said that before," Charles said. "Thank you." He reached down to pet the goat. Its fur was as soft as a kitten's. Two bumps on the top of his head would soon become little horns, Charles thought. "You should probably take him home," he said.

"Would you walk with me?" Martin said.

"Sure," Charles answered. He had made it his mission to return this kid to his family and tonight he was going to get that job done. It felt good to be close to a little victory.

Martin started walking back up the hill with the goat following as close as it could. Charles followed behind them, baseball bat held ready, checking over his shoulder every few seconds.

"I didn't want to have to tell the bees about Pan," Martin said quietly.

"Tell the bees?"

"My grandfather said that if someone dies, you've got to go out to your hives and tell the bees. They're part of your family so it's just being polite. But I didn't want to do it."

Charles kept looking in every direction. They had only taken a few steps when something caught his eye at the bottom of the hill, moving slowly up the gravel driveway. A lone figure on a pale horse rode up the hill casually with no attempt at stealth. In the dim light, Charles could tell the rider was a woman with long dark hair. Her body rocked gently from side to side with each step the horse took. Charles froze in panic.

"Does your mother ride a horse?" Charles asked.

"Everyone rides a horse sometimes, " Martin said. "But she likes the buggy much better."

"That woman would never ride in a buggy," Charles said grimly.

"What woman?"

"It doesn't matter. We need to hurry." They started to run. The woman on the horse continued her methodical pace up the hill toward them.

"Do you know where you live?" Charles asked. "Or where you're camped?" They were both running toward Charle's house.

"Pan likes to sleep under the porch," Martin said. "He feels safe there. Sometimes I sleep with him. We keep each other warm."

"You better come inside," Charles said.

"Pan gets in trouble when he comes inside. He eats curtains. We'll just stay with the dogs."

"I don't think it would be a good idea to take Pan in with my dogs," Charles said.

"They won't hurt Pan," Martin said. "He's a pet. They're all friends." He said it with such certainty Charles believed him.

"Won't your parents worry?" Charles asked.

"They're in Alaska. Your dogs will keep me safe."

None of it made sense, but he was right about the dogs. No coyote or villain would get past them. Charles opened the gate and corrected himself. Except maybe that Arapaho woman.

"At least for tonight, why don't you all sleep on the porch?" Charles said. "A coyote can't get through the door so my dogs will be safer. So will your goat. Plus the screen keeps out mosquitoes." He looked back down the hill. The woman on the horse was getting much too close.

"OK," Martin said. Charles opened the dog's gate and ushered dogs, goats, and boy all into the porch, then latched the door.

"Thank you very much," Martin said. He reached into the pocket of his pants. "I found these by the sunflowers," he said and he pulled out three small blue feathers. "I find lots of stuff by the sunflowers. I never saw blue feathers before, so I think they're magic. But not as magic as Pan. I want you to have them to thank you for saving him."

"I think they're blue-jay feathers," Charles said. "But you don't need to thank…" Martin reached up and put the feathers into Charles' shirt pocket, then turned away. The strange little boy and his pet goat lay down in a corner of the porch. The dogs settled down beside them.

The lights of Denver in the distance seemed very normal and reassuring. The moon was beginning to rise, casting long shadows. Charles could no longer make out the form of a woman on horseback riding slowly up the hill. He'd probably imagined it.

I might feel safer out here too, Charles thought. But that would be silly. He went inside and up to his bedroom, still carrying the baseball bat.

Chapter 16

The next morning, Charles took a sandwich to Martin on the porch but he was gone. He must have found his way to his own house, or to his tent or whatever, Charles thought. It was a relief not to feel responsibility for a lost kid and his goat, but it had also been nice to talk to someone who knew the names Ivanhoe and Merlin. It was a pleasant change to be the older kid, the brave one, the one with more experience. Well, if Martin lives nearby, Charles thought, I'm sure I'll see him again.

For several days, Charles's life returned to normal patterns. His experiments with magic made him feel like one of the early scientists. Maybe van Leeuwenhoek who invented the microscope using a water drop as a lens. Before anyone knew that tiny creatures writhed and swarmed in oceans the size of specks of dust, no words existed to describe that secret universe. Without the right vocabulary, it remained hidden. Maybe magic is like that, too.

Then one night he suddenly awoke, startled as if someone had pulled his hair. A thin shaft of moonlight streamed through the window, its dim light cast exaggerated shadows on the floor. Nothing was out of place.

He lay perfectly still, breathing carefully, listening intently.

Just when he was sure he'd been wakened by his own dream, he heard a distinct tapping and sat up. The sound came from near his window, but the moonlight illuminated only a few miller moths. He wanted to pull the covers over his head and ignore it.

No, he told himself. A scientist is not afraid of the unknown. And a magician is part of the unknown, it's his natural environment. He got out of bed and crept to the window.

Outside the window, the roof to the porch slanted away. It would be easy to open the window and step onto the roof, but he'd never done it. His parents made it clear that he was forbidden to go out there. It was dangerous and he might damage the old wood shingles.

But something had tapped on his window three times, very clearly, in quick succession. With his nose practically touching the glass, he stared out. He thought of Poe's raven; could a bird have done it? Some sort of woodpecker that works at night? Maybe a raccoon?

He opened the window halfway and poked his head out.

"I didn't mean to startle you," a voice to the left said softly. Charles jerked upright, banging his head on the window. Martin stood on the roof of the porch, right next to the window, leaning against the wall.

"What are you doing out there?" Charles said, trying to keep his voice quiet so he wouldn't wake his mother. "How did you get up here?"

"I think they got Pan," Martin said. Before Charles could react, the boy crawled past him through the window and stood beside him inside the room.

"I think they got Pan," Martin repeated more urgently.

"Your goat? Who would take your goat?"

Charles knew the answer as soon as he said the words.. He'd seen those men in old-fashioned clothes and derby hats trying to kill the goat once before. Charles changed the question.

"Why would they take your goat?"

Martin stood to one side of the window, more in shadow than moonlight. He looked down, studying his bare feet.

"It's hard to say in words," he said slowly. "He can do things."

"Do things? What kind of things? You mean like tricks?" Charles said.

"No," Martin shook his head slowly. "Not exactly. Not like a circus goat or something."

Charles kept quiet to let the boy think. After a moment Martin spoke again.

"It's not that he does things himself. He sort of helps me do things."

"Like climbing hills?" Charles said. "Does he pull you like a sled dog?"

"No," Martin said, then paused. "No, no, not like that. Things like this. Coming to visit you. Going places. Seeing things."

"So he's like a magic goat?"

"I'm not supposed to talk about magic."

"Why not?"

"My father doesn't like it. Modern, civilized people don't talk about magic."

"OK, so we won't talk about magic. How does Pan help you go places?"

"Thank you," Martin said, relieved that Charles wouldn't get him in trouble with his parents.

"Before Pan came, I was alone all the time. Then he came and he was my friend. Like your dogs are your friends. I could pet him all day long and he slept beside me at night."

"It's good to have friends," Charles agreed, then waited. After a moment Martin spoke again.

"Yes. One day I was petting him and I remembered the orchard where my mother and I gathered apples. We had a picnic under one big tree and my mother told me a funny story. I was trying to remember the story and Pan was laying with his head in my lap. I scratched his chin and said, 'If I remember, I'll tell it to you.' Pan moved his head so I could scratch his chin better. When I looked up we were in the orchard, sitting beneath the big old tree. But my mother wasn't there and I still couldn't remember the story."

"Maybe you were dreaming," Charles said. But what he was thinking is that this kid hallucinated the same way he did. He saw things that weren't there and finally his parents had him committed to a sanitarium. Just like Raymond said.

"That's what I thought at first. It was like a dream. Everything is sort of like a dream. But there were apples in the orchard and they tasted sweet so I know they were real. Pan ate one too. Nobody owns the orchard anymore, so it's OK." He paused again.

"A spider bit me in the orchard. Not a black one, but a little gray one. See? I still have the mark." He held out his arm. His skin was very pale and his arm was thin. A big red welt stood out on the back of his forearm. "So I don't think I was dreaming."

After all Charles's experiments with magic, he didn't casually dismiss things he couldn't understand. Some very weird things were true and some very logical things were not. A scientist does not make assumptions.

"So, does Pan… help you… like this very often?"

"Yes," Martin said quietly. "We've been practicing and I'm getting better at it. We can go places that seem very far away. Even here in my own house with you seems far away sometimes. But it's not magic. It's just that Pan knows how to do it."

"And those men want him to help them too?" Charles said. He noticed the kid referred to this house as his own. If he had been Martin's parent, he would have had him committed too.

"Maybe," he said. "Or maybe they just want to stop me. They want to hurt my father. I heard them talking. But they don't know where he is. I think they're afraid of me, but I don't know why. I haven't done anything to them."

"Maybe they think you will someday," Charles said. "They haven't had good luck near the house here."

Martin just nodded in the dim moonlight.

"If they want to keep you away from Pan, they'd take him somewhere you won't follow," Charles said. "Where would that be?"

"I don't know," Martin said mournfully. The boy sounded like he was going to cry.

"It's OK, we'll figure it out. They wouldn't take him to your favorite places, right? They'd take him to your least favorite places."

"I like every place."

"Fine," Charles said. Then he had an idea. "Are there any places you're not supposed to go? Places your parents told you to stay away from?"

"I can't remember," he said.

"Your father might have said something like, young man, don't ever let me catch you at this place. Or Martin, you stay away from…"

Martin looked up suddenly. For a moment, his face was illuminated by the moonlight coming through the window and Charles saw him clearly. His face was sweet and calm, almost pretty. Thick brown hair covered his forehead to his eyebrows and was piled like disorganized wads of cotton on top of his head. Uncombed, it looked more like an animal's hair than a little boy's. His eyes opened wide as he remembered something.

"The cemetery," he said softly. "Martin, you stay away from that old cemetery. Good Christians don't play…" he stopped.

"The cemetery at the Pillar of Fire?" Charles said.

"My father calls it Westminster College," Martin answered firmly. "You call it Pillar of Fire. It has gravestones and a metal fence."

"OK, tomorrow morning we'll go there in the daylight," Charles said.

"No!" Martin said. "Tonight! They have Pan! What if they try to hurt him?"

Charles remembered watching the men with the goat and pictured their knife.

"OK, but I'm not supposed to go out at night. We'll have to be very quiet. The floor squeaks."

"I know," said Martin. "We won't step on those spots."

Chapter 17

It took a while for news about President Lincoln and the impending civil war to reach the thinly populated Great Plains, but what news did reach settlers set everyone on edge. Even hardscrabble farmers in the remotest parts of the Kansas Territory tried to keep track. Between those dire rumblings and the growing conflicts with the Arapaho and Cheyenne, no one felt safe.

The Carter family's twenty-acre farm, eighty-five miles south of Denver City, clutched the dry dirt beside the satirically-named Bubbling Creek. Bubbling Creek did not bubble. A hundred years earlier, French trappers had called it The Fountain Creek, but there was no fountain either. It was a small muddy ditch that carved a shallow track through the flat clay. Perhaps its headwaters in the mountain to the west had splashing ripples and leaping trout. But by the time it wandered onto the prairie it had lost all enthusiasm for gurgle or shimmer. It trudged like a flat brown worm toward assimilation into some larger brown river or, perhaps, mere evaporation. It didn't care which.

Each summer it shrank to puddles and mud, and the swath of green weeds on each side shrank with it. A few cottonwood trees clung to its banks; their shade allowed some of the luckier weeds to remain green until August when they coughed up seeds, dried into brittle sticks, and blew away. Still, for most of the year this failure of a stream provided enough water to sustain small herds of cattle or sheep. Confident that irregular rain showers and well water could supplement it, optimists from eastern cities settled the area. They grew potatoes and carrots in desperate little gardens, tended their animals, and dreamed of prosperous futures while their optimism drained away.

As the Civil War was breaking out back east, they lived in fear. Major Chivington had sent special messengers to warn them: Lincoln's war required soldiers. Most of the soldiers in Denver City that protected the small farms were gone. There was nothing to deter the Arapaho and Cheyenne—especially the brutal Dog Soldiers— from swooping down on a farmhouse, killing the men and children and taking the women and livestock. They'd all heard the story of Mary Winter who'd been tortured and raped over several months and then traded to another tribe for more horrors. She'd finally hung herself. The Dog Soldiers left her body hanging from a cottonwood tree to rot. It hung there for a very long time.

Before the sun rose over the frontier prairie, little Benjamin Carter tiptoed outside, careful not to wake his parents. He felt grown-up and brave, but also a little naughty to sneak outside. His parents said there were dangers beyond the cabin but Benjamin was nearly five years old and afraid of nothing.

Amazed at his good luck, almost immediately Benjamin discovered something just outside the cabin door. He rushed back inside, face flushed with excitement, leaving the door open.

"Daddy, look what I found!" He shook his father's shoulders and the man startled awake.

"What is it, Ben?" he asked, rubbing his eyes. "What time is it?"

"The sun is already up," the boy said. "You slept through the rooster. Look! I found it by the door but I don't know what it is."

He held out his hand. It held a strand of leather, twisted together to make a bracelet. Bits of iridescent pheasant feather were twisted into it like little jewels. "Can I keep it, Daddy? It's pretty isn't it!"

Benjamin senior sat up suddenly, all the sleep gone from his face.

"No, son, you can't keep it. It's a message from the Dogs. They've marked our farm. We need to leave right now! Martha!!" he yelled. "Martha get your coat! We have to leave right now."

"I'm not afraid of dogs," little Ben said. "I would just pet them and give them food."

"These are not that kind of dog, son. Martha!" he yelled again while he struggled to put on pants. "Get your coat on. I'll hitch the wagon." He put his boots on and raced out the door without bothering to lace them tight.

Little Ben pulled a small box from beneath his bed. His parents had warned that if Dog Soldiers came, the family would have to flee with no time to pack. He put the bracelet he'd found into his box of secret treasures—a perfect dry and hollow crawdad skeleton, a magpie skull, a bit of petrified wood— and buttoned his coat. By then his mother was pushing him out the door. She carried only a basket of dried vegetables.

"Quickly!" she whispered. "And don't make a sound. There are some very bad men out today."

Ben climbed into the back of their little two wheel buggy and hid beneath the blankets in the back. The buggy lurched into motion, bouncing harshly as its wooden wheels navigated rocks and gullies.

Ben poked his head out from the blanket. An early morning mist gave their familiar farm an other-worldly appearance, softening the straight edges of their house, blurring their little herd of goats. Beyond the house, beyond the little corral made from rough pine poles, was a small hill that Ben often played on. He watched as a lone horseman came slowly over the hill, moving casually toward the house. It seemed that the horse materialized out of droplets of fog, like a cloud coalescing in the dim light of dawn.

Riding the horse was a woman with long black hair, wearing a dark cloak. Around her neck, a necklace made of bright white pieces of wood or stone gleamed against the dark cloth. Sapania rode down the hill, watching the little buggy race away. Puffs of dust followed behind each wheel.

"She's riding toward the new goat!" Ben whispered loudly to his mother.

"Quiet," his mother whispered back, although the clatter of the buggy and the clomping of the horse's hooves made silence moot. "That kid doesn't belong with our herd anyway. He's surely the product of some unnatural breeding, with his one brown ear. Now you hush and get back under those covers!"

Sapania dismounted near the white kid with one brown ear grazing quietly near the corral. It did not resist when she looped a rope around its neck and led it to the corral where a dozen larger goats were tied. Her horse followed her.

Yes, Sapania thought. Fear is a strong weapon, a useful tool. Combined with a magic horse, it was powerful indeed. She had paid no price for this livestock, had spent no arrow; not even a word. She had left a worthless bracelet near the door and these fearful ones gave her their most treasured possessions. Now she had only to picture the camp of the Arapaho women near the flatiron mountains. She pictured the cooking fire, the smell of buffalo meat steaming.

She herded the goats to one corner of the corral, close to her horse. It seemed to work better if they were all close together. The goat with the brown ear looked at her quizzically, as if it had its own thoughts. It did not avert its gaze when she stared at it, nor did it whimper like the others. Its stare unnerved Sapania. She removed the rope from its neck but the goat didn't try to escape. "So you are unafraid, little one? You will learn a lesson tonight. The others I shall sell or barter. But you shall be my dinner."

As quick as she said the words, smoke from the cooking fire burned her eyes and she heard a group of old women gossiping and laughing. She sat on her horse as one by one the women looked up to noticed her and the dozen goats beside her.

Singing Bird looked up in surprise. "Sapania! We did not hear you ride up. Have you bartered for goats?"

"No," she said. "They were a gift." She started to tell them to cook the little one, the kid with a brown ear, but that small goat was no longer among the others. "The tastiest one has escaped," she said. "Perhaps it understood my intentions."

Chapter 18

"I know where the steps squeak," Charles whispered. "You just step where I do. Do you understand, Martin?" The younger boy nodded,

Charles quickly put jeans on over his pajamas. With a flashlight in one hand and carrying his shoes with the other, he walked carefully down the hall as Martin followed. The floor did not squeak.

On the porch, Charles picked up the baseball bat that leaned in the corner. He opened the outside door slowly so its hinges wouldn't complain and closed it behind them just as slowly. He sat on the porch steps and put on his sneakers. While he did, he talked softly to his dogs lying on the dirt a few feet away in their pen. "It's OK, " he whispered. "Just going for a little walk. No need for you to wake all the way up."

Fritz wagged a sleepy tail, making slow whacks against the ground. The boys walked toward the Pillar of Fire.

The moon provided enough light the boys could see where to step without feeling too exposed. They moved deliberately and silently until they were a safe distance from the house. The lights of Denver stretched out in the distance like Christmas lights on a snowy tree.

"We should have brought your dogs with us," Martin said.

"They get excited," Charles answered. "They mean well, but they like to bark and chase things. I'm not strong enough to hold them back if they want to run. This might be a time we need stealth."

"Pan likes them."

"You'll have to explain that to me some day."

The outline of the huge castle-like building loomed like a giant against the dim sky, growing more distinct the closer they approached. With each step, Charles felt an increasing sense of dread. "It's OK, Martin," he told the younger boy. "Everything's going to be fine."

The cemetery on the old campus was only a fourth of an acre, surrounded by a wrought-iron fence five feet tall. The vertical stakes had sharp pointed tops, like a fence made of spears. The gate was padlocked.

Small, worn headstones stood in neat rows. Between the rows, a few sad, barren, dwarf fruit trees guarded uneven grass and patches of brown dirt. The graves were so old that no living person remembered the souls they marked. No one left flowers or came to visit. Even in the daylight, it was land of shadows; any human walking past seemed a ghost's reflection. At night it was a Shakespearian dream.

"Let's just watch from outside," Charles said.

"OK," said Martin.

They sat in the bushes, looking left and right like military sentries anticipating an ambush. Gradually, as nothing happened, Charles relaxed a little. The moon made the headstones look white as dried bone; the long shadows they cast were perfectly black. A bat swooped past in hot pursuit of a moth. It flashed across the sky, then was gone.

Martin nudged Charles with a sharp elbow and pointed. The white goat stood as still as a marble sculpture near the center of the cemetery. The rope Martin used as a leash was tied to a heavy cast-iron grave marker. The goat didn't seem to care that it couldn't escape. After glancing at the boys, it turned its attention to a scraggly rabbitbrush near the grave. It calmly chewed the tough stems until bluish-green leaves protruded comically from both sides of its mouth.

"Where did he come from?" Charles whispered. "How did he…?"

Martin put one finger to his lips, signaling to be quiet. Two dark forms several feet beyond the goat shimmered like shadows on water then came into focus as human forms. Perhaps it was a trick of the light, but Slim and the Reverend, the men Charles had seen from his window, simply appeared among the graves. Even softened by moonlight, they were hard-edged men in their long black coats and derby hats.

"Mr. Smith said bring it back dead or alive," the Reverend said in a hushed voice. "I figure dead and cooked fits that bill." He laughed quietly. The men stood a few feet away from Pan and leaned toward each other, speaking quietly as if they feared the goat could understand them. In the still air, their voices carried very well.

"It's a lot easier to lead a live goat that carry a dead one," Slim answered. "And I'd as soon drink some rum with my dinner and let the cooks at Soapy's place do the workin'."

"What's so special about this particular goat anyway? Looks about average except for the one dark ear."

"It ain't for us to question Mr. Smith's reasons," Slim said.

Martin tugged at Charles shirt sleeve.

"They want to kill Pan!" he said in a loud whisper. "I'm going to stop them. I bet I can sneak in there and untie him before they even notice me."

"That's crazy," Charles whispered back. But Martin was already running toward the cemetery fence. "Come back here!" Charles watched in horror as Martin ran straight to the fence. Somehow, he managed to climb it, pull himself over the sharp top, and jump to the grass without the men seeing him. The men continued their argument while Martin crept toward the goat.

"All I know is that some little boy owns it and when they're together they cause Mr. Smith problems. So if Mr. Smith has the goat, the kid goes away. Both kids."

Martin reached the goat and started trying to untie the rope, but the knot was too tight for his little fingers. As he struggled with it, Slim happened to look in his direction.

"Well, well!" he said quietly. "Maybe we can roast two ducks on the same spit!" He pointed at the boy. "You circle round behind him in case he tries to make a run." The Reverend nodded and walked toward the fence. Martin was so focussed on the rope he didn't notice them.

"Get out of there!" Charles said in his loudest whisper. He didn't want to attract attention to himself, but the men were getting too close to Martin. Martin kept working on the knot.

There were no good choices. If Charles climbed in there, the odds were good they'd both be captured. But he couldn't simply sit watching. He stood up and started running toward the fence. There was no point it trying to stay stealthy.

"Look out!" Charles yelled. "They're trying to catch you, too!" Martin heard that and looked up. The two men also looked up. "Run!" Charles yelled while running himself toward the enclosed cemetery. He still held the baseball bat in one hand, which made it more awkward to run, but he wasn't going to drop it now.

Martin stood up and ran away from the Reverend, who was in front of him and nearly ran into Slim who was waiting to ambush him from behind. But Martin was quick and agile and he avoided them both. He ran toward the darkest area of the cemetery, where a big old oak tree shaded the moonlight. "Get Pan!" he yelled to Charles. His voice sounded thin and frightened. Like the two men, Charles didn't understand what was so important about the goat, but he didn't have time to think about that now. He set the bat down by the fence so he could reach it easily through the bars and pulled himself up the wrought iron fencing. By the time he managed to climb the fence and run to Pan, the two men were entering the shadow of the oak, still chasing Martin, and had apparently forgotten about him completely. In their minds, they already had the goat secured and now they were intent on catching Martin. Charles could hear them yelling at each other.

The knot was tight, but Charles worked it loose. As soon as Pan felt the rope go slack, the goat bounded away several feet and then stopped to examine the fresh weeds at that location. From the shadow of the oak tree, Martin yelled out. "Let go of me! You are bad men!"

Charles leapt to his feet, retrieved the baseball bat, and raced toward the sound of Martin's voice. The Reverend had his arm around Martin's waist and held him up off the ground, kicking and squirming and yelling. Charles ducked behind a tall granite gravestone to watch and figure out what to do.

"Slim, you go get the goat and we'll take our prizes back to camp. Soapy said something about a bonus."

Slim slouched away.

"You let me go!" Martin shouted. "Let me go, I say! My father will be very angry at you!"

"I ain't a'skeered of your pappy like I'm afeard of Mr. Smith," the Reverend said. "Now stop wiggling around like a stuck pig, you little guttersnipe, lessen you want to feel my Arkansas toothpick."

There wasn't going to be a better time for Charles. The man was distracted, his partner was looking for Pan. This might be his one opportunity to save Martin. Charles stood up holding the baseball bat in both hands, over his shoulder as if waiting for a pitch. Holding it like that, he ran across the dark grass and swung the bat, aiming low at the back of the man's knees as hard as he could. It would hurt a lot but wouldn't kill the man. He had no intention of becoming a murderer.

The bat connected with a loud thunk. The man's knees buckled, he grunted loudly and dropped Martin to the ground. The man fell, clutching his knees with both hands.

"Run!" Charles said.

"Did you untie Pan?"

"Yes. Now you climb the fence and I'll got get him."

"No," Martin said. "If he's not tied up he can jump over this little fence. "Let's get out of here!"

The two boys raced toward the fence and climbed it quickly. Despite his sickly appearance, Martin climbed as nimbly as a monkey and was on the ground outside before Charles got to the top.

"Hurry!" Martin said. "I'll call Pan." Then he whistled a very specific series of notes, the complicated call of a meadowlark. His imitation was excellent but seemed out of place— meadowlarks don't sing at night.

Charles jumped down from the top of the fence to join him. The moon had dipped behind a cloud and the cemetery was much darker. Pan did not come.

"He's too far away," Martin said. "I wish I had my bell."

"I have a bell," Charles said. He wore the missionary's bell beneath his shirt and now he pulled it out. "Would this work?"

Martin stared at it. "It looks just like mine," he said. "Pan can hear that from a mile away. Ring it quick!"

97

"It doesn't have a clapper," Charles said. "But I can hit it with a stick." He looked around, frantically searching for some twig he could use.

"You've got a big stick in your hand!"

Charles looked down at the baseball bat. "Why not?" he said. He tapped the bell with the bat and it made a loud, clear tone. From the shadows, the goat came trotting into view

Martin repeated the bird call. Like a dog responding to its master, Pan burst into a quick run, jumped onto a tall headstone and without pause leaped to the top of the fence. In one smooth move, the goat bounded to the ground and trotted over to the boys. Martin held tight to the rope leash and rubbed his forehead against the goat's nose in a bizarre greeting ritual.

Slim chased after the goat and tried to climb the fence but, without cross-bars or footholds, the metal was too smooth for a grownup to climb. The Reverend limped behind him, brandishing his long knife, yelling threats and curses with every painful step.

"Let's get out of here," Charles whispered. He and Martin started running back toward the house with the goat cheerfully trotting beside them.

After only a minute or so, Martin stopped. With one hand on Pan he said, "They can't catch us now. We can walk."

Charles glanced over his shoulder; no one was chasing them. Martin was younger than Charles, maybe he couldn't run as fast. If he needed to walk, then they'd walk. But it was crazy to think they were safe. The men who meant them harm knew where Charles lived.

"Why don't you think they can catch us?" Charles said.

"Because they can't find us. We're very far away and they don't know where we went."

Chapter 19

"I don't think…" Charles started to argue but then stopped. Something had changed but he couldn't put his finger on it.

He looked around. The moon had moved lower in the sky, the breeze felt a little cooler. Another bat flashed across the sky. He watched as it darted south, fluttering like a huge silent leaf in the wind.

And then Charles realized what was different. Against the moonlit sky, he could see the outline of the mountains in the distance. The castle-like form of the Pillar of Fire stood like a giant behind them. But no lights were lit in Denver. Where the twinkling city should be, there was only darkness, a huge lake of black ink on the prairie. Denver was gone.

Charles stopped walking.

"Where…?" started to ask and then stopped. There must have been a massive power outage. That was the only logical explanation, yet it didn't feel right.

"What…" Charles began again. Martin was staring at his feet, his right hand on Pan's head. Martin held the end of the rope in his left hand. He seemed fascinated by his feet, like a kid who's been naughty and hopes no one notices him.

"You know what's going on, don't you?" Charles said. Martin didn't respond.

"Martin!" Charles said. The harsh tone startled Martin and he looked up.

"What?" he said innocently.

"What's going on? You know, don't you?"

"Everything is pretty confusing," he said.

"You know what I mean! " Charles said. "Why can't those men follow us? Did you do something to them? And what happened to Denver?"

"I don't exactly understand. Denver City is where it always is. I didn't do anything."

"Then tell me what you think."

"OK." Martin paused, as if he was still deciding exactly how honest to be. "I told you Pan helps me go places. Sometimes the places change."

"What do you mean change?"

"Like tonight. The lights are gone. Maybe next time the lights will be on."

Charles watched the boy's face. It gave no clue of intentional deceit. He was, after all, only eight years old. Charles softened his tone and asked again.

"You're sure the men can't find us?"

"Oh no, they can't find us again tonight. It will take them some time."

"Good," Charles said. "Let's just sit down on the ground and talk about it, OK? Nobody's mad at you."

"OK," Martin said. They sat on the dry dirt and stared out across the black prairie that was usually filled with sparkling lights, a galaxy tossed into a massive heap of cosmic laundry. Charles had postponed many questions. Who were those men? Why did Martin's family leave him behind? How did he know the men couldn't follow them?

Martin avoided answering direct questions. Charles decided to start indirectly.

"It's interesting that you and I met each other, isn't it? How did that happen?"

Martin nodded. "Yes," he said with a little smile. "You started it."

"Me? How could I..." Charles started to argue but stopped himself. He had to be gentle if he wanted the boy to keep talking.

"That's interesting," Charles said. "Tell me about it."

"You lit your little fire," Martin said. "I woke up and saw it. It looked nice. So I tried to go to it, but then it was gone. I kept having nightmares."

Jim Baker mentioned his campfire, too. Two similar bits of data. Not enough for a hypothesis but enough to spark some curiosity.

"Then what happened?"

100

"Well, I woke up. I must have been dreaming. But then it happened again. This time I got close enough to see you. You had a butterfly on your finger."

Charles resisted the impulse to react. No one had ever seen him hold a butterfly. How did this kid know about it?

"Why didn't you say anything?" Charles asked.

"I don't think you could see me. It would have startled you."

"Yes, I bet it would have. But why couldn't I see you?"

Martin fidgeted nervously.

"I can't explain," he said.

"Try," Charles said. "I helped you get Pan back, didn't I?"

"Yes." Martin paused for a minute, staring out at the darkness. Then his face brightened.

"At night, when the candles are bright you can't see outside into the dark. But if you go outside, you can look in through the window and see the candles just fine. It's the same window but sometimes you can see things and sometimes you can't. It's like that."

"And when you watched me and the butterfly?"

"I was inside, in the dark. You were out in the sunshine, I could see you but you couldn't see me."

"Does that mean sometimes I can see you and you can't see me?"

"I don't know. Maybe."

"And the men who took Pan — you don't think they can see us now?"

"They can't see us because they can't find us. We're too far away."

"It doesn't seem like we're far away. Maybe two hundred yards."

"It looks the same but it isn't the same."

"What do you mean?"

"Maybe next time it will be the same again. But now it isn't."

Charles sighed, "OK," he said. "Maybe I don't need to understand it all right now. Let's go home."

They both stood up. Martin rubbed the goat between its ears and it rolled its head like a cat begging for more petting. "It works just the same," he said quietly.

"What?" Charles asked

"Whether you understand it or not," Martin said. "It works just the same."

Charles nodded, pretending that Martin made sense, and they walked toward Charles's house. Toward the two big dogs who would protect him, toward his own cozy bedroom.

But something was different at the house, too. The moon had set, the ground was dark. In the crystal clear air the stars stood out against the black sky like a billion little flashlights. The night was oddly quiet, for once without the faint hum of distant traffic.

Even the old wooden steps up to the porch door looked different. Over the years they had become cracked and dilapidated. Somehow, while the boys had been gone, someone had replaced them with new steps, straight and strong. Why would someone come in the middle of the night to make repairs? No, Charles' parents must have hired someone in the last few days and he just hadn't noticed. It was probably their little joke— how long before Charles notices the new steps? Charles looked around and realized that more had changed than the steps. The dog pen was gone, and so were the dogs.

He stopped in his tracks and stared.

"Where are my dogs?" he whispered. "Martin!" There was panic in his voice. "Someone stole my dogs!"

"No," said Martin. "Your dogs are fine."

"But where are they?"

"Things change," he said. "And then they change back."

"Did you take my dogs?"

Martin smiled. "Nobody took your dogs. We just can't see them from here."

"We're right beside the dog pen!" Charles said. "Or at least where it's supposed to be. Where it's always been!"

"It will change back."

"Can you change it? Can Pan? I want my dogs!"

"I can't change them. At least I don't think I can. I just go visit."

"Well let's go visit my dogs then!"

"The bad men will go looking there. It's safer here."

"What if they hurt my dogs?"

"They don't care about your dogs. They only want Pan. I'm sleepy. Pan and I like to sleep under the porch. Tomorrow we can visit your dogs. There's going to be a parade tomorrow. I like to watch parades."

Martin skipped away with his goat until both disappeared under the porch. Everything seemed terribly strange, but there must be a scientific explanation. Maybe I've been drugged, Charles thought, and now I'm hallucinating. Or maybe I'm much crazier than anyone suspects.

Charles ran his hand over the new wooden steps, smooth as a cotton shirt. He traced a line from The Big Dipper to the North Star, the axle the other stars pivot around. The mountains silhouetted against the horizon had also not changed. The tree he often climbed was…he stopped. The huge hackberry tree was gone. In its place was a sapling scarcely taller than him.

"Martin!" he whispered loudly but no one answered. He wanted to go inside and ask his mother what was going on but was afraid she wouldn't be here. Suddenly he felt very alone standing outside his own home. A coyote howled in the distance, a bleak, lonely song in the dark desolation. The world had suddenly become vast and vacant. Charles shivered.

He crawled under the porch. Martin and the goat were laying on a big pile of loose straw against the wall. There was no smell of dogs, or old tires, or gasoline. Just straw and alfalfa. Martin was curled up with his head on the goat. They breathed slowly and evenly, deep in contented sleep.

Charles sat against a wall. It was his duty, somehow, to stay awake and stand guard over them. But he was very sleepy…

103

Chapter 20

A dozen people gathered on a Denver City street watching a short, neat man standing behind a small table, talking fast and loud. "Jefferson Smith's the name," he said. "And Three Card Monte is the game— the game that might make you rich by dinner time!"

Sapania stood several feet behind the crowd, observing as carefully as if the people were pheasants to snare. She hated these foreigners, these aliens, but had learned to conceal that hatred strategically. By now, after a few years living close to the city, she knew how to blend in with the townspeople. Her buckskin outfit was unadorned by any necklace of teeth or claws, her face was unpainted and her black hair was pulled back and tied with a strip of leather. She wore a heavy black wool cape, less for warmth than for the secret pockets inside it. From a distance, she was unremarkable.

To a closer observer, she radiated a wildness that set her apart and lit her like a fire. Her dark eyes had an animal gleam as they darted about searching the crowd for danger and prey. The men in the crowd glanced at her repeatedly but were careful not to stare. The women ignored her aggressively.

She edged close to an older man with a big belly. He wore a holster with a lovely ivory-handled pistol. The gun wasn't strapped into the holster and as he moved, it jiggled and looked likely to fall out completely. Without ever looking directly at the man, she she deftly removed the gun and slipped it into the inside pocket of her cape. The man thought he felt something. He frowned and looked around. Sapania looked right at his face and opened her eyes very wide, blinking several times, looking to him like a sweet fawn surprised in a dewy meadow. The man smiled and nodded at her, as she moved toward another man who wore a pocket watch that might be one good tug away from freedom.

Jefferson Smith glanced in her direction casually, then glanced away. Almost immediately his eyes returned to her, the striking woman with long hair and the smooth skin of youth in a rustic leather clothes. He raised one eyebrow, but did not pause in his patter.

"Step right up, gentlemen," he said. "And ladies too." He pointed toward Sapania at the precise moment a lonely pocket-watch had begun to savor the warmth of her hand. "Yes, you, the lovely lady in the back. Always room at Jefferson Smith's table for pretty girls. Don't be shy, come on up here!"

Sapania had tried to be inconspicuous, but when Smith pointed at her, the others turned to look and she stepped forward. It would only draw attention if she objected. She slid her new watch casually into her cape and stepped forward, away from the watch's previous owner.

"That's better," Smith said. The man's voice had a hypnotic quality. "I'm about to conduct a scientific demonstration of the fallibility of the human powers of observation." The crowd parted like water around a boulder in a creek as Sapania moved through it. "Now, before we begin, let me remind you all to keep a close watch on your valuables. Denver City is full of pickpockets and thieves."

Without thinking, Sapania touched the priest's bell that hung around her neck.

The slightest hint of a smile moved across Smith's face as he glanced around the crowd, taking careful mental notes. Several other members of the crowd had also revealed where they kept their most valuable possessions. This made his crew's work so much more efficient, and the fools always fell for it. Sapania's face revealed no emotion, but she kept one hand near the blade hidden beneath her coat. Then she remembered there was no blade there today. She had left it, along with her bow and arrow, in a sack hidden under a bush near the Flat River that flowed through the city. If captured, her best defense would be a look of frightened innocence, as usual. Still, for a moment she panicked and felt vulnerable.

"What's your name, darling?"

"I am called Sapania."

"A lovely name. You remind me of my dear cousin Natana. You'd never guess from my pale skin, but my mother was Arapaho. You wouldn't have a bit of Arapaho blood in your veins as well, would you?"

"It is my tribe," she said in surprise. "But you don't look…"

He laughed—a loud, confident laugh that sounded quite different from the grunts emitted by the men she knew. She felt an unfamiliar stirring within her and her face warmed uncomfortably. She ignored that as she saw the gold coins on the table near the cards Smith continued.

"I am like the rare white buffalo, or the magical white antelope. Sometimes the Great Manitou plays trick on parents.

"You know of the Great Manitou?"

Smith motioned for her to keep her voice down. "We can talk of such things later," he whispered. Then he continued speaking to the crowd in his loud stage voice. "Three Card Monte is a game for kings and gentlemen," he said. "And, of course, for beautiful young women." He gestured toward Sapania, winked, and shot her a big smile. "Won't you help me demonstrate?" He pushed several coins nearer to the cards.

"I don't have any money," she said.

"I would not expect my beautiful volunteer to use her own money for our demonstration." He motioned to his assistant, a sullen and stocky man standing near the table. "Hand our new friend three dollars." The man reached into his pocket and gave her the coins. Smith turned back to the crowd. "If she loses, she only loses my dollars back to me. But whatever she wins is hers to keep. What could be more fair?"

Sapania nodded, but her gaze kept returning to the coins on the table. She imagined the collection that probably hid in the man's pocket. They were good for trading, and no one could prove whose pocket they came from. This one man might be a richer pond to fish than the rest of the crowd combined!

Smith taught her the game while the crowd watched intently. Despite her distrust, she found the bright colored cards fascinating as they flashed through Smith's practiced hands. They reminded her of fluttering butterflies opening and closing their wings. The game itself made no sense to her at all.

She lost the first few hands and a dollar left her for the more familiar home of Smith's pocket. But then her luck turned. She won more hands than she lost and by the time she understood the game, she had ten dollars in her hand.

The crowd pushed closer. One man muttered to the man beside him, "If Tipi Woman here can beat this soap salesman I can empty his pockets in ten minutes. Hey!" he shouted. "Let someone else have a chance!"

Others shouted similar sentiments and pushed their way to the front.

"Very well, very well," Smith said to the crowd. He turned to Sapania and spoke very softly. "My dear, now that you have taken so much of my money, and my pride, and a good deal of my heart, I hope you grace me with your company over lunch. My treat, of course."

"I have errands to run in town..." she said, looking down at the ground as she imagined a shy woman would. The opportunity to divest this man of his coins was very exciting and being alone with him was the first step.

"Oh but I insist! Meet me in that cafe on the next corner as soon as I am done here." It wasn't as much an invitation as a command. He flashed such a disarming smile that her skin flushed and for an instant she felt confused. This pale man was her enemy, she would not forget that. But then, he wasn't a wasicu—a white alien—he was really an Arapaho, just like her, and knew many things about cities that could be useful. No, she reminded herself. He is mere prey to be approached cautiously.

She nodded toward Smith slowly.

Soon they were sitting in a cafe that featured animal heads on every wall and a long wooden bar. They sat across a smooth pine table from each other. A small vase on the table contained several small wild roses. The flowers were common and free, a pitiful attempt to create the illusion of civilization and style. The bartender, a haggard man in a white apron, brought each of them a steaming bowl of food and a cup of tea. Sapania smelled the food cautiously, dipped a finger in, and licked it off. She made a face.

"What is this food?" she asked.

He laughed. "That, my dear, is prairie stew. Mostly beans and barley, but they don't spare the spices. Here, a sip of your tea helps quench the fire."

"I have not seen you sip your own tea," she said.

"Merely being a gentleman," he said, and noisily slurped some of his tea. They each had identical porcelain cups, more delicate than the rest of the furnishings in the place. "Ah!" he said, wiping his mouth with his hand. "Rose hip tea! Approved by both the Arapaho and the heathen whites!"

She took a small sip. The flavor was not unpleasant and she set the cup back down.

Smith pulled a small bottle from the inner pocket of his suit coat. "I hope you will excuse me," he said. "My wrists give me pain from so many hours of working with the cards. This is the one European medicine I allow myself." He showed her the bottle. It had a picture of a young woman in bed with two small children, all looking perfectly content. "Mrs. Winslow's Soothing Syrup," he said. "It's for children who fuss from the pain of new teeth. But I have discovered that it soothes my own pains too." He measured out two spoonfuls of the concoction and added it to his tea. He stirred it gently, then licked the spoon. "You may have some too, if you like."

"I do not drink their poisons," she said.

"Wise indeed," he laughed. He plucked one small rose blossom and dropped it into his cup. "It may be my imagination, but I think the scent of an actual rose augments the flavor of the tea. Now please, you must tell me all about yourself."

"I am a simple Arapaho girl," she said, her eyes watering from the spicy food. "I cook, I help with the skinning, I tend the fires. There is no story to tell."

"I doubt that," he said with a smile. "Surely a beautiful woman like yourself has many stories. But we don't need to talk too much. Eat your food." He motioned to the bartender. "My good sir, I believe we need a bit more tea over here. Thank you very much."

This was a different kind of hunting than she was used to. She needed to keep this man interested in her company until she could take his coins. She told stories of fish that she'd caught, and of going along on an antelope hunt. But even as she relaxed, she did not talk about being a captive to her uncle, or being tortured by Blue Cloud. She certainly did not mention killing him or the priest. She knew not to speak of Flatpipe, her horse with the remarkable powers. Instead, she invented the life of a

108

simple girl and told that story. It felt as real to her as the truth, maybe more. Smith listened intently, as if a story about being chilly sleeping on the ground on a summer hunt was the most interesting thing he'd ever heard.

She regretted having left her blade by the river. This man would not give up his coins without a fight.

The bartender had been cutting some fruit. He got up to pour a customer's drink and left his knife on the bar. Maybe she could pick it up and conceal it before he noticed.

Outside, a man yelled "Thunder and Buttons! Get away from that donkey!"

"Why look!" Smith said. "It's Prairie Dog O'Byrne and his team of elk! He's a bit of a legend around here. Look through that window!"

This was exactly the sort of diversion Sapania had been hoping for. She got up and walked to the window, casually grabbing the knife from the bar as she passed it. Outside, a man in a small carriage was yelling at the two elk that pulled it. Sapania had never seen such a thing. She turned and went back to the table.

"I did not know elk could be trained," she said.

"No one did," Smith said. "He got those when they were very young. Don't let your tea get cold."

She picked up her tea and smelled it. She looked over at Smith's tea with the little rose blossom floating in it. As if sensing her paranoia, Smith took a big drink of his tea. "My wrist already feels better," he said. "Thank you, Mrs. Winslow!"

Sapania sipped her own tea. She was eager to leave before the bartender realized his knife was gone. She finished her tea quickly.

Smith patted his vest pocket.

"Goodness," he exclaimed. "I seem to have allowed my supply of cigars to dwindle to ephemera. Will you accompany me to the general store to replenish my supply? Perhaps you will find a notion you fancy as well."

With a long, sharp knife hidden inside her cloak, this was the perfect next step in her plan. There would be some hidden alley or dim room along the way. The man could lead her according to his own dark plans, completely unaware that it would be his final seduction.

She walked with Smith a few blocks to the store. They stepped inside a dimly lit room cluttered with items of every description. As her eyes adjusted, she was overwhelmed by the confusion of products. Smith quickly located the cigars in a cedar humidor and picked up a handful.

"I'll just be a moment," he told her. His eyes flickered down to the bell she wore, but only for an instant. "Explore the store while I purchase these cigars. I'll be back before you miss me."

While Jefferson Smith was at the counter negotiating the price of his cigars ("Double or nothing on one cut of the deck…") Sapania looked at the shelves jam-packed with cans and bags and boxes. She had never been inside such a place. Bags of flour and beans were stacked nearly to the ceiling. Stirrups and boots filled an entire section so tightly she had to turn sideways to pass between them. Two old dogs and a bored cat slept in one corner of the floor where a square of sunlight fought through the dusty glass of the window to warm them. Above them, hats of all varieties filled shelves. Some were leather with broad brims, a few were derby hats favored by gentlemen from large cities. Some seemed completely out of place.

This little aisle between shelves was perfect, she thought. No one could see whatever happened there. She waited for Smith in the narrow aisle lined with hats and sacks of flour and adjusted the blade in her pocket so the hilt was aimed upward for grasping quickly.

Something felt strange and yet familiar about this particular spot. It reminded her of the night when her horse, Flatpipe appeared and helped her escape her uncle. She looked over at the dogs and cat sleeping on the floor. Could those sleeping animals have some of the same magic her horse demonstrated? Is that what she sensed? They seemed like unlikely magicians…

"Do you want a hat?" Jeff Smith had come up behind her. His voice was joking but she didn't realize that. She was preoccupied with the strange sensation.

"I don't know," she said. For a moment, she was barely conscious of the man behind her. What was it about this place that reminded her of that night? "I rang the bell that night," she whispered. "And then the horse appeared, as if I called it. I don't understand…"

"Well, maybe you should ring it again," he said. "We can always use another horse." Now he was so close she could feel the warmth of his body radiating against her back. "Sometimes we know things but don't realize we know." He wasn't touching her, but she could feel his breath on her hair, smell his spicy cologne. It was hard to concentrate.

"Anyway, I'd love to hear that lovely bell." He put his arm around her waist. The shelves were so tall, no one could see the two of them and she knew the danger that could be approaching. "Just stay very still and I'll ring it for you."

She had felt men's hands before— her uncle and Blue Feather— and they had always aroused pain and disgust. But this was different. She felt relaxed; a calm warmth spread across her skin. Still, she reached into the pocket and her fingers closed on the hilt of the bartender's blade. Smith's hands moved slowly across her chest to the bell.

The bell's note was pure and musical. It sustained for a long time. Smith's other arm squeezed her waist, pinning the hand that held the blade against her side. She watched the animals on the floor. One dog lifted his head sleepily then lay back down.

At that precise moment, a hat fell from the top shelf and landed with a soft plop on the floor. It was large and white, much too large for Sapania. A wide, flat brim extended in a circle around it. It was a ridiculous hat; it looked like a big white pancake with a white cantaloupe in the middle. Or a big fried egg with a white yolk.

"A white hat?" Smith said with a laugh. "One of John Stetson's "Boss of the Plains" style, but white as a sheep? Not only would it look dirty in about one minute, it would stand out in Denver like a big painted sign!"

Sapania felt dizzy and very tired—as sleepy as when she'd stayed awake for three days to learn a ritual. Strange emotions surged through her. The warmth of the man whose arm remained around her waist— memories of the night she rang the bell and her magical horse appeared— surprise at the white hat launching itself onto the floor…

"You should buy the hat for me," she said quietly.

111

Smith laughed but kept his arm around her waist and she couldn't move. The smell of his witch-hazel aftershave confused her. It reminded her of the sweet and spicy scent of black walnuts before they ripen. She felt weak and confused.

He grasped her wrist and pulled her hand with the blade from her pocket and easily unwrapped her fingers from its handle. She did not resist.

"I'll return this to the bartender so he doesn't think someone stole it," he said. He picked the hat up off the floor.

"It probably thought you were calling it when I rang the bell."

Her eyes opened wide with a new understanding. She should have said nothing. But the room seemed hazy; everything moved so slowly it felt like a dream.

"Yes," she whispered, to herself. "The bell has magic, but it is small magic. That's what I did not understand. It can call a manitou. My mother said that small magic can call great magic..."

Later, she would understand she should have said nothing more. Back at the cafe, in the few seconds when she stole the knife and watched the cart being pulled by elk, Smith had employed a skill honed by years of keeping a straight face while switching playing-cards. Smith had switched their teacups, and even switched the little rose. Mrs. Winslow's Soothing Syrup contained medicine made from poppies. The soothing syrup had confused her, the smell of black walnuts triggered distant memories, and she forgot to be careful. She repeated herself.

"I think the bell can call to a manitou."

"You mean the Great Manitou?"

"No. Most magical things are small."

"Are most of them hats? Or are some boots and britches magical as well?"

She didn't realize he was joking. "I don't know. When I close my eyes, my horse can take me places without moving. You should buy the hat and give it to me. Because we are both Arapaho."

Smith smiled. He knew when a mark said too much. "A magical spirit that looks like something ordinary and can transport its owner with a mere thought. That sounds like the superstitions that rise from campfire smoke after a long hunt. Do you believe this hat is magical? That it can transport me like a train?" He stared at the hat with sudden interest. Sapania saw the look in his eyes, realized her mistake, and pulled away from him.

"No, of course not," she said and tried to laugh a little. "It's just a story the old women whisper to each other while they cook. I have not learned to make jokes in the pale man's words."

Smith set the white hat on his head carefully, as if it might be dangerous. It was a completely normal hat. There was a small mirror on the wall and he surveyed himself with some amusement.

"Why, come to think of it, an unusual hat might be good advertising. A way for my customers to find me. I think I'll buy it."

He moved toward the register, then stopped.

"And how about that bell?" he asked. "If you could use some more cash I'd pay you a fair price."

She clutched it with both hands. "No, the bell is not for sale. A priest gave it to me."

"You were friends with a priest?" he joked.

"Not for very long."

"So how do you operate this hat?"

"I don't think it works for men."

"Then there's no harm in telling me, is there?"

She felt confused. Smith had set the knife down on a shelf, if she could distract him for a few seconds he would be dead before he could use her words against her.

"I close my eyes," she said quietly. "And then I see the place where I wish to be."

"Like a dream?"

"Yes. When you close your eyes, can you still see these sacks of flour over there?"

"I can't see anything when my eyes are closed."

"Well then the hat will be of no use to you. I should go now." She took a step toward the knife, but he slid his left arm around her waist again, and then his right arm. He held her too tightly to move.

"No, don't go yet," he whispered into her ear. "I haven't bought my new hat yet. Let's try it out first. I'll close my eyes and picture some destination."

"I'm so sleepy…"

"Yes, I know. Just relax. Let's go somewhere more interesting than an aisle of baking staples in a mercantile."

"I need to sit down…"

"You'll feel better after a little nap."

Sapania closed her eyes.

When she opened them again, she was lying on a hard narrow bed in a strange hotel room. It smelled of old cigar smoke and dirty clothes. She was alone. She sat up and her head throbbed with pain. Smith was gone. The bartender's knife was gone, the coins she had won were gone, the pocket-watch was gone, the pistol with the ivory handle was gone.

And the bell was gone.

Chapter 21

"Wake up!!" Martin said, shaking Charles's shoulders. Charles stirred, still more asleep than awake. He vaguely remembered trying to stay alert beneath the porch to guard against coyotes, but he must have dozed off. His brain swirled with images of cemeteries and dark cities. Confusing as it was, he was tired and didn't want to wake up, so he just kept his eyes closed and turned away from his strange new friend.

"The parade's going to start!" Martin said excitedly. "You don't want to miss the parade!"

"You go without me," Charles said and tried not to wake too much.

"But we're already there!" Martin said. His voice was very excited.

"What?" Charles said with a start and opened his eyes.

They were no longer on the straw beneath the porch but were in an alley between two buildings. The dirt they sat on was cold and rocky; the brick wall Charles leaned against was even harder. He sat up straight, looking around quickly, panic filling him.

"Where are we? How did you…? What in the world…?"

"It's OK," Martin said. His white goat quietly munched on a dandelion. The yellow blossom dangled from its mouth like jewelry, bouncing gently up and down with each bite. Men's voices spoke quietly, not too far away. "You get used to it," Martin said. "We're in downtown Denver City."

"But how?" Charles asked.

"I was thinking about the parade when I went to sleep," Martin said. "I think Pan was too. My father takes me to it. Sometimes there's a circus, sometimes there's cowboys."

"So you just think about places and then you go there?"

"Sometimes. Or I think of a place and nothing happens. Come on, get up. You'll like the parade."

Charles stood up and brushed the straw and dirt from his jeans.

"My mother will be worried about me," Charles said. "I should call her."

"I don't know how to do that," Martin said.

"As soon as we find a pay phone I'll show you."

"OK, but let's go find a good place to stand."

Charles had never seen this part of Denver. The sturdy brick buildings looked well-cared for. The street was unpaved and without stop signs or traffic lights. Few people walked through the early morning. No cars or buses stirred. On one side of the street, a wooden sidewalk jutted out from the buildings. It reminded Charles of the old frontier towns in TV westerns. Someone probably designed this street to attract tourists who still thought of Colorado as the wild west. Of course, the scenes on TV were only in black and white, while this street looked shockingly vivid. The brown wood grain of the sidewalk contrasted tastefully with the red brick buildings and the blue sky. A few pots containing green plants with bright flowers punctuated the sidewalk. Television could never capture all that, Charles thought.

"I wonder if that's how it really looked?" Charles said, daydreaming.

"What?" said Martin.

"Nothing," Charles said. "Just thinking out loud."

A block away, a dozen people milled about.

"That's where we stand," Martin said. They started walking in that direction. A stately brick building loomed behind the little crowd; at three stories it was taller than most. A sign above its doors said "Bank" in big letters.

"I need to tell you something," Martin said. He slowed his pace and kept his eyes on the dirt in front of his feet.

Yes, I think you do Charles thought. "What is that?"

"I visited here before. You know, with Pan."

"OK," Charles said.

"And the people can't see me."

"Well, you're pretty short. Adults often don't notice kids."

116

"I don't think that's it. I'm not sure if they'll see you either."

"Interesting," Charles said. "But we're scientists, right? Any data like that could help us form a working hypothesis."

"I don't know those words," Martin said, furrowing up his forehead. "I just didn't want you to be scared in case you're invisible."

"Thanks," Charles said. He wasn't worried about being invisible, he was too busy being confused. What science would allow an eight-year-old boy to transport himself around the state? He needed more information. Later he could organize information into a theory then devise an experiment to test it. That's how science works. And, he believed, it's also how magic works.

A young mother was trying to herd her excited little girl toward the bank building. The girl wore a light blue dress, her hair was tied in pigtails. She kept throwing a brown ball about the size of a softball into the air and then chasing after it. She tried to catch it but she never did.

"Child, you come back here and walk with your mama!" the woman yelled after her.

"Just one more," the little girl yelled back. She threw the ball as high as she could. It flew over Charles's and Martin's heads as she raced toward it.

The ball landed on a low roof overhanging the wooden sidewalk. It rolled very slowly down, but stopped a few feet short of the edge.

"Mama, my ball!" the girl wailed. Her mother caught up to her and tried to reach the ball, but it was too high for her. She looked around for a stick or a stool but found neither.

"Now see what you've done, child," she said. "Your father will not be pleased."

"Maybe there's a man with a ladder!" the girl pleaded. She turned and looked straight at Charles. "Do you have a ladder?" she asked.

"I'm sorry, no I don't," he said. Then, as an experiment he continued, "What's your name?"

"Melissa," she answered. "But everyone calls me Lissa." Obviously she could both see and hear him.

"I'm sorry about your ball, Lissa," he said

She nodded sadly as her mother took her hand and and led her away.

When their backs were turned, Charles had an idea. Back on his porch he had moved a tennis ball. At least he thought he did. He had focused his mind, generated an emotion, then looked away. Charles stood in the street, just below the spot where the ball remained perched. He held one hand up in the air, closed his eyes and concentrated.

"What are you doing?" Martin said, distracting Charles for a moment. The ball dropped into Charles's hand and he closed his fingers around it.

"That's what I'm doing," he said.

"You lit the campfire again," Martin said quietly. That remark made no sense so Charles ignored it.

"Lissa!" Charles shouted and ran after the little girl. She and her mother stopped and turned around. "Your ball rolled off the roof." He gave it to her. Her eyes lit up and she thanked him several times.

Jefferson Smith stood in front of the crowd, behind a little table. A box of soap bars sat open on the ground beside him. In a loud dramatic voice he proclaimed the excellence of his soap. It sounded medicinal and magical and maybe even Biblical. The crowd stared at him, transfixed, as if he were a dancing snake.

"There!" Martin said. "That's my father." He pointed at a serious man holding a boy's hand just behind the main group. He was about thirty years old with an evenly trimmed mustache and wore a neat coat and pants of dark blue wool. He was dressed better than the others and looked like a businessman, but had a lean, muscular build. He seemed confident in a physical way, like an athlete, and watched the huckster with an intensity different from the others. He was observing the scene more than participating and the frown on his face suggested he thought something was amiss. The boy beside him turned and Charles could see him better. He looked a lot like Martin, only shorter. That must be his younger brother, Charles thought with a burst of excitement. Maybe he had managed to get Martin back to his family without realizing it! Charles's father lifted the boy to sit on his shoulders for a better view.

Charles and Martin were still twenty feet away, with people jostling between. Martin's little brother craned his neck to look down the street, hoping to see the parade before it got to them.

"Frank!" a man yelled and Martin's father turned at the sound. "Frank Whiting! When is that dang-fool railroad line going to get finished?"

"I did my part," Frank replied with a smile. "But I'd be delighted to forward your complaints to the construction boss."

"I believe he lights his cigars with my complaints," the man said. The two men were obviously friends, joking with each other.

Frank smiled. "Well, today let's just enjoy the parade, shall we?"

Martin became very excited and ran ahead of Charles. "Father!" he said. Frank Whiting didn't hear him. Martin shouted, "Father, it's me, Martin! Right here!" His father paid no attention to him and neither did anyone else. Martin's brother looked confused for a moment, as if he'd heard something in the distance, and turned around to look. Then he looked away again.

"He can't hear me," Martin said, dejected. "My voice is invisible too!"

Two men on the other side of the crowd wearing derby hats and dark wool coats walked toward him.

"Those men!" Charles whispered to Martin. "Slim and the Reverend! How did they find us?"

"You lit the fire," Martin said.

"I didn't light any fire!"

"Yes you did. With the ball."

"I don't think they've seen us," Charles said. "Let's get behind that wall."

The boys moved quickly to the side of the bank building. They could still see Jefferson Smith selling soap and Martin's father, Frank Whiting, but the crowd obscured the two men in derby hats. Smith started to talk louder.

"Yes, this is the finest soap in the world, imported directly and exclusively by my company from Paris, France," Jefferson Smith shouted. "And I can tell this is a sophisticated group, discerning in taste but cautious in matters of finance. So I'm going to make an extraordinary offer to you gentlefolk gathered here today, and only you. The modest price of a bar of soap is only one dollar. To sweeten the deal, I have wrapped a one dollar bill in some of these bars. If you should happen to buy one of these, your cost will actually be zero!"

He held a dollar bill up for all to see, then wrapped it around a bar of soap. Then he took some brown wrapping paper and wrapped it around the bar, hiding the money inside.

"That's one," he said. "Let's do more." He wrapped another dollar around another bar of soap and covered it all with brown paper. He pulled a box out from beneath the table and opened it. He held it at an angle so everyone could see it was nearly full of wrapped bars of soap. He threw the bars with hidden money on top of the others in the box.

"In the interest of time and expeditiousness, I have secreted money inside a goodly number of these. Frankly, I was saving this box for my expedition to the grand city of San Francisco, California. To induce those wealthy women to try our product, I gave an extra incentive. Not only are there a number of single dollar bills wrapped with bars of soap, I included several wrapped with a one-hundred-dollar bill!"

The audience gasped. The man reached into the box, pulled out a bar, unwrapped the brown paper and pulled out a one hundred dollar bill. He held it up for all to see.

"You there in front," he said. "Can you attest to the fact that this is, in fact, a one-hundred-dollar bill?" Slim stepped up to inspect it. He turned the bill over in his hands, held it up to the light and nodded his head.

"Yes, sir, Mr. Smith," Slim said loudly. "That's a crisp Watermelon Note, with the picture of Admiral David Farragut as plain as day. Not that I've seen many working for the Briggs coal mine up by Boulder Creek. They prefer to pay us in three-cent nickels." The crowd laughed. It was reassuring that a working man had inspected the bill.

"My good man," Mr. Smith, the salesman said. "Would you be so kind as to wrap this bill around this bar of soap and then cover the whole thing with wrapping paper?" Slim did as he was told.

"Now, sir, would you be so kind as to re-deposit this valuable package in with its fellows? Careful so I don't know which one it is. In fact, I'll avert my eyes." Mr. Smith turned away from the crowd. As he did, he told them, "Friends, you watch him carefully so he does not abscond with your future fortune." The crowd laughed.

"Now, just to be fair, I must inform you that many of the bars of soap contain only the finest soap in the world. My boss wouldn't be happy if I just gave away his money would he?"

The crowd laughed again. In the distance a drum and some trumpets began playing a march.

"It's the parade!" Martin whispered urgently.

"We can see it from here," Charles said.

But Martin wasn't listening. Holding Pan's rope he scurried out of the alley and up the bank steps until he stood just outside the bank's doors. "This will be better," he said. "Come on!"

With everyone preoccupied by the soap salesman and their own imminent windfall, no one looked back at the bank. Charles joined Martin. Smith's voice grew louder and more excited as the parade approached. More people gathered around him. Some paid their dollar and bought a bar of soap. Most were disappointed that they had purchased only soap, unadorned by the riches they deserved.

"I got one!" a man in the center of the group yelled. It was the Reverend. He held up his bar of soap in one hand and a dollar bill in the other. The crowd clapped enthusiastically. Other buyers stepped forward.

"Me too!" someone yelled, and a hand shot up above the heads, waving a dollar bill. The crowd surged toward the salesman. People held money out before them, eager to spend it on soap and the dream of a quick profit.

"One at a time, please," Mr. Smith said with a laugh. "I must insist on order. There's plenty for everyone. And that hundred-dollar bill remains undiscovered."

Far from calming the crowd, they pushed and jostled hoping to buy the lucky bar, desperately hoping their neighbor would not beat them to the good fortune.

Not quite everyone, Charles noticed. Martin's father remained aloof from the crowd. Frank Whiting wore a stern, intent look on his face as he stroked his mustache thoughtfully.

"He's trying to figure something out," Martin said. "He always looks like that when he's solving a puzzle."

"Look," Charles said and pointed to the wooden sidewalk near the bank. The Reverend and Slim had casually slipped away from the group and were walking toward the bank doorway where the boys hid.

"We've got to hide," Charles said. Before he could look for a better spot, Martin had opened the bank door and led his goat inside. A little bell on a spring above the door jingled when it opened and again when it closed.

"That's not a good idea," Charles said under his breath, imagining the commotion a goat might cause among bank customers, but it was too late. The men were approaching fast but hadn't seen him yet. Charles followed Martin into the bank.

A red leather couch and chair near the door were arranged like a living room, inviting and comfortable. A goat's leg incongruously stuck out from behind the couch. The cashiers were all clustered around a window behind the counter, watching the soap salesman and waiting for the parade as eagerly as Martin. No one looked up when Charles walked over to join Martin in his hiding place. He pulled Pan's leg behind the couch.

"I thought you said they couldn't see you," Charles whispered. "Why are you hiding?"

"Most of them can't" Martin said. "But you can and those two men can. I don't know all the rules."

Because the cashiers were all looking out onto the street, they didn't notice the boys. There weren't any customers to serve, not during a parade.

The bank door opened a few inches and the little bell jingled merrily. Charles peeked out from behind the couch. The cashiers glanced over, but no one entered, so they turned back to the window. The Reverend had opened the door and was just outside, crouching on the ground. Kneeling beside him, Slim glanced over his shoulder, then nodded. The Reverend crawled on hands and knees and propped the door open with a big rock. When he was sure no cashier had noticed him, he crawled across the lobby and over to the cashier's counter. He remained low and hidden by the counter, below the cashiers' line of sight.

In a moment the Reverend crawled through the doorway and joined him. With the door propped open, the little bell did not jingle. The sound of a marching band in the distance wafted intermittently on the breeze; a slow crescendo of crisp brass instruments punctuated the steady beat of drums. That music and the crowd noise mixed with the soap salesman shouting his urgent patter camouflaged any noise the intruders made. Two more men crawled inside and joined the first two outlaws.

A man's voice outside rose to compete with Jefferson Smith's. "This man is a charlatan," he said. "He is perpetrating a ruse upon us."

Martin's eyes were bright and there was a big smile on his face. "Father!" he said proudly.

"Someone dispose of this rabble rouser!" Mr. Smith shouted. The crowd noise increased as people argued with each other.

"Only his collaborators find the hidden money," Frank Whiting said. "They are shills and they've slipped away into the bank to hide!"

The men hiding by the counter ignored the commotion outside and crawled to the left, away from the wall with the window. When the the man they called Reverend reached the end of the counter, he stopped and pulled a long revolver out from beneath his heavy coat. Then he crawled around behind the counter. In a moment Slim and the others joined him. They stood up and Reverend pointed his gun toward the cashiers staring out the window, their backs to the robbers.

"They're going to rob the bank!" Charles whispered. "We have to do something!"

"Wait," Martin said, putting his hand on Charles's shoulder, gently holding him in place. Voices just outside the bank argued. Peeking out from their hiding place, the boys could see several men.

"You will find the conspirators in here," Frank Whiting said. "Upon questioning I'm sure you'll deduce, Mike, their role in this despicable affair." Mr. Whiting stood with Martin's brother by his side.

Sheriff Mike Spangler stood beside them, a burly, athletic man of about forty. He came from sturdy German stock, and was smart as well as physical. He'd been a banker before he became Sheriff. His reputation for being a tough man with a temper started when he picked up two drunks and carried them out of a local bar before tossing them onto the street. Today, his brown pants and blue shirt were freshly laundered for the parade, a shiny metal star was pinned to his leather vest. He walked toward the bank door mildly irritated he had to follow through on trivial complaints on a day he was supposed to simply look official, drink lemonade, and let the women flirt with the him, the most eligible bachelor in town. But Whiting was an old friend and not given to fanciful stories.

When Spangler stepped through the door and saw the situation, his eyes narrowed and his jaw clenched. Without a word, he pulled his revolver from its holster and aimed it directly at the robbers. Reverend saw him and quickly ducked down behind the counter. He did not warn his partners in crime.

"Empty your hands, Slim Foster and reach for your Maker's heaven," Sheriff Spangler said firmly. "Or prepare to meet Him personally."

Slim hesitated briefly, then he and the others dropped their weapon to clatter on the wooden floor. The outlaws raised their hands above their heads. The cashiers turned from the window in surprise, their heads pivoting in perfect synchrony, like baby birds watching mama bird land with a big worm. Until they heard the Sheriff and the clatter of the guns on the floor, they hadn't realized they were in jeopardy.

"This ain't what it looks like," Slim said in a calm, conciliatory tone. "It's all a big misunderstanding. We're putting on a play here. Part of the festivities. No need to make a fuss."

Sheriff Spangler nodded. "That's just fine," he said. "Now, Slim, you and the other gentlemen come on on out here where customers are supposed to stand. And then you lay down on this floor, facing down,

124

hands behind your heads. That's it. Is Reverend Bowers back there with you, Slim?"

"I don't know any Reverend," Slim said.

"I agree Bowers isn't very holy," the Sheriff said.

"No idea who you're talking about."

"Have it your way. The rest of you lay down there too. Nice and slow. I been hunting rats in my barn and my trigger finger tends to squeeze at any sudden movement."

The men did as they were told. The cashiers remained behind the bar, frozen with fear. "Anybody get hurt back there, Dolores?"

"No, Mike, we're all fine." The cashier, a plain woman of about forty tried to warn him that one outlaw remained hidden back there, huddling on the floor, his gun aimed right at her. Her eyes widened. Her voice was shaky.

"Well that's good news for these boys," the sheriff said. "But I do believe I seen a rat go hide behind that counter. I bet I can shoot him right through the wood without even seeing him. When I count three, you gentle folks cover your ears, cause this 44 makes a heck of a racket. One…"

The Reverend reached up and set his gun on the counter, then slowly stood.

"See, I was right," Sheriff Spangler said. "There was a rat hiding back there. You come on out here and join the rest of your congregation."

"Lucky you didn't hurt anybody," the sheriff said. "Maybe you won't get hung after all. Dolores, would you go over to my office and bring Henry back here? Hate for him to miss all the excitement."

"Of course," she said and walked briskly out the door.

"Would one of you kindly tie some hands behind some backs while I try not to shoot these vermin. The twine you use to tie up cash bags should be fine."

Martin's father had been standing just outside the door. Despite all the excitement, Martin hadn't taken his eyes off him. Frank Whiting and Martin's brother stepped inside.

"May I be of any assistance?" Frank asked the Sheriff.

"I believe we have the situation well in hand," the Sheriff said. "Your instincts were correct, sorry I doubted you. Thank you for the tip."

"One does the honorable thing," Frank said. "But I'm afraid their leader escaped. He bundled up his wares and ill-gotten profits and spurred his horse at the first sign of controversy. He rode west out of town. He could be to Golden by the time you get up a posse."

"Jefferson Smith is well known in these parts," the Sheriff said. "If he doesn't flee the territory, we'll find him."

"Then I believe my son and I have a parade to attend." Frank picked up Martin's brother and carried him out the door.

"It's not done yet," Martin whispered. With his goat beside him he walked toward the door. Charles followed behind them.

"Young man, stop right there!" Sheriff Spangler barked and Charles stopped in his tracks. "Are you related to this group of entrepreneurs?"

"No sir," Charles said. The sheriff's speech reminded him of the vocabulary and cadence of the old books he read. This might be one time all that reading could work in his favor. The sheriff might believe he wasn't part of the outlaw gang if he didn't talk like one of them.

"No sir," he repeated. "I have been drawn unwittingly by unfortunate and inexplicable circumstance to this place. I've had no congress with these miscreants before today."

Sheriff Spangler smiled. It worked, Charles thought.

"Was that your goat?"

"It belongs to a friend," Charles said. Interesting, he thought. The Sheriff could see him and the goat but he didn't mention seeing Martin.

"Well, you'd best catch up to it before it joins the marching band."

"Yes sir," Charles said and walked quickly outside.

Neither Martin nor his goat were anywhere to be seen.

Charles stood outside the bank building, scanning the crowd frantically. He finally saw Martin trotting along behind his father and brother. Pan bounced along beside them on spindly goat legs. People had gathered on both sides of the street as the sound of the marching band got louder. Martin's father stopped at a corner with Martin's brother on his shoulders, the boy's thin legs straddling the man's head and both arms wrapped around his neck. The boy's big grin looked just like the one on Martin's face as he stood beside them.

Martin nodded happily at Charles and they watched together.

An energetic drum major led the band. He wore a white suit and marched with precise, exaggerated motions, raising a baton into the air every fourth step. A line of trombone players followed him, then the other musicians. The crowd clapped in time to the music; children marched in place, most imitating drum majors.

After the band came people and animals from the traveling circus. Two pretty girls perched gaily on horses, waving to the crowd. A dark man in flowing robes and a turban rode a huge camel. Four clowns wearing bright costumes and painted grins cavorted behind them. They tossed a hoop to each other, sometimes catching it with the most improbable gymnastics, other times stumbling in an elaborate manner only to have one of the others bounce the hoop high in the air with a kick and then look around as if confused when it landed in their hand. The crowd roared with laughter.

Behind the clowns walked a giant, a man two feet taller than any other man in the parade. He was an impressive, muscular figure with shaggy black hair and a massive black beard. His shirt was tight and too short; his wrists and hands stuck far out of the sleeves. His pants barely reached his knees.

Martin's eyes were bright and intent as he watched each act passed before him. When the giant drew near, he waved broadly at the huge man. "Hey George!" he yelled. "Hey, over here!"

The giant's face lit up with delight and waved back at him. The giant danced a goofy little dance, turning like a ballerina and pointed at Martin.

Martin's face exploded into an even bigger smile. He suddenly looked childlike and happy, no longer stiff and formal. The giant kept walking.

"You're not invisible to George," Charles said. "That's interesting. Who is that behind him?" He pointed at a man in a little buggy.

"That's Prairie Dog O'Byrne," Martin said. "My father says he consorts with sinners but has a good heart."

"Are those…?"

"Yes, two elk with big antlers pull his buggy. People pay him for rides from Colorado City to Colorado Springs. Sometimes the elk scare people's horses and he gets thrown in jail, but usually nothing happens." O'Byrne waved and Martin waved back. In the back of his carriage a round wire cage spun around, powered by a prairie dog that ran in place.

"Mr. O'Byrne's father laid railroad tracks, so my father knew him." Martin added proudly.

After the parade passed and the sound of the marching band faded in the distance, the crowd began to break up and go home. Mr. Whiting and his little son walked off with the rest of them. But Martin stood still, watching the nearly vacant street.

"It's still not over," he said.

Chapter 22

Sapania's head ached, as if the card-player had struck her with the handle of his gun. She knew better than to trust a wasicun, a person not born of the prairie, men with strange ways and odd clothing, and worth no more than an insect. She sat up in the hotel bed and thought her whole body would explode. She had been careless, she knew that, trying to play the wasicun's game. She had no memory of what happened after the card game, but the fact that she was in a city hotel room told her all she needed to know. There was no need to try to piece together the details.

She walked to the window, one slow painful step at a time.

On the street below she saw her horse still tied to a railing. It would have been worse if she'd lost the horse. She was not helpless. And the man would pay. They all would pay.

There was a pitcher of water next to the window. After smelling it and sipping it to make sure it wasn't another trick, she drank deeply. Her body was a desert.

These white men were all evil. They deserved no mercy. Not just the white men, she corrected herself. Blue Sky was just as evil. Her uncle was just as evil. They should be cleansed from the earth. All of them. They deserved whatever pain she could direct toward them. She took another deep drink from the pitcher.

Most of her clothing was on the floor, some of it newly ripped. She got dressed as well as she could, then walked down the stairs and stood by her horse. Her legs were too weak to mount it so she waited for strength to return. Something was different about Denver City since the last time she'd snuck in to liberate molasses and ammunition. The street was very quiet. An old woman trudged down the wooden walkway carrying a heavy basket of potatoes. Sapania caught her attention.

"Old woman!" she shouted. "Where are all the soldiers?"

The woman stopped, put down her basket and stretched her back.

"Well, don't put me under oath and make me swear, but I got a good idea." She spit on the boardwalk, then looked into the distance. "The men folk been talking about Sand Creek." She waved a pesky fly away from her face. "I heard that Chivington's soldiers headed out there yesterday. Something about a big party, but I didn't hear much. If it's a party, you can be sure there will be drinking and card games with my worthless husband right at the center of it. They stopped short of inviting me."

Sapania had been to the Sand Creek camp once with Left Hand. It was a new settlement for the Arapaho, several miles east of Denver City, out on the plains where tribes could be separate from cities and soldiers. Left Hand had been involved in negotiating it into existence. It was desolate, dry land, but he hoped it would bring a more stable peace between his people and the white settlers. It was the unlikeliest site for city people to hold a party. Then Sapania realized the old woman had been tricked. It wasn't going to be the kind of "party" the woman believed. No, it was where evil men would do evil deeds. Yes, that is where the soldiers would be, perhaps the wasicun salesman would be there too. First she would retrieve the weapons she'd hidden by Flat River. Then she would join their "party."

They had a head start. It normally took two days to ride to Sand Creek. But she would travel in a different way.

When she was ready, she closed her eyes and remembered the camp. It looked like a temporary camp for a large hunting party— dozens of tipis clustered around a few cooking fires, horses gathered outside the main area shuffling their feet and swatting at flies with their tails; children yelling and chasing each other through the dusty heat. A month ago, when she rode there with Left Hand and the others, they had paused on a low hill before they rode the last bit of the journey, and she remembered that spot clearly. A few cactus clung to the dirt amid tough blue sagebrush; spiked yuccas with their green swords; a few stubborn cottonwood trees a half mile away near the creek itself; prairie dogs that sat up and chattered their urgent chirping warnings. One granite boulder protruded a foot from the dirt on top of the hill, covered with the scratchings of hundreds who had stopped to rest at just that spot.

A gunshot snapped her out of her reverie.

Chapter 23

"It's still not over," Martin said, pointing down the nearly vacant street. "Just watch."

In a few minutes, a lone horseman came riding slowly up the street. His horse was large and glossy black. The man wore a big floppy leather hat and held a rope casually in one hand. It was Jim Baker, only younger and healthier than before. His piercing blue eyes flickered back and forth. Now he didn't look old and menacing. He looked young and menacing.

Trailing a few feet behind at the end of the rope, Mr. Jefferson Smith, the soap salesman walked. The rope looped under his arms and his hands were tied behind his back. His dark suit was covered in dust and so was his hair and beard. He walked defiantly with his chin held high in the air. Baker stopped just as Sheriff Spangler and his deputy Henry, led the group of bank robbers out of the bank. Their hands were tied behind their backs with sturdy twine. A rope was tied around each man's waist, linked both to the man ahead of him and the man behind them, creating their own little forced parade.

"Let's stop right here, gentlemen," he said to his train of prisoners. "It looks like we may have one more guest join our party. I think Jim Baker's been trappin' vermin instead of beaver."

The young version of Jim Baker nodded.

"Mornin' Jim," the sheriff said.

"Mornin' Mike," Jim Baker replied. "Nice weather we're having." There was a noticeable pause as both men contemplated the weather.

Sheriff Spangler nodded. "Respectable weather," he said. "Highly respectable."

Another pause for introspection and meditation.

"You puttin' together a church choir?" Jim Baker gestured toward the bank robbers.

"Something like that. And you?"

"Oddest thing," Jim Baker said. "Mr. Smith here was flying out of town like the Devil himself was chasing him for a gambling debt. That put to mind the time Mr. Smith managed to win all the money I'd saved up for two years to buy a little place. Won it all in one night of Three-Card Monte down in Albuquerque. His remarkable good luck saved me from a life of leisure and tranquility but I never did get the chance to thank him."

"I can see how you'd want to express your gratitude."

"It was the very least of what I hoped to express to him. Then I seen him high-tailing it, looking sort of anxious. So I said to myself, by gonny, that poor sinner needs to join a church choir! Being sympathetic to Samaritan impulses of all varieties, I determined to help him out."

The Sheriff nodded slowly. It took a while for either man to process that many words.

"And has Mr. Smith been properly appreciative of your altruism?

"Well, you know, I believe he's still searching for the appropriate words of gratitude."

Jefferson Smith, the soap salesman, spit in the dirt. "You live beneath the tyranny of a government, of rules and foolish conventions," he said, his voice dripping with disgust. "Card dealers and girl managers are not the criminals. Men who buy horses from the desperate and sell them to the ignorant for a reasonable profit—these are not treacherous miscreants as they are labeled. No, the villains are the men who hide behind laws, who use words as weapons. The tyrants control you and don't even realize it. My men and I resist their evil. We are the real heroes, but we get no credit!"

He stood with his chin thrust upward, his legs spread in a solid, confident stance. He would not let being captured and hog-tied interfere with his image. "I win games," he said. "It's the way of nature. Outsmart some sucker, take his money, move on before he thinks about it too much. You can't let 'em think, that's the key. Some say it's wrong but they don't say that about a cougar. He outsmarts a stupid rabbit and doesn't feel remorse for his dinner. It's the way of Nature, the way of God. How can the way of God be wrong?"

Jim Baker nodded slowly, then turned back to the Sheriff.

"Just as I was telling you, Mike: he's a religious man It may profit the lot of them to spend an hour praying together in a quiet cell," he said.

The sheriff nodded. "This visit will be a little longer than usual. We have a witness who watched the fraud perpetrated, with a new variation. This time they weren't satisfied with bilking our citizens and disappearing into the crowd. This time they tried to rob the bank. We caught these foxes in the henhouse with chickens in their mouths. They'll be praying in jail until the circuit judge has time to have a conversation with them."

"Is your witness reliable?"

"Indeed he is. Mr. Frank Whiting, a civil engineer for the Colfax Railroad Line. An eye for detail, an excellent memory, and an upright man. With his tip, I captured them in the middle of their bank heist. I think we have them this time."

"Then I believe I'll go find me a city breakfast. I'll stop over later to retrieve my rope." Jim Baker reached into his saddlebag and pulled out a large but crumpled white hat. "Don't forget this. He calls it his lucky hat."

"Then he probably has some aces hid in it. I'll give it back to him when he's safely locked up."

Jim Baker pulled an old bell out of his saddle bag. "He had this thing, too," he said. "Looks like something a preacher might carry. You should probably give it back to him in case he feels the urge to save some souls."

The Sheriff smiled. "I think it highly unlikely that Jefferson Smith will be saving many souls. Leastways, until Saint Pete starts offering a dollar bounty per soul. Why don't you just keep that as a symbol of our gratitude."

"I don't much care to have what don't belong to me," Jim Baker said. "Just put it with his other stuff in a drawer or something. We don't need to follow his bad example." He handed the bell to the lawman.

The Sheriff led his captives down the street. Jim Baker turned his horse to walk away.

"Mr. Baker!" Charles yelled. "Honest Uncle Jim Baker!"

Baker stopped and turned his horse to face the boy. He stared at Charles for a moment displaying no hint of recognition.

"Do I know you, son?" he asked.

"Pillar of Fire... I mean, Westminster University, north of Denver," Charles said. "You helped me with some... some hooligans. I had an owl..."

Jim Baker's expression remained blank.

"I been considering building a little house up north of town. But I ain't explored it much yet."

"You saw... you saw my little campfire."

"I'm not saying you're wrong, son. I been on on the trail a while and I seen some campfires. But I think you got me confused with someone else."

"You're Honest Uncle Jim Baker, aren't you?"

"I been called that. Like I said, I'm not saying you're wrong. Just confused."

There was no way to explain it, let alone argue the point.

"I'm sorry, sir. I guess I'm mistaken."

"No need to be sorry," he said.

Charles had a thought. An experiment, really.

"Do you know my friend here?" Martin stood right beside him holding Pan's leash. Pan was nibbling at some nasty-looking bindweed clutching the dirt street. Charles pointed at Martin.

"I don't think he can..." Martin started.

"Your goat?" Jim Baker said.

"You only see the goat?" Charles asked. "You don't see my friend?"

"A goat is as good a friend as most men," Baker said. "Just be careful. My wife's a Shoshone princess and she swears goats are magic. You start leading one around and pretty soon it's leading you around instead." He gave a short snort of a laugh. "Sort of like Shoshone princesses, I guess." He leaned back his head and laughed long and loud at the sky. Then he abruptly stopped and looked down at Charles. "You have a pleasant morning, young man. You and your goat too."

"You too, sir."

Baker rode away and Charles turned to Martin.

"So he can see me and the goat but not you?"

"I think so."

"But the giant could see you?"

"We can always see each other. He's my friend."

"And your father can't?"

"No. I wish he could. But I like seeing him."

"Is it always exactly the same?"

"Oh no. Sometimes father wears different clothes, sometimes he looks younger. Once Mr. O'Byrne's elk started a stampede. Then the circus camel got in a fight with a horse. I don't always get to see the bank robbery."

Charles tried to collect all the information. The Sheriff saw Charles but not Martin.

"Can everyone else see the goat?" Charles asked.

"I don't know. My friend's name is George," said Martin.

"Can the other people see George?"

Martin looked down at his shoes.

"I don't think so," he said softly. "He waves at the people but no one waves back. He doesn't notice and I don't want to tell him. He loves being in the parade. He walks in every parade he can find."

So George and Martin saw each other but others couldn't. It was very confusing.

"And the men that are after you, the ones who stole Pan. The Sheriff called them Slim and the Reverend. Those were the bank robbers."

"Yes. They aren't nice men."

Charles just nodded. The two boys started walking down the street although Charles had no idea where they were heading. "Who was the boy with your father?" Charles asked. "He looks a little like you. Is he your younger brother?"

"There wasn't any boy with my father," Martin said.

Charles started to argue then thought better of it. Martin couldn't see that kid standing beside his father, riding his shoulders, grinning at the parade. Charles had a theory about that, but it was too weird to be right so he didn't say anything.

"You knew everything that was going to happen today, didn't you?" Charles asked.

"My father took me to the parade."

"And then you remember it while you were touching Pan? Is that how it happened? And then somehow I could see your memory too?"

"This is an easy place to go."

"So you've done it before?"

"Oh yes. Many times. It's exciting and nobody gets hurt. I like to see my father."

"But why would I remember it with you?"

"Pan likes you. He likes your campfire. It's easier when you're with me."

"I see. So when do I get my dogs back?"

"It's probably safe there now. I like your dogs."

"Fine. How do you do it?"

"I'll show you. Let's try it together. I like to use smells. Your dogs' house is made with hay. If we can find a stable with some hay, that might help."

A building that looked like a barn incongruously stuck in downtown Denver had a sign said "Livery. Horses Bought, Sold, and Stabled." The big double door wasn't locked or guarded so they walked right in with the goat between them.

Immediately the smell of hay and manure and horse sweat flooded over Charles. If Martin used smells, they'd come to the right place. Charles sneezed loudly.

"Shh," said Martin. Charles sneezed again.

"It's so dusty," he said. "I think I'm allergic to the straw."

"It's not straw, it's hay. Maybe if you cover your face with something," Martin suggested.

Charles stepped back outside and looked around. A newspaper that looked fresh and clean had blown against the building. It wasn't ideal but he picked it up and covered his nose and mouth.

The room was divided into a series of horse stalls. Horses peered out of several, hoping for carrots or apples.

"There's an empty stall," Martin said. "Back in the corner." Charles followed him to it, ducking low under its gate. The stable was dark, the floor was covered with loose hay a foot thick and the smell did remind Charles of the area beneath the porch. It felt safe.

"Let's hide in the hay," Martin said. "Sometimes it takes a while."

They lay down on the hay and pulled a thin layer over their legs and stomachs. A casual observer might not notice them there. Charles covered his face with the newspaper.

"Pan, you lay down between us," Martin said. Charles could feel its boney warmth as the animal snuggled beside him.

"Now, Charles, let's both think about your dogs and their little home."

"There aren't any magic words?" Charles asked, joking.

"Maybe," Martin answered seriously. "But I don't know them."

Charles pictured his dogs greeting him, jumping on him, wagging crazily. He could see their eyes and feel their warm drool on his cheek. But nothing happened.

"I told you sometimes it takes a while," Martin said.

Then Charles had a thought. Jim Baker referred to his "campfire" and so had Martin. They thought he'd lit a fire when he'd been trying to do some magic. Maybe that was the secret ingredient.

With one hand on Pan beside him, Charles relaxed his mind. It should be something small, he thought. Something he'd practiced. In the quiet stable, he heard a fly buzzing the loud irritating buzz of a fat, late-summer fly.

OK, Mr. Fly, Charles thought. You are under my porch and I don't want you to pester my dogs. He concentrated on the sound of the fly. I want you to land and shut up.

Almost instantly the buzzing stopped. But nothing else had changed. He could still feel the newspaper on his face, still feel the goat's soft fur, still smell the stable.

"It's not working," he said and pulled the newspaper away. With one hand he brushed straw from his shirt, with the other he stuffed the newspaper into the back pocket of his jeans. It might come in handy if they tried again. "There must be some other trick," he said. "Maybe…"

He was interrupted by Fritz, his rambunctious dog jumping on him, pushing him back down into the straw and licking his face enthusiastically.

Chapter 24

Sapania sat on her horse at the very spot she'd pictured, near the Sand Creek settlement, on the top of a gentle rise, with the stone outcropping a few feet away. But it was not a peaceful scene.

Smoke rose from burning tents below and made her eyes water. A half mile to the left, soldiers on horseback chased after women and children who were desperately trying to escape. The air was full of screams, and shouting, and gunshots, and terrified horses.

"I can get him from this distance!" An excited soldier knelt on one knee to steady his rifle. He was closer to her than most of the activity, not fifty yards away.

"A dollar says you can't," a soldier on horseback said. He was grinning from ear to ear.

"You're on!" the soldier on the ground said gleefully, steadying his rifle. Sapania followed his aim with her eyes. A hundred yards down his his line of sight, a little boy perhaps ten years old ran away from them, yelling "Mother! Mother! Mother!" over and over again. His mother had gotten ahead of him, now she turned and stopped.

"Quickly!" she said "Run like the antelope…"

The soldier's rifle interrupted her. The little boy stumbled forward as if pushed from behind. A red stain spread on his back and he lay motionless on the ground.

"No!" his mother screamed and ran back toward him.

"You owe me a dollar," the soldier said, standing up with a satisfied smile on his face. "But I'll let you take the woman. If your gun can shoot that far."

Sapania pulled two arrows from her quiver. She was too far away to have any chance of hitting the soldiers with her hunting arrows. And they could easily shoot her with their big guns if she rode closer. She was already easily in handgun range if they had glanced behind them but they were intent on their game. Sapania's face felt hot as if she stood too close to a campfire. A thousand cicadas buzzed in her brain.

It wasn't a thought that came to her. Nothing as organized as a plan. She just realized there was another way, something she could do that no one else could. She nudged her horse with her knees and it took a few steps forward. Some previous horse had left a steaming pile of excrement on the dirt. She leaned over and jabbed both arrows into it until the arrowheads and several inches of shank were brown.

She notched one arrow and looked down the hill at the soldiers. She knew exactly what to do, as if it had already happened and she was merely remembering. She needed to be behind the two men and a little to the left. She pictured it carefully. And then she was there. She was in exactly the spot she pictured, but the scene had changed, as if a fog had settled over the prairie. She shook her head to clear her cloudy brain but it didn't help. In a moment the soldiers would turn and see her. Before they could, she raised her bow and pulled back the string.

But the man had changed. He was no longer standing, joking with his friend. Now he knelt, his rifle aimed at the frightened boy who still ran screaming toward his mother. Perhaps there was still time... she released the arrow.

The instant she did, a flash of fire shot out from the end of the rifle and a puff of smoke rose from it. The gun made its terrible loud thunder, the boy plunged forward to lie still on the ground.

Sapania's arrow flew straight and true lodging deep in the man's thigh. He screamed out in pain and surprise, spinning to look at her, losing his balance and falling. His rifle flew several feet away. He pulled his handgun from its holster, but now she was right beside him. She wrapped her legs tightly around her horse's neck while she leaned over and simply jerked the gun away from him. One second later, she was ten feet away looking at him with amusement.

"It will be a slow and painful death," Sapania said, calmly notching the other arrow. "The poison from the horse shit loves white meat, but it eats slowly."

"Shoot her!" the wounded soldier screamed at his partner, who was too stunned to react. He regained his composure in a heartbeat, raised his rifle, and fired directly at the woman.

But she was no longer there.

Suddenly the mounted man felt a sharp pain in his back. He twisted around and fired again at the woman who was now somehow, impossibly, behind him. Despite the close range, the bullet missed its mark as well, for the woman was now on the other side of his horse, reaching across him to slash at his right arm with a long blade. He screamed again as the blade sliced through his skin, and his rifle fell to the ground. An arrow protruded from his back, blood seeped out and soaked his uniform. Sapania smiled.

"You may survive until the next full moon," she said. "But your life will be only pain."

"Your horse needs to run," she said and slapped the horse's rump. It startled, jerked, and started galloping across the field, with the soldier clinging to the saddle horn and emitting horrible grunts and screams with every step.

She turned back to the wounded soldier on the ground. He was trying to crawl over to his rifle. Sapania guided her horse with her knees until she blocked the man's path. Then she frowned. "How many did you kill today? Or did you count them?" The man didn't answer. "You didn't even count them," she said simply. " I begin to understand the games you light-skinned ones play. I shall learn to play them too."

The man writhed in agony.

"I will enjoy your slow death as you enjoyed shooting the boy. It's a good start." She watched him for a moment, then she frowned.

"But it's not enough," she said. "You butchered children of the prairie. I must help you repay your debt. I will find your own child."

"I don't have a child."

"You lie, like like every other man! I will know your child when I find him. I hope it's a little boy. And then he will pay."

Chapter 25

"Well, Mr. Frank Whiting! I'm surprised you're still in Denver City." Sheriff Michael Spangler stood and extended his hand as Whiting entered the small room. The sun was just setting and the light from a single high window near the ceiling bathed the room in a dim golden-rose hue.

"Yes, all that commotion this morning put me behind schedule. I sent the boy home with Millah and her brother visiting from Chicago. My children love their 'Uncle Kruck' dearly, and he entertains them well with stories of his adventures as a scientist collecting specimens in jungles for the museum. I'm supposed to meet Bill Cody tomorrow, then talk to the Colfax Railroad folks after that. I need to take some measurements tomorrow. Anyway, when Millah and "Uncle Kruck" get to talking they wouldn't notice if I sprouted wings and flew over them."

"Well, welcome to my office and the local jail," Spangler said as they shook hands. "Sometimes I'm not sure if I'm in charge or if I'm an inmate. You're welcome to sleep on the bench over there. It's not comfortable, but the price is right,"

In the back of the room, several men grumbled behind the bars of a crowded jail cell. At the back of the cell, the Reverend and Slim leaned against the stone wall, a thin man in rough clothes that reeked of whiskey slept in a corner, four other men stared glumly through the iron bars. Jefferson Smith stood tall near the front and tried to look proud.

Mr. Whiting smiled.

"Thank you, sir. I might at that."

The sheriff nodded. "You sound busy."

"Too busy. Bill Cody wants me to help design a dam on the Shoshone River up in Wyoming Territory. Big project. If it works, I expect he'll build houses there and name it either 'Buffalo Bill City' or 'Cody Town.' And what's new in the world of law enforcement? You arrest Doc Holliday again?"

"Nothing that exciting. I got one regular customer, a local named Streeter who drinks too much and gets in trouble. He ain't bright, but he's harmless. Plus, as you know, I got Soapy Smith and a passel of his ruffians." he said. "They're getting to be regulars here. Con men, grifters, and general hooligans. Don't get too close or they'll talk you out of your wallet."

"Was Mr. Smith happy to get his white hat back?"

"Yes, sir. . He looks at that hat the way most men look at pretty women. I confiscated most of their personal property because this group might use any harmless object as a weapon or key. "

"I can imagine."

"This group had an odd assortment." The sheriff opened his desk drawer. "Here we have a lovely ivory-handled pistol, six knives, some saloon tokens. Soapy even had this old bell, although I can't imagine why. Looks like something a Spanish friar might carry back in conquistador days. Can't imagine Mr. Smith having any use for that. But it makes a nice sound. Here, try it yourself." The sheriff handed the bell to Frank Whiting.

"Yes, it is a lovely sound," Whiting said as he rang it softly a few times. "Very musical. It may be the closest Mr. Smith ever gets to religion."

The sheriff put it back in the drawer and closed it firmly. There was a quiet knocking at the door, the sheriff opened it.

"Well, hello little fella," he said. A small white goat stood out there all alone. As soon as the door opened, the goat snuck into the office and rubbed its head against Whiting's leg.

"Looks like you got a new friend," the sheriff said with a smile. Whiting petted the animal's head and neck.

"He's a cute one indeed," Whiting said. "Never seen a goat with one brown ear. Who do you suppose owns it?"

"I've never seen any goats here in Denver City," Sheriff Spangler said. "Whoever lost it will stop in here sooner or later to report it. Unless it escaped while they were just traveling through."

"Well, if you need someone to take care of it until the owner shows up, I've got several children who would volunteer," Mr. Whiting said. The goat nuzzled his leg like a pet cat.

"The way I see it, it's your goat, not mine," Sheriff Spangler said. "Take it on home. If someone claims it I'll let you know."

One of the prisoners cursed loudly. Sheriff Spangler and Whiting turned to look.

"What's going on in there?" the sheriff asked.

"Nothing to concern you," the Reverend said.

The sheriff walked up to the cell. "Where's Soapy?" he asked.

"Soapy who?" the Reverend said smugly.

"Don't recall ever meeting anyone with that name," Slim added.

"Streeter!" the sheriff shouted. "Somebody kick Streeter, he's only pretending to sleep!"

"Ouch!" Streeter rolled over. "Can't a guy take a little nap?"

"Did you see Soapy Smith absquatulate from these premises?"

"I didn't see nothing," Streeter said and rolled back over to resume his nap.

"Well, we'll see about this," the sheriff said, opening the door to the street. "I've got a deputy outside." He stepped outside the door and yelled. "Henry! Are you still out there?"

"Yes sir," Henry yelled back from the alley. He hurried to the street. "What's wrong?"

"Soapy seems to have disappeared! Did you see anything?"

A thin young man with very dark skin came to the door.

"Nobody came or went out here. I been watching real careful."

The sheriff and his young deputy stepped back inside with Frank Whiting. The sheriff faced the cell. "Streeter, one more time: did you see Soapy?"

Streeter didn't hide his irritation. "Just when your man put him in here. He dusted off his clothes, stood up proud, then marched himself into the cell smiling like he was going to church. Then I took a nap."

Henry looked down at his boots, and the sheriff stared at him.

"You know something else, don't you?"

"No sir. I didn't see a thing. But I've heard stories,

"What sort of stories? And keep it brief. Not like one of your campfire palavers."

"It ain't the first time he's disappeared," Henry said. "A posse had him surrounded up in Cripple Creek. He was spotted in the lobby of the hotel and two minutes later he was gone. Just vanished. They had guards on every door and window. He moves like a ghost, that one does."

"I do not believe Mr. Smith is a sorcerer who vanishes at will," Mr. Whiting said firmly. "No more than this little white goat is. He is a con man and this is just another confidence game. He employs either science or bribery and a careful observer will deduce his method."

"That ain't as bad as the time outside Leadville," the deputy continued. "He skedaddled out of the Silver Dollar in a hurry because of a business disagreement about the proper number of aces in one particular deck of cards. He got a couple of miles out of town with three of his men when one of the horses went lame. They hadn't seen anybody following them, so they just camped out on the rocks, not a tree for a quarter mile. They was sitting around a campfire when some men who'd been unlucky in the card game rode up. Being outnumbered with no place to hide, Soapy finally agreed to a restitution plan.

"I got your gold right here," he said, standing up. He put that white hat on his head, like he was getting dressed up to go to a fancy dinner. Then he kind of squinted and pointed off in the distance.

"That ain't a bear, is it?" he asked with some alarm.

The men from town looked where he pointed.

"I don't see nothing, one said, turning back to Soapy. But Soapy wasn't standing there any more. There wasn't any place to hide; there was enough moonlight to see clear. He just vanished."

"Sounds like the kind of story you could pay men to tell," Frank Whiting said.

"You're probably right. He don't seem like much of a magician except when he's swindling someone at cards. But it's the story I heard."

145

"I agree with Mr. Whiting," the sheriff said. "Perhaps he's switched clothing with one of the other prisoners, hoping they'll be released sooner than he would be. Let's get a lantern over here so we can see them better."

"I guess we could count them," Henry the deputy said. "We booked eight prisoners in."

A quick count indicated the cell now held seven men.

"I don't know how he did it but he's gone." the sheriff said. "He probably had an extra horse stashed somewhere around town for this kind of situation. By now he could be anywhere."

"Well, he's a bad penny, he'll turn up soon enough," Mr. Whiting said. "Perhaps the best remedy for an unhappy day is a very rare buffalo steak at Highland House? I believe the railroad I work for would be happy to invest in good relations with local law enforcement."

Sheriff Spangler laughed. "I'm completely in favor of good relations with all the railroad companies. Why don't you leave your new friend here until we return." He pointed to the goat.

"Indeed. His owners would not want him wandering at night in a dangerous city."

They left Henry, the deputy, in charge of watching seven prisoners and a goat and rode off to the restaurant. Highland House was small and dark, but the staff knew to be kind and generous with a sheriff. The beer was unusually cool and refreshing and the night had grown dark by the time they returned. No additional prisoners had escaped, the goat had been content to nap on the wooden floor of the office. The sheriff relieved his deputy. "Go on home, Henry," he said. "Get something to eat. I'll hold down the fort until you get back." Henry left.

"You can keep the goat here overnight," Spangler said to Whiting, "But would you take him out for a little night air first? After all, until further notice, he's your goat, and he's been inside for a while now."

Frank Whiting fashioned a short rope leash and took the goat outside. He sat on the boardwalk. "This is a reward for your good behavior," he said and gave the goat a firm red apple he'd purchased at the restaurant. Whiting rubbed the goat's neck while it devoured the fruit.

"Where do you suppose that scurrilous miscreant absconded to?" Mr. Whiting asked the goat. He had no intention of degrading his vocabulary in the vain hope that an animal would understand simpler words. Whiting looked down the street, suddenly confused. "And who would light a campfire in the middle of town?"

A few blocks away, beyond the shadowy buildings, a small fire flickered in the night. It seemed completely out of place. Whiting still felt a bit tipsy from the beer he'd consumed with dinner and he shook his head to clear it. "We could probably both use to stretch our legs a bit," Whiting told the goat. "Let's walk on down there before we call it a night."

Within a few steps, a sudden cool breeze chilled his neck and he turned up his collar. A light fog, unusual in Denver City, drifted between buildings. The street they walked down was empty and none of the windows were lit, giving the scene a lonely and desolate flavor.

A small fire burned in a vacant lot. Tall pine trees made it look like an isolated woodland clearing. A lone man huddled by the fire, warming his hands. He wore a white hat with a round brim. He didn't notice Whiting approaching until the firelight lit him.

"I would have thought you'd travel a bit farther from town," Mr. Whiting said. Soapy Smith's eyes grew wide and he stood straight up.

"How did you find me?"

Whiting smiled. It seemed like an absurd question; he hadn't walked three blocks. "My goat here was a bloodhound in a previous life. Now maybe we should mosey on back to the sheriff's office where you can sleep in a warm cell." He turned to point back to the jail, but it was no longer there. There were no buildings, no road. Now there were only trees and bushes. All evidence said they really were far away in the mountains. "I don't understand…" Whiting said, turning back to the fire. He was completely disoriented.

But Soapy was no longer listening. The con man climbed onto his horse and galloped into the darkness, leaving Whiting alone without a horse or hope of catching the escapee again.

"How did he do that?" Whiting said, speaking to the goat, which found some grass and nibbled at it. "This makes no logical sense. We walked a short distance on a city street and now we're in a forest. I must have drunk more than I thought, But at least we have a fire for warmth. Come over here, little Capricorn."

"It's an illusion of some sort," Whiting said, warming his hands and talking to the animal as if it were a pet dog. "We walked directly here from over there. It should be a simple matter to return. Perhaps I simply did not notice the trees before and it looks much different from this perspective." There was no point to staying there. "Come on, boy. Let's get back to the sheriff's office. We could see the fire from the sheriff's office, so as long as we can see it behind us we should be able to figure this out."

He walked slowly, turning back often to see where the fire was, but the forest did not thin and no buildings came into view. "I have taken an inaccurate bearing," he said to himself. "As if the fire were the axle of a wheel and I picked the wrong spoke to follow homeward. Listen, you," he said to the goat. "The people I work with would mock me mercilessly if they discovered that a civil engineer in their employ was so easily confused by simple geometry. You must assure me you will relay this incident to no one." The goat looked up at him with the strangely-shaped horizontal eyes that makes goats look so different from most animals. It cocked its head to one side, as if listening. Mr. Whiting laughed. "I will take that as your vow of secrecy. Now let's try a different spoke before the night gets chillier. I wonder where Smith went?"

The next bearing he took was no better. It led only into deeper woods. Again he retraced his steps. He scratched a line in the dirt to indicate each direction away from the fire he tried.

The fourth attempt was different. This time, the space between the trees opened up as he walked, becoming a path and then a dirt road. Buildings rose from the fog ahead of him and he quickened his pace. Lights poured the windows of one building. He heard laughter and conversation within. Whiting pushed the door open and entered the room, with the goat following close behind him.

He stood in a crowded bar, full of men who wore denim clothes and muddy boots. A single harried bartender, an overweight man with a thick brown mustache, poured whiskey and beer as fast as he could. Several men stood at the dark wooden bar, drinking and talking loudly. One man wore a white hat with a round brim. Whiting went over and stood next to him.

"Whiskey, sir?" the bartender asked him.

"No, I don't think so," Whiting answered. "I'm just here to take Mr. Smith home." He motioned toward the man beside him. At the mention of his name, Smith turned. His face registered total shock. He stood abruptly and took a step backward, bumping the man on the other side of him.

"You!" Soapy said in disbelief. "It isn't possible! You're the do-gooder with the goat! How did you…"

"Hey, who do you think you're jostling," the man behind him said angrily and pushed Soapy in the back. Soapy stumbled toward Mr. Whiting, losing his balance for a moment. His hat fell off and, landed neatly on the bar directly in front of Mr. Whiting.

Whiting picked it up.

"I believe you have a reservation at the Hotel Hoosegow," he said. "We wouldn't want to keep the staff waiting, would we?"

"I'm not going anywhere. And give me back my hat!"

"You seem awfully fond of this hat. Perhaps I'll hold it for you until you're back in your accommodations," Whiting said calmly. "Just to keep it safe."

Soapy lunged for his hat, Whiting pulled it away. "I think it's time for us to go," Whiting said. "Don't you agree?" he looked down at the goat. The goat cocked its head to one side, as it had done before.

Mr. Whiting looked back up at Soapy but everything had changed. Smith still stood there, but now there were iron bars between the two men. Whiting looked around and stepped back. He was in the sheriff's office; Smith was in the jail cell with the rest of his gang, most of whom were sleeping and snoring loudly. Whiting still held Smith's hat, the goat was still beside him. But the saloon had vanished along with the bartender and all its patrons. Whiting was utterly baffled.

"Give me my hat!" Soapy yelled from within the cell.

"It shall be returned in good time," Whiting said. "Along with your other effects." Whiting counted the prisoners. Eight men were in the cell. The sheriff dozed in his chair. Whiting looked at the goat.

"I suspect that you, sir, are a delusion derived from some adulterant in the beer I drank. And this entire episode is merely a drug-induced dream. Tomorrow I shall have a conversation with the proprietor of the Highland House about his standards."

Whiting stretched out on a bench by the wall and quickly fell asleep. Jefferson Smith paced angrily within the cell for a few minutes. Finally, he stretched out on the last cot and fell asleep almost immediately, too.

A few minutes later Henry entered the office for his shift of keeping watch. It wasn't uncommon for a trusted guest to rest in the office after visiting John Barleycorn or nipping a bit of nose paint. Henry nudged the sheriff, who jerked upright.

"I can handle this from here, sir," Henry whispered. "I won't disturb your friend."

The sheriff nodded drowsily and left.

There was no activity in the jail cell. Henry paced back and forth, bored and restless. From the cell, Streeter watched him through half-closed eyes and then sat up.

"Man, I'm sleepy," Streeter said, yawning loudly. "Wish I could get out of here and get some whiskey."

"Go to sleep," Henry said. "I got things to think about."

"Yeah," Streeter said, ignoring his comment. "If I was out there, I'd go down to that saloon down the way. I heard some new girls come up from New Orleans. You know what they say about them cajun girls."

"Shut up and go to sleep!"

"Yeah, it's pretty important you watch us hard criminals sleep. Very important job. Hey, them girls might still be working by the time you get off. When's that next shift take over? Two in the morning, right? Or is it five? Did you bring a book to pass the time? Books are better than new whiskey and pretty cajun girls any time, right?"

Streeter laughed a little, then rolled over on his side. In a moment he was snoring with the others.

Henry paced back and forth for another half hour, listening to the men in the cell snort and sniffle and grunt. When he opened the door to get some air, the sound of honky-tonk piano music and laughter taunted him. He closed the door and continued to pace. The men in the cell were all fast asleep, he told himself. Even if they weren't, they couldn't get out. And the sheriff's friend was out here. He'd wake up if they tried anything. There really was no point to a deputy watching over them every second. No harm in taking a ten-minute break.

He put the key to the jail cell in his pocket and walked out the door, locking it behind him.

The moment the door closed, Streeter stopped snoring and sat up. He pulled an iron key out of a little pocket sewn into the inside of his hat. Careful not to wake Whiting or his cell-mates, he reached through the bars and unlocked the door. He pushed it slowly open in case it might squeak, stepped free of the cell, and locked the door quietly behind him. He carefully opened the drawer of the sheriff's desk. There was an ivory-handled pistol in there, and an old bell, and some silver dollars. He put them into a burlap sack from the shelf. He found some extra ammunition, and a big sack of raw sunflower seeds and a small tin box of Barber matches, with pictures of pretty women on the cover. He grinned at the pictures. "Hello, ladies," he whispered and put the tin in his pocket. Beneath some loose papers in the bottom drawer, he found the sheriff's private stock of liquor and his face broke into a broad grin. The bottle had a picture of an elderly gentleman. "Clarke's Pure Rye!" he whispered to himself. It was a full bottle of better liquor than he'd ever tasted. Things were looking good.

In the morning, Sheriff Spangler counted seven prisoners, just like last night. He frowned as he realized that one of them was Soapy Smith. Well, his deputy Henry had a heart of gold and was completely trustworthy but also young and uneducated. The sheriff himself had sipped more than one beer with dinner and could have been confused. Surely an honest mistake had been made. He gave it no more thought.

By the time the sun began to slide behind the mountains through a symphony of red-tinged clouds, Streeter sat on top of a hill a few miles north of Denver City. The hilltop was barren but it had a fabulous view of the setting sun, the purple mountains, and the dry plains in between. If anyone approached, he would see them long before they got close. Using a trail of raw sunflower seeds and a lot of patience, that afternoon he'd lured a jackrabbit into range for a lucky shot from his new ivory-handled pistol. He'd collected enough scraps of twisted wood from a few dead pine trees to make a little campfire and now the jackrabbit was roasting on a stick over it. Streeter sipped whiskey straight from the bottle while dinner cooked. As the sips became more generous, he started to sing: "Carve dat possum, children, Carve him to de heart; "

The smell of roasting meat filled the air beneath the red clouds of sunset. The sunflower seeds would make a tasty side dish, he thought, especially if he could roast them. But he didn't have a pan. Inspired to creativity, he dug out the old bell, another of his new possessions and inspected it.

It would be a tiny pot, holding less than a handful of seeds, but the smell of roasting seeds might be worth the effort. That little clapper inside would get in the way, but it was only attached by a small wire. "You'll make a fine little roaster," he told the bell as he shook it. It made a pleasant enough sound, if a little loud. He shook it a few more times, removed the clapper, then set the bell upside down it on some hot coals at the edge of the fire. He spilled some seeds as he filled it, but that didn't matter. There were more in the sack, and sunflower seeds were cheap because people thought of them as animal feed. He could always buy more. He would cook these few, then cook a few more.

The sky darkened, the red clouds over the mountains faded to dark gray then to black. The night grew colder. The rabbit sizzled and the gentle aroma of roasting seeds made the crude camp smell like a fancy restaurant. Streeter took a swig of whiskey and realized he had an urgent need to answer Nature's call. Might as well get that done before dinner, he thought. He stumbled fifteen feet away from the fire, undid the buttons on his overalls, and began to water a spiny yucca plant.

He looked up and saw a pair of bright white eyes glowing in the darkness. Two more joined them a few feet to the left. They moved slowly toward him. Another pair of eyes appeared behind the others. He reached for the ivory-handled gun but realized he'd left it back by the fire. In his drunken state he thought he was being visited by supernatural creatures. He scrambled to pull up his overalls and retreat back to the fire, but the figure of large dog-like animal blocked his path, snarling like a devil.

Wolves' eyes reflect light very efficiently. On a dark night, when they look toward a light such as a campfire, their eyes glow like white-hot coals. Wolves are larger than most dogs, stronger than any, and twice as large as a coyote. In fact, they often prey on their smaller cousins. They hunt in relentless packs, taking down antelope and even buffalo as they wander the plains and mountains.

In the last ten seconds of his life, Streeter did not have time to remember any of this.

Chapter 26

"OK, boy, OK. I'm glad to see you too." Charles managed to sit up. "How did you do that?"

But Martin was gone, Pan was gone. Charles was alone with his dogs in the familiar hideout beneath the porch. The smell of straw mingled with the aroma of old tires and dog fur. Keisha, always calmer than Fritz, slept a few feet away. The air felt cooler than a moment ago.

"Have I been gone, Fritz" he asked, petting the big dog between the ears. "Or have I been sleeping? Or am I crazy?" Everything had seemed so real — the bank robbers, the Sheriff, the stable. Had he eaten something unusual? Or were vivid hallucinations a natural part of getting older, just new hormones inebriating the imagination? If this was something that happened to everyone, he wished someone would have mentioned it to him.

He crawled out from beneath the porch and stood up. The sky was dimly gray, the eastern sky barely tinged in pink. His family wouldn't be awake this early. He closed the gate behind him quietly and snuck into the house. The porch door didn't have a lock, but the door from the porch into the house did, so he retrieved his key from his pocket, reassured at its tiny familiarity. Then he frowned. Something was different.

It wasn't the key that was different. It was the steps. He looked back down at them. They were as old and worn and faded as always. He smiled.

"Well, of course they are," he said quietly. "You just dreamed someone came in the dead of the night and replaced them with new steps." He shook his head. It's easy to fool yourself with your own dreams.

He unlocked the big wooden front door and crept up to his bedroom. As long as he let his weight fall only on the extreme left and right of each stair, it hardly creaked at all.

Without undressing, he got under the covers and pulled them up to his chin. If one of his parents looked in, he didn't want to explain why he was up so early. He relaxed and turned over. There was some paper in his bed and it crackled when he rolled on it. He smiled again. Sometimes you hear or feel something when you're asleep and incorporate it into your dream. If he'd rolled over some wad of paper in his sleep it probably inspired the newspaper of his dream. Once again, science explains something that seemed weird. Before he threw it onto the floor, he pulled his flashlight out from beneath the pillow.

It was a page from the Denver Evening News, a newspaper he'd never heard of, fresh and new but crumpled, dated July 1897. He rubbed his eyes and stared at it for a long time. Then he set the paper down on the table carefully. Maybe he was still asleep, he thought. He decided to lie in bed until it was time to rise. There had to be a scientific explanation.

If I'm crazy, Charles thought, that would explain everything in one neat sentence. He could imagine Mrs Klein telling his parents, "I'm sorry, but your kid is insane." But he didn't want to risk incarceration in the sanitarium of his nightmares, where mean doctors conducted cruel experiments. There had to be another logical answer. Maybe the newspaper had been on the floor when he went to bed. He'd used it unconsciously as both inspiration and theatrical prop in his complicated dream. Maybe it had been in some old book he read a year or two ago, preserved like a dried flower and his conscious mind forgot it. Maybe it somehow got mixed up with his stuff at the library. Maybe his brother had planted it in his bed as a weird joke. However it got there, it looked crisp and new.

"My dream," he said aloud. "has started to deliver newspapers."

A week passed and he did not see Martin or the goat, or any frontier scouts or bank robbers. Not in a dream, not anywhere else. He was careful not to eat anything unusual, and nothing too spicy. Luckily, his mother kept to her standard menu of familiar dishes— spaghetti, tuna casserole, meat loaf etc.

He studiously avoided experimenting with magic. A fly buzzed around his room one night and he ignored it. He just let it buzz for as long as it wanted. He rode along with his mother to the Granada Fish Market on Larimer Street in Denver, a store that sold weird fresh fish and Asian ingredients.As they drove, they hit many red lights and Charles made no effort to change them with his mind. Until he could explain that old newspaper to his own satisfaction, he wasn't taking any chances on "lighting a campfire" that might attract dangerous specters in the night.

Westminster's library was about a mile from his house, an easy walk on country roads and sleepy residential streets. It was even easier on his three-speed bicycle. The library was small, about the size of a modest house. He visited it nearly every week, usually checking out two books at a time. But today his mission was researching the date of that old newspaper. If someone had printed up a phony newspaper for an advertising campaign, for example, did they choose that date at random?.

"Hello, Charles," the librarian greeted him. She was tall and pale with short brown hair, about his mother's age. Her glasses had thick dark rims. She wore a tasteful dress with a repeating pattern of small blue flowers, and over that a gray sweater to warm her always-chilly shoulders. Her perfectly erect, regal posture and the calm dignity of her voice made her seem like an ambassador from some relentlessly civilized British colony.

"Hello, Mrs. Alexandria," Charles said.

"Are you returning books today?" she asked. He wasn't carrying any books, just a notebook. She was either making a very dignified joke or wondering if he'd somehow forgotten the objects of his visit.

"No, ma'am, not today." he said. "I'd like to do some research. Do you keep very old newspapers? Like from fifty years ago?"

"A few. Is this for a school project?" she asked.

"No, it's just for me. I found part of an old newspaper and it made me wonder about that day."

She pulled a small square of paper off the neat little pile of scratch paper. "Which paper?" she asked.

"It's one I never heard of," he said. "It's the Denver Evening News. July of 1897, I think."

She smiled. "That paper changed its name some time ago. Now it's called the Denver Post. If it's that old, we won't have physical copies but we probably have it on microfilm. Have you ever used our microfilm viewer?"

"I don't even know what that is."

"Well, let me get you started." Charles followed her to a small room in the back. A machine with a blue plastic screen that resembled a TV screen sat on a desk in the center. A wooden cabinet with many small drawers occupied most of one wall.

"Let's see," she said. "Eighteen ninety five, eighteen ninety six… here we are." She opened the drawer and pulled out a roll of plastic. "Let me thread it for you," she said. "It's a little tricky until you get the hang of it." While she fed film through the proper rollers, she explained.

"They take pictures of the newspapers," she said. "Do you know how an enlarger works?"

"Sort of," he said. "You project an image through a lens and make it bigger."

"Exactly. A microfilm works like that except they use the opposite kind of lens. It makes a tiny, tiny picture of the newspaper on the film. You can fit hundreds of them on one roll. We use this machine to blow the image up again. It projects it onto the screen."

She reached down the base of the machine and flipped a switch. The screen began to glow bright blue. "This knob is the focus," she said. "And this one rolls the film forward and backward." She turned a big wheel and shadows flashed across the screen. "See, this is June 4." She turned the focus knob and the screen got blurry and then came into focus again. "Turn it this way…" She turned the wheel and the image on the screen moved so fast it was a blur. "And this is June 22. Why don't you try it?"

Charles turned the wheel very slowly and page after page flashed across the screen. When he stopped, the image was blurry.

"See if you can focus it," she said.

He turned the focus knob and it got even worse. He tried the opposite direction and gradually the image became sharp and clear. "It's like magic," he said.

"There is no such thing as magic," she said. "Don't be silly. We let people use the microfilm for up to one hour. But since you're such a good customer, feel free to use it as long as you like. Unless someone else wants to use it, of course."

"Thank you," he said. She left the room. Charles spent a few minutes looking at random pages, just for the fun of getting a glimpse into Denver's past. In 1895 a hotel was destroyed in a big explosion. Twenty-two people died, they blamed the guy who ran the steam boiler and said he was probably drunk.

So much had changed in the ensuing fifty years! Back then, people rode horses, trains were a still news. There were plans to build rail lines linking distant towns to Denver City. Those towns were now suburbs linked together with highways.

Charles easily found the exact newspaper he'd discovered in his pocket.

The front page of the newspaper on film looked exactly like the page he'd found. Nothing remarkable happened at all on that date. But in his dream, there had been a parade and an attempted bank robbery and a fugitive captured and thrown in jail. If anything like that had really happened, it would have been in the paper.

He turned the handle to move the film and read the second page of the paper, but there was no mention of those events. He read every page of the paper. Clearly those events had not happened. One small article interested him. Its headline read "Gold nugget found in Skagaway, Alaska." Prospectors had flocked to that area since 1893 in hopes of finding gold. Most found only wishes and daydreams. Opportunistic criminals followed these naive new victims. With every nugget found, enthusiasm grew and activity surged. The population exploded from a handful of solitary men until the town had 15,000 residents. A man named Frank had been the engineer who laid out the town plan as it grew, but it was Frank Reid not Frank Whiting. There was nothing at all about a parade or a bank robbery.

Charles was disappointed. That newspaper obviously arrived in his pocket by some very ordinary means. He just hadn't discovered it yet. He turned off the microfilm machine and went out to the main library.

"I guess I'm done," he told Mrs. Alexandria.

"Was your research successful?"

"Well, yeah, I found the right paper. It disproves my theory, so that's a success. The microfilm is pretty fun." She just looked at him without saying anything for a minute.

"Let me show you how to change film," she said. "If you're careful, you can come back and look at nearly any date. And there are other records as well."

"That would be great," he said. Even though he hadn't made any progress on the newspaper itself, the microfilm made the past seem vivid and alive. It gave Charles a little thrill to do something so adult.

She smiled and led him back into the microfilm room. She demonstrated how to remove the film and insert a different roll. She explained how films were filed.

"We have the whole history of Colorado contained in this one little room," she said. "But most people don't even know this room exists."

"I bet fifty years from now everyone in the world will have their own microfilm machine" Charles said. "Things change so much."

"In 2005? Maybe," she said. "But no one can predict the future."

Chapter 27

If a person had never heard music, logic couldn't persuade them that it exists. Words couldn't describe listening to it.

Maybe some people are like that with magic.

The best explanation for all the weird things that had happened to Charles was magic, improbable as it seemed. Raymond's theory of an overactive imagination didn't explain the old newspaper. Insanity didn't explain the scratching sounds and sad wailings emanating from the walls of his bedroom. By now, everyone in the family had started to hear them.

Now Charles was testing the idea that maybe his attempts at magic, while not often successful, in some way triggered the supernatural events. It seemed like an odd idea but it would explain a lot.

For his experiment, he carefully avoided magic for a week. His life went on as usual. No scary visitors arrived. Now it was time to try some small magic and observe the results. Whether the trick itself worked or not wasn't the point because they rarely worked. He wanted to see if the attempt itself caused anything else weird to happen.

Tuesday afternoon he started walking toward his piano lesson a half hour earlier than usual. The curving sidewalk of the Pillar of Fire campus felt familiar. Tall trees shaded the peaceful grass in a very ordinary way. When he was sure no one was watching, he would try to influence how a coin landed or some equally innocuous trick.

He stopped beneath a big oak tree near the castle building. The leaves on one branch were dead and brown and clung by their fingernails to a shaky perch. The slightest breeze would release them. He selected one large brown leaf balanced precariously between its history as a photo-synthesizer and its future as mulch. He focused his attention on the leaf and pictured it drifting to the ground. He tried to keep all other thoughts at bay, but he realized he was hungry. He'd have to start over. Before he did, he whispered to the leaf, "I wish you were an apple instead," then smiled at his little joke and focused on the leaf again.

"I was just thinking about you," a voice behind him said. Startled, he whirled around. Martin and Pan stood quietly on the steps leading up to the castle's front door.

"How long have you been standing there?" he asked.

"I don't know," Martin said, shrugging. "Why do you like that tree?"

"It was an experiment," Charles said.

"What's an experiment?"

"It's when you try something to see if an idea works."

"Oh."

"I had a question for you," Charles said. He took the old newspaper out of his back pocket. "Does any of this make sense?"

Martin looked at the paper, but in a casual way. Maybe he couldn't see very well, Charles thought. Or maybe he can't read.

"Let me read some of the words to you," Charles said.

"Is it a story?" Martin said. "I like stories."

"It's a newspaper," Charles explained. "It tells about different things that happened on a particular day."

"I know about newspapers. My father sometimes reads them to me. Why do you like this one?"

"This is the paper I got at the stable and I wanted to see if anything was interesting in it. See, this story is about a train coming to Denver that had engine trouble. This one is about horses getting sick in Aspen. This one is about a big gold nugget someone found in Skagaway, Alaska."

Martin's eyes got big.

"That's the town!" he said. "It's where my family went! I remember now. Skagaway, Alaska!"

Charles read the article quickly. One nugget does not make a gold rush, it said. If more were found, the town would build a railroad line to transport gold from the hills above town down to where it could be processed and shipped on a boat.

"Your father works for the railroad, doesn't he?" Charles said.

161

"Yes, he makes the plans they use to build them. Can we go to Skagaway?"

"It's a long way away," Charles said with a smile.

"Pan could get us there," Martin said. "If we both thought about it. I just couldn't remember the name."

"Maybe," Charles said. "But not today. I need to do some research."

"What's research?"

"It's learning about something. I don't know anything about Skagaway; maybe it's cold. Maybe there's polar bears. We could wind up anywhere."

"Does research take a long time?"

"Not if you have a good library," Charles said.

"OK," Martin said. "I'll wait." He sat down on the steps.

Charles turned to walk away.

"Don't forget your apple," Martin said. Charles looked down at his feet. A perfect red apple sat in the grass. He picked it up. It probably fell from some kid's lunch sack but he sure hadn't noticed it before. Unless he had, unconsciously, and that's why he told the leaf he wished it was an apple.

Charles took one bite to convince himself it was real. It was sweet and juicy and definitely real. He carried it over to Martin.

"You and Pan can have it," Charles said. "Eat out of this side so you don't get germs where I bit it. Pan can have the rest."

"Thanks," he said. "I don't know what germs are, but Pan loves apples."

"Listen," Charles said. "Why don't you come back to my... to the house with me."

"I want to go to Alaska!"

"It might take me a while to learn about it. You know, so we can picture it right."

"OK. Will you visit me tonight?"

Charles paused. "Sure," he said. "I'll visit you tonight.

162

Chapter 28

That night, Charles crept down the stairs and went outside. Martin and Pan were waiting for him.

"Can we go to Alaska?" Martin asked.

"Not yet," Charles said. "I have more questions to answer first. Do you remember Jim Baker?"

"I don't think so."

"He was at the parade. He caught the bad man trying to escape."

"I usually just watch my father."

"It's OK. I think he might be able to help us," Charles said. "Can you travel to a person, not just a place?"

"Sometimes. If I think about you, I can find you. But I can't find my parents. They're too far away."

"What would happen if we both touch Pan and I picture this man? Would we find him?"

"I don't know."

"Shall we try?"

"Will it help us go to Alaska?"

"Maybe. I'm newer at this than you are."

"OK."

Charles put his hand firmly on the goat's neck. He was nervous and his throat was dry. It felt like he was about to jump onto a moving train and didn't want to get thrown off. Martin stroked the goat's head. Charles thought about Baker, how he'd looked when he scared off those teenagers.. Nothing happened. He closed his eyes and tried again.

A cracking sound startled him and Charles opened his eyes.

They were no longer standing in front of his house. Now they stood on some other hill, surrounded by yucca plants and weeds all eerily gray in the dim twilight. More stars than Charles had ever seen peppered the sky.

If not for the Big Dipper and North Star, he would have believed they were on some strange, distant planet. Fifty feet away, a blazing campfire shot sparks into its own swirling smoke. Jim Baker sat beside it, calmly smoking a pipe, not threatening, not intimidating. He looked peaceful.

"You ought get closer to the fire," he said quietly. "Bit of a nip in the air tonight."

The boys didn't move. Charles was completely stunned that the idea had worked and couldn't remember how to move his legs. He was also completely disoriented. Was he hallucinating? Or had they actually traveled across space, and maybe across time? It was not scientifically possible. Yet he could smell the woodsmoke, feel the cool breeze on his cheek.

Baker nodded and hummed quietly to himself. A glowing ember hissed and flew from the fire, twirled lazily in the air like a firefly and landed near Baker's foot. He kicked it back toward the larger flames.

"Suit yourself," he said. "Them coyotes probably won't harm you none."

At the mention of coyotes Martin and Charles quickly moved to the campfire, pulling Pan along with them. Several logs, each two feet in diameter and six feet long, were arranged on the ground around the fire, circling it like big uncomfortable couches.

"Have a seat," Baker said. "Unless you're Comanches come to scalp me. If it's that, I hope you got the good manners to let me finish my smoke before we get messy."

"I have some questions," Charles said as they sat down on one of the logs. Baker still frightened him, but logically he should proceed anyway.

"Questions is fine," Jim Baker said. "But I got more buffalo jerky than I got answers." He picked up a leather pouch filled with little slabs of thin dried meat that looked like cooked bacon and tossed it to them. Charles and Martin each took one. "So what's your questions?"

"I don't know how to put it, so I'll just say it." He hoped his question would not enrage this dangerous man. "What's going on?"

"Well, there's a fire," Jim Baker said calmly. "And there's stars and jerked meat. Got a little pipe tobacco. That's about all that's going on." He poked at the fire with a stick. "Nice nights like this, I sleep outside. Can't sleep inside a room where the air don't breathe around my face. It's like sleeping with a corpse on top of you."

"That's not what I mean," Charles said. "How did we get here? How did you get here? And Martin here, and his goat— I just want to understand…"

Jim Baker smoked his pipe and contemplated the stars. The fire cracked and a new flurry of tiny embers lifted into the night sky like furious little hot-air balloons. The man started humming a song again, ignoring the question, or maybe having forgotten the question. Beyond him in the darkness, beyond the firelight's flickering fingers, Charles saw movement. Coyotes, he wondered? Or worse? He looked around for something he could use to defend himself with, but there was only dirt.

A man approached them slowly, gradually becoming illuminated by the fire's dancing light. With Charles's mind full of ghosts, it seemed like he just materialized out of the darkness. He was tall and muscular, with long black hair pulled back behind his head into a pony tail. He wore the same sort of buckskin pants and jacket that Baker wore. He had high cheekbones, like Baker's. Except for having darker skin and hair, he could have been Jim Baker's brother.

The man carried a very long rifle using both hands, keeping the weapon aimed down at the ground in front of him. Beside the man walked a large dog. Its tail curled upward like a husky's as it confidently trotted along. Its head had a vaguely triangular shape, like a wolf. Its oval eyes were a yellow amber-color.

"So now even city boys can sneak up on the great woods-runner," the man said as he approached. His voice was deep and a little hoarse.

"If they'd been as noisy as you," Jim Baker said, "I would of shot them just on principle."

The man gave a short laugh. "Yeah, you might get off one lucky shot in the dark. I'd prefer a morning death, I think. Somehow that would seem less final, more hopeful."

The man stood behind Baker. The firelight on his face and clothes created the illusion that he was moving a little, like pond water rippling in a breeze. He took some jerky out of the pouch while his dog sniffed at Pan. The goat held very still for a moment, then kicked a hind foot at the dog. The dog easily dodged the kick and moved away.

"Now Flint, you mind your manners." The stranger sat on a log near Baker, across the fire from the two boys. "It's a good night," he said, chewing the jerky and poking at the fire with a stick. Without looking up, he asked, "You got some new scouts?"

Charles jumped to his feet. "My name is Charles," he said, reaching out his hand. "And this is my friend Martin."

Jim Baker motioned toward the stranger.

"And this is the worst excuse for a friend ever created," he said. "His name is Murphy."

"Pleased to meet you, Mr. Murphy," Charles said. The stranger's grip was strong and his hand was rough.

"Not mister," the man said. "Just Murphy. That's my name: Just Murphy."

Baker laughed quietly. He seemed calm enough, even friendly, but Charles didn't relax. Crazy people can transform in an instant. Jim Baker pointed with his pipe at Murphy and explained his friend's name. "Back in Ireland he was born Bill. Then his folks moved to America and the Iroquois stole him when he was a tadpole. They didn't know his white name, so they called him Tear because of that ugly mark on his face. But by gonny, he was too much trouble even for the Iroquois, so they give him to the Huron. By the time he got back to civilization, nobody knew where he came from, so they give him the whole new name Tim Murphy. When he got tired of that, he dropped the Tim part. Anyone asks, he says "I'm Murphy. Just Murphy." After a while 'Just Murphy' stuck." Baker laughed again, reached for a metal cup, and took a swig.

"I done things people know about," Just Murphy said in his deep voice. "Some thinks they was good and some thinks they was bad. I got tired of explaining. Now I'm 'Just Murphy' and that suits me fine."

"So you guys have known each other a long time?" Charles asked.

"Don't remember a time Just Murphy wasn't causin' me trouble," Baker said. "He showed up when I was a pup with bad advice and crazy stories."

"I'd put it different," Just Murphy said. "I think I get the credit for every scrap of fun you ever had."

"Yeah," Jim Baker said. "And most of my scars. I wouldn't have got mauled by them grizzlies if you hadn't run off on me."

"You was the one thought fighting two grizzly cubs with a hunting knife sounded like fun. I just wanted you to have more of that fun. And I did teach you how to shoot."

"Fair enough," Baker said.

The two old friends seemed about the same age, maybe forty and no more wrinkled than you'd expect from men who spent most days outdoors. And yet Just Murphy must be much older. There was more going on than they let on.

"What kind of dog is that?" Charles asked.

"Flint's a Huron dog," Murphy said. "Bred from wolves. They kept the smart ones." He paused and looked at Charles for a long time. It was like he was trying to decide if he should tell him something. Finally he said, "Huron dogs are smart in a special way. Some folks call them manitous." He reached for another slab of jerky and took a bite before he continued. He looked at the sky while he spoke, apparently talking to the stars. "Flint is a lot like your goat. He moves around a little different from most dogs."

Charles looked at the dog, then looked back at Just Murphy. Did he mean the dog had the same odd talent Pan had? Is that what they meant by "manitou?"

Just Murphy looked Charles straight in the eye and nodded, as if reading his mind. "I got shot pretty bad— lots of us did. They piled a dozen of us into a little church." He paused. "We was all just waiting to die. That dad-blame church bell kept on ringing. If I coulda reached my rifle, I would have shot it. Then Flint strolls in and sits on my legs. Wouldn't leave. He's been with me ever since. That was the night I... changed. And the night Baker here was born. Flint and I just joined up with him, kinda took care of him. It was like starting over. Didn't think it was odd at the time."

"And you're like…" Charles looked over at Baker who was poking the fire with a stick.

"Yeah, I'm like them. Only I know it and they don't."

"Why don't you…?"

"Tell him? Wouldn't work. People only see and hear what they're ready for. They know we're talkin' right now, they can hear the sound. But the words don't mean nothing to them. It's like we're talking a different language. After a second or two they get busy with their own thoughts." He chewed on his jerky and pushed some dirt around with his moccasin.

"I would have stayed back tonight, just watchin'" he said. "When I seen his campfire and then yours I figured I should join you."

Martin leaned closer and whispered, "Are you going to ask how we get to Alaska?"

"In a minute," Charles whispered back.

Jim Baker took some tobacco out of a pouch, refilled his pipe and lit it with a burning twig from the fire. He started humming a song again and rocking back and forth on the log. The fire crackled and popped. The only other sound was the soft whispering of insects in the dim, blurry night.

Everything seemed so fragile, as if they were all part of some delicate spell that could shatter if anyone said the wrong thing. It felt like carelessness might harm these ghosts, or whatever they were, and wake them from their dream. Just Murphy was watching Charles carefully.

"Aren't you worried," Charles said slowly, trying to think of the right words. "about… changing things?"

Just Murphy nodded and the campfire lit his face in flickering shades of yellow and orange. Charles had asked the correct question.

"A Huron wise man once told me, 'Little Teardrop, you are a stone in a mighty river. Yes, you affect the water. But not as much as you think."

"So you are…?"

"Real?" He laughed a little in his deep voice. "Yeah, I think I'm real. My question is, are you two real? Or am I just dreaming you. I've had a lot of dreams with Baker here. You guys are something new."

"Can Martin see you?" Charles asked.

"I don't know. You see what you look at, what you pay attention to. Out in the woods you get along just fine on your own. But back in town you walk past a saloon and get a whiff of perfume and all of a sudden you're a madman. Can't think of a dad blame thing but women. And I tell you what: they know it, too." He stared at the stars for a moment, then continued.

"Anyway, what you pay attention to gets real."

Charles wanted to come right out and ask if he was a ghost, but he didn't. He had an uncle in a wheel chair, paralyzed by polio, and once Charles asked if he could still walk in his dreams. His uncle said yeah, he could, but his face changed when he said it. He'd never really thought about that before, he said, he just enjoyed his dreams. For half of every day he wasn't trapped in that wheel chair, a prisoner in that helpless body. Charles was sorry he'd asked him the question, afraid maybe now his dreams would change. This felt like that. He changed the subject.

"Your old guns," Charles said, changing the subject. "Are they muskets?"

Jim Baker looked up from his humming as if he could suddenly hear Charles again.

"Nah," he said. "They're rifles. Muskets are smooth inside the barrel. Rifles got scratches inside that makes a bullet spin. Goes straighter and farther. But if they ain't made right they blow up in your hand and take some fingers with it."

Maybe he was remembering something that happened to him. When Charles first saw him, looking old and bedraggled, he was missing his thumb and a couple of fingers from his right hand. Charles had seen it distinctly, but now he had all his fingers and seemed much younger. He was somehow a younger version of the old man who wandered up the driveway and smoked his pipe. It made absolutely no sense. Maybe he had an accident with a gun, but as he sat by this fire, it hadn't happened yet. Or he was remembering himself as a younger man and Charles was eavesdropping on his memory.

"Now, Murphy's gun, that one's kind of special," Jim Baker said. He leaned forward and whispered, sharing a secret. "Just Murphy got famous for shooting a general from so far away no one knew where the bullet come from. Some say he saved a lot of lives, maybe even won the war. But it eats at him. Felt like murder. He don't talk about it, don't tell anyone his true name if he don't have to." Then he spoke louder, looking toward his friend. "Why don't you tell the boys about Eunice."

Just Murphy smiled and nodded and set his rifle across his knees.

"John Golcher made this special for me," he said. "Two barrels, one on top of the other. Don't have to wait to reload to get off a second shot. That second shot surprised a few Apaches and a few lobsters too."

"Lobsters?" Charles said. "You hunt lobsters with a gun?"

"It's a rifle, son. I was in the war with Dan Morgan's boys. They called us The Shirt Men. Lobsters is what we called the enemy."

"Why do you call it Eunice?"

"Named her after Golcher's wife. I wanted a rifle that could spit fire as hot and sure as she did." He patted the rifle affectionately. "I think she'd be proud."

"Were you in the war too?" Charles asked Baker.

"I been in wars my whole life," he said. "Mostly buffalo wars and railroad wars. Apaches and Sioux. But not Shoshone. I married a Shoshone and they're sort of family."

"My father works for the railroad," Martin said.

Jim Baker looked at him like he was noticing him for the first time.

"Is that right?" he said. "What's his name?"

"Frank Whiting," Martin said proudly. "He plans out how to lay the track."

"I knew a Frank Whiting," Baker said, puffing on his pipe. "He done that Colfax track out east of Denver. Worked for Bill Cody up in Wyoming on a dam." He thought for another minute. "Him and me worked on a

170

railroad plan from Denver to Salt Lake. Smart man with numbers and papers, and he'd work till candle-lighting most days. Honest, too. You say you're Frank's boy?"

"Yes sir," Martin said. "Only he went up to Alaska and I want to go there too."

"That's a far piece," Baker said. "Never been that far. How about you, Murphy?"

"Never been," he said. "Might be better for you to just wait for him to come back."

"I been waiting a long time," Martin said.

Nobody said anything. Finally Charles turned to Just Murphy.

"Sometimes I think I recognize people who can't really be there." Charles hoped Just Murphy would understand what he was really asking but the other two wouldn't.

Just Murphy looked at Baker and then at Martin and nodded.

"Could be. Sometimes I'll visit an old friend," he said. "Just to see them, not to say something. If there's a crowd, I just walk along for a minute and then turn a different direction. Maybe I'll sit by their campfire, in the back where they can't see me so well. If they notice me, I see the surprise in their face, but by then I'm gone and they think they're just making somethin' up. It don't harm nobody. Sometimes it makes both of us feel better."

"You talkin' about liquor?" Jim Baker asked.

"Only if you got some," Just Murphy said.

"Happen to have a jug of kill-devil right behind this log. Finest drink in the world," Baker said. He pulled out a jug of dark liquid.

"These pups are a little young," Just Murphy said. "And you know we tend to get in trouble once the kill-devil starts giving the orders. We both seen it at The Slaughterhouse doggery in Denver."

"I'm mending my ways, Murphy," Jim Baker said. "I got some cider heating up in a coffee-pot in these embers over here. Make us up some stonewalls. Young scout, you ever drink kill-devil?"

"I've never even heard of it," Charles said.

"After they make sugar out of the cane stalks, the left-over slop's called molasses. Distill that out and you get kill-devil. City folks call it rumgullion. It's a fine drink all by itself. If you add some molasses back to it, stir it into hot cider, you got a drink guaranteed to make you healthy as a young buffalo." He laughed. "They call it a stonewall."

"After Stonewall Jackson?" Charles asked.

"I think Jackson got his nick-name from the drink," Baker said with a laugh. "Anyway, by the time you dilute the kill-devil down with cider it's about like drinking Brad's Drink, down at Bradham's Drug Store in New Bern. More like medicine for babies than whiskey. Perfectly safe."

"Somebody say kill-devil?" a voice to the right startled Charles. An old man was sitting on the log just a few feet away. He had not been there a moment ago and Charles hadn't noticed him join the group. He wore a neat white shirt buttoned up to his neck and a white linen coat and pants with a folded handkerchief in the breast pocket. He looked like pictures of Mark Twain, with quick piercing eyes and a shock of disorganized short white hair atop his head. He sat erect, thin and tough as a strip of jerky. A very old rifle leaned against the log beside him. He moved his feet closer to the fire and grinned.

"Well, John Burns, I should have known you'd come calling if there was kill-devil involved." Jim Baker said.

"Never been much of a drinking man," Burns said. His voice was high and thin, an old man's voice. "But I do enjoy the company."

Just Murphy laughed. "Don't get Mr. Burns here started about Mr. Lincoln. He's sort of an expert."

"Only met the man once," Burns said, stroking his chin and gazing into the distance. "But it was a proud time. We walked to the Presbyterian church together. He admired my rifle, only it was one I borrowed."

"Who is Mr. Lincoln?" Charles asked.

"Greatest American who ever lived," Mr. Burns said.

Jim Baker poured a cup of hot cider into a metal cup, added a shot of molasses from a small jar and some kill-devil from his jug. He took a sip to taste it. "Now, that's a real lally-cooler if I say it myself!" He handed it to Mr. Burns. Just Murphy looked at me.

"Mr. Burns has some stories," he said. "Says his great grandaddy was an Irish poet."

"Scottish," Burns corrected him.

Just Murphy smiled. "Right," he said. "I forgot."

"You forget every dad-blame time," Burns said.

Just Murphy turned back to Charles and spoke under his breath. "Burns is a fine shot himself with a long gun, but his stories are starting to fade. Don't see him too often." He paused. "He don't have a dog or a goat."

"What were the Indians like?" Charles asked.

"They're like anybody else," Jim Baker said. "Some's crazy, some's serious. If an Arapaho don't know you, he'll steal you blind. If he knows you, he's your best friend. Marina was a Shoshone. Her daddy made me part of the tribe when I married her."

Just Murphy looked at Charles. "Might be why me and Baker found each other," he said quietly. "We was both partly raised by tribe-folks. Took some of the good and some of the bad from both sides."

"But I thought you said you shot them."

"More than once," Baker said. "And they shot me. And then I married one. And then I married another one of them. Life ain't simple." He stared at the stars and watched the smoke trace lines between them. "Marina," he said softly. "Now, she was a jammy bit of jam."

He sipped his drink and nodded toward the cabin. "In the morning, I still sit at the kitchen table drinking a cup of coffee and when I look across I always expect to see her, but she's not there. Sometimes I pretend so hard I think I see her, just for a second. And so I talk to her. Tell her it's a sunny day, the kind she liked. I tell her about the garden and the little scarecrow I made to shoo off the birds. It won't work, she tells me. Crows are too smart. They'll figure it out. Probably so, I say. They can tell when something's not real." He paused, looking at the stars.

173

"But it helps for a little while, and that's the truth," he said. "For just a while, it's better."

Just Murphy looked up suddenly and his expression changed. Now he looked nervous, like he'd just thought of some danger. "Might not be smart to do too much remembering," he said.

"Why not?" Charles asked.

"Remembering is the past and dreaming is the future. They move back and forth."

"I don't understand."

"Because of the dog and the goat," Just Murphy said. "I thought Flint was the only manitou left. When I seen you two with that white goat, I knew right away. You got to be careful. Today can change yesterday, it ain't a one way deal. Water in a creek can't see the beaver dam in its future, but the water slows and spreads onto the bank behind it just the same. Beaver-pond water reaches back and touches upstream like fingers. The future affects the past the same way. We just ain't got good words for it."

"The future affects the past? How can that be?"

"Flying Fawn, she understood things. She made that bear-claw necklace for Baker. She said sometimes two totems work different if you use both of them. Maybe stronger, maybe just different. If Baker starts remembering things too hard, with these two animals here… I don't know what might happen."

"Are you afraid of Mr. Baker's memories?"

"Yes sir, I guess I am. Him and me, we're both woods-runners and riflemen," Murphy said. "Something about shooting a long gun at something so far away most folks can't even see it. You got to focus your brain on that one thing and picture where that bullet's gonna go. Maybe the way you hold your brain counts as much as how you aim your gun. You sorta' think that bullet to the target. And when Baker starts to focus his brain on a memory… well, he's a helluva shot."

"So it's like magic," Charles said.

"I just know that if he starts remembering stuff too hard, especially with the kill-devil chiming in, we're all likely to be right there with him. And some of his memories ain't any places for young pups like you two."

Jim Baker looked up from the fire. "So, if you're Frank Whiting's boy, you must be from Denver."

"North of Denver," Martin said. "By Westminster College."

"I spent some time in Denver," Baker said. "Sold a year's worth of beaver pelts there. Saved up a thousand dollars to buy a little farm." He stared off into the distance, smiling and nodding. "I felt so rich I bought a suit and and some fancy boots. Lost it all in a card game, and I don't believe it was a fair game, either, by gonny. Got broke and lonesome in a hurry. Being rich felt pretty good for about a week, though. Stayed at a nice hotel..." He puffed on his pipe and got a faraway look in his eyes.

Just Murphy's eyes widened. He recognized the far-away look on Baker's face. He looked at Charles and motioned frantically in Martin's direction. He said, "Get that kid out of here!"

Charles turned to Martin. "I think we should go back to the house."

"What?"

Charles leaned closer and whispered right in his ear. "I think we should go back to the house. It's getting late."

"But the fire feels good," Martin complained, sounding exactly like the eight-year-old kid he was, protesting about bedtime or eating broccoli.

"Yes, it does," Charles said and looked at the fire. Only now it wasn't a campfire. It was a fire in a big stone fireplace. Instead of sitting on hard round logs, they sat on thick carpet a few feet from the flames. They were in the lobby of a nice old hotel with dark wood paneling and old gaslight chandeliers hanging from the ceiling. Jim Baker was lounging off to one side in a fancy padded chair. Just Murphy sat in another chair with his dog Flint laying across his feet. He looked over at Charles and exhaled loudly, obviously relieved.

"This ain't bad," Just Murphy said. "We been lots worse places. Maybe it'll be OK."

Pan, the goat, sprawled on the carpet between Charles and Martin. Charles put one hand on the animal's back. He didn't know where they were or how they got there but he wasn't going to risk getting stranded. Keeping one hand on the goat felt like the safest insurance against that.

Martin seemed completely unconcerned. "It's a nice fire," he said again, perhaps not even realizing it was a completely different fire.

Then, in the blink of an eye, the fire was gone, the carpet had vanished along with Just Murphy and Jim Baker. Charles was beneath the porch of his own home, in his own time, and all alone. His dogs lay outside in the sunshine.

"It was a dream," he said to himself, but he wasn't sure.

Chapter 29

As he rode his bike down to the library, Charles remembered what Just Murphy had said: "Yes, you affect the river. But not as much as you think." That was reassuring. Even if he was traveling back and forth in time he probably wasn't powerful enough to destroy the universe. He grinned to himself. He hoped he was getting good advice from his hallucinations.

"Hello, Charles," the librarian said.

"Hello, Mrs. Alexandria."

"What are we researching today?"

"A town in Alaska called Skagaway. I've already read in our encyclopedia about it. It's a port town and was big in the gold rush. I'm just wondering what it was like back then. Back in 1898 or so."

"We have some older encyclopedias in the back," she said. "But nothing that old. We replace reference books as they become outdated. I think that town is now called Skagway, not Skagaway." She pointed toward a hallway.

The reference room smelled dusty and was quiet as an empty church. One wall was filled with sets of encyclopedias: The Book of Knowledge, American Educator, Colliers, Funk and Wagnalls. Charles sat at a table and began reading. The books were old, but he learned a lot.

Because of the promise of riches from gold, during the 1890s Skagway's population swelled from a handful of tough loners to a thriving mass of 15,000 souls. It got its name from the Tlingit tribe's word, which means 'place where the north wind blows.' It had a good harbor, and it flourished for a few years because of the White Pass and Yukon Route Railroad, which allowed gold to be transported from inland. By the 1950s, fewer than 4,000 lived there.

Charles wrote down the dates the railroad was built. If Whiting had actually moved to Alaska to help design it, that would be evidence that Charles wasn't crazy. Figments could not provide true historical information.

177

Kenn Amdahl

None of the books mentioned Frank Whiting but that only proved that he wasn't encyclopedia-level famous. Maybe he'd been better known in Colorado. Charles went to the front desk.

"All done, Charles?" Mrs. Alexandria asked.

"Not quite," he said. "Do you think I could use the microfilm reader again? I'd like to look for an obituary."

She smiled. "Of course. Let me get it set up for you."

He followed her back down the hall. She unlocked the microfilm room and turned on the machine. "Let's see, you were interested in 1897, weren't you? Or was it 1898?"

"I'd like to start with 1897 and work my way forward," he said.

He started with the day of the newspaper scrap. Was Martin's father alive on that date? The first page of the paper was identical to the scrap he'd found. The few obituaries on the last page weren't interesting.

He rolled the microfilm to the next day and stopped quickly in surprise. The headlines were about the attempted bank robbery the previous day, the circus parade, and the arrest of notorious con man "Jefferson Smith, also known as Soapy Smith."

Of course! Newspapers always report the news a day late! It takes them time to write the stories, set up the printing press, print the pages and deliver the papers.

He read each article carefully. The stories matched his own experience with a few embellishments. The paper made everything sound more exciting and dangerous, but the main facts coincided with what he'd seen.

Charles leaned back in the library chair. His experiment had demonstrated something useful already: he could not have imagined those events from before his grandfather was born. Not so clearly, not so accurately. He had been there. Or he'd seen the memory of someone else who had been there. But he still wanted to learn about Martin's father.

He quickly fell into a routine. The obituaries were always on the last page so he rolled the film forward until he saw the big headline on the following day's paper, then scrolled back slowly. It only took a glance to

178

confirm there were no Whitings listed. Charles moved through the pages with increasing efficiency.

When he finally did see the name, he scrolled right past it without his mind registering immediately. A second later he realized he'd seen "Whiting" and scrolled backward slowly. Sure enough, on the previous day's paper, there was a Whiting obituary. He read it carefully, then read it again. It made no sense.

The obituary was not for Frank Whiting at all. It was for eight-year-old Martin Bates Whiting. His father was Frank Whiting, the respected civil engineer who worked for the railroad company, his mother was Millah Whiting. About a year after the attempted bank robbery the boy got an infected tooth. The infection spread, he became very sick and died at home in his bed. The family lived north of Denver City in an area called, at that time, Gregory Hills.

Charles stared at the screen, his hands holding the heavy metal microfilm machine as if it were an anchor. Its cold hard steel was certainly no hallucination. Martin was no hallucination either. But what was he?

Maybe it was possible to communicate with a living child across time, even over the vast distance of fifty years. Maybe people left memories behind like a scent, and a sensitive person might "remember" a life the way they "remember" a woman's presence by the perfume she left clinging to drapes when she walked through a room. Or maybe ghosts exist.

You don't need to understand everything, Charles told himself. It's nothing to be upset about, you can't understand most things in life. You accept them, make decisions, and take actions.

Martin heard his parents talk about moving to Alaska before he got sick, that was probably true, but when they moved, he stayed behind. Maybe he'd been too sick.

Charles stopped in mid thought. Or, by the time the Whitings moved Martin wasn't sick at all. Maybe they moved after the date of the obituary. Martin could never join his parents again, not in the way he imagined.

Yet he could still see them, at least when he "travelled" with Pan. Watching his family in Alaska might feel comforting, like seeing old pictures, even if he was invisible to them. It might eliminate his sad nightmares and cure Charles's house of its haunting. He had to help the boy travel to Alaska.

If this "traveling" could be controlled, Charles didn't understand the mechanism. He couldn't bear the thought of stranding Martin in some bleak Alaskan wilderness, more alone than ever. Ghost or not, Martin was still basically an eight-year-old kid, too inexperienced for a solo trip to a distant, dangerous destination. His thoughts were unpredictable and his vehicle was a stubborn baby goat on spindly legs that was easily distracted by any interesting weed. But if Charles went with them, he risked being stranded in Alaska forever.

If only he had a second manitou to get him back if it worked… As soon as he thought that, he got an idea. He knew someone else who owned a spirit animal.

Chapter 30

Jim Baker looked young; his right hand had all its fingers as he stuffed a pinch of chewing tobacco into his mouth. His hair was neatly combed and he wore a black suit and shiny leather boots. The way he squirmed and twisted his head from side to side revealed that he was uncomfortable in the city clothes. On the floor, Martin stared at the fire that writhed and hissed like snakes within the huge fireplace. Pan sniffed at the hotel-lobby carpet. Charles looked from the goat, to Martin, to the two men. He didn't think ten seconds had elapsed since he'd left this scene.

"Sir," Charles said to Just Murphy. He hurried to speak because he knew he might not have much time. "I need some help getting Martin back to his parents in Alaska. I need someone with a dog like Flint."

"To help you return if you're successful."

"Yes sir."

Just Murphy looked far into the distance, considering the idea. Before he could answer, Jim Baker spoke up.

"I ain't never gonna get used to these dad-blamed store-bought boots," Jim Baker said to Just Murphy.

"Damn waste of money," Just Murphy agreed. He was still dressed in buckskin and moccasins.

"They hurt your feet and they're noisy as a crow," Jim Baker said. "Not even you or me could get close enough to a deer to get off a shot in these things."

"I think I'll stick with the moccasins," Just Murphy said.

"Yeah," said Jim Baker. He turned his head to the right and spit out his chewing tobacco, which flew in a graceful arc across the room and landed like a dead bird on the fancy carpet. While he jammed another wad into his cheek, a skinny kid, maybe twelve years old, scurried into the room carrying a shiny brass bucket which he set right on top of the tobacco mess on the floor.

"Here's a spittoon, sir," he said.

Baker paid him no attention.

"I've got half a mind to take the damn things off and walk around Denver City barefoot," he said. Murphy smiled and nodded.

"That would be the first time you done that," Just Murphy said. "At least cold sober."

Baker turned his head to the left and spit out his tobacco onto the carpet on that side. The kid ran out again and moved the spittoon to cover the new mass of brown goo.

"Perhaps you'd prefer it over here," the boy said politely. Again, Baker didn't respond at all. He was deep in his own thoughts and didn't notice much else.

"Gonna use my savings to buy some land," Baker said. "Build a little cabin, raise some potatoes, do a little fishing. Maybe ferry folks across one of them little rivers by Denver City. Shoot, you or me'd just walk across them, but them city folks don't like to get their shoes muddy." Baker spit once more, this time onto the carpet directly in front of him. Once again, the kid moved the spittoon to the carpet in front of Baker.

"Whatever you like, sir," the kid said with a sigh.

Baker looked at him. "Young feller, that's a fine pretty bucket you got there. But if you keep moving it around I'm likely to spit tobacco right into it."

"I think that was the idea," Murphy said. "Fancy people spit in them things all the time."

"I ain't gonna get civilized if it means I got to get stupid," Baker snapped. "Why would you mess up the prettiest thing in the room by spittin' tobacco into it?"

"Ain't much chance of you getting civilized," Just Murphy said. "I think we ought to get back to your campfire."

"Least we got tobacco these days," Jim Baker said, ignoring Murphy. "Remember that time we had to rescue Captain Frapp at Bastain Mountain?"

Just Murphy looked at Charles and stood up quickly. "That ain't a memory for these pups," he said.

Baker took a long drink of dark brown whiskey from a glass. "That was quite a time," he said. "Apache warriors screaming, chargin' up the hill at us, shooting and hooping. And that mad Arapaho woman leading them all."

"You boys get out of here!" Just Murphy said urgently. He motioned wildly with his hand and turned back to Baker.

"What about my idea?" Charles asked. "Would you be willing to help me?"

But Just Murphy wasn't listening. He was talking to Jim Baker.

"Someday you'll have a nice little cabin outside Denver, Jim." Murphy spoke with quiet intensity, trying to distract the trapper. "A place with a view of Vasquez Fork, maybe have a little pump organ inside, play them old songs you like. Can't you just picture that?" Just Murphy said. "Them little prairie dogs you feed might come right up to you, like pets. At night you can have a campfire outside. Put some big cottonwood logs around it to sit on. Stare at that fire and just be peaceful."

Baker wasn't listening.

"That Arapaho woman, she was scarier than a grizzly bear," he said.

Murphy stood up and pointed at Charles.

"This ain't going any good way," he said with an urgency Charles had not heard before. "You two hang onto that goat and get yourselves back to someplace safe!"

The fear on his face indicated he was very serious.

"Martin," Charles said. "We need to get back to the house right now!"

"But I want to hear the story," Martin said. "I think he's going to tell a story!"

"We was on the wrong side of the Little Snake River," Baker said, as if he were talking to the fireplace.

"Charles!" Just Murphy said urgently. "You put your hands on that goat and do whatever you do to travel. Get you and the boy out of here! One thing I figured out is if something... something really bad happens to you or your animal, it can't be fixed."

Charles held the goat with one hand and Martin with the other and pictured his house on the hill, and his dogs. For just a moment it felt like he was there. But then the light dimmed, a cool wind blew through his hair and he knew it hadn't worked.

Chapter 31

Baker stared at the flames dancing in the hotel fireplace and smiled. His mind was far away. "We'd shot a couple of buffalo and was dressing them out. Remember that, Murphy?"

"Come on, Martin, " Charles said. They had to try again. "We need to go!"

Martin was staring at Baker, transfixed. Baker continued his story.

"Across the river, up top of the ridge we seen more buffalo running like they was being chased. Only we hadn't done nothing to spook them."

Charles tried not to picture the scene as Baker spoke: The dead buffalo on the ground, the two men in buckskins kneeling beside them holding hunting knives in hands red with the animal's blood. Flint, the dog, sat patiently beside Murphy while flies buzzed around its face. The dog's mouth was open, panting in the heat. Behind it, the dry weeds of August clutched the dirt like sad ornaments. Pine trees lined the edge of the level clearing which ended abruptly where a steep ravine swooped down to a sparkling blue stream. Near the water, the valley on both sides of the river glowed bright green with vegetation. Charles tried very hard not to picture the scene that Baker described.

"Hey Vandusor, what do you make of that?" Baker pointed at the buffalo on the horizon. Across the top of the hill, silhouetted against the bright blue sky, a series of buffalo ran one after another. They churned up a cloud of dark dust. Charles had no idea who 'Vandusor' was. Did another invisible friend lurk on the prairie?

"Arapaho," Just Murphy said, answering as if his name was Vandusar. "We better get back to the fort. We ain't got much chance out here by ourselves."

"My horse outrun a few arrows in his day," Baker said. "But then he was bred for running. You think your beat-up old nag can make it down the hill and across the river?"

"I don't know," Murphy answered. "Straight down and cross the river's our shortest shot. But over to the left ain't as steep. Might be better odds."

185

The men abandoned the buffalo carcass and mounted their horses. Baker's was a huge black stallion, Murphy's smaller horse was a mottled tan. Baker's horse was fast and confident; it headed straight for the short but steep course and got to the edge first. Without hesitation, the black horse started down, picking its footing carefully. Murphy cursed loudly but followed, his horse complaining at the sudden and unusual request for speed. Flint trotted along beside.

Murphy's horse stumbled a few times but caught its balance. By the time Murphy reached the river, Baker and his stallion were halfway across the river, the big horse swimming powerfully. Murphy's horse followed bravely but the current was too strong. Horse and rider drifted downstream as quickly as they moved toward the opposite shore. Flint was a strong swimmer and followed right behind them.

Not far downstream, a huge cottonwood tree lay prostrate on the opposite bank, its massive trunk broken and jagged. Half of its root system still anchored it firmly, but the top part of the tree dangled in the water with many branches and twigs submerged. Sticks and weeds were trapped in its network of branches creating a tangled web of debris. The current carried Murphy and his horse directly toward it.

The horse swam as fiercely as it could but it was no use. Its saddle became ensnared by the natural dam. Flint calmly climbed out of the water onto the tree and sat on the largest branch.

Baker, whose horse had already scrambled onto land, saw the situation and galloped downstream to their position.

"I told you you ought get yourself a real horse," he shouted.

"I'll consider that advice," Murphy shouted back. "You got more suggestions to improve my life than a preacher. You'll make someone a fine wife."

Baker threw a long, sturdy rope onto the river a bit upstream. It floated down to the stuck horse. Murphy grabbed it and tied a loop around his saddle horn while Baker tied the other end to his own saddle. Murphy scrambled onto the tangle of branches. Clinging to the tree with one hand, legs dangling in the muddy water, he broke off the limbs that had snagged his horse's bridle and saddle. "OK," he yelled and Baker backed his horse over the green grass. With this extra help, Murphy's horse swam easily to shore.

"Them Arapaho ain't gonna wait for you to finish your bubble bath," Baker said.

"I should have known better than to follow your lead," Murphy said. "That flat spot upstream would have forded easy." He climbed back on top of his horse and the two men galloped away with the dog following close behind.

Charles's hand clutched the rough bark of the cottonwood tree, the part that still lay on the ground. The trunk was nearly four feet in diameter and the grooves in its bark were large enough his thumb could easily fit into them and trace their pattern. Everything seemed perfectly normal and he forgot where he was. The sun felt hot on his face and a meadowlark sang somewhere near the river. A bee buzzed past his face and instinctively he closed his eyes, shook his head, and waved his hand to chase it away. This isn't such a different world, he thought. Between my own magic and Pan's, if I concentrated, maybe I could get us back to my house.

When the bee left a second later he opened his eyes. His fingers were still touching a cottonwood log, but it was not the same one. An arrow whizzed past his ear so close he heard it cut through the air. Terrified, he ducked as fast as he could, his whole body shaking. The arrow stuck in the dirt just behind him with a thunking sound and vibrated for several seconds.

"Stay down!" Just Murphy shouted. "This ain't a place for young-uns!"

They huddled against a makeshift wall three feet tall that someone had hastily constructed of logs and twigs. A very crude fort. The same intensely blue prairie sky covered them as it had near the dead buffaloes, but now frantic activity and noise surrounded them. A dead horse lay on the ground beside them. Men shouted, guns fired, the air was thick with the smoke and smell of gunpowder. On the other side of the wall, whoops and yells jumbled together with horses neighing and galloping. These sounds were punctuated by shorter screams of pain that ended abruptly. Behind them, men were moaning and crying out.

"They want our horses!" Just Murphy yelled in Charles's direction above all the noise. He was out of breath. "And they say they'll let us live if we give them over. Only that ain't how this tribe operates. They don't deal fair. And even if they aim about as steady as drunk miller moths, with so many dad-blame arrows and bullets flyin' around they already killed just about all our horses by dumb luck. They just don't know it yet."

An arrow flew over the wall and stuck in the carcass of the horse beside them.

Martin sat upright beside Charles, eyes wide, his head and shoulder above the log, curious but completely unafraid. Pan lay on the ground, instinctively staying low. The one big cottonwood log seemed their best shelter.

"You stay down behind this log," Charles said firmly. When Martin didn't move, Charles pushed him down into the area between the big log and the dead horse and lay on top of him. "The dead horse will protect you!" Charles said.

"I want to go home!" Martin yelled.

"The dead horse will protect you! Here, keep Pan right next to you. You need to protect him!"

Charles's hands shook and his brain buzzed with fear. He desperately wanted to be anywhere else, but leaving would require concentration. Only there wasn't any way to concentrate with death flying all around him. He wanted to be the brave one for once, the older kid, protecting Martin and reassuring him but he was too scared to do any comforting.

"We need to travel back home!" Charles shouted. Martin didn't answer. As if he was in a trance, he just kept repeating "The dead horse will protect you."

Jim Baker was yelling at the other men. Two dozen frightened young men dressed in buckskin and denim aimed long guns over the wall. Some wore identical blue jackets. Baker was clearly the leader.

"Make every shot count!" he yelled. "They got Frapp and they'll get us too if we ain't smart. Get a buddy, the guy next to you. You reload while he shoots. Them savages won't get too close until everybody's reloading at the same time."

Suddenly the whoops and yelling on the other side of the wall got louder. Just Murphy moved a few feet to crouch nearer the boys, using one knee as a rifle stand to steady his aim.

"Here they come again," Baker yelled. "One at a time now boys! No wasted shots!"

Half the men looked over the top of the little wall, aiming their rifles down the hill, while the rest huddled lower, biding their time. Arrows flew through the air from the attackers, and many gunshots came from that side as well. It was a furious volley and it seemed like there must have been hundreds of attackers. The trappers fired back, slowly and methodically. It was less furious, but someone was always firing. Charles peered through a crack between logs. The Apaches were racing uphill toward them on horseback, between trees and hillside on the left and a little creek off to the right. The attackers screamed and waved their bows and rifles in the air. As soon as they got within range they all fired. Their gunshots were rapid as popcorn, their arrows flew like a flock of geese in a loose formation. Then, just as suddenly as it started, the attack ended and the Apaches retreated.

"They all shoot at once," Baker said, not yelling as loud now. "And then they have to drop back to reload. They ain't strategic. They'll want to bargain again pretty soon."

"We need to leave," Charles told Martin.

"I don't know how," he answered. Now he sounded tearful and afraid.

"Just the same as always," Charles said.

No arrows or bullets were coming from the other side for a moment, so Charles raised his head. Smaller logs and branches were stacked on top of the biggest log providing a good view between them. At the base of the hill, a mass of men on horses milled around. The water in the little creek looked pink. Despite the danger, the scientist in Charles wondered what sort of mineral deposit could color the water that way? Iron maybe?

As if reading his mind, Baker's voice rose again. "They're dragging their dead to the creek," he said "From the color, you can see how we're doing."

Charles looked at the creek again and felt a little sick to his stomach. Behind him, men dragged several dead horses next to the wall. Once in place, men crouched behind them, using the carcasses as shields against the bullets and arrows. Other men lay on the dirt motionless, covered with blood, arrows protruding from their bodies at crazy angles. A few injured men sat on the ground with a dazed look on their faces as they pressed their hands against bleeding holes in their stomachs or legs. Some writhed in agony, shrieking like animals. Healthy men struggled to drag the wounded to relative safety behind the dead horses. Men screamed as they were moved, then went silent as they lost consciousness.

Beyond the wall, several of the Arapaho's horses lay twisting on the dirt, making their own pitiful sounds. Individually, every sound was horrible and frightening. But somehow all the screaming and moaning and yelling and gunfire blended together into a sort of hum that merged all the sounds together into something muted and less terrifying. The sound was almost lovely. Charles found it deeply disturbing that his brain could combine so much horror into something that didn't bother him at all.

Martin tried to sit up, but Charles pushed him back down. "You stay down until I tell you to get up," he shouted. Martin looked stunned. I'll apologize later, Charles thought. Assuming we survive. Charles moved some twigs to see better. His mouth fell open and he shivered, despite the heat.

The Arapahos were riding up the hill again, but slowly, in an orderly way. One rider led them, staying a bit in front of the others. They did not get as close this time before they stopped. The first rider carried some sort of staff, a big stick with feathers on the end. It was Sapania, the woman who had ridden into Charles's yard by the sunflowers, the one who killed the jackrabbit and wanted his bell. It wasn't possible, yet there she was. She waved her staff and the riders behind her stopped. Her eyes were no longer milky white, or covered with a film. Now they were as clear and bright as an eagle's eyes, the whites like snow and the irises and pupils nearly the same shade of black. They glistened when she opened them wide and shouted up the hill to Baker and the others.

"We shall talk again, foolish pale men," she yelled. "Give us your horses now or I shall bring the spirit of the desert down upon you!" She

190

paused, waiting for a response, but Jim Baker did not reply. She continued, even louder, raising her arms to the sky. "Hawk Brother! Visit us and shame these imposters into leaving. Sweep down on golden wing with a wind to frighten mountains. Blow their bullets back to them. When they shoot at us let them pierce their own hearts." To Charles, it sounded like she was chanting some incantation, creating a magic spell. Or at least trying to convince the men that's what she was doing.

Her voice was young. Maybe she was even pretty, beneath all the war paint and strange clothing; maybe that's why all the young bucks seemed so eager to follow her. But today, with dead birds hanging around her neck, that was hard to imagine.

She spoke again, louder this time. "Fear the blossoms with thorns like daggers! We bloom in the night! The heat will devour you and spit out the dust of your bones!"

The band of black paint that covered her eyes seemed darker than before. Her cheeks were still streaked with horizontal white lines. The thin red lines on her forehead and cheeks looked even more like blood in this setting, with so much actual blood everywhere. The feathers stuck in her long black hair looked like arrows impaling her from crazy angles. Her buckskin outfit and black cape looked fresh; her necklace of dead birds dangled and danced like puppets. Some of them might still be twitching. Her eyes gleamed brightly like the eyes of a wild predator intent on prey.

"The wind hears every whisper, every prayer, but it answers in moans, a sad ghost without a tongue."

"You say you want to talk, but you ain't talking sense. Just a lick and a promise," Baker shouted down to her. "You spout out a bunch of loco words and then you shoot."

The woman laughed. It was a loud, disturbing cackle, the sound a rooster might make if it tried to laugh.

"We only want horses," she said. "You took all our buffalo, pay us now with horses. And then you may go away free."

"I don't think we'll be giving away any horses."

"Your horses do not belong to you, they belong to the land. The spirit of the land is Arapaho, so you must return our horses to us."

"You sound like a Denver City lawyer," Jim Baker said.

"White man lawyers only know thieving and trickery. I speak the voice of the tumbleweed, the song of the coyote. I am the Spirit voice and I demand you send my horses back to me."

"Pretty sure we got a receipt when we bought these ponies. I don't recall Mr. Spirit signing it. Maybe you confused them with some other ponies."

In a quiet voice Murphy said, "We ain't got much ammunition left, Jim. We might hold 'em off for one more charge. But maybe not."

The woman leaned back and spoke to the sky in the chanting voice of a preacher. "The magpie speaks, he does not sing. The grasshopper leaps, he does not dance. The moon weeps in her meadow of stars. Only the snake hiding in the weeds watches and understands. He rattles the truth, a single word: death."

"That woman is the problem," Baker replied. "They think she's magic."

Murphy looked startled. He stared at the woman for a moment, then nodded as an idea sprouted within him. "Maybe she is at that, " he said.

Chapter 32

Just Murphy kneeled by Charles and spoke with a keen intensity, as if he had a special message and this might be his only chance to give it. "Nobody told Flint he had to live in just one time. So he don't. And sometimes, if he's with me, I don't either. We mostly live in whatever world we believe in but you can't always control what you believe. This is a time to get serious about what you believe." He turned back to Jim Baker and spoke louder. "See if you can stall them off a bit."

Baker nodded, then yelled at the woman. "How many horses you think might be a fair trade?"

She laughed again.

"All the horses! That's a fair deal! And now is the time, before the rain shall kiss the lonely cactus. Or I will touch your secrets and make them mine."

The woman fit into this hostile environment as surely as sagebrush did. Ancient demons lived here: the gods of rattlesnake and beetle summoned by smoke and lonely drums; the goblins of thorny, cunning plants too wicked to die. This furnace of a landscape was haunted by nature itself; it rightly inspired fear in any sane person. But this crazy woman didn't fear the fiends of sunstroke and sudden death. She teased them and flirted with them.

Murphy steadied his rifle on the wall. He was aiming at the woman.

"It's too far," Baker said under his breath. "Don't waste your ammunition."

"Maybe too far for them old-fashioned smooth-bore guns these trappers got from their Grandpa," he said. "But not for you or me. Not for Eunice." He patted his rifle affectionately. "Anyway, I ain't aiming at the woman. I got a bigger target. You keep negotiating."

Baker nodded.

"How about half the horses?" Baker yelled. "We need something to get us home, don't we?"

"Spirit has made this a good day for walking," she yelled back. "You give me all the horses, you go free."

Murphy was concentrating on his shot. But he was also muttering something and Charles listened carefully.

"That scrappy flea-bit horse reminds me of a certain dog," Just Murphy said. "And a certain goat. Easy to convince Arapaho boys you're a powerful shaman if you got a manitou."

Charles didn't see anything special about the woman's horse but it made sense. If magical animals were common, some of their owners would likely be evil, or crazy, or greedy. Throughout history, both good and bad people had unexplainable influence over others; maybe spirit animals had helped them.

Pan remained huddled beside Martin, unconcerned. If something happened to that goat...

Charles swallowed hard. We'd be stuck here, he thought, in this place and time, surrounded by an army of angry young men who want to kill us. They'd be even madder once they discovered we didn't have many horses to trade them.

Unless this was still some sort of dream. It did not feel like one.

The sharp sound of Murphy's gun broke his thoughts. Smoke curled up from the end of the rifle barrel like the wisp of a child's breath on a cold morning. Murphy held perfectly still.

Across the clearing, the woman did not realize what had just happened,.

"No more talk!" the woman yelled. "You give us horses now."

A red circle formed on her horse's head, right between its eyes. Its head jerked backward. The woman looked confused for a moment, then she understood. The horse's front legs buckled and it lurched to its knees.

"Not you!" she shrieked. "Not my Flatpipe!" She slid off the horse's back and pushed on its side as if to hold it upright, to stop something she had no power to stop. The horse paused, frozen in place for less than a heartbeat, its cells instinctively struggling to live after there was no hope for the creature to survive. Then it collapsed on its side and stopped moving.

194

"No!" she yelled, all her eloquence abandoning her. She turned back to the men behind her. "No! Not Flatpipe!" she shouted. "Not my Flatpipe!" She shouted other words in a strange language and screamed, a loud terrible wail that echoed from the hills and rose to the sky. Standing beside the dead horse, she spread her arms, palms facing upward, as if pleading with the gods of the cactus and rattlesnake. Over and over she screamed in anguish.

Then she turned and shook her fist at the men who shot her horse. "This is not over! I shall track you down and kill each one of you! In your sleep, when you least expect it!" Then she turned and walked down the hill.

None of her fighters knew what to do and they sat on their horses looking at each other in confusion. In a minute, the baffled warriors turned and followed her. As Charles watched from behind the little log wall, the mass of men and horses moved slowly away.

Baker stood and straightened, no longer concerned with being an exposed target.

"Lucky shot," he said to Just Murphy.

"Not for her it wasn't," Murphy said. "Eunice feelin' feisty today." He stroked his rifle affectionately. One by one the other men stood, looking dazed at being alive. One by one they gradually seemed to awaken and move more quickly, attending to normal things that had seemed inconceivable a few moments earlier. Bandaging a wound, taking a drink from an iron canteen, removing a boot to shake out a pebble.

Jim Baker spoke to Just Murphy. "You think they all pulled foot?"

"I do," Just Murphy said. "Without their magic leader pushing, they ain't got much idea to attack. They might regroup in a day or two, but I think we're safe today."

Baker nodded, then walked off to help with the injured.

Charles was trying to understand what had just happened.

"So that woman," he said. "She was… like you?"

"Maybe," Murphy said. "Or maybe like you. That's where I'd put my money."

"I still have so many questions," Charles said.

Murphy nodded slowly.

"Sometimes there's reasons things happen," he said. "Sometimes there ain't."

Charles frowned at that imprecise and indifferent attitude. Where would the world be if Newton and Galileo had been frightened by things they didn't understand? We'd still be living in the Dark Ages. And what would happen if people got scared by magic before they really understood it?

Exactly what has happened, he realized. They would stop trying to learn magic, stop talking about it, stop believing in it. They would forbid their children from hearing about it. It would remain forever in the shadows labeled superstition and fairy tale. Just like science would have if a few people hadn't been brave.

The only cloud in the sky, a mere puff, moved until it obscured the sun, dimming the scene. Charles glanced up as the light continued to dim.

"I want to go home!" Martin said again, tugging at Charles's shirt.

"It's all right," Charles said. "We'll be home soon..."

He stopped. That was no ordinary cloud. The light continued to fade. Was this an eclipse? He started to ask Just Murphy, but the rifleman had frozen in place like an old photograph and as the light grew ever dimmer, the man seemed to fade with it until he disappeared. The air continued to get darker and within a few seconds it was dark as night. Charles shivered as a cool breeze swept over him.

"I'm going to go to sleep," Martin said.

"That's probably a good..." Charles began, turning to face him. But Martin was no longer there, either.

Charles stood amid the familiar weeds near his house, but it was night. The sunflower patch was barely visible to his right. As his eyes adjusted to the darkness, he gasped. Someone sat on the dirt a few feet ahead of him with his back to Charles, staring in the direction of the mountains. The smell of cigarette smoke floated from the figure and a glowing red tip of a stub lit his fingers.

"Raymond?" Charles said in disbelief. "Is that you? What are you doing…?"

Raymond jerked around, startled. He quickly smashed the cigarette into the dirt, trying to hide the evidence. When he realized it was just his younger brother, he relaxed again.

"I heard it too," he said, his voice shaky. "It was so clear. A child's voice, over and over, the same words. "The dead horse will protect you. I want to go home." He shook his head, trying to clear it. "The dead horse will protect you. What does it mean? The house really must be haunted, and by a lunatic."

Charles sat on the dirt beside his brother.

"A lot of things are scary that aren't dangerous," he said. "And our imaginations enlarge things like a movie projector does."

"It seemed so real."

"Did you tell Mom?"

"No, not yet. I didn't want to wake her."

"I tell you what," Charles said. "Let me do a little more research. Maybe I can fix this problem."

"You? What could you do?"

"I've got a plan. Don't you tell Mom about this until I try it. And I won't tell her about the cigarette. Deal?"

Raymond nodded.

Chapter 33

"Do you ever travel to your own house?" Charles asked Martin the following night. Once again he had snuck down from his bedroom after everyone else was asleep. His dogs wagged and sniffed but didn't make any noise.

"I'm already at my house," Martin said.

"Yes, I understand that. But do you ever want to visit when your parents are here?"

"They aren't here. They're in Alaska."

"Yes, I know. But we saw your father at the parade. Do you ever see him here, in the house?"

Martin looked confused.

"He's in Alaska."

Charles decided to try a different strategy. "It might be easier to find him if I knew a little more about him."

"He works for the railroad," Martin said.

"Yes, that's a start. Did he have a room in the house where likes to spend time?"

"He works in his office."

"Great," Charles said. "Which room is that?"

"It's right next to mine," he said.

"OK," Charles said. "So could you visit him there?"

"He's not there. He's in Alaska."

"Right. Well, would it be all right for me to go into his office? Maybe I'd get some idea about how to find him."

"He doesn't like anyone to go into his office."

"Well, do you ever visit your own bedroom?"

"Sometimes," he said softly. "But then I always go to sleep."

"I'd like to see your bedroom," Charles said.

"It's the same as yours," he said. "Only it has my things in it."

"Well, I'd like to see your things."

"But I might fall asleep!"

"That's OK," Charles said. "It's fine to sleep. Anyway, we'll take Pan. Then after I look around for a few minutes, I'll wake you up and we'll come right back here."

"Promise?"

"Of course."

"You're going to go into my father's office, aren't' you?"

"I'd like to take a look," Charles said. "But I promise not to disturb anything."

"He'll be mad if he comes back home and something's been moved."

"I won't move anything. I just want to look."

"Well, OK then. Just this once."

Charles put one hand on Pan and Martin did the same. Charles tried to keep his mind completely blank so that Martin's thoughts would guide them.

In the blink of an eye Charles was sitting on the floor of his own bedroom, with his hand on the goat. Martin lay on a small bed, obviously asleep, with his hand dangling over the side, also resting on Pan. He was very pale and his chest hissed with every breath. Charles knew it was his own bedroom; he recognized the tall window above the porch and the small square one, high on the wall facing the mountains to the west. But nothing else was the same.

Bright floral-patterned wallpaper covered the walls; the floor featured thick gray carpet. Two little chairs flanked a small wooden table. The table was just the right size for an eight-year old child, but too small for Charles. Several hand-carved wooden toys were lined up neatly against the wall.

Piano music came from from downstairs, faint and muffled. Two men were conducting a quiet but intense conversation downstairs as well, but Charles couldn't make out what they were saying.

Charles looked down on Martin sleeping on his small, old-fashioned bed. Pan lay on the floor beside him. Could he leave them alone for only a minute or two? Probably not. Martin might dream some eight-year old fantasy and transport himself to some distant place or time. That would leave Charles stranded in his own house but years before his parents were born. He might become an invisible ghost to Martin's family, a sad ironic twist.

Gently, Charles lifted Martin's hand off Pan's back and set it on the pillow.

"Come on, boy," Charles whispered to the goat and nudged it. "Let's go exploring." He led Pan by the rope that served as his leash out into the hall. A light glowed in Martin's father's office but no one was there. Charles pulled Pan gently into the room.

"Don't eat anything," he whispered sternly.

The room was a shrine to efficiency. A sturdy oak desk sat against one wall, its wood dark and polished, its surface holding one neat stack of papers and a small lamp. A yellowing black and white photograph in a frame on the left side of the desktop showed a very pretty young woman in old-fashioned clothes. The woman's bright, defiant eyes sparkled as if she was staring through a tiny glass window. Charles picked it up and looked more closely. Her eyes and mouth were like Martin's. Perhaps she was his mother, he thought. Or even his grandmother. He set the picture back down exactly where he'd found it.

A heavy chair and wooden file cabinet matched the desk. A neat blue rug covered most of the floor. A few items hung on the white walls: a framed certificate and a series of art prints, probably copies of famous old paintings that had been tinted by hand. Their colors complemented each other, suggesting they were chosen by someone seeking the orderliness of matching colors rather than artistic merit. Without any real plan, Charles walked over and looked at one, a print depicting burly peasants on a town square. An exhausted bagpipe player sat near the left edge of the picture while the villagers danced with drunken abandon.

Concentrate on your mission, he told himself. Don't get distracted by trivia. You might not have much time.

Nothing in the room gave him any better sense of Martin's father. No picture of him, no coat hung carelessly across a chair. But nothing sinister or dangerous happened, either, so he became a bit bolder. He led Pan out of the room and down the hallway that was both completely familiar and totally strange. Charles crept down the stairs and smiled when he realized that the steps creaked and squeaked in exactly the spots he knew. He went down a few steps until he could see the living room below but remained hidden on the dark steps. Charles's father sat across from another man. They were deep in intense conversation. The piano music came from farther away, perhaps the dining room.

"You would be serving your country," the man said. Charles could only see the back of his head.

"There must be others more suited to such a mission," Martin's father, Frank Whiting replied.

"None who would have your credibility," the man said. "They need an engineer with specific railroad experience. No one would question your credentials."

"But the collecting of evidence and the law enforcement aspect—of those I have no experience."

"You have your honor," the man said. "You have experience in being truthful. In the battle against swindlers and liars, that may be the most important credential."

The piano music stopped and a woman's voice, obviously irritated, loudly said, "Brahms, you are an unkind soul! The flats and sharps with which you infect your music!!"

The men in the living room chuckled, despite the gravity of their conversation. The piano music resumed.

"Millah does not normally berate the composers of the music she learns." Mr. Whiting said softly. "She is distracted. Our son is ill and she is a bit off her gentle temperament. As am I, I'm afraid. The doctors are of little use. I cannot make such a trip at this time."

"I understand," the other man said. "And we would not interfere with your family. If the situation…" he paused. "If the situation changes, and your son regains his health, we will, of course support the move of your entire family. This would not be permanent, of course. We will assure that your house here in Colorado remains secure. Once in Alaska, you will perform your regular duties with the railroad. The line does, in fact, require your engineering skills."

"Not that I am considering your proposal but, hypothetically, how would I communicate?" Frank asked. "By telegraph?"

The other man shook his head.

"The only telegraph in Skagaway is a fiction existing in Mr. Smith's criminal imagination and nowhere else. He extracts money from workers to send telegraphs back to their family. His men tap on the key, but no wire is attached to his building."

"That's unscrupulous!"

"Unscrupulous defines the entire operation. This is why the government needs an honest observer. The man remains at large for lack of evidence. You will communicate with the captain of a ship that visits the post regularly."

"Surely others can provide evidence."

"Indeed they could. But Mr. Smith is both charming and cunning. He well understands how a few gold coins strategically placed can fog a man's memory. That's another reason you fit our parameters so well. Beyond your sense of honor, your success makes you less vulnerable to venal temptation."

"I appreciate your confidence in me," Frank Whiting said, standing up. "I understand your concerns with these men. The Devil loves chaos. When the inmates revolt, the loudest madman rules the asylum. It sounds like Mr. Smith and the Devil enjoy a comfortable working arrangement. If the need remains when Martin recovers his health, I shall consider it." The man understood the meeting was over and also stood. They shook hands.

"We all pray for that outcome," the man said. They walked to the door. The piano music stopped again; the woman complained again about the composer's morality and motives.

"Goodnight, ma'am" the man said loudly.

"Goodnight indeed," the woman yelled from the other room. "And pray, take Mr. Brahms along with you!" Then the music resumed.

Charles tiptoed back upstairs and went into Martin's room again. It felt very strange to be in his own bedroom that was not his bedroom. He looked around one last time. On the table beside the bed was a glass of water and several books. The top one was Ivanhoe. The book looked new, but Charles recognized a scratch on the cover. It was the same copy of the book that he read. Or that he would read, fifty years from now.

A few other books on the table seemed appropriate for a boy Martin's age, but others seemed aimed at an adult reader. One was a yellow cloth book with the title "Dracula" in bright red letters. Charles wondered if that book had been the origin of the movie? His parents wouldn't let him attend the movie, it being too disturbing for a boy his age. He'd never seen the book and it hadn't occurred to him that the movie might have been based on an old book. And yet here it sat on a younger boy's night table. Charles opened the book at random and smelled the pages. They definitely had the smell of fresh ink and new paper. Unable to resist reading, he read a few pages, then set it down and picked up a book by Morgan Robertson called "Spun Yarn." He opened it at random to a short story called "Slumbers of a Soul." That seemed an odd coincidence and he closed the book. It reminded him that he did not want to become trapped in someone else's dream.

The first stair creaked as someone started up.

"Wake up, Martin, it's time to go!"

Martin did not stir. His breathing remained slow and labored. "Martin! We've got to go!" Charles said. He whispered as loudly as he dared, glancing back at the door to the hallway. Martin did not respond. Charles put his hand on the boy's forehead. It was hot as a black stone in the summer sunshine. Charles shook his shoulder, but the boy remained asleep.

Martin was obviously very sick with a high fever. From his limited science background Charles guessed Martin already had the infection he'd read about in his obituary. Why didn't the doctors give him an antibiotic?

With a start, Charles realized that antibiotics had not yet been discovered. In the year 1897, World War One was still 18 years in the future. Fleming discovered the first antibiotic, penicillin, after that war and it wasn't manufactured until World War Two. The first vials were shipped on D-Day and helped the allies defeat Hitler.

He shook his friend's shoulders more vigorously. Martin opened his eyes and looked in his general direction but without recognition. "Father is that you?" he said. "I don't feel very well."

"No, Martin, it's me, Charles."

"I must have been dreaming," he said. "Father would you read to me?"

"Can't you see me?" Charles said as panic grew within him.

"I wish Father would come in," Martin said. He could not see or hear Charles. Charles had not anticipated that problem.

"Pan, I think we have to do this one by ourselves." Charles nudged the goat so his face was near Martin. The second stair creaked, then the third.

"Hello, Pan," Martin said.

Good, Charles thought. At least he recognizes his manitou. Charles put his hand on the goat's neck and closed his eyes. He tried to hold his mind very still, with no thought other than his dogs.

"Hi, Fritz," Charles said softly to the dog in his brain. He pictured the straw bales beneath the porch, the smell of his secret hideout. "Come here, boy," he whispered. But nothing happened.

The floor creaked in the hallway outside Martin's bedroom. "Come on, boy," Charles said again, more urgently. Mr. Whiting was coming to check on his child. It seemed like the sick child was alive in the bed and his ghost was also there, dreaming with him. Mr. Whiting probably wouldn't think it odd to see the pet goat there. Charles was the only one who did not belong in that room at that moment in time. What would happen to him if he was discovered?

"How fares my young gentleman?" Mr. Whiting said softly as he entered the room. The room was dim, it would take the man's eyes a moment or two to adjust. Charles was frantic. As Mr. Whiting walked toward them, Charles got down on the floor and slid beneath the bed. It was a tight fit, and dusty. Charles stifled a sneeze. Mr. Whiting sat on the edge of the bed and the bed sank until it was pressed on the boy's back.

Charles didn't know if he'd managed to get his entire body into the hiding place but he didn't want to move and risk making a sound. What if his foot or elbow protruded? He kept very still and imagined himself to be invisible, a shadow in a dark room. He reached out to touch Pan again, but the goat was not there. With increased panic, Charles moved his hand around as much as he dared, but did not encounter the goat. It must have moved away when Martin's father entered the room. Sweat trickled down his forehead as he tried to remain calm.

"And his noble steed Pan," Mr Whiting said. That was good. The goat was still somewhere in the room. "Haven't seen you in a while." The man moved books around on the table.

"You must rally, my son, like Ivanhoe." His voice was kind, but concerned.

Maybe Charles could travel without touching Pan. Just Murphy said that was possible for some people. He closed his eyes and concentrated on his dogs, their straw, the way the air felt, and the abandoned spider web collecting gray dust in one corner. He pictured their dog-food bowls and the smell of Purina dog food. But nothing happened.

If Mr. Whiting led the goat outside, Charles might be stuck there for a very long time. More than a lifetime. He must distract the man for just a few seconds and touch the goat.

From beneath the bed, he couldn't see anything beyond Mr. Whiting's boots a few inches from his face. If one of the books fell off the table, that would startle Mr. Whiting. He dismissed the idea because the book would fall right next to him. The distraction should be farther away, perhaps outside the window.

The book Dracula on the table gave him an idea. He didn't know much about the book except that it somehow involved an evil monster and blood-sucking bats. Bats probably don't fly into windows, the way birds do, because their natural sonar system warns them away. But if one did, the sound of the collision would certainly be distracting. He imagined a bat colliding with the glass.

Just as he began his experiment, he heard fluttering wings and a quick squeaking sound. In a bizarre coincidence, a bat had flown into the room.

The window must have been open. The creature whizzed past Mr. Whiting who instinctively waved his hands to shoo it away. His elbow nearly knocked over the cup of tea on the bedside table. The bat flapped frantically from wall to wall. Mr. Whiting stood quickly. He strode to the window and opened it all the way. Then he moved around the room, waving his arms, trying to herd the frightened little mammal toward its escape. After a few moments, the bat flew back out into the night.

Mr. Whiting closed the window firmly, with a little thumping sound and kept looking outside for a moment. Charles cautiously reached his head out and saw Pan curled up in a corner of the room. While Mr. Whiting was still distracted, Charles tapped the floor quietly with one finger, but the goat ignored him.

"And peace shall be restored," Mr. Whiting said softly. "Listen to them, what music they make!" He turned and walked back to his son. Charles quickly withdrew under the bed. Mr. Whiting lit the lamp on the table, and opened a book. When his vision adjusted to the dim lamp light, Mr. Whiting wouldn't see in the shadows as well, Charles thought. It was one tiny thing to hope.

"Now, my young man, where did we leave Ivanhoe and his merry band? Ah yes, here it is." he spoke in an exaggerated theatrical voice. "Chivalry!---why, maiden, she is the nurse of pure and high affection---the stay of the oppressed, the redresser of grievances, the curb of the power of the tyrant ---Nobility were but an empty name without her, and liberty finds the best protection in her lance and her sword." He paused. "Sorry, son. Chivalry gestured too enthusiastically and I'm afraid some of my tea got on your book." He wiped it dry with his shirt but his son did not stir from his fevered dreams.

Whiting read more, his voice sadder and less dramatic. Then he closed the book and sighed.

"Perhaps your sleep is too deep for even Ivanhoe to reach, young Martin. I shall save it for another time, when we may enjoy it together."

Charles exhaled as quietly as he could. When Mr. Whiting left the room, he'd be able to crawl out and concentrate on getting back to his own time. But Mr. Whiting did not move right away. He just sat there watching his son sleep and listening to his labored breathing.

"My friend Fritz Delius sent me a new book all the way from London," he said. "He's endured his own travails." Mr. Whiting laughed softly to himself, trying to sound cheerful. "He knew how to grow oranges in Florida and knew how to write music, but only had a passion for music. Had his passion been agriculture, he might not now be considered the most hated man in Norway. He says this book distracted him admirably but warned it might not be suitable for one of your tender years. If there are passages for your ears, I will share them with you. Perhaps I can have a brief part in one of your dreams."

Great, Charles thought. He's going to sit here and read to himself. The room seemed very quiet. Charles tried to keep his own breathing slow and quiet and in time with Martin's. His left foot developed an itch that demanded attention but he remained still and in agony. Finally Mr. Whiting spoke.

"This line was written for you, Martin." Mr Whiting said. "There are darknesses in life and there are lights and you are one of the lights."

Mr. Whiting was focused on the book and his sick son, so he did not hear what Charles heard. Outside the window, below on the hard dirt, came the distinct sound of horse hooves walking around the house. The sound stopped, then a moment later it resumed. Someone was riding a horse around the house very slowly, as if looking for something.

Charles was sure he knew who it was. Then the sound stopped.

Mr. Whiting continued reading and the only sound in the dark room was the intermittent rustle of pages turning. Charles pictured the Arapaho woman, Sapania, dismounting and stealthily entering the house. She could be climbing the stairs right now, holding her long knife, looking for the boys. He had to escape but how? He could not reach the goat. As Charles frantically searched his brain for ideas, Mr Whiting spoke again, calmly reading another passage. He had not heard the horse outside.

"'There are things which you cannot understand and yet which are.' That is certainly true, Martin. I have told you many times that foolish men do not trust their intellect at all but even more foolish are those who trust it over-much." In a moment he read another line, "'Indeed, some people see things that others cannot.' " Mr. Whiting closed book with a snap and stood up. "This book is too dark for you now, but it has moments of truth. When you are healed and a few years older, you may find it interesting."

He looked down on his sleeping child sadly.

"As the book says, 'souls and memories can do strange things during trance.' I hope your own soul and your own memories are all delightful this night, while you are in the trance of illness. I wait fondly for your return."

Then he extinguished the lamp and left the room.

Charles slid out from beneath the bed. Outside, a horse whinnied. Pan was sleeping in the corner. Without much concern for the animal's comfort Charles grabbed its two hind legs and pulled it closer to the bed. It looked up in surprise but did not protest.

Keeping one hand on its back, with the rope wrapped around his wrist, Charles gently pulled Martin's hand to rest on its neck. Even unconscious, Martin instinctively stroked the soft fur. "OK, Fritz," Charles spoke to the dog he hoped to see very soon. "I know you're not magic. But come here, boy, come here."

Nothing happened. Remain calm, Charles told himself. It had been easier when Martin was awake. But then Charles had seen Jim Baker when neither Martin nor his goat were around. Surely he could master this. It was not a trick it was an experiment. It was science. He tried to recall the procedure he'd noted before. Think only of the destination. Concentrate as if you're conducting an experiment in magic. He pictured his dogs and their area. Now try a bit of magic. Move a tennis ball, direct a flying insect to land. He remembered the scent of vanilla the first times he'd seen Martin. "A scent of vanilla," he said to himself. "I wonder if I can conjure a scent?" He closed his eyes and pictured the smell. It was very pleasant and reminded him of Christmas. But there was another smell, too, also pleasant and familiar.

He opened his eyes.

Charles stood in the kitchen where his mother was removing two loaves of bread from the oven. She was a heavy woman with thick glasses and brown hair going to gray. Classical music came from the record player in the dining room and his mother hummed along cheerfully. The kitchen air was thick with the smell, not of vanilla, but of freshly baked bread.

"Your timing is excellent, as always," she said when she noticed him. "I'll need someone to sample this when it's cooled for a few minutes. Do you know where I can find a volunteer to test a fresh warm heel with some raspberry jam?"

She set the loaves on top of the stove and turned to Charles. He stood motionless, wanting to believe he was really home, but still feeling confused.

"Where did you get the goat?" his mother asked. Having spent her childhood on a farm in Kansas, animals did not bother her in the least.

Charles didn't respond at first. He just stood there, staring at his own familiar kitchen. His mother looked at him more intently, concern showing on her face. Finally Charles managed to speak. He tried to sound casual, but his voice was weak and unsteady. "I'm watching it for a friend."

"Which friend is that?"

"His name is Martin."

"Is he a new friend?"

"He's sort of both old and new."

His mother smiled. "A mystery, eh?"

"A deep mystery," Charles said smiling back. "I think Martin is my shadow and I'm his reflection. Or maybe one of us is imaginary."

"Or maybe you don't know whose goat it is and you're taking care of it until they find him? And maybe hoping no one shows up to claim him?"

Charles laughed. "The dogs like him," he said. "And he's not scared of them either."

"He's a pretty fellow," she said. She leaned over and petted Pan's head. "But he doesn't belong in my kitchen."

"OK," Charles said. He started to lead Pan out then stopped, turned back, and gave his mom a tight hug around her waist. She laughed a little.

"What's that for?" she said teasingly. "Have you been up to mischief?"

"No," he said. "Just glad to be home. And hungry for some bread and jam."

"Well, get busy then and take your little sidekick outside. Before I decide to cook up the both of you into a stew." She swatted Charles' back playfully as he scooted out the door.

Sapania crouched in a dark corner of the livery stable, keeping quiet and still. Dirt streaked her face, her hair was a tangle of twigs and straw, her buckskin outfit was dusty and ripped in several places. She cursed the white men for killing Flatpipe, her manitou. Without magic, the journey across the prairie to her tribe's camp near the Creek of Boulders had been an ordeal that consumed many days. She had no concern for her appearance.

On the other hand, it had been easy to sneak into this Denver City stable earlier tonight, when the guard was busy settling a new horse in a stall. She had already tested every pony in her village and was becoming desperate. She would not consider the possibility that Flatpipe had been unique. So she remained still and waited.

Now, as the night wore on, all activity gradually diminished until even the guard nodded in his chair by the door. Sapania stood and moved slowly toward the first horse.

She put her hands on its neck very gently, soothing it with soft words. "Take me to the camp by the Creek of Boulders," she whispered. "I see it before me, with sparkling water and slick green rocks. If you are to be my new manitou, you see it as well."

Nothing happened. This was the last livery stable in Denver City, and so far it was as unlucky as the others. A dozen horses stood in their stalls, waiting to be rented to customers. A handful of others were being boarded for their owners. They were used to strangers and didn't complain.

Sapania moved to the next horse and stroked its neck. "Can you see the sparkling water?" she asked it softly. "Can you smell meat cooking and wood smoke? Do you hear the drumming of the boys and the old women arguing?" The horse ignored her.

One by one, she tested each one, hoping to find a replacement for Flatpipe, the horse that could move through time and space. Without the bell that summoned a manitou, this was the only thing she could think of to try.

None of the horses gave the slightest hint they possessed a hidden magical nature. Sapania slipped past the guard and out into the night.

She could easily navigate Denver City on such a starry night. Most of the businesses were closed, the streets were dark and deserted. Small groups of men sat on chairs outside the hotels, smoking and making small talk. Only the saloons remained raucous and lively, but their customers had no interest in the few pedestrians outside. When men stumbled out, it took time for their eyes to adjust to the dimness. More than enough time to hide in a shadow.

Sometimes Sapania encountered a foolish drunk who saw a lone young woman as an opportunity for mischief. With her right hand inside her cloak, holding the hilt of her blade she smiled at the thought. Many of those men had carried coins or other valuables. Perhaps tonight she would be lucky and such a man would insist on becoming her prey.

"Now, Billy, why don't you just sleep in back on the cot tonight." A man shouted from a side street and Sapania froze. "You ain't in a condition to ride all the way back to the ranch!"

Sapania crept closer, keeping to the darkest shadows. An older man wearing a ragged apron stood in a doorway speaking to a younger man who was trying to mount his horse but having a little trouble with his balance.

"Nah, Rupert, I'll be flyin'. I mean fine" Billy laughed and used both hands to aim his boot into the stirrup. After three tries, he managed to pull himself onto the horse. "Ol' Hopscotch knows the way better'n I do. I just climb on and he does all the work."

"It's a good hour's ride," Rupert said, exasperated. "You'll fall off your dad-blame horse by then!"

"Listen," Billy said in a conspiratorial whisper. "I'll tell you a secret." He motioned for Rupert to come closer. "It don't take us an hour. It don't take us any time at all. In fact…" he looked around to make sure no one else was listening. "I get home about an hour before dinner time every night."

"Your wife don't make dinner until midnight?"

"No, no, not like that. I go out and drink, and then I get on Hopscotch and tell him I want to go to the barn while she's cooking. Most nights, I'm in that barn before sundown. Sometimes I even have a little nap before she hollers to come in."

"OK, now I know you're drunk. You're talking nonsense. You get on inside and sleep it off."

"I appreciate the offer, Roop, I surely do. But you seen me ride off a hundred times and I always come back. But your own wife's gonna wonder about you if you don't high tail it. I'll be fine."

Rupert shook his head, shrugged, and went back inside. Hopscotch started walking down the street, with Billy precariously balanced on his back.

Sapania did not hesitate. She emerged from the shadows and ran after the horse and rider as they strolled away and quickly caught up to them. Without pausing, she leaped at the man, grabbing his coat to pull herself behind him. Before he realized what was happening, she had both arms around his waist and wrenched him sideways.

"What the...?" he yelled as both of them fell to the ground. When he hit the ground, he did not move. Sapania jumped up, knife in hand and stood over him. The man was unconscious and deliciously helpless.

She tied the horse's reins to a hitching post. "You stay right here," she said to Hopscotch. Then, still holding the knife in front of her, she returned to the man on the ground and looked around furtively. The street was empty; she could do with him whatever she wanted. She pressed the blade against his throat but did not slice him immediately. Clearly he was known by others, he had a wife. Killing him might cause more problems than she needed. The Sheriff would investigate, Rupert would report his conversation about the strange power of Hopscotch. No, she thought with some disappointment, it would be smarter to leave evidence that the man was crazy than to leave a carcass to investigate. .

She removed the saddle from the horse and set it on the ground. Her tribe had no use for saddles and no white would buy one from an Arapaho. A small saddle bag contained a few trinkets which she removed. Then she went back to the man and went through his pockets. A pocket knife, three coins, a box of matches. Hardly worth the effort, but she put those into her cloak.

Then she removed the man's shirt, and his overalls and set them in a pile beside him. She removed every scrap of his clothing and left him sprawled, naked and unconscious on his back in the middle of the street. No one would ask about his wounds or his horse. They would be laughing at his ridiculous situation. They wouldn't believe anything he told them. She looked around one more time before leaving.

The wind had piled dried tumbleweeds next to a building across the street. Using one of the man's matches, she lit it and a fire quickly blazed up. It crackled and spit, perfuming the air with the angry smoke of burning weeds. Flames licked at the wooden wall. Almost immediately, fire raced up the dry wood. She turned and walked past Billy, sleeping on the street, and climbed onto Hopscotch. As the fire behind her grew, the buildings beside her flickered and danced. She nudged the horse forward.

"The Creek of Boulders," she said softly. "With boys drumming and women cooking venison. I can picture it very well. Can you, Hopscotch? Let's go there."

The horse did not move.

"You miserable meat-bag" she yelled. "You know where I want to go! Now take me there before I sell you to an Apache cook!" She kicked the animal hard with her heels. "The Creek of Boulders! The camp of the Arapaho! The women by the cook-fire!"

Startled, Hopscotch lurched forward, then began walking. The street remained silent; no one had noticed the fire yet. Sapania and the horse walked slowly into the darkness.

Then they were no longer there.

Chapter 35

The next night, when he was sure everyone was asleep, Charles tiptoed down the hall and down the stairs in his stocking feet, carrying his shoes, careful to avoid the spots that squeaked. His dogs scrambled to the gate and jumped up to greet him. Their tails wagged enthusiastically but they didn't bark. "Good boy, good girl," Charles whispered, then sat on the steps and put his shoes on.

"Hey guys," he whispered to his canine buddies. "Don't get too excited." He opened the gate and crawled under the porch. Martin was asleep on the straw and Pan slept beside him.

"OK, Pan," he said quietly. The goat looked up at him quizzically. "I don't know how this works if Martin's sleeping. Try not to wake him and we'll see." The goat probably couldn't understand words but maybe it could get some sense of the meaning anyway. Charles explained their mission.

"I'd like to visit Jim Baker's campfire again, the one by his house in Denver. I want to help Martin visit his parents but if you stay there with him, I could get stranded. So I need a second manitou for the return trip, and I need a guide. Maybe Just Murphy can guide me. His dog Flint is a manitou. But I don't want Martin to hear anything that might upset him, or set his hopes too high That would be bad for him and bad for my family, too."

The air was warm, filled with the rich organic smells of straw and dog fur. In the distance, a train called out low and sad; a dog answered by barking and howling. Crickets chirped relentlessly. Charles took a deep breath, wondering if there were other pitfalls he hadn't even considered.

"OK, now I'm going to close my eyes," he said quietly. "I'm going to picture Jim Baker's campfire just the way it was. I'm going to remember the smell of the woodsmoke and the sound of coyotes. And then I'm going to try some small magic. Some little thing. Maybe I'll make this bit of straw on my forehead slide off. A tiny breeze…"

The memory of the woodsmoke suddenly became sharper and Charles' eyes burned.

The campfire lit Jim Baker's face as the woodsrunner sat puffing on his pipe. Just Murphy sat beside him, his dog Flint sprawled across his feet. Charles sat on the same huge log as before, still holding Pan's rope. Martin slept on the ground beside him. The older man, John Burns, sat on another big log sipping killdevil from a metal cup. It all looked the same as before. The fire danced bright and hot. The men's faces glowed as if lit from within, while the space behind them on this moonless night was black as a cave. Charles thought he saw shadowy movement beyond the campfire, as if other people lurked back there, unseen but not quite invisible.

Just Murphy looked at him and nodded.

"Kind of unusual," he said. "You showing up again."

Baker looked over and realized someone had joined his campfire. It took him a moment to remember Charles.

"You're that little scout, ain't you?" he said "Was it Charles?"

"Yes sir."

"You develop a taste for the killdevil? I got plenty."

"No sir, but thank you. I need some help."

"What's your problem?" Just Murphy asked.

"We need to get to Alaska."

"Where's that?" John Burns asked.

Charles thought back to his history class. "Seward's Folly," he said. "All that land way north of California."

"Why Alaska?" Just Murphy asked.

"After Martin … got sick, his parents moved up there. Now he stays at his old house where my family lives. He's so lonely. He cries a lot…"

"So you figure you'll help him visit? Or help him move there?"

"Yes sir. But I can't picture the place well enough. I pictured his father but by the time we got there Martin was already very sick. Too sick to help me. I think that's how it will be every time I try it with Martin and Pan. And I don't want to get, you know…"

216

"Stuck in a snowstorm without a sled." Just Murphy said. "I ain't had much desire to go explore. There's another problem for Jim and me."

"What's that?"

Just Murphy nodded slowly. "See, it ain't a big thing visiting memories. That don't use up our time. But doing something new, well, we only get a certain amount of new time. Once we use it up, that's it. No manitou can give you extra time."

"I'd rather use up my time than waste it," Jim Baker said.

"I mostly follow ol' Jim around. You don't know anybody who's been there? Someone who can help you picture it?"

"No," Charles said, but then stopped. He had recently encountered someone who mentioned Alaska.

"There were some bad men," he said. "They tried to kill Martin's goat. They said something about taking it back to Alaska."

Just Murphy sipped his killdevil.

"You say they almost killed the goat?"

"Yeah."

"What stopped them?"

"I guess I did, sir." Charles said.

"With a gun?"

"No, sir. I just told them to stop."

Murphy nodded.

"You told them to stop, eh? Did you yell it so loud you scared them?"

"No, I just whispered it. And I was too far away for them to hear."

Just Murphy didn't seem surprised.

"So you aimed at them like you had a rifle and sent them words right into their brains." He took another sip. "That's how long-distance shooting works too. You might turn into a sniper yourself if you practice up."

"Maybe someday," Charles said.

"So why did these men want to kill the goat?" Murphy asked. "If they wanted a manitou, they would have taken it with them. Not kill it."

Charles hadn't thought of that. It made sense and he felt dumb he'd overlooked it. Jim Baker took his pipe out of his mouth. He blew a long thin cloud of smoke into the campfire.

"Martin uses his goat to travel, like someone might ride a horse," Charles said. "Maybe they want to make sure Martin can't travel."

Murphy frowned. "But he's just a kid."

"He's kind of a special kid, " Charles said. "He must pose some danger to them. The men tried to rob a bank. Their leader was selling bars of soap."

Baker sat forward, suddenly alert. "Them guys part of Soapy's old gang?"

"I don't know his name."

"Probably Slim and Reverend. That sound right?"

"Yeah, I think the Sheriff called them that."

"And this kid's Pa, Frank, he gave them outlaws some grief, didn't he? Old Soapy don't forget stuff like that."

Baker took a few more puffs on his pipe. Then he took a sip from his metal cup. He rocked back and forth on the log as he watched the flickering light.

"So these men want to hurt the kid's goat. They want to hurt him too?"

"I think so. They chased us pretty hard," Charles said. "We need a guide."

Just Murphy smiled. "It don't need to be a willing guide, does it?"

"That's what I was thinking," Charles said.

The plan was simple: capture the two outlaws and follow them to Martin's family. Murphy nodded.

"Could work," he said. "Might not, but it could. Hey, Baker, you interested in trappin' some critters?"

Jim Baker looked up.

"Seems like a long time since I seen a beaver," he said.

"Not beaver. More like rats. Human rats. Charles here has a plan."

"What's the bait?" Baker said.

"Don't need bait," Just Murphy said. "Charles here, he's got a way of whistlin' up critters. Critters like you and me and maybe these coyotes. He aims words the way you aim a bullet. He thinks them to the target. Like your wife Marina did."

Baker turned to face Just Murphy directly. "So your plan is to whistle a couple of desperados into the camp of these two pups and hope they don't get theirselves killed?"

"We'd be there behind him like a posse."

"Like you was behind me when I fought them grizzly cubs?"

"I'd appreciate you not thinking too hard on that memory," Just Murphy said with a smile. Then he turned to Charles

"You got a talent," Just Murphy said. "Like Jim and John Burns here. You can move around a little…" he waved his hand at the campfire and the dark hills beyond it. "…without an animal at all. Maybe all their old stories act like a manitou." He looked over at Burns a little sadly. "But stories fade." He paused.

"Me, I can't. Your little friend, maybe he can't either."

"What's the worst that can happen?"

Just Murphy looked at his dog and thought for a minute.

"Different for everyone. For me the worst would be going back," he said. "Back where people know my name and know what I done."

"I don't have much time," Charles said.

"There could be a price to pay," Just Murphy went on. "It's one thing to follow a guy around, even go back in his memories from time to time. But going forward, where we ain't been before. I don't know. There could be a price." He sighed "Might be the last thing we ever do. But if you need some help, we'll be there."

"Thanks," Charles said. "I don't want you to take the risk unless I'm out of options. I'll try to do it by myself first, without the outlaws. Maybe I won't need you at all. But if I do…"

Quietly, they devised a plan. Then Charles put one hand on the goat's head and the other on Martin's back, closed his eyes and pictured his dogs sleeping under the porch. He remembered the smell of dog fur and straw.

When he opened his eyes he was under the porch. Martin and Pan still slept in the straw. Fritz and Keisha slept a few feet away.

"It's OK, guys," he said softly. "It's just me."

Fritz wagged his tail in his sleep but did not rouse.

Quietly Charles crawled out into the warm summer night and closed the gate behind him. The lights of Denver twinkled in the distance. He inhaled the dry air before he went inside and tiptoed upstairs to his bedroom.

It felt like he was the only living thing awake on the planet.

Chapter 36

The next afternoon, back in his own familiar bedroom, fortified by a bologna sandwich and a glass of milk, Charles sat on his bed to contemplate the situation.

A ghost was sleeping under the porch with his dogs. When dreams frightened that ghost, he cried in his sleep and kept Charles and his family awake. The ghost was a kind and gentle little fellow who meant no harm to anyone; he only wished to be reunited with his family, all of whom were surely ghosts by now, too. Their lives were all in the past, gone like tumbleweeds disbursed by the prairie wind. They no longer existed; Charles should have no concern for them, no feelings of any kind. And yet he did.

He rationalized that he did not want the house to be haunted by a sad ghost. The sounds frightened his family and maybe he could stop that. He was doing all this for his family, he thought. And he was doing it to be kind to a stranger, something he was taught every week in Sunday School. Plus wouldn't it be the smart, scientific thing to relieve Martin's sadness a bit, reunite him with his family, help him move on to where he belonged? Charles smiled at that thought. He was rationalizing whether or not to help someone that science and common sense told him did not exist.

But that wasn't really it. He didn't think of Martin as a ghost. He was just a little kid who needed help and for some reason. Charles was the only person who could help him. He felt honored to have stumbled across something so rare and fascinating. In a weird way, it reminded him of the time he caught a very fat horned toad and put it in a cardboard box to watch for a while. As he stared at this miniature dinosaur, it moved forward an inch, leaving a glob of mucous behind it. In all his years of observing reptiles Charles had never seen such a discharge.

Then the glob of mucous moved. Perhaps the horned toad had eaten an insect that had somehow survived a trip through its reptilian alimentary canal. As Charles watched, transfixed, the glob continued to move and take shape, like a slide coming into focus on a screen. Within seconds, as if it shrugged off a misty coating, the formless mucus transformed into a tiny version of the horned toad itself.

221

It certainly felt like magic, and yet this must simply be the way of these little desert creatures. Like all reptiles, they lay eggs, but their eggs apparently consist of goo that disintegrates within seconds. The little mother gave birth to several more creatures while he watched. Charles carried the box into undisturbed prairie and released the mother and her children far from his cat, far from car tires. As they scurried away into the weeds, he said "thank you" out loud to no one in particular. It felt like he had been visited by grace, something powerful, benign and undeserved, and the only appropriate response was gratitude.

The honor of meeting a ghost felt like that, and conveyed a similar responsibility; Charles needed to carry Martin's metaphorical cardboard box somewhere safe and release him.

There were problems, of course. If they made it back to 1897 and arrived in the bedroom the two boys shared a half century apart, Martin would be sick and asleep. They had already done that. The little ghost's dreams might make them veer off course. Navigating back to the present was even trickier. Like attempting to influence a fly or a tennis ball, the results were unpredictable. And if the obituary was correct, simply returning Martin to that time wouldn't do him any good. He had to try one more thing, too.

Magic isn't something you learn in a lecture hall and this —whatever it was — wasn't either. He knew what he had to do. He needed to practice.

"Let's take a walk in the sunshine," he told Martin after he found him sitting on a bale of straw in the little hideout beneath the porch. Pan stood beside him, munching on a scrap of cloth from an old T-shirt.

"OK," Martin said. The sunlight felt incongruous because they usually met at night, but there was no good reason for that except that it seemed like ghosts probably come out at night. Plus, Charles felt safer while his parents were at home, sleeping in their room but that was silly. If he intended to fly around through space and time armed only with a sleepy goat and a weepy child, he should abandon the false comfort of believing his parents could rescue him. There would be no rescue.

They stepped out in to the morning sunshine.

"It's bright," Martin said.

"Yes," Charles answered. "But you get used to it."

This was the first time Charles had seen the boy in full sunlight. His clothes were old fashioned, but not ragged. Only his brown shoes looked scuffed and worn. His face was sweet and earnest; a tangled mop of brown hair tumbled over his forehead and eyes.

They walked down the hill, through the dry weeds and low cactus, avoiding the spiked yucca plants that jutted up like green porcupines. The air was dry, the sky clear and blue. The mountains in the distance had a light frosting of white on their highest peaks. Pan followed along, amiably snatching a mouthful of weeds from time to time. Martin held the animal's rope, but gave it a long leash.

"I think I need to go looking for your family alone," Charles said. "Just at first."

Martin didn't say anything and his expression remained blank. Finally he spoke. His tone was not argumentative, but sad. Once again, he was going to be left behind.

"Why?" he said.

"Because I need more clues. Those clues are probably at your house. But you go to sleep when we travel there. What if you dream something? What if I can't…"

"Can't find your way back?" he said.

Charles sighed. "Yes. What if you're asleep or dreaming and we get stuck there? With you asleep and me as far from my family as you are now?"

"These weeds are stickery," Martin said, changing the subject.

"They're at the stickery part of their life," Charles answered softly. "They were seeds, then they were soft and green and now they're stickery."

"They turn to seeds," he said.

"Yes," Charles said. "That's part of it too."

"I don't want to be stickery," Martin said.

Charles smiled. "You will always be soft and green."

"Promise?"

"I promise. And Pan will always be soft and white. That's how we can tell you apart."

"You want to take Pan with you, don't you?"

"Yes. But I'll bring him back. If you loan me your goat I'll loan you my dogs. They won't let anything hurt you."

"I like your dogs," he said. "They are very strong. But they don't know how to travel."

"I'd never run off and leave them, right? That's how you know I'll bring Pan back. And maybe I'll figure out how to get you together with your parents again."

"Nothing else has worked," Martin said.

"I know. But maybe this will. If I can get a little better at this traveling thing."

"You can read," he said. "That might be useful."

"It often is. You could make a nice little bed in the straw behind the bales where my parents won't see you. I bet I'm back before your nap is over."

"I don't think your parents can see me anyway. Would you take good care of Pan?"

"I'll treat him like Sir Walter Scott treated Maida, his own dog."

"Who was Sir Walter Scott?"

"He wrote Ivanhoe. And he loved his dogs, especially Maida."

"I never heard of Maida."

"OK, then, I'll treat him like he was Archimedes"

"My father said that name but I don't know anything about him. Was he an old Greek guy?"

"Yes, but I'm talking about Merlin's owl."

"Merlin was smart and also scary. But I didn't know he had an owl."

"There were some other books about King Arthur and Merlin that your father hasn't gotten to read you yet. One of them talks about Merlin's owl named Archimedes. The owl says something like 'The best thing for being sad is to learn something.' And I want to learn about your family so you won't be sad. Anyway, don't you think Merlin would take good care of his owl?"

"Yes, he would."

"Well, I'll take that same care of Pan."

The book that talks about Merlin's owl would not be published until fifty years after Martin and his family left this house. If he survived his infection, if the newspaper obituary was wrong, he could read that book when he was sixty years old. And I would still be eleven, Charles thought. I probably would not recognize Martin as a sixty-year-old man if I saw him tomorrow at the Granada Fish market buying halibut. And he would probably have no memory of me. Charles wondered if they would somehow notice each other and feel a remote connection?

"OK then." Martin handed Charles the rope-leash. "You go with him, boy, but remember to come back for me."

They walked back up to the house. Meadowlarks whistled. A hawk circled in the sky, swooping and gliding effortlessly, as if it were the eternal tip of a paintbrush tracing invisible curves on the permanent blue canvas.

"Will you stay until I'm asleep?" Martin asked. His brown eyes were so sad Charles nearly cried.

"Of course," Charles said. Martin crawled behind a bale and lay down in the narrow space between it and the stone wall.

"Sweet dreams," Charles whispered. "Please."

Chapter 37

With one hand on Pan, Charles recalled his last visit to Martin's father. Weird little details popped into his head as he tried to picture Mr. Whiting. He remembered the books on Martin's table, the bat that flew in, the photograph on Mr. Whiting's desk, the sound of the piano. Charles went through all the details he could recall, then did it again, trying to hold his mind in a suitably mystic posture.

Nothing happened. All those details blurred together. Focus on the office, he thought. Not the bedroom where Martin's father was reading to his unconscious son. Just remember the office. He closed his eyes and tried to picture it, but his mind wandered. His nose tickled, his feet hurt and then, to his great consternation, he sneezed.

The voice of a woman startled him. He opened his eyes.

"A bat came flying round and round us, flapping its wings heavily," the woman said. She spoke in a low, urgent, conspiratorial stage whisper. She gave no indication she'd heard Charles sneeze.

Pan and Charles stood in the corner of a small, dark bedroom, but not a room he'd seen before. In the opposite corner a thin, pale boy about Charles's age sat erect in a simple wooden bed with a patchwork quilt drawn up to his chin against the chill of the night. The boy's mother sat beside the bed on a plain wooden chair. A small table held a single candle, its flickering light the room's only illumination. The woman's red hair was hidden, except for a few wild strands, beneath a faded wool scarf. Her skin was pale and smooth, her face thin, her cheekbones prominent. She wore a thick gray sweater that came down nearly to her knees. When she turned, Charles saw that she was pretty. But her intense expressions and dramatic gestures left only one impression on Charles: this woman is a witch.

Charles stood very still in the darkness and observed. She was telling her son stories, punctuating them with huge bold movements of her expressive hands and thin arms. Her voice rose and fell, like an actress on stage before a vast audience, conveying the story to the back row. She often held her eyes wide open as if surprised or frightened, making each event of the tale seem large and important.

The boy in bed stared at her, utterly transfixed by her compelling act. A wild shock of dark hair made his thin face seem even more pale. His alarmingly thin and pale arms suggested he was sick, like Martin. He was living the story as if it were his own life. The candlelight flickered on his eyes as they peered out from the dark caves below his eyebrows. They seemed to glow like the hot coals of a hardwood fire, burning deep in some quiet forest where mortals slept and stars kept watch.

Charles felt completely disoriented. What year is it and who are these people? The woman wasn't really a witch—was she? Is that intense boy a sorcerer, or ghost, or just a kid who loves stories? More important: what had Charles done to land himself here? And how would he get back? He wanted to run toward the door and escape this room but he forced himself to be still. Don't run like prey, he told himself. Just think. Look for clues. Be a scientist. Observe first, then make a hypothesis, then a plan. Look around, collect data, notice patterns.

In many ways, the scene was identical to the one he'd visited earlier: an adult was reading stories to a sick boy in a bed. That's a good place to start, he thought. He had been thinking of Martin, a sickly boy in a lonely bed and a parent reading him stories. The strange chariot Charles rode seemed as influenced by careless whim as resolute, determined thought.

The mother and son were too engrossed in the story to notice Charles in the dimmest corner of the dark room. The good news was that he had managed to transport himself somewhere, using whatever extra charm a manitou provides. He had done it once, so he could do it again. He would stay for only a moment, gather clues, decide what he'd done wrong and transport away before these people even noticed he was there. He massaged Pan's neck gently, as much to calm his own panic as to keep the goat still.

The room had one window, but Charles couldn't see outside from where he stood. Cold rain drizzled down the glass. A horse whinnied and Charles froze. Had Sapania followed him somehow? He held the goat with both hands. A moment later, a horse's hooves clopped on a stone street outside, wooden carriage wheels rolled slowly on the uneven surface and a man's voice, muffled by the weather, urged the animal on. The horse and carriage moved past the window and faded away. Charles relaxed just a little. Horses exist in many times and places.

"'Twas the land of Ir-Na-Nog," the woman said softly, moving her arm grandly, her fingers extended as if she were indicating a wide rolling field before them. "Ir-Na-Nog is a fine, magical land, my boy, where all are young and healthy." She spoke with an accent that Charles had heard on T.V. A policeman on a comedy show talked like that, and the other characters said he was from Ireland. Not proof, he reminded himself, but a clue. Perhaps she's from Ireland, too.

"I'd like to go to Ir-Na-Nog," the boy said. His accent was the same as his mother's.

"Aye, Abraham," she said. "You'd be a good fit for such a land, being handsome and young. Alas, 'tis a land for the fairy folk alone."

"But I could visit!" he said.

"Aye, perhaps, perhaps. But humans can not enter." She did not pronounce the "t" in "not," so it sounded like 'cannah enter'. "Not without invitation from the wee ones."

"Well I would befriend one and then he'd invite me!"

"Sure, sure. But how would ye travel there? No man knows the location."

"The phooka could take me."

"Aye, indeed. Your memory is sharp I'll give ye that. But the phooka is a trickster and from a different tale. But, for the sake of conversation, if ye had a phooka, what form would it take?"

Little Abraham thought for a minute.

"A bat!" he answered. "He'd be small enough to slip among the city folk undetected, but could fly o'er the rooftops and into the dark forest."

"Aye, a bat would be a fine choice. The phooka often takes that shape. But ye must not underestimate its power. Recall what happened in the talk of Tehi Tegi. Let that be a lesson to ye."

"But you've not told me that tale!"

"Oh, sure you must be mistaken. Tehi Tegi is the enchantress. Tis a famous tale. But the night grows old and your father will soon return from working at the castle. Perhaps another time."

"No!" Abraham pleaded "How may I sleep when the story of the enchantress remains untold? When a lad is sick, surely he is owed the consideration of one small story!"

The woman laughed.

"Lad, you are sure to be a solicitor. The way ye twist words to your own design!"

"A short one, at least," he entreated. "Like medicine for a wee, helpless lad, constrained to his bed by illness, 'twould be indeed. "

"Aye," she said with a smile. "A solicitor or a druid, spinning magic with his words. There is no 'short one' when you're in the story," she said. "But perhaps we can try." She leaned her head back and closed her eyes, collecting the story in her mind, deciding on which persona she would become as she acted it out.

"Ooo…" she said, a long drawn-out sound that rose and fell softly like the beginning of a song. "Oooo" she said again. Abraham grinned and leaned back against his pillow.

"One could hear the banshee wail in the distance," she whispered, her voice now sounding raspy and old. An observer who heard that voice might decide it came from a withered old hag stirring her caldron. "A sound like the calling of a wolf, but with the Devil singing the harmony. Oooh… ahhhh… oooh."

The woman knew how to make a story come alive. Charles realized with a start that he must guard against being drawn into the story too much. He might accidentally transport to some even stranger land of greater peril. Yet he had no choice but to listen. And now he heard something else: another horse approaching. He tried to ignore that sound as well as the woman's story.

"The distant howling should have warned the people of Dublin to stay safe inside their homes and churches. But alas, no. 'Twas on this very street she came…"

"Who came?"

"The lovely witch Tehi Tegi. As beautiful a young woman as ever breathed. On a small white horse she rode. Beautiful she might be, for she had the magic to change into whatever form she wished. So why not become the most beautiful young woman ever seen by the eyes of man?"

"Was she a good witch?"

"No, my son, she was not. She had the gift of making men love her. But they knew not her heart. Her heart was black as a dungeon and cold as a lump of wet coal. She once loved a man but killed that love and her own heart with it. Now she chews the memory of her old love as if it were dried fruit, tough and brittle, but still faintly sweet with an under-taste of summer."

"But if she was evil, how could she fool the men?"

"Ah, my child. One day you will understand how blind men can be in the presence of beauty."

"Like Kate Kearney, in the song?"

"Aye, a bit like that. But Kate's magic involved more than her own beauty. She had the magic potion of strong poteen whiskey and a friendly disposition. Few men can resist such a combination. But you try to prolong the story with your diversion," she said.

The boy grinned and pulled the covers up against his chin again.

The woman closed her eyes, picturing the scene. Once more, her voice became that of an old witch telling the tale of a young witch. "So Tehi Tegi rode her horse right down this very street."

Charles was sure he could hear a horse right outside the wall, moving slowly toward the window. He stared at the window.

"What did she wear?" the sick boy asked,

The woman smiled.

"The most beautiful gown, of course. Twas a light rose color with lace about her neck…"

"And a red sash!" the boy interjected.

"Why yes, as it happens. She did have a red sash. I nearly forgot that," the woman said.

"Did she come right in front of our house?"

"Aye, that she did. As fate would have it, she stopped right outside that window there."

She pointed toward the window. The boy's eyes widened.

"Before our very house?" he said.

"Indeed. Why I can almost see her there now…"

They both looked toward the window and Charles tensed. The wind blew a branch to scratch at the glass and all of them jumped. The woman smiled at the coincidence. She still did not notice Charles and Pan, precariously concealed only by darkness. If she moved the candle at all, the shadows would forsake him.

"Then all the men," the woman continued. "they came out to the street. And as if a bell sounded within each one, they fell madly in love with her. But she ignored them all and rode down toward the river."

"And did they follow her?"

"Indeed. What choice did they have? There were entranced by her spell. Dozens of men followed her like puppies following a milk pail…"

"Perhaps it was hundreds!" the boy chimed in.

"Why yes, now that you remind me, I'm sure it was hundreds. Thank you, Abraham."

"And they followed her to the river? And was the spell broken there?"

"Alas, no," she said. "No, she led them to the river and by her enchanting made the river look as shallow as a creek. With smiles on their faces, the men gladly trooped right into the water. And then she caused a great wind to arise which pushed the water into a wall to devour and crush the men."

"Oh, goodness, she really was evil!" Abraham said with a grin.

"Aye, lad, beware the lovely ladies. Ye never know what darkness their beauty conceals."

"And then did she ride away?"

"Not at all," she said. "She transformed herself into a bat and flew away."

"So she chose the bat to be her phooka, just like me! But she left her white horse?"

"No, the horse transformed into a porpoise and descended into the depths of the water never to be seen again."

The boy leaned back and closed his eyes.

"Tis a lovely story," he said. "But none such as her dwell among us in these modern days. Else we should surely see them."

"Be not so sure," his mother said in a conspiratorial whisper. "Think ye of the Ribbon Men who live among us still. For years un-noticed despite the spot of green ribbon in the buttonhole of their coats. None paid notice until their sign was made known. Perhaps the magic ones walk among us now but we know not their sign. There are things we cannot see and things we cannot understand. Ye must keep an open mind, both to the ordinary and the strange. Tis a pity to be trapped in the cage of one or 'tother."

"But the ordinary seems so sad and dreary!"

"Aye, so you should think, being born as ye were in Black '47, the hardest year of the Bad-Life times. And being as you are plagued by illness and grief that's no fault of your own. But despite it all, ye know King Laugh makes all dance to his merry tune."

She reached over and began to tickle the boy. He squirmed and giggled like a rag doll on a string. Finally she stopped and he sank back, obviously happy and exhausted.

"I've a wee secret for ye," she said in her soft, urgent, story-telling voice. "A visitor comes soon to fair Dublin. And he shall give a talk ye might find of interest. Assuming ye are well enough by then, of course."

"Who is it? Who's coming to town?"

"It wouldn't be much of a secret if I blabbered it aloud so easily, now would it?

"A hint then! A clue!"

"Very well," she said. She thought for a moment then launched into her most theatrical voice. She moved her arms broadly, like the great wings of a swan and her eyes grew wide as saucers. "The curtains of his bed were drawn aside," she said. "He started up into a half recumbent attitude and found himself face to face with the unearthly visitor who drew him as close to it as I am now to you."

The boy's eyes also grew wide, then he smiled and put on his own grown-man dramatic voice. He pointed a thin finger at his mother.

"You may be an undigested bit of beef!" he said. "A blot of mustard, a crumb of cheese, a fragment of underdone potato! There's more of gravy than of the grave about you, whatever you are!"

The woman smiled. "Aye, ye have it."

"Scrooge is coming to Dublin!"

She laughed. "The closest thing to it. Mr. Charles Dickens is coming to Dublin to perform at the Rotunda from his works. And if you are an exemplary lad who eats his soup and recovers his strength, ye shall be there to hear him."

"I can picture him well," the boy said. "But he could not perform his words as well as my own mother does."

She laughed again. "Spoken like a solicitor before a judge."

"If I am to regain my strength, perhaps I should drink one more cup of hot broth."

"And then straight way to sleep?" she said with a smile.

"Indeed, your honor," he said. The woman left the room. Charles knew this was his chance to escape. He closed his eyes and pictured Martin's father. Before anything happened, Abraham spoke again.

"She can't see you, but I can," he said sternly.

Charles hoped the boy in bed was talking to himself so remained still and silent. Abraham sat up even straighter.

"You in the corner. I see you and your goat as well. My mother will return shortly, so we have little time. What is the purpose of your visit?" He suddenly seemed more adult, not the little boy he played for his mother to get stories and broth.

Charles stepped forward into the candlelight, holding tight to Pan's rope.

"We mean you no harm," he said. "We are here by accident. The strange craft I ride has been blown off course and come to an unfamiliar land. I wish only to be back upon my journey."

"So, you have crossed an ocean?"

"In a way. We have crossed an ocean of time."

"And the goat. Is it your phooka?"

"I've not heard that word before tonight," Charles said. "But perhaps it's something like that. The wild men who live in America call it a manitou."

"Ah, the indigenous tribes! Can it change shapes?"

"Not that I've seen," Charles said. "But it does have a gift. It helps me to travel to the places I picture."

"So it's like a book or a story? Those are my best friends."

"In a way. But it feels more real than any story."

"So you are one who believes in things you know to be untrue." His voice was a child's, but he spoke with the confidence of an educated man occupying a child's frail body.

"As are you, I suspect," Charles said.

Abraham nodded. "As are all wise men," he said. "They learn not to fear what they don't understand. It's not always easy."

"Yes," Charles agreed. "Are you sick?" He felt a connection with this kid. Abraham obviously read books, knew many words, and was curious about the supernatural. It would be a mistake to stay too long, but Charles couldn't resist staying for a moment in the warm glow of a candle, with the comforting murmur of rain tapping on leaves and windows, talking to someone who felt like a potential friend.

"I am always sick," Abraham said. "But I hope to recover. It would be a grim sort of purgatory to survive too long in a sick body, a kind of monster, condemned to sleep in a tiny dark room—a wood paneled coffin—while others walk through the sunlight with the smell of pine trees and fresh grass. You'd have to pay me well to endure such a life."

"Is there enough money in the world to pay for that?"

Abraham thought for a moment,.

"Not money," he said. "You can't spend money in a coffin. Some sort of power…"

"It would have to be significant power," Charles said.

"Indeed." Abraham nodded. "Significant power…"

It was a surreal conversation with an apparition from the past who was probably his own imagination. But at that moment it didn't matter whether that person was real. "I believe in magic," Charles said. "At least in small magic. But I don't understand it."

"Inconspicuous magic moves the universe," Abraham said, nodding and closing his eyes. Then he shook his head. "But you are almost certainly the product of my own delusion, a Marley's ghost conjured by spoiled food. I am pathetic to engage in conversation with such a specter." The boy sighed. "This bed is a lonely vessel to transport a life, so I will agree with you, Marley. Any observant person must believe in magic. Leaves mature into blazing flags that nudge Earth round its axis; roosters crowing and robins whistling raise the sun each morning; massive clouds whisper shadow-stories to each other before they crash together and drizzle their sadness and thunder their rage."

Charles smiled. "You talk like one of my old books. I'm careful not to talk like that with most people; I bet you are too. I'm sorry you're sick."

Abraham smiled and shrugged.

"Words are my drugs and stories my pharmacy," he said. "I must get well before she tries to feed me more garlic. To her, 'tis medicine but to my tongue 'tis poison. How may I assist you?"

"I'm very new at this," Charles said. "I know that I must be calm, that I must focus my mind and not be distracted."

"Aye, that makes sense," Abraham said. He thought for a moment, then nodded. "My mother will return in a moment. I always welcome visitors from the shadows and shall not betray you. Perhaps she will sing a soothing song to calm you on your way. When she does, I shall close my eyes and leave you undisturbed." A wave of gratitude swept over Charles.

He reached into his shirt pocket and pulled out one of the three blue-jay feathers Martin had given him.

"I have nothing of value to repay your kindness," Charles said. "But let me leave you with a small blue feather. Believe me when I say, it has traveled a path more improbable than any of your own invention. If luck rides a twisted path, this token will surely bring health and good fortune."

Abraham took the feather with both hands, carefully, and his face opened as if astonished by the gift of a gold wand or ruby.

"'This is as precious as the harp of Dagda," he whispered. "The bright color of your gift reminds me of a Spring day, too temporary to be real. While this long cold drizzle feels permanent, a cold gray blanket laid too firmly on the soul."

Footsteps approached his door.

"Quick!" Abraham said. "Get ye back to the shadows!"

Charles pulled Pan back to the corner and sat cross-legged on the floor. Abraham's mother entered the room carrying a cup. A moment later the rich meaty aroma of salty broth induced a twinge of hunger in Charles. Abraham hid the hand holding the feather beneath the covers as his mother handed him the cup. "Now drink that up and be off to sleep," she said.

"Thank you, mother," Abraham said, once more the little boy. "You have me in mind of Kate Kearney," he said. "You well know, Mrs. Stoker, that the tune will not leave me in peace until it has been sung."

The mother smiled. She knew she was being played, but that was obviously part of their game. She sat in the chair and sang a slow sad song:

"Oh have ye not heard of Kate Kearney; she lives on the banks of Killarney; From the glance of her eye, shun danger and fly, for fatal's the glance of Kate Kearney."

The song was soothing and Charles let the haunting music wash over him. Mrs. Langford would be proud that he could tell it was written in a minor key. When the song ended, Abraham's mother stood and kissed her son on the forehead.

"Good night, dear 'Bram," she said. "May your dreams be all sweet water and sunshine."

Then she left. Distant thunder haunted the sky. As promised, 'Bram remained quiet. Charles held Pan close with both arms around the goat's neck, pictured Mr. Whiting's office, and closed his eyes.

Chapter 38

Before he opened his eyes, Charles smelled food. The aroma of cooking meat and toasting bread mixed with the sweet steam rising from a warm apple pie; the smell of beer and woodsmoke and ginger and bacon merged together in a confusing blend. A bagpipe blared nearby, a woman laughed loudly, many footsteps stomped on the ground in time to the piper. People shouted, but individual words did not register with Charles, they just created a background jumble of voices singing, yelling, and laughing. The breeze was cool but dusty.

He opened his eyes. He was in the midst of an outdoor party, a festival of some sort. Middle-aged people in old-fashioned costumes danced and laughed around him. It was like the Octoberfest he'd seen on TV, where European adults celebrate the harvest by dressing up, drinking beer, and being silly. Maybe he'd managed to get back to his own time and Octoberfest. He looked around for clues.

A tall, heavy man as old as his grandfather stumbled past, trying to drink beer from a heavy mug. An equally old woman wearing a big white scarf around her head chased after him. Neither moved very fast, but the man was just fast enough to stay ahead of the woman. Charles could not understand her words but deduced from her motions that she wanted a kiss. The man splashed beer on Charles as he hurried past but didn't stop or apologize. Neither adult seemed to notice Charles in any way.

Instinctively Charles backed up, pulling Pan along with him. The goat was completely indifferent to the noise and the crowd, but was fascinated by a patch of mint growing in the hard dirt. Charles stepped up on a wooden vegetable box to get a better view and to avoid being trampled by heavy people.

He was in the town square of a charming old city. It looked like an antique postcard. There were pointed roofs, quaint windows, and cobblestone paving. A church spire rose above the far side of the square, a tavern with a sagging wooden sign stood nearby. Despite the seated piper's obvious exhaustion, people tried to coax him to stand up again and keep playing. The villagers wore simple clothing. Many shirts were ripped or frayed. The women's skirts reached their ankles, the men wore loose, blousy shirts and baggy pants. Those who were not dancing stood in groups on the periphery drinking beer and laughing loudly. Several couples sat on grass beneath shade trees at the edge of the square kissing each other sloppily.

They spoke some language Charles had never heard and the words were nonsense to him.

Then a strange thing happened. Their words didn't change but gradually they became clear and he could understand them, at least a little. Now the words made sense, but many of the sentences did not. The woman in the white scarf chased the old man close to Charles again.

"Claus," she said. "You know you cannot escape by dancing. What can smoke do to iron? We shall marry under the broomstick! You stand in your own light!"

Another woman followed them. This new woman stopped in front of Charles, frazzled and out of breath. Her hair was a tangle of black, her simple brown dress was wrinkled. She stopped and stared at Charles. Then she pointed her bony index finger at his forehead and said, "There is more in it than an empty herring,"

"I should hope so," Charles replied.

She pointed at the goat. "He has rung a bell and brings a nixie!" She started shouting, "This one brings a nixie! Call the watchmen!"

"It's not a nixie," Charles said, desperately wondering what that meant. "It's… it's a Spanish goat. Very rare."

"Ah, a goat," the woman said. "That makes sense."

Apparently satisfied, she turned and stormed away. Claus, the man being pursued, noticed the commotion and came back to stand in front of Charles. The man stood, his hands on his hips, and sized up this boy who did not look like he belonged.

"Your goat's not dancing," he said.

"No," Charles said as politely as he could.

"A goat at a party should be dancing and doing tricks. Else he should be part of the stew."

"He's a pet," Charles said. "With many talents. But I've not seen him dance."

"Where did you get that costume?"

"My parents," Charles said truthfully.

"Calvinists then?" Claus asked. From his tone it sounded like a trick question with only one correct answer.

Charles thought quickly. "I think you would approve of my parents."

The woman chasing Claus stood beside him now, impatient with this new distraction.

"Dance with me, Claus," she said. "The herring does not fry here. And the roof has laths."

"Woman, you gnaw forever on a single bone."

She smiled, as if that were some sort of an inside joke.

"Horse droppings are not figs," she said.

Claus looked at Charles shrewdly.

"From your look, your parents don't strain to reach from loaf to loaf," he said.

Charles had no idea what he meant.

"They rarely speak of loaves," he said.

"Those that have the world spinning on their thumb need not talk of small matters," Claus said. "It proves my case."

"I guess so," Charles agreed.

"Have you paid your admission?" Claus asked.

"Admission?"

"The piper must be paid, the beer man encouraged to pour generously. Did you think a party like this grows out of the windows?"

"I had not intended to be here."

"Which every drunk says to the bartender when his bill comes due! But I am a kindly man. I will convey your payment to the master and not tell that you tried to enter as a thief." Claus held out a big, beefy hand, palm upward to receive payment.

"I have no money," Charles said.

"Parents whose roof is tiled with tarts would not send their child out as a beggar!"

"As I said, I had not intended to be here. I'll just leave and thank you for your hospitality."

"No money, you say? Very well, I'll take the goat."

"The goat is a pet and not available for barter."

"Fine. I'll just hold him until you go to your parents and return with coin."

"No, sir," Charles said. "my parents would be angry if I came home without Pan. I'll just leave."

Charles pulled Pan from a choice clover plant growing on the street and tried to walk away. But the burly man clamped a meaty hand around the boy's elbow and restrained him.

"I think you have something of value. Some contribution to the beer and piping."

Charles instinctively covered his shirt pocket with his hand. The only thing he had of value was his library card, which he carried in that pocket when he rode his bike. He could feel the feathers Martin had given him, and that sparked an idea. He would let the man outwit him.

This massive man's hand was strong and he squeezed even tighter. He repeated his demand for money more forcefully. His speech was slurred.

"Sir, I have only two things of value and would be in desperate trouble with my parents if I came home without either."

"Two things?" Claus was suddenly more interested.

"Did I say two? I meant one. Only the goat."

"Do not gaze at the stork!" Claus said, shaking his finger in Charles's face. "I was not born on the full moon! What is your other treasure?"

241

"'I misspoke," Charles said emphatically. "There is no treasure."

"Out with it, child! Or you'll be roasting on the spit beside your billy." He squeezed Charles's arm until the boy cried out. In old fairy tales, rough men captured children and actually did roast them. Could those ancient tales have begun in a place like this, with a man like Claus? Was he in greater danger than he knew?

"It's a feather," Charles said, hanging in his head as if ashamed the man had coaxed the most secret information from him. "Only a feather. There is no magic to it at all."

Claus's eyes widened.

"A magic feather you say? You have a magic feather?"

"No! I said it is NOT magic. It's the goat that helps me win at games of chance, not the feather!"

"Let me see this feather that is not magic," Claus insisted.

"Please sir, take the goat not the feather."

"I only wish to see it," the man said. "But I will see it this moment!"

"Very well," Charles said. With exaggerated carefulness, he removed the tiny blue feather from his shirt pocket.

"It's a bluejay feather," Claus said. "I see no magic."

"That's right," Charles replied, sounding relieved. "Just as I explained. It is not magic." He started to put it back in his pocket but Claus caught his hand.

"I need a feather for my cap," the man said. "Perhaps this will pay your admission. It has, indeed brought you luck!"

"No sir, my parents…"

But Claus had already plucked the tiny blue feather from the boy's hand and slid it into his hat's headband. Then, wearing the hat at a jaunty angle, he laughed and danced off into the crowd with the woman in eager pursuit.

A dozen feet to the left, a man stood painting on a huge board about the size of a full sheet of plywood. He looked both sane and sober and

242

therefore out of place. The painter was intent on his work. As he got closer, Charles was no longer so sure about the 'sane' part.

The man had the wild disheveled look of an old man who no longer cares about his appearance. A neat round cap covered the very top of his head, but a rat's nest of hair stuck out in every direction beneath it. His eyebrows were so long they hung over his eyes. His beard was trimmed in an unusual way. Rather than coming to a point below his chin, it ended in two points, one to each side of his chin. He looked out at the crowd with the intensity of either artistic concentration or lunatic frenzy.

"You are a painter?" Charles asked, immediately realizing how foolish the question was.

"Anybody can see through an oak plank if there's a hole in it," the man said. He stared out at the crowd, then dabbed some paint.

"Right," Charles agreed. "What is the festival?"

"It is no iconoclastic riot," the painter said. "Nor Calvinist gathering, nor council of blood. It's the better use of the tenth penny," he said.

"It looks like everyone's getting their money's worth," Charles said. He hoped that sounded like a joke.

"Many drag the block," the man said, wiping paint on his pants. "But a few are sea beggars to be sure. Or do you hang your cloak according to the wind?"

"I'm a stranger here," Charles said. "So I hesitate to answer for fear I mistake your meaning."

"You are wise to let geese be geese if you are not to be their master."

"Do you mind if I watch you for a minute?"

The painter shrugged and said, "You'll put no spoke through my wheel." He turned back to his painting and mumbled to himself. "I should paint the sleepers first. I hold an eel by the tail. But you'll carry the day out in baskets."

"Can you tell me what year it is?" Charles asked.

The painter had been watching the crowd and dabbing paint on the board while he talked, ignoring Charles. But at this question he stopped and eyed the boy more carefully.

"There hangs the knife," he said suspiciously. "Or have you a hole in the roof?"

"I've traveled a great distance," Charles said. "And have grown tired and confused. I'm no longer sure what is true and what is dream. And this scene…" He waved broadly at the crowd "does not reassure me."

The painter stared for a moment. Then he shrugged again, convinced the boy was harmless.

"It's been one-thousand-five-hundred-and-sixty-nine years since our Savior's birth. It's the one thing both Calvin and the Pope might agree upon."

"Fifteen-sixty-nine?" Charles said in amazement.

"And some of these won't see fifteen and seventy," the painter continued. "Some may well not see the morrow at this pace."

What caused me to land in this place at this time, Charles wondered? It's like no place I've been. Yet, as he looked around more carefully, he realized that it all seemed oddly familiar: the painter, Claus, the woman chasing him — had he read it in a book?

When he looked at the panel the man was painting he realized where he'd seen it— Mr. Whiting's office had a copy of the painting now being created before his eyes. It was familiar only because of that. It was completely foreign, a place of incomprehensible phrases where his science and vocabulary meant nothing. He did not want to be stranded there.

He worked his way through the crowd toward the old church, pushed open its heavy door, and stepped inside. Pan walked beside him. The thick walls muted the sounds of revelry, the air was musty and cool. A thousand Sundays had worn the pews shiny with a yellow-brown patina of varnish and memories; the stillness felt holy.

Several rows of pews were divided by a single aisle down the center. Near the front wall, a table was covered with white cloth. A silver bowl sat on the table, a rough wooden cross hung on the wall behind it. Above that, the walls angled together to form a peak. A large circle of stained glass lit the room as it glowed red and blue from the sunlight behind it. He walked about halfway down the aisle and sat in one of the pews.

Charles felt out of place, an intruder, a burglar stealing the sacred peacefulness. On the other hand, maybe he wasn't so different from the parishioners. They believed in things they couldn't understand, in a God they never saw, in mysteries and commandments passed down from previous generations. Maybe he wasn't so out of place in this church after all.

Should he try one more time to reach Mr. Whiting's study? Or should he give up and aim for his own place and time?

One more try, he told himself. It's what Edison would have done. He closed his eyes and pictured Mr. Whiting's study, remembered the desk and the cabinet. He avoided thinking about the prints on the wall, or the picture of the woman on the desk. There had been a large oval rug in the middle of the floor, he remembered that now. He tried to recall Mr. Whiting's voice talking with the man in his living room. He heard the piano music farther away, heard Martin's mother complaining about the composer.

"That's the kid that hit my legs!" the Reverend shouted from the back of the church. "Looks like we got him cornered this time!"

Charles opened his eyes. He was still in the old church, but now the Reverend and Slim, Soapy Smith's thugs, stood at the back, pointing at him.

"You go get him," Slim said. "I'll block the door. He ain't gettin' away this time."

Charles closed his eyes again and pictured Frank Whiting's office in the house in Colorado. He could hear the Reverend's limping footsteps coming toward him.

Suddenly the air felt heavier.

Chapter 39

Piano music! I've done it, Charles thought before he opened his eyes. No, wait. Something was burning with a familiar, distinctive smell. It took him a moment to identify it: cigar smoke! He opened his eyes.

This was not right at all. He was in a large living room, with the dated feeling of an antique, maybe even older than the Whiting's house, but it was not the Whiting's living room. He was sitting on a worn brown leather couch next to an old piano. A large, gruff-looking man sat playing it. This bear of a man, whose huge belly made it hard for him to reach the piano keyboard, was playing the same tune Martin's mother had played, only he was playing it easily, as if it were simple. The man wore a rumpled black suit coat and wrinkled black pants. A massive white beard straggled down over his shirt and a fat cigar dangled precariously from his lips, threatening to ignite the beard. Charles coughed from the smoke but the piano player didn't seem to notice.

The man played effortlessly, almost casually. Even in old age with stiff fingers, he was much more skillful than Mrs. Langford, Charles's piano teacher or Mrs. Whiting. "Good music deserves to be played loudly," the man said, without looking up. "Unless it is very gentle music, like this. Then you must play as you would kiss a baby's cheek."

Against the far wall, two bored men stood holding violins, a third sat on a stool holding a cello between his knees. A very thin young woman stood in the hall just outside the doorway, whispering to someone Charles couldn't see. She had the alert look of a nervous bird and wore what might have been a man's suit. Despite looking neat and controlled, she radiated urgency. The room's inhabitants were as pleasantly worn as the oak paneling or the faded blue rug covering the center of the floor. The musicians conversed quietly, obviously taking a break from rehearsal while the old man played piano with desultory carelessness.

The old man turned and looked directly at Charles with deep blue eyes showing just a hint of inquisitiveness. He glanced down at at Pan but did not interrupt his playing. Despite his gruff manner, Charles thought the man winked at him before turning to the other musicians.

"Gentlemen," he said. "I believe we have a new audience, filled with creatures I have not yet insulted. No merely-human brain could contrive such a miracle!"

Suddenly there was a disturbance out in the hall and something crashed against a wall. All heads turned and the music stopped. Had Sapania or Soapy Smith's men somehow followed him? A gray wool blanket was folded neatly on the arm of the couch. Charles pulled it over himself and Pan. "Quiet, boy," he whispered. "Just keep quiet and still."

An instant later, a huge shaggy Saint Bernard dog burst into the room like an unexpected hurricane in calm weather. The woman in the doorway shrieked, "Marco, no!"

But the dog was a force of nature and bounded straight toward Charles and Pan. Charles gripped Pan's leash tightly. Books cascaded off of a small table, and sheets of music flew into the air as if caught by the wind. The dog knocked the cello stand completely over; it clattered noisily against the wooden floor. The woman at the door looked horrified. "Oh, Doctor Brahms, I'm so sorry," she said. "Marco, come here at once!"

The dog ignored her and slid to a halt before Charles. It stood wagging its massive body and sniffing at Pan, who had thrown off most of the blanket. The goat stood very still until the examination was complete. The big dog obviously thought it wonderful that a goat interrupted the rehearsal. Its wagging tail stirred up a breeze that Charles could feel.

"Think nothing of it, my dear Oboe." Doctor Brahms shouted toward the woman while leaning over to pet the great beast enthusiastically. "Your dog senses a kindred spirt." His blue eyes twinkling like a mischievous child, Brahms glanced at Charles. The grouchy old bear had been transformed somehow; now he was cheerful and charming. No one else gave any hint they saw the boy or the goat.

"My name is Ethel," the woman in the hall firmly corrected Doctor Brahms as she squeezed past two men in the doorway. She remained embarrassed at the commotion her dog caused, but not so much she would back down from the pianist. "Not Oboe. Ellie to my dearest friends. Had an old man like you possessed breeding or manners you would surely refer to me as Miss Smyth."

Ethel Smyth entered the room the way a cloudburst enters the desert— sudden and powerful. Her boisterous enthusiasm woke the other musicians from dormancy, transforming them into living things, suddenly alert. But the old man at the piano didn't stop petting the dog. He held up his hand at the woman, who hovered nervously a few feet away.

"Don't be harsh with Marco," Dr. Brahms said. "He has been discouraged since he was dethroned and disenfranchised by the cat who kittened in his bed. I welcome his first burst of exuberance since his abdication."

"Actually," Ethel said. "his first exuberance of any sort since before that, since we lost our dear Ford."

That surprised Charles. He had presumed this scene was in a time before automobiles. And why would a dog grieve for a car? The huge dog still sat near Pan, but now a very young woman sat cross legged on the floor behind the animals. She smiled at Charles. Charles nodded and smiled back, certain she had not been there a moment ago. The young woman hugged Marco's neck, petted his chest, and rubbed her cheek against his nose. She was slender and startlingly pretty, with gray twinkling eyes. Long black hair flowed down her shoulders like a liquid. Both Marco and the woman seemed very happy.

"I'm Ford," she said to Charles. "I've missed my dear Marco so desperately." She looked at Marco's owner, Ethyl, who stood a few feet away. "And my dear Ellie as well. I think I have been on a journey. Now that my headaches are cured, perhaps she will take me back."

Dr. Brahms spoke to Ethel.

"A dog is usually better company than a musician," he said. "I have fond memories of one, a story I'm sure I have not told you. It seems quite appropriate."

"A story you have not related ad nauseam? That seems unlikely," Ethel said, rolling her eyes.

"Years ago I visited with friends at a cabin near Grindenwell," Dr. Brahms said, ignoring the woman. "It was harsh country and dangerous weather. I arrived before them, and as they journeyed to meet me, their little Scotch terrier ran off and could not be captured. The coach would not wait for fear of the weather stranding them all. The little dog was left behind. When they reached the cabin, my joy at seeing old friends was nearly destroyed by the sadness of the loss. I confess, I'd looked forward to seeing little Argos as much as my friends.

"Days later, as I prepared to leave, I arose early to a scratching at the door. Imagine my delight to see Argos, thin and dirty but wagging his entire body with joy." Doctor Brahms looked down at the Saint Bernard, who was still wagging its own body, and rubbed it between the ears. "My friends calculated that Argos must have run along behind us without stopping for three full days. So such things do happen and are not just sportsmen's stories."

"Yes, Doctor," the woman said. "Animals can have remarkable stamina."

"Indeed," he answered. "Although sometimes I wonder if they don't have other gifts for traveling we do not understand."

At this, he looked directly at Charles and winked again, as if they shared a secret. Ethel was obviously relieved that the old man wasn't upset. Her eyes twinkled and she cocked her head sideways in a playful pose.

"Even cats, Doctor?" she asked.

"Now that Mr. Wagner's grave has had time enough to smooth his many sharp edges, yes. I have also made my peace with cats."

The cello player, a thin man with short neat hair and a tasteful mustache looked confused. "I don't understand," he said politely. "Did Wagner dislike cats?"

The old man smiled grimly. "That we shall never know. It was me he disliked, despite my admiration of his music. Perhaps my own was too advanced for him. When asked about me, the best he could answer was, 'The evil only starts when one attempts to compose better than one can.'"

"I remain confused," the young man said. "What has this to do with cats?"

Ethel glanced at Brahms, then answered for him.

"You must forgive Doctor Brahms," she said. "He is as honest as God but as good as the Devil. It would be preferable to have those traits

249

reversed. Are you sure," she asked the old man, "this feud is cold enough to speak of?"

"I never thought of it as a feud," he shrugged. "How can one feud with God? Wagner surely saw himself as God." He paused for effect. "Or perhaps even as Beethoven himself."

Ethel turned to the young cellist. "But even God could be jealous of Doctor Brahms," she said. "Wagner made comments. He started rumors."

"We can't know for certain," Brahms said, shaking his head.

"Why Doctor, if Marco can soften you thus, he should attend every rehearsal!"

"I'm only taking a pause," the old man said. "I shall be sure to insult each of you at least twice more before we finish here. Especially the upstart Oboe here."

Ethel smiled. "Of that I'm sure." She turned back to the younger man. "The Doctor feels every person resembles some instrument, so he names them as he feels appropriate. As we all know, an oboe is a lovely and elegantly thin instrument."

"With a loud and piercing voice," the Doctor corrected her.

"Soon I shall begin calling him contra-bass. Or perhaps tuba. He is an unutterably sad and bitter man. Whereas I have been intoxicated by the desert sky and gone star-mad, dazzled by joy and beauty." She smiled at Brahms. "He understands that I only tease him, just as he teases."

"As to cats," she continued, "Wagner started a rumor that the Doctor shot cats with a bow and arrow from his balcony. Each arrow had a long string attached so it acted as a harpoon. The Doctor, according to the story, pulled in the pierced animals. As they howled and screeched to their death, the Doctor took note of the sounds they made and incorporated them into his music."

"Surely no one could believe such a tale!" the young man said.

"The truth can't compete with a vivid story," Ethel said.

The Doctor nodded. "Baudelaire once said he preferred the sound of a desperate cat clawing on a window to the music of Mr. Wagner. I'm sure that's where Richard got the idea. I do not credit him with that level of originality. Baudelaire opened the cemetery gates to let the curs inside. It was his finest joke. Perhaps his only joke."

Ethel smiled. "Now there's the Doctor Brahms I've come to admire."

"Oboe wishes she'd been born a man," the doctor said. "She spends her time in the manly pursuits of tennis and golf and musical composition. And, of course, riding bicycles and trying to convince the Queen of England that women should be given the vote. None of these, of course, are suitable pastimes for a woman."

"Ah, but for an oboe?" the woman replied. "What's proper for an oboe has yet to be decided!"

"Leipzig is not ready for either a woman or an oboe to tinker with composing. She writes sonnets and music yet knows nothing of counterpoint."

"I take it as a compliment that the great man is familiar with both my poetry and my music," she said. "Come, Marco, I must save you from this madman."

The pretty young woman on the floor who called herself Ford kept her arms draped around the dog's neck and petted him fondly. She looked at Ethel with a wistful, affectionate look. Then she looked directly at Charles.

"I think she'd like it if you told her I was here," she said.

"I'm not sure I should," Charles said.

Ford looked at Charles and tilted her head playfully. She stuck out her lower lip like a pouting child and opened her eyes very wide, like a puppy or a fawn. Even though he was too young to fully appreciate the woman's beauty he could not resist her playful charm.

"I think Ford is here now," Charles said.

Ethel smiled, but sadly.

"Of course she is," she said. "I feel her essence all the time, especially when Marco is happy. When you whisper certain names to yourself a cathedral lights up in the dark recesses of memory. Ford is one of those names." Then she turned to leave. "Come, Marco," she said, but the big dog ignored her.

Ford smiled at Charles and blew him a kiss. She mouthed the words 'thank you.'

Doctor Brahms looked at the two of them. "Wait one moment, my dear Oboe," he said, and the woman paused, hands on her hips, impatient. The old man looked off into the distance and spoke softly. Only Charles was close enough to hear his words clearly. "We think we own other people when we merely share a moment of life with them." he said. "We stand beside them and look away, when we look back, mid-sentence they've disappeared. She can't see you, or the goat, or the young woman."

"And yet you can?" Charles said.

"I've had a bit of experience," Brahms said, still whispering. To anyone else in the room he was speaking quiet nonsense to the big dog. "It takes a while for a person to... to notice. She may hear your voice as if it were a memory within her, or her own daydream." He kept petting the dog, scratching it between the ears while Ford, the young woman, buried her face in the fur of the dog's neck. "Sometimes people see things only after someone points to them," Brahms said. "Each observation trains the mind for the next. If you study music you will understand."

"I don't think I'll be studying music," Charles said.

"Pity." Brahms shook his head sadly. "What is life without music?" Then, in a much louder voice he turned back to Ethel Smyth. "Oboe!" he said sharply. "There's someone here who requires your attention."

Ethel, bored with the old man's incomprehensible mutterings, had started to walk away, quietly singing a sad slow song that began "At the mid hour of night." Brahms's louder pronouncement reminded her that she had not removed her dog and stopped walking. "Of course," she said. "Marco, time for us to take our leave. That song tends to make people cry anyway." She snapped into action, moving to grab the dog's collar. "Come, Marco! You're disturbing the doctor. We must go outside at once."

"The dog is the most pleasant part of this entire dismal rehearsal," Dr. Brahms said gruffly. "The one who requires attention is not Marco."

"I don't understand," Ethel replied.

"Of course not," he said. "It's a failure of imagination common to those who pretend to create."

"Well, I certainly bow to your superior understanding of such people," she said. "You have a lifetime of personal experience."

"There is a young goat standing next to your dog," he said. "Absolutely invisible to those who do not expect to see it."

"You have completely lost your mind," she said. "Or else you are reverting to language idioms from your extremely distant childhood that do not translate to English."

"His name is Pan," Charles said, trying to be helpful.

"Whose name is Pan?" Ethel asked. She could obviously hear Charles to some degree. She glanced in his general direction but did not focus on him. The fact that she heard a voice when she saw no person didn't seem to bother her at all.

The pretty young woman, Ford, looked at Ethel wistfully and spoke. "Pan is the goat's name," she said. "He has some sort of magic."

Ethel looked confused. "Who said that?" She looked at Ford and then at the doctor, and then at her dog Marco. The doctor spoke softly.

"Be patient, my dear," he said. "Imagine there is a young goat right beside your dog. If you reach your hand out, you may be able to touch it. It is as real as a melody you have yet to write."

"I see no goat," she reached out her hand as if to illustrate and then stopped speaking. Her hand was on Pan's head.

"What…?" Ethel said. She looked up in surprise.

"There is a goat here!" she said. "Where did it come from? Who let it in? It's no wonder Marco rushed in here…"

One of the other musicians, who saw neither ghosts nor goats, responded to that. "The great composer prefers we not refer to him as a goat." he said.

"His name is Pan," Ford said quietly.

Ethel looked in the direction of the younger woman. Her face was confused, then gradually became focused, like a painted vase being slowly raised through murky water. Her eyes opened wide in surprise.

"Ford!" she whispered, her voice full of urgency and astonishment. Then her face exploded into a smile, then contracted again in confusion. "But how?"

"I don't know," Ford said, beaming happily. "I think Pan, the goat...perhaps he helps people see things. Or to see them out of order. Today and then yesterday. It's confusing."

"An inordinate animal!" Ethel smiled, proud of her pun, but baffled by the scene.

"I don't know the word," Ford said. "You have always known so many words."

"I'm sorry, I was making a small joke. Pan seems to be an inordinate animal in both senses of the word; extraordinary, which he certainly seems to be, and also the meaning "out of order." For surely seeing you now is...out of sequence."

Ethel kept looking back and forth between the goat and the young woman. Her fingers could not resist scratching the soft hair between the animal's floppy ears.

"Pan, you say? And somehow he helps you come to visit me after... after so much time."

"I think so."

"Well, if such a charming fluff of fur can help you to visit me, then I shall have my own Pan. And he shall be with me at all times." Then Ethel frowned. "Can you stay?"

"Maybe for a while," Ford said.

"We must continue our rehearsal," one of the other musicians said. "If you can stop communing with the wall for a few moments, please."

Ethel looked around and nodded. Then she began to sing the song she had begun earlier, but now it sounded cheerful. Charles realized that her singing was a code that only Ford would understand. Her voice was lovely:

254

"Come o'er the sea, maiden with me, Seasons may roll but the true soul, burns the same where e'er it goes." The words were an invitation for Ford to follow her. She reached out her hand and Ford happily took it and stood up. Ethel kept her hand near her side so it looked perfectly normal to the other musicians. With Ford holding her right hand invisibly and Marco's collar in her left hand, they strolled out of the room as if on their way to a Sunday picnic, singing a song with meaning only for its secret audience.

When they left the room, the cello player remarked, "Sir, you mentioned Miss Smyth's poetry. I did not know she wrote poetry."

"A clever woman is nothing," Brahms said as if reciting lines from a stage. "So let us become stupid, for that is the only requirement to admire Doctor Tuba." He laughed, the others in the room looked confused.

"Poetry from the heart of Oboe herself," he explained, shaking his head and finally smiling a small, grudging smile of appreciation. "Indeed, she could be my own child."

"Do I detect an uncharacteristic note of affection?" the violinist said, with a hint of a smile.

The old man scowled. "Should you ever repeat such a hateful accusation you shall meet the same fate as Wagner's cats. And an unplayable violin part shall bear your name. You shall be reviled by every violinist for generations."

"Then at least my name shall become immortal, right along with yours."

"Yes, that would be too kind of me. I shall instead name it "Concerto Number One" or some other faceless appellation. Yet we shall both know."

"In that case, I'll not accuse you of affection for any human."

"Thank you for that, at least. I suppose it's the most I can hope for from the likes of you."

The violinist smiled and nodded stiffly from his waist. "And anonymity is the highest praise I can hope for from you," he said.

With both hands on Pan's soft back, Charles closed his eyes and pictured home.

Chapter 40

In the blink of an eye, Charles travelled from a musician's apartment in Leipzig, Germany in the 1800s to a dusty area beneath an old porch north of Denver in the 1950s. Clearly, he could not control manitous and time-travel by himself yet. But he had to try again.

There's a cost to magic, a secret price magicians pay. As he considered the wailing in the night, the scratching in the walls— as the thumps and bangs increased— Charles realized there was also a price to pay for ignoring the unknown. A week after his last adventure, he and Martin walked through parched dirt and lifeless weeds toward the Pillar of Fire, with Pan trotting along behind them.

"Don't let go of the rope," Charles said, but there wasn't much chance of that. Ever since the coyote had attacked them, Martin held Pan's rope tightly. Charles looked over his shoulder, remembering the wild canine's gleaming white teeth.

He chose this night for the experiment mostly because it had a full moon. Not much logic to that decision he knew but, in stories, magic blossoms on full-moon nights. Maybe there was some truth to the stories. At least the bright moonlight made it easier to see where they were going.

As the tower of the gloomy old castle rose high in the air before them, like a giant's raised fist, Charles shivered. If magic responds to atmosphere, the old campus was a perfect setting. The sky beyond the big building was clear and black as ink, sprinkled with white stars. The edges of a half-dozen somber clouds glowed with pale yellow moonlight as they drifted aimlessly. The clouds are like sad ghosts, Charles thought. Wandering.

"We're going to the old cemetery again, aren't we?" Martin said. Crickets sang with the slow urgency of late summer their one last song before the inevitable frost ended their concert forever.

"I think that's where we have our best chance."

"Don't tell my father," Martin said.

"I won't."

The full moon hovered low above over the eastern horizon. Every weed, tree, and fencepost cast an elongated silhouette on the ground. Their own thin shadows followed Martin and Charles, creeping like huge spiders behind them.

Finally they stood outside the wrought-iron fence that enclosed the dismal cemetery. Each modest headstone threw an exaggerated shadow that stretched beyond the grave it marked. Beyond the life it represented.

"I don't like it here," Martin said.

Charles just nodded.

"Remember those two men who wanted to hurt Pan?" Charles said.

"I don't like to think about them," Martin said. "If I think about them, they might come."

"I know," Charles said as calmly as he could. He did not want to frighten the boy. "But tonight, that's what we want."

"I don't want them to come here!"

"It will be fine," Charles said. "I think they can lead us to your father."

"They won't do that," Martin said. "They'll try to hurt us."

"Yes, but they won't be able to. This time we'll be prepared. They know where your family is in Alaska. And I think we can make them take us there."

"No," Martin said and his voice was very firm.

"They want to hurt your family," Charles said "but maybe we can stop them. It's not just about you and me." As he said it, he realized he believed it. Those men had appeared for some reason and their motives were not benevolent. They wanted to kill the goat, perhaps to keep Martin away from Alaska. But how could Martin be a threat to them?

"I think your father needs our help," Charles said.

When Martin spoke, his voice was very soft. "But what's your plan?"

Charles took a deep breath. Frightening Martin would be both cruel and counterproductive. Charles shook his head at the irony . He was worried about frightening a ghost.

"Sometimes you think of a place or person and then they come to us," Charles said. "I've seen it."

"It doesn't always work."

"I know. But sometimes it does."

"It helps if I'm with Pan," Martin said.

"Right. I do the same thing in a way. I'm just not very good at it. But if both of us try to summon these men, maybe they'll come here. Then we'll make them think about your father and maybe we'll all go to him."

"Won't we be bringing the bad men to my father?"

"Yes. But if my plan works, they won't be able to hurt him."

"What would I have to do?"

"You have the most important job," Charles said. "You have to imagine."

A cloud drifted across the moon and the light dimmed for a moment. Despite the warmth of the evening, Charles shivered. The moon lit the clouds with a pale yellow glow but everything on the ground — the spooky castle building, the skeletons of trees, the fence, the headstones in the cemetery — looked black and gray, like a very old photograph. Suddenly Charles was not at all sure he was being smart about all this.

"Last time, they were right over there," Martin pointed at the middle of the cemetery.

"Not yet!" Charles said. "Don't think about them yet. We don't want them to get here before I have everything ready!"

But it was too late. In the center of the cemetery, a dark bush stirred. Then a second bush stirred. Their leaves moved as if in a gentle breeze, small branches wrapping together and clinging to each other to form larger limbs. Twigs congealed into vague thick branches. As the cloud drifted away from the moon, the scene was illuminated. The bushes became two men sitting on the ground, turning their heads this way and that. They wore old fashioned derby hats, round with small brims.

Pan perked up his ears and turned to look at them.

"It's them," Martin whispered. "What do we do?"

"Just stay quiet and hope they don't notice us."

As soon as Charles whispered the words, Slim pointed at them and he and the Reverend started walking toward the boys.

"This way!" the Reverend shouted, turning toward the padlocked gate. He took out his hand gun and shot the lock. The boys jumped at the loud sound. The lock split into several pieces which clattered against the fence as they flew away.

The two men walked through the gate and strode toward the boys with long intimidating steps. The Reverend's gun was still in his hand.

"Did I make a mistake?" Martin asked. "Wasn't I supposed to imagine them?" He sounded frightened. "Shouldn't we run away?"

"You did great," Charles said. "Plans never go exactly the way you think they will. Let them get closer."

"Well, look what we got here!" the Reverend said when they reached the boys. "It's the little hero and his goat."

Maybe they can't see me, Charles thought. As if reading his mind the man looked right at him. "And I see you brung along the kid in the window too. Just give us the goat and we'll let you two run along."

Charles ignored that comment. "You were in Skagaway, weren't you?" he said. "And you know Frank Whiting."

The question startled the Reverend and he looked at Slim. They hadn't planned on a conversation.

"What if we was?" he said. Then he snorted a little, like he'd heard a joke, trying to downplay his surprise. "Frank's part of the Committee of 101, wants to make it hard for honest businessmen like us to make a fair living. But that's all ending tonight. Mr. Smith has put together his own Committee of 303. He'll make short work of it."

"So why don't you want Martin to be there?" Charles asked. His directness surprised the two men again, and they looked at each other, not knowing how to respond.

"Don't know what in the Sam Hill you're talking about," the taller man said. "Mr. Smith just said take care of the goat."

"Why does he care about a goat?"

They looked confused for a moment, then got more belligerent.

"Mr. Smith don't have to explain himself. And sure not to children." Slim pulled a long knife out of his belt and advanced toward the boys. "'Whatever you got to do' was his words. So just hand it over!"

Martin and Charles stood on each side of the goat. Instinctively, both stepped in front of Pan, blocking the man's path. The Reverend holstered his gun and pulled out his own long knife. He wore a nasty grin on his face as he stepped toward them.

"So, Slim, looks like we get a little bonus," he said. "We won't even charge Mr. Smith for the boys. I want the one on the left. I owe him a little something. Plus, he's got the better scalp."

Terrified but trying not to show it, Charles improvised. These guys were evil but they didn't seem very smart. Charles raised one arm and pointed it at them. Sometimes people believe ridiculous things, especially if you say them with confidence. It was worth a try. Maybe it would buy them some time.

"Those knives won't work here," Charles said.

The weird comment surprised the men and they stopped moving forward. Almost immediately they grinned again.

"I believe they'll work just fine," Slim said, stepping closer.

It was too late to try some different plan, Charles had to plow forward. He forced himself to smile. Then he gave a little laugh. They would never believe him if he faltered. His confidence must be supreme.

"No, sir," he said, a little louder. "They won't work. At least not for you two." His mind raced, trying to think of something else to say. This was a stupid plan. The men took another step toward the boys. Finally, in desperation Charles blurted, "They won't work for you... because they're too hot."

The men laughed.

"I warned you," Charles said, in his deepest most grown-up voice. He pointed directly at Slim's knife, clearing everything from his mind but searing heat. The heat of a pan steaming on a stove. The heat of glowing coals in a campfire. He pictured the hot ember Jim Baker used to light his pipe, the flickering twig lighting his face. The heat of a welding torch shooting sparks in every direction, so hot you'd hurt your eyes if you look at it directly. Hot as the sun.

The man holding that knife stopped and stared at his hand. "What the…" he said, and then he dropped the knife on the ground. Charles wasn't sure if he'd actually done anything to the knife or if the power of suggestion merely convinced the man. Either way, it remained his only option, he turned to the Reverend.

"Stop playing games, Slim," the Reverend said. "Let's do what we set out to do and get back to the saloon." By now Charles was pointing at that man's knife. Uncertainly flickered across the Reverend's face, only for a moment, but that was enough. He didn't believe Charles could do anything to him or his knife, not really. But he wasn't completely sure. His eyes got wide. A moment later he dropped his knife too., shaking his hand to cool it.

But the men remained fixed on their mission and now were angry beside.

"We don't need knives or guns to kill a dad-blame goat," said the Reverend. "Come on, Slim. I'll just break its little neck. And then I'll do the kids just for sport."

He took a step toward the boys, but they did not move.

A dried weed crunched behind Charles as if someone stepped on it. The men stopped cold and the boys froze, startled by the sound.

A man's voice, deep but quiet, spoke very slowly.

"That's one way this night could go," Jim Baker said. "With you killing a goat and a couple kids. Maybe collecting a scalp or two so your friends think you're a mean woods-runner and brave as a Comanche." He paused. He spit chewing tobacco and stepped forward to stand next to the boys. "But I kind of doubt it."

"Who are you?" the Reverend asked, stepping backward. "Wait, I think I seen you somewhere…"

Baker looked at the two men for a minute, sizing them up.

"I'm a woods-runner," he said. "And I prefer fights that are just a little bit fairer."

"Get out of our way, old man!" Slim shouted.

Jim Baker just stood there and put a fresh wad of tobacco into his mouth.

"I said get out of our way! Move! Or I'm likely to start shooting!"

Baker nodded and looked at the younger man. He looked down at the man's shiny leather shoes and his neat city clothes. His glance landed on the man's new derby hat. Then he spoke very slowly and said, "Yeah, you might start shooting. You surely might," he said. "And when you do, young feller, I'll tell you when to stop."

Slim and Reverend looked at each other, then turned and started to walk away quickly. They only took two steps before they stopped again. Another man had somehow snuck up behind them, silent as a cat, and blocked their path. He was tall and muscular with long dark hair pulled back, and dressed in buckskin.

"Honest Jim didn't tell me there was going to to be a party," Just Murphy said. The Reverend and Slim stood still. They were effectively surrounded.

"Looks like the little scout already has things under control," Jim Baker said. "He disarmed them before I got here. Except for them little guns. If I was them, I'd just toss them into the grass right now before they get theirselves hurt. The little scout might not be quite done with them, you think, Murphy?"

"He's got a bit of the Huron shaman in him, for true," Just Murphy said. "Ain't that right, Flint?"

The dog beside him panted and wagged its tail. Its tongue lolled happily out one side of its mouth.

The Reverend and Slim tossed their handguns aside. They stood uneasily shifting their weight from foot to foot, calculating their next move. Maybe they could run away and get lost in the darkness before one of these riflemen could get off a shot. Maybe they could tackle the men in buckskin and disarm them…

Just Murphy gestured with his long rifle in the general direction of the two men. "This one on the left has the look of a deer just before it makes a run for it." He didn't aim the rifle at the man but lifted it casually, as if loosening his muscles preparing to take a shot. "You know, that look they get right before they turn into venison." The men stared at that long two-barreled rifle and turned back to the boys and the goat.

"What do you want from us?"

"We have no interest in you at all," Charles said. "We just want to follow you to Skagaway, Alaska. To Mr. Whiting and his family. Then you can do whatever you want."

"Whiting? The guy with the White Pass rail company? He sticks his nose where he ain't got business. Darn shame his house burned down."

"His house burned down?" Charles had not expected that news.

"Twice. Him and his wife Millah and all them kids had a place above a bar. Dad-blame shame it burned down. For a fellow supposed to be smart he ain't a fast learner. Pretty unlucky to have that second place burn down too. People who get crossways with Mr. Smith— why it's like getting crossways with God. They tend to get unlucky."

Jim Baker interrupted him. "From where I stand, you ain't in a good position to call someone else unlucky or un-smart. Not by a jugful. Mr. Smith reminds me of Mr. Jonah when he decided to go fishin'. Why don't you just mosey on back to him, and we'll follow along."

"Follow us? I don't know what you mean."

"You were in Skagaway, Alaska with Mr. Smith," Charles said. "And now you're here. How did you get here?"

The men looked genuinely confused.

"We're in Skagaway now," Slim said. "You're crazy, kid."

Charles hadn't anticipated that they might simply be unaware of what they were doing or how they were doing it.

"Does this look like Skagaway?" Charles asked.

The men looked around.

"We ain't been in every part of the territory," Slim said. "But we been here a few times and it looks about right."

"So where is the town from here? Where do you go?"

"I don't get your meaning."

"How do you report back to Mr. Smith?"

"He just calls us and we come."

"Well, I think he's calling for you now," Charles said.

As if on cue, yet another man's voice called out from the shadows. Charles looked around, startled, wondering if they had transported to Alaska without realizing it. But no. They still stood near the cemetery, the full moon still rose behind the Pillar of Fire castle. Had they accidentally summoned Mr. Smith instead of traveling to him in Alaska? Whoever spoke was hidden in the shadows but the voice was clear.

"I like it out here," the man said. "Not so crowded. Not so many voices." He sounded agitated. "But it's too close! They'll find me here! They'll make me go back!"

Mr. Peters, the disturbed man the nuns had caught and returned to his room, stepped out from behind a tree, looking left and right to make sure he wasn't being followed. He wore ragged jeans and a faded denim shirt. His hair stuck out at absurd angles like straw glued randomly to a scarecrow's head.

"What are you doing here?" Charles asked. Mr. Peters looked around frantically, trying to locate whoever spoke to him. In his agitated state, it took him several seconds to locate Charles.

"It's a free country, ain't it?" Mr. Peters said. He swept his hand broadly, pointing to the little group of people but also the entire cemetery and lawn beyond it. "You're the ones who won't shut up. Won't let a man rest." His eyes settled on Charles.

"You!" he shouted. "You understand You're just like me!"

"You should go back to your room," Charles said as sternly as he could. "It's not safe here."

264

"It's not safe anywhere!" Mr Peters answered. "Angry, angry! Sad, sad! Lonely, lonely! Crying… that's the worst. Can't shut out the crying!"

Mr. Peters glanced at each of them furtively before averting his eyes, like a fugitive in a strange country, baffled by a different language and strange customs, careful to hide his own identity while searching for clansmen who share his vocabulary, rebels who sympathize with his crime.

"It's probably quieter in your room," Charles said. "We're busy here."

"No!" he shouted. "Quieter here!"

Suddenly Martin shouted. "They're getting away!" He pointed to some shrubs near the cemetery fence. While Mr. Peters had distracted them, the two outlaws had slipped away and were now running full speed into the shadows. Charles started to chase them but before he'd taken two steps, the men stumbled and fell. Incredibly, Martin was clinging to their ankles. They'd been running side by side near each other and somehow the boy just transported himself to their location, grabbed an ankle in each hand and tackled them. A moment later, Jim Baker and Just Murphy loomed over them as well. They tied the outlaws' hands behind them and began herding them back toward Charles.

Mr. Peters and Charles remained where they were, fifty feet away. Charles held Pan by his rope.

"See?" said Mr. Peters. "You're like me, not them. But they don't… bother you? Keep you awake?"

"No," Charles said. Suddenly he understood. "You see more of… them, don't you?"

"Hundreds," Mr. Peters said. He looked right at Charles and for a moment he seemed completely sane. "Don't you?"

When Charles didn't answer right away, the man's expression changed. The tormented man was shocked at a sudden realization. He was a prisoner who just discovered his own punishment was far more severe than the other prisoners'. In an instant, loneliness became helpless desolation.

"We're leaving here," Charles said. "You should return to your room."

265

"Take me with you!" Mr. Peters implored, grabbing the boy's wrist in a tight grip. "Don't make me go back..." he shuddered and motioned toward one of the buildings. Then he whispered, "Back there."

Charles tried to imagine what it would be like to see every ghost that might linger near the cemetery. All the young couples who had walked hand in hand down that path, all the students who had sat studying on the lawn. Their whispered comments, their colorful clothes, their urgent problems, their sad confessions, their upset stomachs and headaches. The old men who remembered only the songs of their childhood; the children who could not imagine an elderly version of themselves.

As Charles thought of these departed souls, he started to see them. First as vague shadows between the trees, as wisps of fog floating above the grass. Surely his imagination was playing tricks, he thought. Gradually they became more solid, more vivid, like actors in a movie coming into focus. Nearly all of them were talking or singing or crying or laughing. Their voices merged together like the humming of a beehive. Some of the voices near him were louder, insistent, but disconnected: people arguing with themselves or with invisible companions. It was completely distracting and impossible to ignore.

A little girl in ragged clothes stood beside him.

"Where's Mama?" she asked, looking up at him with sad eyes. "I've been waiting for her like a good girl..." She continued talking but by now a middle aged man had reached Charles as well. He wore a faded military uniform from some long-forgotten war.

"Reporting for duty, sir," he said. "They ambushed my platoon. Somehow I got separated from my men..." He continued talking oblivious to the little girl who also continued to speak. The people swarmed and swirled like a river around Charles.

One man stepped out of the foggy darkness and approached him directly with more urgent intent that the others. "Tell her!" he said. He was a short thin man with white hair and a kind face. "Tell her it's beautiful." He shook his head in frustration. "That's not good enough. I don't know the words," he said. "She always had the words. Tell her the flowers glow. The tall grass sings. The gray cranes rattle and scream. And the colors. So many colors I can't describe them." He paused. "Tell her to smile." He shook his head again, frustrated at his limited vocabulary. "She will know the words. Tell her it's beautiful. Thank you."

A woman of about twenty pushed forward through the crowd and reached Charles. She was pale but very pretty.

"He'll be home soon," she said sweetly. "And I've baked him a cake."

Charles tried to back away, but the man holding his arm was too strong. Mr. Peters eyes grew wide and he became excited.

"You hear them!" he said. "I can tell you do!"

"We have to shut them out," Charles said. "None of this will work amid so much commotion."

Mr. Peters put his hands over his ears and shook his head.

"Somehow we invited them here," Charles shouted. "Surely we can ask them to withdraw!"

Mr. Peters kept his hands over his ears and shook his head. "They don't listen," he yelled. "They only talk! And they never stop!"

It was no wonder the man felt helpless and acted crazy. Anyone would. But there had to be a way.

Maybe Charles could try something like he'd done with the outlaws, convincing them their knives were hot. He reached out his arm like an orchestra conductor trying to get the attention of unruly musicians. He moved it from left to right, from the string section to the woodwinds to the upright bass.

"You must withdraw!" Charles shouted as forcefully as he could. The noise did not decrease. In fact, more of these creatures seemed to direct their attention toward him. Their faces came into sharper focus. Charles was surrounded and they were closing in around him like wolves.

"Stop!" he shouted but they ignored him. "You must all be quiet!" Charles shouted. They continued to advance.

"They can't hear you," Mr. Peters said. "Now that you've called them, they will be with you forever." He squeezed his hands even tighter over his ears and shook his head.

267

"Waiting for instructions, sir…"

"It's a chocolate cake. It's his favorite…"

"Mama said to wait right here. But she's been gone a long time…"

"We were ambushed. I got separated from my men…"

"We'll build a house in the country…"

"I don't know if I should tell the priest…"

"Someday. We don't need to fix it now. Someday…"

"Could I bum a smoke? Don't know where I set them down…"

"Where's my Mama? She told me to wait…"

Suddenly Martin was beside him. Jim Baker and Just Murphy stood on each side of the two outlaws fifteen feet away. Just Murphy watched Martin carefully but Baker paid no attention. He was only interested in the outlaws that nearly escaped him. The scowl on his face said they had offended his honor. Next time, he'd just shoot them.

Martin looked at the little girl who kept calling for her mother.

"Mary," he said calmly. "It's all right. You don't need to worry about your Mama. But my friend can't help you and he needs you to be quiet. Can you do that for me?"

The little girl nodded her head. Gradually she disappeared, fading away like fog in sunshine.

Martin turned to Charles.

"How did you do that?" Charles asked in amazement. A hundred other apparitions continued to talk and sing and laugh and cry. Most still seemed to be moving toward him.

"She was being a pest," he said. "But she's little so she doesn't know better. She just needed me to tell her."

"How about all the others?" Charles said.

"What others?" Martin asked.

"So you don't see…" Charles stopped himself. He hadn't seen them either until Mr. Peters made him look for them. The last thing he needed was for Martin to get distracted by a hundred voices. "Never mind," he said.

Just Murphy spoke quietly.

"I think you can choose who you see," he said. "Sometimes who you hear. Kind of like a sniper chooses his target. You focus on one and block out every other thing. It's too confusing if you don't."

"So Mr. Peters here?" Charles asked.

"He never learned how to choose. There ain't a book to teach it." Charles could hardly hear Just Murphy over all the voices. He watched the man's lips to help understand what he was saying. "Some guys are good shots but they ain't graceful shooters. They can't shut out extra targets. They work hard, but bein' good ain't a sure thing, it ain't a payment for your practice. It's kind of a gift you get by luck."

"So how do I…?" Charles shouted.

Just Murphy shrugged. "No idea. Folks figure it out for theirselves. Most folks learn to ignore stuff before they figure out how to see. You done it kind of backward."

That rang true. Babies don't recognize anything at all; maybe that's because they see everything all at once. Then they learn to see their mother's face and shut out everything else. They don't see distractions because they're only looking at her. Mr. Peters heard all the voices and now Charles did too. He had to remember how to focus on just one thing.

"What's wrong?" Martin asked. He looked up at Charles with his big brown eyes and concern on his face but oblivious to the confusion around them. Charles had an idea.

"Martin, do you see Mr. Peters here?"

Martin cocked his head to one side and stared at the man. "Why isn't he happy?"

"I think he feels lonely," Charles said. "He needs a friend. Could you be his friend?"

"I don't think he can see me," Martin said.

269

"That's OK. We can't always see our friends, can we?"

"No," he said softly. "My father can't see me."

"Here, let me hold Pan's rope for a minute." Martin handed him the rope. It didn't seem to matter who was holding the goat, they both transported together just fine. Still, it gave Charles a tiny sense of control to have the leash.

"Mr. Peters," Charles said. He didn't respond. "Mr. Peters!" he shouted. Mr. Peters looked at the boy mournfully. Charles stepped even closer. "Give me your hand." Mr. Peters shook his head with both hands still clamped on his ears.

"Let me try to make it better," Charles shouted and reached out as if to shake his hand. Still unsure, gradually his face changed. He had nothing to lose. The voices around them made it impossible to hear much else. He winced as he reached out his hand, expecting the volume to increase. Charles took his hand.

"Covering your ears doesn't help, does it?" Charles said.

Mr. Peters shook his head. "Nothing helps."

"I have a friend you can't see," Charles said. "He's a little boy who is very kind, but also lonely. Other people might think that was a crazy thing to say. But you understand, don't you?"

Mr. Peters nodded slowly.

"Martin, would you hold Mr. Peters's hand for a few minutes? I think you could both use a friend."

Martin nodded and took the man's hand. Mr Peters's eyes opened wider and he looked down at his hand. "I feel something!" he whispered and closed his hand partway. His voice was full of wonder. "I can't see anything, but I feel something."

"I think that's a good first step," Charles said.

Martin smiled. Charles hadn't seen him smile very often.

Charles needed to focus his attention on one thing so he concentrated on Martin's smile. He ignored the voices, the faces, the urgent conversations. He wasn't trying to do a magic trick or transport them anywhere, not yet. He just needed some silence. He shut everything else out of his brain and watched Martin. I'm a sharpshooter, he told himself, zeroing in on a target. He was an osprey soaring over a silver river seeing only a single salmon streaking through the water like a shadowy torpedo.

Gradually the voices faded. The urgency dissipated from the strange chorus. It was working! He kept his attention on Martin and finally the dark cemetery was populated only by the small group he'd summoned in the first place: Martin, Just Murphy, Jim Baker and the two outlaws. Plus, of course, Mr. Peters over whom he had no control. Mr. Peters stood beside Martin, holding his hand. A peaceful smile covered his face like a mask, a perfect replica of the peaceful smile that Martin wore. Both of them stood with eyes closed, finding at least for the moment a refuge from their sadness.

Just Murphy stared at Charles. "You've got the gift," he said. "Baker's Shoshone wife had the gift too, but not so many others. Flying Fawn could quiet a whole battlefield."

Jim Baker suddenly seemed to be paying attention.

"I married a medicine woman with that name," he said.

"Yes, Jim," Murphy said, "I was just telling the little scout that she had powerful magic."

"Beautiful woman," Jim Baker said. "Better than I deserved."

"That's a true shot," Just Murphy said

The two outlaws stood between the two frontier riflemen, scowling and glancing around furtively, waiting for another chance to escape. Baker smiled at their discomfort as they calculated their odds. He had watched dozens of men calculate how far they'd have to run before they were safe. He turned and spoke to his friend, but his words were obviously for the outlaws' benefit.

"So, Just Murphy, what's the longest shot you ever hit?"

"You know, Jim, I don't rightly recollect. Don't keep track of that sort of foolishness." There was the trace of a smile on his face. He understood the game they played. "Well, I did hit that red-coat general from 400 yards. I kind of got famous for that one. They say it changed the whole dang war. But it took me a couple tries. His dad-blame horse wouldn't stand still. How about you, Jim?"

271

"Well, down at Kit Carson's big rendezvous, I hit a silver dollar from 100 yards."

"As I recall you didn't hit it dead center, though."

"Yeah, they called it a tie for first. I should have took my time. I always tell folks I took second place and it's my own fault, by gonny." Jim Baker said. "Course, I also tell them that you just got lucky."

The two outlaws seemed to abandon their plans to make a run for it.

"Why don't you just let us go?" Slim said. "We can't help you."

"We're going to let you go in just a minute," Charles said. "Where will Mr. Smith be tonight? If we wanted to talk to him?"

The outlaws smiled.

"Tonight he's going to be with about 300 of his best friends and associates. At a meeting of town-folk," Slim said. "It would be a great place for you to have a little conversation with him. We'd be happy to introduce you to him."

Jim Baker nodded. "Two of us against 300 the likes of you don't seem like favorable odds."

"So you're afraid of Mr. Smith," the Reverend said. "I don't blame you."

"Nah, " Jim Baker said. He spit out some tobacco. "I meant it ain't favorable odds for him."

"Tell me about this meeting place," Charles said. "How big a room will it be in?"

"What's it to you?"

"So you've never been there," Charles said.

"Sure I have. Been to a dozen meeting there. Mostly meetings to make gambling rules and drinking rules. Bunch of do-gooders."

"Does it have chairs?"

"Sure it does. Got some benches too"

"Wooden chairs?"

"What else would they be?"

"What does it smell like?"

"Smells like a bunch of stinking dad-blame gold-rush prospectors that ain't touched soap in two months."

"Can you picture the door Mr. Smith will use?"

"Only one door," he said. "He'll be dragging you and your buckskin simpletons out that door by your heels."

"I can't quite picture that," Charles said. "Can you Just Murphy?"

Murphy shook his head. "No sir," he said. "I think they're making up a story. They ain't ever seen no meeting hall. They don't even know what the door looks like. Little short on details if you ask me."

"It's a sturdy fir door, with a big iron latch," he said. "And three bullet holes from the last time somebody thought they'd regulate Mr. Smith. You want more details? OK. Above that door on the inside is the biggest rack of moose antlers you ever seen. Them antlers might be the last thing you see in this life when they drag you out of there. You take note of them early so you can proper appreciate them."

"Thank you," Charles said. "Although I'm still not sure you've ever been there."

"And a cedar board across the bottom as a door jam. That's gonna scratch your back up pretty good when you get drug over it. But you probably won't be feelin' nothing by them."

Charles' eyes were closed, he listened intently to the words as if they were a tennis ball he wanted to move, or a butterfly he wanted to capture. He pictured a rustic building of rough cut lumber and pine logs on a muddy street in a tiny frontier town. He imagined the smell of wood smoke and pipe tobacco and pine needles.

He could almost hear a chorus of loud, rough men shouting at each other, some angry, some drunk…

"What kind of name is Just Murphy?" Reverend said.

Charles shook his head, frustrated by the interruption. "It's as good a name as any," he snapped, opening his eyes. "You were telling us about a meeting hall in Alaska…" He stopped.

He was no longer at the cemetery in Colorado and it was no longer night. He stood in the middle of a rocky dirt street with small wooden buildings on each side. The sun was low over a hill. A late afternoon summer heat radiated up from the street. Neither Martin nor any of the others were with him. Pan wasn't there, either. He had traveled somewhere, he wasn't sure where, and he'd done it alone.

A crowd of rough-looking men surged past him. A burly man wearing rough, smelly clothes bumped into Charles so hard he nearly fell.

"Get moving or get off the street, you little saphead before I slick you good!!" the man shouted. "I got a meetin' to attend! You hear me?" The man grabbed Charles by the collar of his shirt and lifted him off the ground. The man was clearly drunk. He stared at the boy for a moment and then grinned. "Well, I reckon we got time to find out if you're a soft-horn or a snuffy after all."

Charles tried to get free. He looked around frantically for Jim Baker and Just Murphy.

But they weren't there. And a large man was dragging him off the dirt street and to a dark alley between two buildings.

Chapter 41

Charles struggled and yelled as the man dragged him into the alleyway. The crowd was so noisy he could scarcely hear his own voice. If the others were nearby, there wasn't much chance they heard him.

"You squeal like a chuck-wagon chicken!" the man said with a laugh. "Like a bushwhacker that's got the hemp fever. Well, there's only one cure for the hemp fever."

The man put both hands around Charle's neck and lifted him off the ground. "Don't need a rope for a little creepmouse like you. Anyways, this is more fun." The man started to squeeze Charle's neck.

"That hurts!" Charles tried to yell, but no sound came out. He couldn't inhale, he couldn't exhale. Gradually everything became foggy and dark. The noisy crowd faded away. This is just a dream, he thought. No point in struggling. The light faded as if a movie was about to start and management was dimming the house lights. It's only a dream.

Now the colors were bright, the sounds clear; even the smells seemed vivid. Charles stood in a park near a playground with slides and swings and wooden structures to climb. Many kids were sliding, swinging, chasing each other, screaming and laughing. Several mothers stood at the edge of the area chatting with each other, laughing and trading gossip, but with one eye always on their child. Safety was very important and they didn't want anything bad to happen to their children. Not here. Not in this lovely park. A few wooden benches faced the playground.

An old man sat alone on one of the benches. He looked a little like Charles' father, only older. No, not his father. Some relative, but no one he knew, maybe an uncle he'd met when he was an infant. Thin white hair, windblown and messy, touched the man's shirt collar. He wore jeans and sneakers and a heavy blue long-sleeved shirt. In one hand he held a brown paper sack. Every few minutes he reached in, took out a handful of something and threw it on the grass. Curious, Charles moved closer.

Five chickens crowded around the man's feet. They were intrigued by what he threw out, but careful to remain at a distance until their little poultry-brains decided it was safe. The chickens were brightly colored, brown and white, and red with splashes of green and blue. Charles had never seen such extravagantly-colored chickens. The man threw out a handful of food, they clucked busily and scrambled to peck each morsel from the grass, then scurried back to a safer distance again.

Chickens don't run wild in parks, so the scene seemed incongruous but not impossible. In a moment the man looked up and nodded at Charles. His eyes were kind, with the wrinkles around the edges that people earn by daily smiling.

"What are you feeding them?" Charles asked.

The man smiled and the wrinkles near his eyes deepened. "You're not a park ranger are you?" he asked. "Checking to make sure I'm using approved feed?"

He was obviously teasing, so Charles smiled back at him.

"No, sir. Just a curious scientist."

The man looked at Charles more carefully when he said that. Then he turned away and studied the sky, as if searching for some dim lighthouse whose faint pulse of light could not reach Charles's eyes. Then he turned back to the birds.

"Meal worms," he answered. "Someone lost their pet flock. At least that's what I think. These birds usually eat whatever's in their food bowl. Probably safe and nutritious. But on their own they'll eat sticks and pebbles and whatever potato chip a kid drops until they bloat and die. So I feed them meal worms."

"For the protein," Charles said.

The man smiled and nodded.

"So you *are* a scientist," he said. "Yeah, protein and vitamins. These chickens won't survive long out here on their own. Too many dogs and cats and raccoons. But for today at least, they won't be hungry."

"They don't seem very smart, do they?" Charles said.

"They're smarter than you think," the man said. "It wasn't their brains that got bred out of them, it was their common sense. That's why they do dumb stuff." Each bird ran quickly toward a treat a few feet away, then froze in place, only its head pivoting from side to side, tilted at an angle to see the morsel more clearly. Then it pecked quickly and savagely like a dinosaur attacking an unlucky primitive mammal. They acted like Saturday morning cartoon animals. "But we can learn things from chickens," he said. "From any animal, really." He paused. "Even goats."

Charles pulled back, startled. Pan wasn't around. Charles hadn't said anything about goats. .

"Why do you mention goats?" he asked nervously.

"You remind me of someone I knew a very long time ago. Don't analyze it too much. The most precise analogy can fail in many disastrous ways."

Charles didn't understand what he meant but he didn't argue.

"So what do we learn from chickens?" Charles asked.

"You're asking what I learn from chickens," the man said. "I think the question is what do *you* learn from chickens?"

"I learn that they'd be a lot safer from raccoons if they stay in their pen."

The man laughed. "True, very true. But they'd miss out on some fancy pet-store meal worms."

"Yeah, I think I'd be OK missing out on the worms."

The man smiled and nodded. One of the chickens ran a little farther away, lured by a ladybug on a blade of grass. A bit of dandelion fluff skimmed across the lawn like Tinkerbell.

"I wonder if their owners are sad?" Charles said.

The man thought for a moment before answering.

"Yes, of course they are. But they aren't really 'owners' are they? The chickens and humans have a role in each other's lives for a certain time."

Charles nodded. "Semantics," he said quietly.

The man threw another handful of mealworms. "Anyway, even if they wandered they aren't really 'gone' are they?" he said. "They're right here."

Charles thought about that. Knowing the birds were loose in a city park wouldn't make the owners feel much better.

"They'd still be sad," Charles said.

"Yes, certainly sad," the man agreed. "But look." He motioned to the birds, who thought he was throwing more food and clustered closer. "They're right here. Just like you are. Just like I am."

"I'm right here," he repeated.

The roar of a gunshot awoke Charles.

Chapter 42

Charles fell to the ground, gasping for breath, the lovely park fading away. The gunshot still rang in his ears. It took a minute for his eyes to focus again.

He lay in an alley between two wooden buildings. The man who tried to strangle him lay dead on the ground, face down, blood seeping from a gaping hole in the back of his head. More blood and bits of bone spread from the dirt beneath his face. Just Murphy and Jim Baker stood over him. Wisps of blue smoke rose from Jim Baker's rifle. Martin and Mr. Peters stood behind them, eyes closed, still holding hands, still smiling like statues of saints.

"You okay, little scout?" Jim Baker asked calmly in his deep voice.

"I… I think so," Charles managed to sit up.

"Hope I didn't get any of that old lag's brain juice on your shirt."

"He tried to kill me," Charles said, staring at the lifeless body at his feet.

"Yeah, we noticed that too," Jim Baker said. "Hey Murphy, do we need to haul this carcass down to the bone orchard?"

Just Murphy shook his head. "If he's got friends, they'll probably be more than delighted to handle that chore. Besides, I ain't in a mood to answer many questions. How about you?"

"Let's ease back onto the street and find what we come for."

"Where are the outlaws?" Charles asked.

"They disappeared like smoke when we got to this street," Just Murphy said.

"Doesn't matter," Charles said. "I think they got us to the right place."

They stepped out onto the dirt street and stood near the building. Charles's knees shook, so he leaned against the wall for a moment. Pan found a scraggly weed and chewed it contentedly. Murphy's dog Flint stood beside its master, wagging its tail.

Jim Baker took a deep breath. "I can smell the trees," he said. "And I smell a fresh-water creek. There's beaver in them hills!"

"And rats in this town," Just Murphy said.

Several small groups of men argued on the street, all dressed in rough clothing, all very agitated. No one paid any attention to the newcomers.

"That new guy, Stewart? They flat stole his gold dust," one man said loudly. "Claiming it was a fair game don't hold no water."

"Behind Smith's Parlor? Never been a fair game within a half mile of that saloon!"

"Sheriff Taylor ought to arrest them!"

"And risk his pay? Smith pays him more than the government does!"

"Maybe the Committee can do something."

"Yeah. They'll hold a dad-blame meeting. Smith's boys don't care much about meetings."

"Well, maybe if all of us show up."

"We'll show up all right. Goin' there now. But the Cabrónes will show up too, and better armed than miners."

All the men were drifting in the same direction up the street and all the talk was the same: Some fellow named Stewart came into town with gold dust from his claim. Smith's men lured him into a game of Three Card Monte and got all his gold. Most of the townsfolk said it was a swindle, a few disagreed. Apparently this happened frequently and the town was fed up. Most believed this Mr. Smith had to go.

"Feels good to be in beaver country again," Jim Baker said.

"Is this where my family is?" Martin said.

"I think so," Charles said. "Looks like a small town. Shouldn't take long to find them."

Mr. Peters looked around. "It's so quiet," he whispered. "So very quiet."

Maybe this vast but sparsely populated area harbored fewer ghosts. Fewer memories to haunt a stranger.

"So Jim, where do we start?" Charles asked.

Jim Baker looked around at the buildings, the people milling around, the bright blue cloudless sky. He inhaled deeply as if trying to catch a scent, suddenly more alert. He inhaled again, holding his head up in the air to catch a higher breeze. Suddenly, he looked confused. "By gonny, I don't know," he said. "That's a new one on me. My landmarks are all knocked away," he said. "Don't know where I am, don't know where I come from, don't know where I'm going." He swiveled his head from side to side, trying to catch his bearings..

Just Murphy touched his shoulder.

"It don't matter, Jim," he said. "You're a trapper and a scout and the second best shot in the country. We're just out huntin' varmints like we done when we was young. Ain't a better scout in the world than you. Kid's lucky you're here."

Jim Baker nodded and relaxed a little.

"People all seem heading one direction," he said. "Might make sense to throw a line in the pool that has the most fish."

They started walking uphill with everyone else. Martin held Pan's rope in one hand and continued to hold Mr. Peters's hand with the other. They followed Jim Baker who walked slowly but firmly in the lead. His quick catlike eyes darted back and forth, searching for clues, for signs, for danger. He sniffed the air in quick bursts like a dog hunting for hidden food. He was scouting, tracking prey, listening for the crack of a distant twig.

Just Murphy trailed them all by several paces, his long rifle leaning against one shoulder. He too was in a familiar role: soldier, sharp-shooter, protector. His shoulders rolled from side to side with confidence as he walked. He held his rifle casually, like a fashion accessory, no more important than a cap or belt, but his right hand stayed near the trigger. Eunice could sweep down in an instant, suddenly aimed at a target too distant for any other man on that street to see.

The crowd congregated in front of a larger wooden building. A painted sign above the door said "Sylvester Hall." Being short, Charles saw more rough leather coats, denim shirts, and thick brass belt buckles than faces. Many men wore holsters with handguns. Jim Baker and Just Murphy looked completely calm. They were well-armed too, and much more experienced than the miners and shop keepers in this crowd. Charles exhaled.

The little group of time travelers moved with the crowd and were jostled and prodded through the big wooden door. A rough cedar board served as a door jam, just as Slim had described.

A few men stood near a small stage at the front of the room. The townspeople crowded toward the front and center of the room. Charles and Martin climbed onto a crude wooden bench against a wall and stood on it. Pan hopped up between them.

Near the stage, Frank Whiting engaged four other men in urgent conversation.

"Do you see him?" Martin said happily, pointing at his father.

"Yes I do," Charles said.

"Well, there's a surprise," Just Murphy said.

"What's that?" Charles asked.

"That guy next to him. That's Tom Whitten. I know him from Denver."

"Don't look familiar to me," Jim Baker said.

"He's a good man," Just Murphy said. More men crowded into the room. "I think I smell an ambush," he said. "How about you, Jim?"

Jim Baker's eyes moved quickly from face to face.

"There's some coyote-mean in the air and some scalp-hunting crazy," he said, as if treachery was something you could smell, like smoke from a distant fire or a rainstorm moving across the prairie toward a dry camp. "What's the play?"

"You stay here with the civilians," Just Murphy said. "I'll go up there and ask Tom what's what."

Jim Baker nodded. Murphy eased his way through the crowd. A path opened for the tall, muscular woodsman in buckskin clothes.

"I want to go up by my father," Martin said.

"I know you do," Charles said. "But it looks like he's part of the meeting. Let's wait til he's finished with his business. He's going to be surprised to see you."

"Yeah," Martin said. "If he can see me. I wish that sickness hadn't made me invisible."

At the front of the room, Tom Whitten stepped up onto the little platform and the room got quiet. Murphy stopped near the front row.

"Tom Whitten," Just Murphy said loudly. He raised one arm in the air. "Tom!" he repeated.

Tom Whitten stared at Just Murphy in confusion. Then his face brightened with recognition.

"Ice-Box Murphy!" he said. "You're about the last person I expected to see here."

"I got tired of first names," Murphy said. "Now people call me 'Just Murphy.' I got here today, hopin' to work with Mr. Whiting there on that White Pass Railway. What's going on?"

A man in the crowd yelled out, "Do-Gooders! That's what this is about!" A few other men hooted in loud agreement.

"Shut up," someone yelled. "We didn't invite you rats into the pantry!"

Tom Whitten held up his hand. "OK, OK. Quiet everyone! I tell you, Murphy, what this is about. Our town's got an infestation of con-men and thieves and we've had enough! This meeting is where we figure out what to do."

A man near the door yelled out, "Talk louder! We can't hear you back here and there's fifty men outside trying to listen too!"

"Ain't no law against being a businessman!" someone shouted. There were more hoots of approval and also more boos. A few men shoved each other. More than one put his hand down by his gun, getting ready.

"Stealin' gold dust ain't being a businessman!"

More men argued loudly with each other.

"Quiet!" Tom Whitten shouted and for a moment the room calmed again. "See, Murphy, we got some differences about the law. There's this group of... businessmen associated with a gentleman named Jefferson Smith. Their idea of a fair profit is whatever ain't locked up good enough. And Sheriff Taylor tends to see things Mr. Smith's way. Especially since he developed more refined taste in clothes and horses and women."

There was more angry yelling, fists were raised into the air.

"Man's got a right!" a man yelled. "All you got is lying accusers. Can't shut down a man's business for made-up lies against him!"

"Quiet!" Tom Whitten yelled again. "Quiet, I say!" but the men in the room ignored him.

Just Murphy stepped forward to stand beside him and turned to face the room. The arguments continued and got louder. Just Murphy held his rifle with both hands and surveyed the crowd. Then he raised the long gun into a shooting position with the butt against his shoulder and aimed at a spot above the door. A few men in front stopped talking, watching him. Murphy sighted along the barrel for less than a second and pulled the trigger.

A flash of fire shot out the end of the barrel and the boom of the old rifle startled every man in the room. Most ducked low instinctively, many shouted in surprise or terror before going silent. A few started to reach for their own handguns but thought better of it.

The moose antlers above the front door fell directly onto the men closest to the door. Its sharp corners cut into their shoulders and they cried out, more from surprise than pain. The weight of the mighty rack was spread over six or seven men but it got everyone's attention. The now-silent crowd watched as the men wrestled the big trophy off of them. Then they turned back to the front of the room, stunned.

Just Murphy leaned the rifle barrel back up against his shoulder and his face moved almost imperceptibly in the direction of a smile.

"How did you...?" said Whitten.

"Easy shot," Just Murphy said with a shrug. "Once I seen it was only hung up there with one nail. It was like a shiny little target." He spoke at a normal, conversational volume. Then he stepped back off the little stage to stand behind Tom Whitten. He watched the crowd with an intensity that made Charles shiver.

"I can see we got to postpone the meeting," Tom Whitten said. "Citizen's Committee will meet again tonight at nine o clock. This time we'll meet down on Juneau Wharf where it's a little easier to regulate attendance. I need five or six men to guard the approach to the deck in order that no objectionable characters might be admitted to disturb the deliberations of the meeting. Anyone wanting to attend must walk down that pier to get there."

He pointed at the first row. "You two, Tanner and Landers," he said. "You willing to stand guard? Make sure no ruffians or charlatans gain access?"

"Yes sir," Tanner said. Landers nodded.

Tom Whitten pointed to the man next to him. "Frank Reid, you be in charge of the guarding, all right? Frank Whiting, will you help him out? But we'll want you next to me once the meeting starts."

"Yes sir, happy to help," Martin's father said. "Graves and I have a load of iron rails to get unloaded. I'll get that started and then help the guards until the meeting gets underway."

Just Murphy took a step forward. "I ain't got no part of your quarrel," he said. "But I do enjoy negotiating with bushwhackers and claim jumpers." He smiled and patted his rifle. "I got a friend by the wall there who might also enjoy doing some honest work for a change. A red-headed Shoshone trapper."

Jim Baker smiled and patted his own long rifle.

"Can he shoot?" Whitten asked.

"I believe he's startin' to get the hang of it," said Just Murphy. "He ain't bad on the short-range stuff."

"All right then," Tom Whitten said. "All you members of the Citizens Committee go on home and get some dinner. We'll meet at the wharf at nine o'clock. The rest of you just go home and go to sleep. Or go over to Smith's Parlor and get drunk like usual. But be warned: we're going to lay a chain across the pier and anybody tries to cross it that don't belong is going to get stopped. That chain will be your dead-line if Frank Reid or Just Murphy don't think you belong there."

The crowd murmured, some in agreement, some in anger.

"It was a fair game!" someone shouted. "Sheriff Taylor even said so!"

Other men grunted and hooted dismissively.

"Taylor's Smith's milk-fed puppy," someone yelled.

"The law's the law and that's the Sheriff!" People started to leave.

"Father!" Martin yelled, but Mr. Whiting did not respond. "Father!" he yelled even louder. Mr. Whiting just turned and walked out of the room. Martin looked dejected. "He can't hear me," he said. "My father can't hear me or see me. Why can't he see me?"

"There's a lot of commotion," Charles said. "Let's go to the wharf tonight. Maybe it will be different."

Martin didn't say anything.

"Should we try to get there early?" Charles asked as they walked down the street.

Jim Baker shrugged. "Just Murphy don't need us to set out trivets and doilies."

A few minutes before nine, they stood on a gravel shore next to a bay. Small fishing boats bobbed in the water. Hastily built sheds and bulky metal equipment in various shades of rust were strewn randomly. A wooden sign said "State Street" in crudely painted letters.

The cool, moist air smelled of salt and seaweed. Gentle waves lapped against the rocky shore and glowed with little white caps in the dreamy half-light of the cloudy moon.

Jim Baker inhaled deeply.

"There's salmon in that water," he said. "Don't remember the last time I ate salmon."

"How will they set up security?" Charles asked quickly. He did not want the old scout conjuring some random vivid memory right now.

"They pretty much explained it at the meeting," Baker said. "Smart thinking, for town folk. They'll have their meeting out on the wharf, where they load and unload boats. To get there, you got to walk down that narrow pier right there. Can't go more than two or three at a time. They'll post the guards just a little way down the pier."

"He said something about a deadline?"

"Probably just stretch a chain across the pier," Jim Baker said. "Easy to step over. But if you ain't supposed to step over it and you do, it's your own dad-blame fault if you get shot."

"So it's literally a 'dead line?'" Charles asked.

"It ain't a confusing name."

Fifty feet down the pier, Just Murphy and Frank Reid stretched a metal chain about a foot above the plankway. A child could step over, it was only a symbolic barrier.

"Where do you want me, boss?" Jim Baker yelled.

Just Murphy thought for a minute, then yelled back. "Might make some sense to have backup right about where you are now, on the beach." He paused, nodded, then amended his statement with a completely emotionless expression on his face. "If you think you could hit a cow from that distance, should one try to cross the chain."

"Fair point," Baker said. "Why don't you hold up a silver dollar and let me take a couple of warm-up shots?"

Both men smiled and nodded.

Baker looked around. "We're a little too open right here. Next to that little shack might not be bad," he said. "Good cover, but I'd still have a clear shot if need be." He looked at Charles. "Which ain't likely," he said. "Murphy's got a way of catching folks' attention. Somebody'd have to be saloon-rat drunk and badger-crazy to try to get past him."

The shed hid them on the left, a bright red nine-bark bush hid them on the right, but they had an unobstructed view of the pier straight ahead.

"You gentlemen make yourselves comfortable," Jim Baker said. "But stay hid. This town's got gold dust and whiskey. I'd prefer it was just grizzly bears and Apaches."

Martin and Charles sat on the dirt and leaned back against the rough wood of the shed. Mr. Peters, dazed by the quiet surroundings, finally sat down too.

Jim Baker kneeled and supported his rifle on one knee, aiming toward the pier.

"Not much challenge from this close," he said.

"You're not going to kill somebody, are you?" Charles asked.

"Probably not," Baker said calmly. "Shouldn't have to. A little flesh wound ought to discourage them just fine. Never heard of a meeting so interesting folks was willing to get shot for it. City folks is crazy."

Once they settled in place, mosquitoes and gnats descended on them like tiny demons. Squadrons of flying insects stung their hands and faces, especially near their eyes. Charles swatted at them but it did no good. He had not anticipated this new torment of buzzing pestilence.

"It's father!" Martin said quietly, pointing across the gravel toward another pier. Mr. Whiting marched toward the pier like a soldier.

"Quiet," Charles said to Martin, but the younger boy was too excited. He stood up and waved his arms wildly.

"Father! Over here! It's me, Martin!"

Martin's father did not react.

Mr. Whiting walked up to Tanner and the others.

"Graves and I were unloading cargo," Mr. Whiting said. "Smith passed by us like a tornado. He was armed and drunk and in a foul mood. Graves thinks he's bluffing; I think he's collecting his men. Prepare for the worst."

Tanner responded quietly. "We are unarmed except for our righteousness."

Mr. Whiting shook his head. "That's unfortunate," he said. "I believe in righteousness, but even Moses carried a staff."

"Reid has a handgun," Tanner said.

Frank Whiting joined Frank Reid and Just Murphy near the chain stretched across the pier. Whiting wore a bell about the size of a fist suspended by a leather strap around his neck. From a distance, it looked just like the bell Charles had found, the bell Sapania wanted. Instinctively, Charles reached up to touch it hanging around his neck and was startled to realize it wasn't there. He must have forgotten it this one time.

People started to congregate near the pier; a few ventured out onto it. Tanner and Landers stood on the gravel area where the pier was anchored to land and nodded to the familiar faces as they went past.

Sixty-eight men trudged down the pier toward the meeting, two dozen others loitered on the gravel shore, talking quietly, smoking pipes and cigars, glancing toward the water and the wharf but keeping their distance and waiting. Small groups huddled farther away at the edges of the gravel, like raccoons at the edge of a street lamp's light.

"Keep your eye on them varmints over there," Jim Baker gestured with his rifle. Charles looked in that direction. "And there's Soapy."

Jefferson Smith, the soap salesman walked toward them with a confident but tipsy swagger. He wore a dark suit and a white hat with a broad round brim. Behind Smith, Reverend and Slim walked side by side. As they walked toward the pier, small groups of men fell in behind them until it looked like an army following a general. As they passed from shadow to moonlight a quick glint of light reflected on rifle barrels and pistols.

The mob of drunk men stumbled and jostled with each other. Tanner yelled out from the pier, "Jefferson Smith, you're heading the wrong direction unless you're looking for trouble."

Smith raised his left fist in the air and yelled, "By God, trouble is exactly what I'm looking for!" and increased his pace. He carried a rifle leaned up against his right shoulder the way Murphy had earlier.

Tanner yelled over his shoulder. "Frank Reid! We got some party crashers out here."

"He's going to hurt father!" Martin whispered.

"Shh!" Charles said, and put his hand on Martin's arm to calm him.

When Smith reached the first two guards, he turned to the men following him and held up his hand.

"You boys wait here," he said. "I'll go in and explain what's what. If these do-gooders understand their whole precious town could get burned down and not just Whiting's place, maybe they'll get some common sense."

"Whiting!" Martin whispered. "That's my family!"

"Shh," Charles said and gripped the boy's forearm more tightly.

"Reverend and Slim, you come along with me. You can be my attorneys." The two men smirked and fell in beside him.

"I need a little better angle," Jim Baker whispered. "Too many drunks in my sight-line. You fellers stay hid here." He strode away from their hiding place and knelt behind a huge rusty pump fifty feet to their left

Martin stood up and started to walk toward the water, oblivious to the danger. Mr. Peters leaned against the shed. He looked like he was sleeping contentedly for the first time in his life

"Get back here!" Charles whispered as loudly as he could. "We're supposed to stay by this shed!" Martin stood out in the open, watching the pier, Pan's rope in one hand. He was completely vulnerable if anyone could see him.

But Charles was no longer looking at the pier or watching Martin. Farther down the gravel beach, beyond the crowd of men, a movement caught his eye. The moon lit the water brightly. A thin brown horse walked out of the water, drops of water glistening on its belly and legs. A woman with long black hair sat astride the horse. Her face was painted in streaks of white and red. She sniffed the air, cocked her head to one side, then pointed directly at Martin and nudged the horse. The horse stumbled a bit then walked slowly forward. The milling mob paid no attention to the woman. Each time she approached a group of men, they stepped aside to let her pass, but none gave any hint they could see her. The path opened before her as if by sheer coincidence. She ignored the men as they ignored her.

"Martin, get down!" Charles whispered as loudly as he dared. The surly mob shuffled and stumbled toward the pier, many brandishing guns and knives. Martin stood upright, staring intently at the pier while Sapania rode toward him at a leisurely pace.

"Mr. Baker!" Charles called out as loudly as he dared. He didn't want the gang of men to notice him, but he sure didn't want to have to face Sapania alone. "Mr. Baker!" he said, even louder. But Jim Baker was concentrating on the conflict developing on the pier. Charles looked around frantically for something to use as a weapon or a shield. Sapania ignored him and rode toward Martin.

"You are the soldier's son," she said, notching an arrow onto her bow. "I've been looking for you for a long time."

"Who are you?" Martin asked. His voice quivered.

Charles stood up. He was about twenty feet away from Martin. "No," he shouted. His knees shook and his voice wavered. "You have him confused with someone else. This boy has done nothing to you."

Sapania spun to stare at Charles and sniffed the air.

"And you! I know you! You took my bell! And now my magic Flatpipe is dead! Instead, I ride this crowbait! It is fit only to be stew, not a manitou. You will both pay! When I take my bell from you I shall call a new manitou. I'll leave this one for the buzzards and coyotes. Right beside you two."

Charles noted the irony of one ghost threatening to kill another ghost. "Or two hallucinations, for that matter," he said beneath his breath.

"What did you say? Did you speak to me?" Sapania screeched.

The intensity of her voice sparked a new emotion within Charles. Suddenly he was no longer afraid. Now he was simply angry.

"Go back where you came from!" Charles shouted.

The woman smiled. "Or what? You will challenge me to combat? That would be a story to tell the old women. A very short story."

"I won't let you hurt him!"

"Your father's army couldn't stop me," she smirked. "I'll deal with the little one first, so you can watch, and then you." By now she was only a few

291

paces from Martin. Her arrow was aimed at his chest, and she let it fly. It flew straight and true.

"No!" Charles yelled, raising both hands, palms forward as if pushing something away.

Before the arrow reached Martin, it stopped in mid-flight as if it ran into an invisible wall, then fell harmlessly to the ground. Sapania stared at the arrow on the gravel. Then she shook her head angrily. "The manitou of the desert will eat your tongue," she screamed. "And I shall add your ears to my necklace!" She notched another arrow.

Charles was stunned for a moment. "I think I'm beginning to understand," he said to himself. The way he'd focused both his brain and his emotion on the one single thought, the way he'd pictured the arrow stopping and falling—it was the same process he'd used to move a tennis ball, or convince a fly to land, but with much more force, much more focus. He'd always thought that magic was hard, but this was no harder for him than for a salmon to swim upstream. It was built into him. It just required his complete attention and a sort of relaxation. "I can do this," he said quietly.

Sapania launched another arrow directly at Martin. This time Charles raised only one hand. Again the arrow seemed to hit an invisible wall and tumbled to the ground. Charles nodded. Martin looked confused. Sapania's face contorted with rage.

On the pier, Frank Whiting jogged toward the deadline chain and the bell around his neck jingled. Sapania whipped around to face the sound. "My bell!" she whispered. Charles and Martin forgotten, she nudged the horse with her knees and kicked it with her heels. Startled, it lurched forward toward the pier.

"No!" Charles yelled. He raised both hands in the air and closed his eyes. Be calm, he told himself. Then, in a much quieter voice he said, "That's not where you want to go. Go the opposite direction, toward the cool green hills above the town. Go toward the beaver dams and salmon runs and the smell of pine woods. There will be lush grass for grazing and a cool breeze to chase away the flies. Go far from this place. Do not listen to the woman who kicks your sides."

The horse stopped. Sapania kicked it again, but it ignored her. Then, it turned around and galloped away from the water carrying a very angry Sapania. She tried to dismount, but the horse was going too fast and the ground too rocky. "Stop, you worthless buzzard bait!" she shouted. "I am the voice of the wind and I command you!" In a moment, horse and rider disappeared into the trees.

Charles ran to Martin. "You need to get back to the shed! You're too vulnerable out here in the open!"

"That man in the white hat wants to hurt father," Martin said. "And so does the scary woman."

"Well, we can't do much to help them. We should just stay out of the way. Jim Baker and Just Murphy are watching too."

Jefferson Smith walked up the narrow wooden pier toward Frank Reid who stood just behind the chain deadline. Whiting and Just Murphy stood a few paces further down the pier. Sapania had not yet reached the water and none of them noticed her.

"Jeff Smith, you been warned!" Frank Reid yelled. "That chain is a dead-line. Cross it and I'm gonna have to shoot you. That's just the way it is. You caused enough trouble in this town already. Don't make me do what I'd prefer not to do."

"You still carry that old 38?" Smith shouted as he continued to walk forward. "The one that jams about half the time? Since you only keep two bullets in it, then maybe you got one good shot. And you're nervous as hell. Now, my new Colt 1889—it's got 6 shots and it never jams. And I'm too drunk to be nervous. Them size 45 bullets stop a bull in its tracks. I'd wager a Morgan dollar your backup Whiting here, he never shot a gun in his life."

"You'd be wrong on that count. But civilized men have no need of firearms," Whiting said. "The committee will be happy to discuss the results of our deliberations with you tomorrow. In the sober light of day."

Smith laughed. "I hope to God I'm never as sober as you," he said, then he paused. When he spoke again his voice was hard and cold. "We done this once before, Whiting. Same pier, same moon, same deadline. Only that time you cheated, bringing that little kid and his goat to help you. You don't remember it, but I do."

"You are a crazy man for sure and certain."

"No, no. That kid got in my way and I couldn't get a clean shot. He wouldn't have shown up if that goat hadn't been magic. Well, this time I sent my boys to take care of the goat ahead of time. I don't see the brat here, do you?"

"I don't know what you're talking about!"

Smith laughed. "You will, soon enough. This time it ends different. And you there. It's 'Murphy' ain't it? You weren't here last time. I see your rifle's a little out of date, but I heard you could shoot. I could use another sharpshooter in my company. Why don't you just go on home tonight. Tomorrow you stop by Jeff Smith's Parlor and I'll sign you up. As a little hiring bonus, I'll give you a brand new Winchester just like this one on my shoulder. Some museum might give you a buck for that antique you're holding."

"I'm pretty happy with Eunice," Murphy said. "She kind of understands the way I shoot. But it's mighty kind of you to offer."

"This ain't your fight," Smith said.

"Well, I told my friend I'd help," Just Murphy said. "So that makes it my fight. Anyway, I already lived most of two good lives, so I ain't got a lot to lose."

"Suit yourself," Smith said. Reverend and Slim stood ten feet behind Smith, one on each edge of the floating walkway. They each held a hand-gun, inconspicuously down by their sides.

"I don't like this," Martin said. His face was fierce. "Those men need to get away from my father."

"I'm tired of people telling me what to do," Smith said. "Now I'm gonna do the telling. You men get the hell out of my way before I knock you out of the way!" He stepped up to the chain.

"Deadline chains is like laws," he said. "Just rules that do-gooders make up. I got as much right to be at that meeting any anybody else." Smith stepped over the chain.

"Not tonight you don't," Frank Reid said. He started to pull his handgun.

"We'll see about that," Smith said. The outlaw took two fast steps forward. Swinging his rifle like a club, he hit Reid on the side of his head. Reid staggered and fell; his gun clattered away on the wooden pier.

Mr. Whiting stepped between them. "Now see here!" he said. "That is the dark angel of your soul, not the benevolent one of Lincoln! There is no place for violence…"

Smith turned toward Mr. Whiting and raised the rifle to club him as well.

"No!" Martin yelled from the shore. "I'll help you father!"

Suddenly both Martin and Charles were on the pier between the two men. In the blink of an eye they had simply transported there. Pan stood beside Martin, completely unconcerned.

Smith held the rifle like a baseball bat, coiled far behind him for maximum power. He initiated a swing and shifted his weight to smash the rifle barrel down on Frank Whiting.

But he was not as quick as an eight-year-old ghost. Martin jumped up and took hold of the barrel and pulled. The rifle was already in motion and too late to stop, but Martin deflected it enough that it missed Mr. Whiting cleanly. Smith tried to raise it again, but Martin kept pulling on it. Smith instinctively pulled back.

All this activity roused Pan's interest and the goat leaped forward. As Martin and Smith each pulled on the gun, the little goat—whose forehead had grown two small nob-like horns— rammed its head into Smith's knees with surprising power. Startled, Smith lost his grip and staggered backward, falling hard on the wooden pier. His hat fell off, his rifle flew high into the air spinning end over end. When it landed, it bounced and fired with a roar and a flash of light. His inelegant fall made Smith angrier than ever. He crawled toward his rifle, but it had skidded away and he couldn't see it in the dim light. He stood up and scuffed his feet back and forth, looking for it.

Mr. Whiting smiled. "The Lord works in mysterious ways," he said. "And surely He walks with the righteous tonight. I can feel it."

Martin beamed at his father.

Frank Reid made a strange grunting sound. He stared down at his stomach where a red stain appeared on his shirt. "I been hit," he said. "When that rifle went off..." His eyes widened in disbelief, then his knees buckled and he fell down on the pier.

Whiting turned to Jeff Smith "You barbarian!" he yelled "Get off this dock immediately! This is attempted murder!"

Mr. Whiting knelt by Reid's side. He took off his own shirt and pressed it against the wound.

"I can't find my gun," Frank Reid told him in an urgent whisper. "You've got to find it for me."

"Don't worry about that now," Whiting said.

"Don't you get it? He's not going to let us live," Reid gasped. "I've got to find my gun before he finds his!"

"Here it is, sir," Charles said to Reid. Charles picked it up and handed it to the wounded man.

Reid stared at him. "How'd you get here?" he said. Then, without waiting for an answer, "This ain't no place for a kid."

Resting his elbow on the pier, Reid took a shot at Smith. But his hand shook and the bullet only grazed Smith's thigh. Smith stumbled and grabbed his leg. Slim and Reverend ran forward, guns raised. They stopped just behind Smith and spread their legs in a half-crouch shooter's stance. Holding their guns with two hands, they aimed at the men.

Two quick gunshots rang outs. But instead of the outlaws shooting the men on the pier, something much odder happened: their guns flew out of their hands with such velocity they leapt in the air and splashed down in the bay. Incredibly, Just Murphy had shot the gun right out of Slim's hand. Even more amazing: from fifty yards away, Jim Baker had shot the Reverend's gun out of his hand. Slim and the Reverend could not have been more surprised if lightning had struck their weapons. They looked at their empty, bleeding hands then turned and raced back to the shore. When they got to the gravel, they just kept running.

Smith quickly recovered his composure. He was drunk and angry but the pain in his leg snapped him alert. Suddenly calm, he smiled. He stopped looking for his rifle and pulled out his handgun. He walked back toward Frank Reid and Frank Whiting and spoke softly, "I'm gonna heal from this little wound. But you ain't gonna heal from this next one."

Reid raised his hand weakly and tried to get off one more shot, but his gun jammed.

Smith grinned. "That's unfortunate luck," he said. "And it's bad luck to be a witness, too," he said to Mr. Whiting. "The story about tonight ain't gonna include survivors." He aimed at Frank Reid.

Charles knew that antique flintlock rifles need to be reloaded after every shot; Murphy and Baker didn't have time to reload. Baker was too far away for a sure shot with his handgun. It would take several seconds for any of the men in the meeting to get there. Smith had more than enough time to finish off both men, as well as him and Martin. But he paused and played out a little drama for the crowd.

"Oh God, don't shoot!" Smith yelled in mock terror, as he aimed at Reid who was struggling at his feet, frantically trying to make his gun operational. Smith cupped a hand near his mouth, his words obviously intended for the audience on shore. In the dim light, they couldn't be sure of what was happening, but they could hear Smith's voice. "Frank Reid shot me! He intends to murder me!" he yelled. "Oh God, don't shoot!" He wanted every witness on the shore to think that whatever he did next was done in self defense.

Martin leapt up and stood bravely between the gun and his father, trying to use his body as a shield. Charles admired the child's bravery, but someone most people can't see probably wouldn't have any effect at all on a bullet.

Charles had one idea, too silly to try. But it was the only thing he could think of in less than a heartbeat. He closed his eyes.

"What the…" Smith paused and waved his hand across his face, trying to dispel the cloud of insects that had suddenly discovered him. He only waved for a few seconds and then the insects vanished.

Then Just Murphy spoke in his deep, calm voice. "You stop right there and drop the gun," he said slowly. "Or else you can choose my next shot. Left eye, right eye, or heart."

Soapy smiled and reached up to tug at the brim of his hat, as he had done dozens of times before when he felt trapped, the hat that let him move just far enough away to escape. But it was not on his head. The smile melted from his face. He looked around frantically, but the hat that was his secret weapon was no longer by his feet. He caught a glimpse of it ten feet away. A small white goat with one brown ear was chewing on the brim. Soapy took a step toward it. "Give me that!" he yelled, and the goat turned and trotted away down the pier. After a dozen steps it stopped, turned, and continued to eat the hat.

"I'll deal with you right after…" Smith said, turning and aiming his gun at Just Murphy. Murphy's rifle shot interrupted him.

"Shooter's choice then," Murphy said. "Heart it is."

Smith jerked backward and fell motionless, a gaping red hole in his chest

Just Murphy walked up and stood over him. "Folks who know I got an old rifle always forget mine's got that second barrel."

"They killed the boss!" a man on the shore shouted as he ran down the pier toward them. He had a pistol in one hand and was aiming it toward Frank Reid and the others. He sounded hysterical.

"Yeah, and they'll probably kill you too," a man far behind him responded loudly. The crowd laughed.

"You murdered him! An eye for an eye!" The man stopped, his pistol aimed right at Frank Whiting. "And now you'll pay!"

A gunshot interrupted the man and he lurched forward, blood spreading from the back of his shirt. He tried to catch his balance, then his legs gave out and he stumbled and fell off the pier into the bay. He was dead when he hit the water. The splash of the body seemed to wake the crowd and the angry yelling subsided

Charles looked around in confusion. Neither Jim Baker nor Just Murphy had had time to reload. Back on the gravel beach, a thin old man in a white linen suit waved.

"I heard Mr. Lincoln's name," John Burns shouted. There was a big smile on his face. "That's all I needed." He continued to smile and wave but, like an ember in a campfire expiring, very gradually he simply faded away.

"There's a price to pay," Just Murphy said softly. "For all of us. He just ran out of stories. Goodbye, John."

Jim Baker still knelt beside the rusty equipment, but he looked unsteady. He leaned against the equipment and his rifle nearly slipped from his grasp. Just Murphy's voice was subdued when he spoke again. "I think my old friend needs me to be with him. He might be runnin' short of stories, too."

Frank Whiting nodded, "Thank you for your help tonight. And thank Mr. Baker as well." They shook hands and Just Murphy walked down the pier toward land.

Whiting turned to Charles. "You never explained what you're doing here."

"I guess I followed my imagination," Charles said.

"Imagination is a strong if unpredictable horse to ride. You're lucky no harm befell you."

"Father!" Martin shouted. "Can you see me yet? Can you hear me?"

Mr. Whiting did not respond. Martin looked down sadly at his own feet.

"It's OK," Martin said bravely to Charles, though his voice wavered. "I feel better now. Maybe I'm getting over this sickness and pretty soon I won't be invisible." He paused. "Charles, I'm glad you brought me here, even if he can't see me. At least I can see him again. When he goes home, I'll follow him and see my mother and my brothers and sisters, too. And when I get better, we'll all be together. So being here is better. But it's not fair that you aren't with your family too."

He held out Pan's rope.

"You take Pan. He can get you back to your family."

Charles took the rope.

"Just wait until we're not so close to each other or I'll come with you accidentally."

A sudden cold wind slapped Charles's cheek and he shivered. An Arctic cold front, he thought. A faint flash of distant lightning illuminated the scene for a brief flickering moment. In that moment, Charles saw Sapania walking up the pier toward them.

"It's the mean lady," Martin said,

"I won't let her hurt you."

"Who is that?" Frank Whiting asked.

"You can see her?"

"Of course I can see her. She looks like an indigenous medicine woman, but I'm not familiar with the trappings of her tribe."

"She is not a good person," Charles said. "And she wants your bell."

Frank Whiting touched the bell that hung around his neck. "Why would she want Martin's bell?"

"I don't know," Charles said truthfully. "She thinks it has some magical power. It doesn't make sense to me."

"Well, I shant give her a keepsake of my son. Surely she will understand that."

"No," Charles said. "I don't think she will."

Sapania raised her arms and pointed both of them at Charles and the others. In a loud, almost operatic voice, she yelled at them as she continued to approach.

"Wind of the North!" she screamed. "Strike my enemies like knives! Tear at their skin and twist their arms and legs Black water of the abyss— swell and crush over them!"

As she said that, the wind increased and the water in the bay rolled like an angry beast. A wave lifted and hammered down on the pier, sending it rocking.

"She is a charlatan," Frank Whiting said. "A wind blows and she wants credit for the storm. It is the first trick of every imposter."

"Yes," Charles said. "That's certainly part of it. I don't know if she has magical powers. But she has a long and brutal knife and she takes pleasure in pain."

"She certainly does look menacing," Frank Whiting agreed. "I shall go speak with her."

"No," Charles said firmly "This is something I need to do."

"Don't be foolish! You're a mere child." Mr. Whiting began to walk toward Sapania.

"Stop!" Charles said, holding up his hands the way he'd stopped the arrows. Mr. Whiting froze in his tracks, stunned surprise on his face. The wind now whipped around them. The pier swayed from side to side. Icy rain lashed their faces, driven by the wind.

"I shall have what I desire!" Sapania shouted. "Revenge for Flatpipe and She Who Walks! The gods of the desert shall strike my enemies!"

At precisely the instant she said that, a lightning bolt struck a tall fir tree at the edge of the water, illuminating the scene as if in daylight. Thunder shook the air. The tree cracked and split and began to burn. Suddenly the air was full of the smell of ozone and woodsmoke as the storm beat down around them.

"She certainly has a flair for timing," Whiting shouted over the wind. "And a remarkable way with words. I must insist you let me handle this."

But Charles had already started walking toward her. "Martin, you hold Pan until I get back. Just stay close to your father." Martin took the rope from him.

"Who are you talking to?" Mr. Whiting said.

Charles ignored him. "She's not the only one who knows fancy words," he muttered. By now, Sapania stood only a dozen feet away.

"Give me the bell and your deaths will be quick!" she yelled.

"Lebistes reticulatus!" Charles shouted back, and took a step toward her. It was the only Latin that came into his brain: the scientific name for guppies, but he pronounced it as forcefully as if it summoned the dogs of Hell. "Lepidoptera! Coleoptera!" He tried to make the Latin names for butterflies and beetles sound dark and menacing.

301

For a moment she looked surprised, unsure. Then the arrogance returned to her face. She pulled the long knife from her belt.

"I will not give the gods of the sky and water this pleasure," she said. "I want to feel the blade as it slices through your flesh like dog meat. To relish the death shudder. To sing along with the music of your screams!"

"No!" Charles said firmly. "E pluribus unum! Non sequitur!" He pointed at her dramatically as if his index finger were a magic wand. He walked toward her purposefully, aggressively, as if he intended to punch her in the face. He wished he had a weapon of some sort, but the pier was clean and empty of debris. He tried to think of some way to escape if she continued her attack, but the pier was narrow and she was too close. He glanced into the churning black water. He could jump in and swim away, he realized. She wanted the bell more than she wanted him.

Martin stood near his father. Frank Whiting looked confused. Why was this crazy woman attacking the strange boy?

No, Charles realized. If he swam to safety, she would kill Martin's father and take the bell. Martin would be more alone than ever. Plus, if he swam to shore he might not be able to get close to Martin and Pan again. He would be marooned in frontier Alaska forever.

Sapania smiled and took another step toward him.

"Your knife is oily!" Charles shouted, "It is covered in buffalo fat! Can't you feel it sliding loose in your hand?"

"It will soon be slippery with your blood," she said. She lashed out, slashing sideways to cut Charles stomach. He jumped back and the blade cut his shirt but only grazed his skin. But now he was on the edge of the pier. His heels hung over the edge supported only by air. A wave came over his feet, soaking his shoes and he nearly lost his balance. The water was icy on his ankles. Sapania took another step toward him.

"The first cut is not to kill," she said. "It is only to give the blade a taste." Again she slashed sideways across his body. With no place to move, he ducked very low with the quickness and flexibility of an 11-year-old and the blade missed again, flashing above his head. He rolled away from the woman, away from Martin and Pan, toward the land. He stood up and Sapania turned to face him.

"The blade can get a deeper taste in many ways," she said. She raised it to the position she used when she threw it at the jackrabbit.

"Your blade is soaked in the fat of a cooked duck!" Charles shouted, pointing at her again. "It is too slippery for throwing!" He took a step backward. At the least maybe he could lead her away from Whiting and Martin. Even if he couldn't escape, maybe he could give Jim Baker or Just Murphy time to reload.

"It does not feel slippery to me," she said. With the same quick, practiced throwing motion she used the first time Charles saw her, her arm straightened as quick as a scorpion's tail.

But the knife did not fly toward Charles. It slipped from her grasp at the last instant and clattered on the wooden pier. Her eyes opened wide in amazement. Charles quickly retrieved the knife.

"I guess you were right," he said. He flipped the knife end over end a foot in the air and easily caught it by the handle. He'd practiced that trick after seeing a cowboy on TV do it. Then he raised it as if to throw it like she did. "It isn't slippery at all" He then took a step toward her "But it still thirsts for blood, even very cold blood like yours"

This time, Sapania took a step backward, holding her hands out as if to protect herself. But she'd lost track of where she stood on the pier and was right on the edge. She arched her back and waved her arms wildly, trying to regain her balance,

Charles walked right up to her, close enough to pull her to safety or push her over. He put the hand with the knife down by his side and raised his other hand. He pointed directly at her face.

"I am not afraid of you," he said. "But you need to learn some manners. The water is shallow enough here you can walk to shore, if you can't swim. But it won't be comfortable."

She continued to teeter. He pointed down at the cold black water. "Sic semper lamia!" he said. Then he said it again, with more authority and pointed commandingly. "Sic semper lamia!"

With her arms windmilling, she fell into the churning black water. After gasping and sputtering for a moment she began to swim to the shore. She no longer seemed frightening.

"You did it!" Martin shouted, running to his side. "What did you tell her?"

"I sort of made it up. I think it means 'thus always to evil witches'. We need to take her horse somewhere she can't find it. Maybe it's not a great manitou, but I'm tired of her chasing me around." Pan nuzzled Martin. A small piece of white hat protruded from his mouth. "Come on!"

The two boys ran to the shore and easily found Sapania's horse. It didn't have a saddle or reins, just a rope around its neck like Pan's. They led it to the rusty equipment where Jim Baker now lay prone. Just Murphy kneeled at his side. His dog, Flint, sat beside him.

"Is he...?" Charles asked.

"He don't have a manitou. Flint might get him home, but Jim's pretty weak. Can't really even talk." He sounded confused, trying to make sense of the situation.

"Listen," Charles said. "We need to get the woman's horse out of here. What if Mr. Baker held her rope? And you held on to Flint and pictured some memory?" Charles put the horse's rope into Baker's right hand and closed his fingers around it. The man's hand felt cold.

"It's worth a try, Maybe the two manitous together could carry someone in Jim's condition," Just Murphy said. He scratched Flint's head and moved him next to Baker. He set Baker's left hand on the dog's neck. "If we only got one more trip in us, we might not see you lads again. In that case, it's been an honor traveling beside you on your trail."

He nudged Flint a little closer to Baker and kept one hand on the dog's neck,

"Flint might pull the two of us and maybe the old flea-bit cayuse too. But that might be too much. I never tried something like that." Baker looked like he was sleeping peacefully.

Just Murphy leaned close to Baker's ear and spoke quietly. "We had our adventures, didn't we Jim," said Just Murphy. Baker nodded weakly. "And this one was a doozy. But there's a time to chase new dreams and a time to remember old ones. Remember that cabin you built out in the highlands north-west of Denver City? Where you could sleep outside under the stars, have a little campfire, drink stonewalls and smoke a pipe? Can you picture that now?"

A faint smile flickered across Jim Baker's face. Just Murphy closed his eyes too, but nothing happened. Just Murphy opened his eyes and shook his head. He tried a second time to transport back to the cabin and failed again.

"It ain't working," Jus Murphy said. "Jim's too old, Flint's too old, I'm too old, and that horse probably don't understand English enough to help. Well, maybe I can lighten the load a bit." He removed his hand from the dog's back and moved several feet away.

Charles understood what Murphy was doing. "But if Flint's gone, won't you be stranded here?"

"If he's out of stories," Just Murphy nodded toward Baker. "Then I guess I don't much care if I get stuck here. Won't last long for me either, I can feel it in my bones. Flint, you do your best for old Jim here. You old nag of a horse, even if you ain't much of a manitou, you might try to pull a bit of the weight too. Honest Jim's a dang sight better than the woman who's been riding you. "

Then he talked louder so Jim Baker could hear him.

"Jim, if you can hear me, I need to stay around to answer some questions about tonight or else the foxes will just find a new leader and take over the henhouse. A few days, maybe a week. After I finish my business here, I'd be pleased to join you at that campfire if I can figure out the way. Eat some jerked buffalo, listen to you lie. If you're lucky, I could even give you some shooting lessons."

Jim Baker opened his eyes and rolled them, then closed them again.

"Wouldn't it be good to be home again?" Just Murphy said loudly. His voice was a little sad. "With the stars and the coyotes singing?"

Baker lifted his head, summoned some strength and whispered.

"Yes it would! By gonny, yes it would!"

Then he very gradually faded from sight until there was nothing left of him. Sapania's horse faded into invisibility as well. Flint remained sitting on the ground.

"Is he…?" Charles asked again.

Just Murphy shook his head. "I don't think so. No more than he already was. That old horse pulled him through."

"Sapania said it was worthless."

Just Murphy smiled.

"It probably just didn't like her much."

"So is Sapania stuck here? In this time and place?"

"I think so. At least for now, unless she finds another manitou. And if she treats it better. Flying Faun said a manitou can pick its human. If that witch doctor's reputation got spread in the manitou community, they might avoid her this time."

"And Mr. Baker?"

Just Murphy nodded. "Nothing lasts forever. But I think him and me can sit by that campfire dreaming up memories for a good long time. As long as we don't try to get young and foolish again."

Charles started to say something to Martin, but he was no longer beside them.

"Where's Martin?" he asked, with panic in his voice. "And Pan? Did you see them wander off? Martin! Where are you! Come here, Martin!"

"Ain't that him walkin' down the pier with his father? And the goat between them?" Just Murphy pointed.

"But how did he…" Charles stopped. A boy who could travel across time and continents with his goat could certainly slip away from their little group without anyone noticing. Charles wondered where he had gone, and how long he had spent there. And if he'd taken his father with him. He sighed with relief. At least he had a chance to get back to his own place and time.

Charles walked down to the water to join them.

Mr. Whiting stepped onto the gravel beach and stood staring out at the water, its gentle waves sparkling with reflected starlight.

"Hello, sir," Charles said. He looked at Martin. "And where have you been?"

The man was deep in thought and the boy's voice startled him.

Martin looked down at his shoes, sheepishly. "I wanted to see my mother and brother and sisters. I spent three days there. None of them could see me, but now I know where they live."

"Well, hello young man," Whiting said. "It's a little late for a lad to be about, don't you think?"

"A goat protects me, sir," Charles said. If Mr. Whiting had been gone with Martin for three days, then there had been two identical men with the same name in Scagaway for a while. Maybe that didn't change the future very much, but people would probably have created a plausible story to explain it. Two men with the same name working for the same company. Unusual, of course, but not unbelievable.

Mr. Whiting smiled but it was a sad smile.

"I have a fondness for goats and their lads," he said. "I dreamed of one after a night of spoiled beer. It even looked like the one Martin later adopted." Then he shook his head slowly. "In my experience, they provide insufficient protection."

"Father!" Martin said. "I'm right here! Can't you see me? Can't you hear me?"

"Your goat looks much like my lad Martin's pet," Whiting said. "Down to the one brown ear."

"It is him!" Martin yelled. "It's Pan! And I'm right beside him!"

"How I wish I could hear his voice again," Mr. Whiting said.

"I think he's speaking to you right now," Charles said.

"I am!" Martin said. Mr. Whiting shook his head again.

"Would that it were true," he said. "I'm afraid my memories of young Martin remains back in Colorado. He got the fever…" He could not go on.

"The fever," Charles said. "Surely they gave him medicine. Why didn't it help?"

"There is no medicine for the fever," Whiting said. "Broth, a cool cloth for the forehead, rest. The medicine has changed little in a thousand years. Now, I tend the hearth for that is a father's duty. My family requires its warmth. But the light of the dancing flames is gone, for that was Martin. To live with Sarah and the others or to join Martin in endless slumber— that is no easy choice. And I must make it daily."

Suddenly Charles had an idea, a very strange, outlandish idea.

"What if there was medicine?" he said.

"I am not without means," Mr. Whiting said. "If there had been a cure I would have paid any price. But I will not buy carnival potions and gypsy powders."

"Of course not," Charles said.

"Smith and his thugs would sell snake oil to a cobra. We have rid ourselves of such men. Or at least we have begun the process.. They sell false hopes. I'll not be duped."

"I would not dupe you," Charles said. "But sometimes truth lies where we least expect it. From the mouths of babes," he said. "Mysterious ways."

"Young man, it's late. You should go home."

"I have spoken with Martin," Charles said. Mr. Whiting froze.

"What do you mean?"

"Your son Martin. And his goat Pan."

"How do you know the goat's name? What sort of trick is this?"

"No trick, sir. I don't understand it myself."

"Go on home to your mother before I tell her she must lash you for your insolence!"

"It's like a dream," Charles said. "He likes it when you read to him. Ivanhoe was one of his favorites. He spilled tea on the cover. The stain looked a bit like a dog…"

Whiting looked stunned. "Who are you?" he whispered.

"My name is Charles. I live in the house you built north of Denver."

"Ah, so you saw the book there and deduced the rest."

"I understand how it would seem just so," Charles said.

"He can hear you," Martin said "He can see you too! Why can't he see me? How did the fever make me invisible?"

Charles wanted to respond but didn't want Mr. Whiting to think he was trying to pull a bizarre scam on him. He tried to answer them both at the same time.

"We can't understand every mystery," Charles said.

"But why?" Martin insisted.

"Indeed not," his father said. "What is it you want?"

"I'm not sure," Charles responded again to both of them. "I mean you no harm. But I can't answer your questions with authority because I'm confused myself. I can't say why I see the things I do, or why others do not. It's like being in a dark room, but then someone turns on the switch."

"The switch?" Mr. Whiting said. "Are you speaking of electricity? Like Mr. Edison promotes?"

"I speak in imperfect metaphor," Charles said. In the 1890s the concept of turning on a switch would not be such a common image, he reminded himself.

"Assume that I'm inventing a story. A story like Ivanhoe or any of the others a father and son might share. Perhaps that's all I'm doing. There can be no harm in a story, can there?

"I like stories," Martin said.

"Stories can be used for both good and ill," Martin's father said.

"I wonder what the son might say to the father," Charles said. "When he knows it's time to sleep but he doesn't want his father to leave yet." He looked at Martin. "Can we imagine such a thing?"

Martin's eyes lit up. He was beginning to understand the game Charles was playing.

"I would ask about that Spanish priest's bell," Martin said. "The one I found by the sunflowers. They made me sneeze."

"Yes," Charles said. "Perhaps the son would ask about the bell he found by the sunflowers."

"You are making wild guesses, as a confidence man like Mr. Smith would. You know bits of truth and hope I will provide more clues to continue your ruse."

"I see what you're doing," Martin said. "If you make him remember me better he'll be able to see me again. It's like he's been put into a trance by Franz Mesmer. He told me about that."

"Perhaps the son would say you were under Doctor Mesmer's influence." Charles stopped and listened to Martin. Then he smiled and repeated it for his father. "But he'd be glad you're not quacking like a duck."

Mr. Whiting again looked stunned, hopeful for a second. Then his face darkened again.

"It's a cruel prank you play," he said softly. "Devised with care and detailed research. But my God is kind and methodical and he devised a world to run in straight lines and precise equations. What you suggest is witchcraft."

"Did not your own God send his people signs and prophets? Was that also witchcraft?"

"Of course not!"

"Then please, at least keep an open mind. We may not have much time. If you could speak to your son right now, what would you tell him?"

He paused and swallowed and looked down at his feet.

"Not that I believe you, understand. But I would tell him I love him. I will always love him. And I miss him." He smiled "I miss him more than he missed…" he paused and looked at me. "Well, he would know who he missed."

Martin whispered. "Noceratops"

"Excuse me?" Charles said.

"Never mind," Mr. Whiting said. "He would know."

"Noceratops." Martin said. That wasn't even a real word as far as Charles knew, but he repeated it.

"Noceratops?" he said without much confidence.

Mr. Whiting stared at him in utter disbelief.

"How could you know?

Martin smiled. "He was my very favorite horned toad. He looked like a little dinosaur. So I was going to call him triceratops, except he didn't have three horns. So he wasn't triceratops, he was noceratops."

"His little reptile," Mr. Whiting said. "He was very sad when it escaped."

"I've had pet horned toads too," Charles said. "They like black ants best."

Mr. Whiting just nodded. "Indeed," he said.

"They discovered the first triceratops bones when I was a baby," Martin said. "It was near Denver. Once upon a time, I think a triceratops sat on the hill where I live. Maybe he watched the sun set over the mountains, just like I do. Maybe Noceratops was his grandson. Remember father? Remember when we talked about that?" Mr. Whiting gave no suggestion that he heard anything.

Bumps might be Noceratops's descendant, Charles thought. Then he focused again on Mr. Whiting,

"I don't intend to be cruel," he said. "But our time is probably very limited. If I could find something that would be useful against the fever, I would need to get it to you before... that is, while the fever was in its earliest stages. But that would be before now, before you have any memory of me or this night. How could I then convince you of my sincerity?"

"I see your quandary," Mr. Whiting said. "And it is interesting in at least a theoretical way. Hubert G. Wells contemplates such things in his books. It would be my fondest wish that a doctor from the future could ride Mr. Wells' machine back to save my son. But that is idle fantasy." He paused. "However, I miss my own son's fantasies and you have brought him closer to my immediate thoughts this evening. For that I thank you. There is only the remotest of chances that you are anything but a trickster or a lad under the influence of a trickster. Yet, when employing an entirely philosophical spirit, there is always the faint hope."

"Perhaps the size of a mustard seed," Charles said. Biblical references hadn't changed much in the last few centuries.

"Yes. Faith and hope the size of a mustard seed." He removed the little bell that hung around his neck. He handed Charles the bell. "I don't need this to remember my son. You were brave this night, brave like my own small son. I'd like you to have it."

Charles put the bell around his neck. It felt very familiar and comforting.

"Thank you, sir."

"Love is strongest when we give it away. Remember that, son."

Mr. Whiting thought for a moment, then continued. "Very well. My mother told me a story of how she chose my middle name. She said she never told another soul. I will tell you that story."

At the word story, Martin perked up.

"Tell him there will be time tomorrow for another story. Tell him!"

"Martin says there will be time tomorrow for another story."

"That's what I said to him every night," Mr. Whiting said. "How can you possibly…"

Before he could finish the sentence, the light changed. It was suddenly very bright, as if something had exploded. Charles' face felt hot. He looked around. frantically.

He was standing in the center of the Pillar of Fire cemetery. The sun was high above, beating down with a baking heat.

He was all alone.

Chapter 43

Charles stood in the middle of the cemetery for several minutes, overcome by the sense of being alive in this exact place in this specific moment. The gratitude he felt was mingled with the profound sadness of having left Mr. Whiting alone before getting some clue that would help if he could ever return. He inhaled deeply the smell of grass and clover, spiced by a whiff of the bitter perfume of dry weeds being burned by a distant farmer. A grasshopper leaped into the air near his feet, buzzing like a little motorboat in the summer air. A sparrow chirped; a meadowlark whistled its distinctive melody from some unseen fencepost. Charles lifted his face to the sky and the warm sun felt like opening the oven door to smell chicken cooking on Sunday afternoon. In the distance, a truck shifted gears to labor up a hill.

Did Martin travel with him back to this time? If so, did that mean the boy was still trapped in his sad dreams and would continue to haunt the house. Or did he stay with his family? If so, then how did Charles manage to get here?

Old headstones surrounded Charles. Some gray stones were worn by years of weather, the names and dates blurring into non-language. Not too far a way, a woman called out urgently. "Mr. Peters!" she yelled. "You simply must come back right now!"

"Where in the world has he gone this time?" another woman asked her.

"He must be near. Keep looking!"

Not this time, Charles thought. Mr. Peters has relocated. Perhaps he steers a lonely fishing boat, far from land, where only seagulls argue. He can finally argue back. The women continued their loud conversation.

"Well, Sylvia Peters, I'm sure this is not what you signed up for when you married him!" the first woman said. "Caring for a crazy man who wanders off every chance he gets. It's simply not fair to you!"

"He can't help it," Mrs. Peters said. Her voice sounded very tired."When he was young, he was the most dashing fellow you ever saw. The life we had together was long and wonderful. Until the last few years, of course. I've been fortunate the administrator has let him live here with me for so long. But it may be time to put him into a more appropriate setting, where trained people can take care of him. Maybe they can quiet the voices he claims to hear." She sounded sad but resigned.

"Well, Sylvia, we have to find him first." Then she yelled again, "Mr. Peters!" But Mr. Peters could no longer hear her.

So this was not the location of the sanitarium after all, Charles thought, if such a place even existed. It's just where one man who heard voices lived with his wife. He could not explain to the woman that her husband was gone but content. He walked home and looked under the porch.

Martin was curled up and asleep behind the bales of straw. He did not look well. The boy rolled over and moaned, as if in pain. Of all the memories to relive, somehow he'd gotten stuck in a loop that returned him over and over again to his feverish days of pain and frightening delusion.

Charles went down the hill and sat in his little tumbleweed cave to think.

He wanted to change one event in the past, to improve an outcome. But what if he did something that changed all of history? If he helped Martin survive a while longer Mr. Whiting might not go to Alaska. Without Mr. Whiting, the outlaws might continue to defraud the town, growing stronger every day, perhaps even gaining national power.

He went back up to the house. He sat at his usual chair and watched guppies chase each other through the water plants. The males spread their colorful tails, showing off for the females. Two little catfish scurried around on the bottom, busily searching the sand for bits of food. Their entire life was the cheerful hope that one more flake of fish food would settle like a tiny feather to the bottom of the tank.

"You're pretty lucky," he told them. Charles reigned over the guppy universe benevolently. Sometimes the god of a universe has to make sad choices; other times, he cures a pandemic and saves the world. He doesn't always know which he's doing.. Charles opened the drawer beneath the tank and pulled out a little vial. Only two pills remained.

It was an absurd idea to begin with but completely unreasonable with only two pills.

There wasn't time to get to the pet store and back before his parents got home from work. For the rest of the afternoon he would conduct research out on the front porch. He would also watch clouds drift over the mountains, birds streak across the sky, and flies beat themselves crazy against the screen.

If his experiment failed, he might never have another chance to do those things.

He carried one big volume of Encyclopedia Britannica out to the porch. He needed to convince himself that the medicine that cured his guppies might also cure a little boy, years before anyone ever heard of it.

 The problem with both science and magic isn't rarity; it's that they're everywhere, exploding around us like land mines, swarming us like bats. Sometimes, we try to ignore science, the way Mr. Peters tries to shut out voices. Other times, we try to quiet any hint of magic. People who succeed probably feel confused much less often than Charles.

The other problem with both science and magic is that they're dangerous. Especially to beginners. But Charles owed Martin and the other souls he had disturbed one more try.

His plan was simple. He was going to buy some fish penicillin down at the pet department of Woolco. It came in 500 mg tablets and didn't dissolve easily in the tank. When his fish got a disease called "fin and tail rot" he treated the water with penicillin and it cured them. The pills were cheap, even for a kid, and fish medicine didn't require a prescription. But was it identical to the medicine they gave humans? He didn't know. Would it be effective against whatever fever Martin was dying from? Obviously, there was no way to predict it. So he read the encyclopedia.

Penicillin was first mass produced during World War Two. That was more than forty years after Martin got sick and a dozen years before Charles was born. It cured many kinds of infection and helped the Allies win the war. It was especially effective against the main bacteria that caused gum infections. So maybe.

But fish aren't the same as humans; maybe fish pills contained dangerous chemicals. Common sense argued against that. The aquarium market was too small to justify building a separate penicillin factory. More likely, they swept up pills that fell on the floor, the ones they couldn't sell as medicine, and packaged them for fish stores. The pills were probably identical to the ones sold for humans, only with dust on them from the broom.

The encyclopedia described dosages and treatment protocols and side effects and dangers. A few people are allergic to the medicine; even one pill could kill them. There was no way to know ahead of time and it wouldn't be worth the risk unless a life were at stake. But of course, Charles thought, one was.

At Woolco, he bought three times as many pills as he thought he'd need. If he could transport himself back to Mr. Whiting and convince him to try it, maybe Martin would not die of the infection. Perhaps his family could have many more happy years together, and the house would no longer be haunted by a sad and lonely spirit.

Charles would have to explain to Mr. Whiting how to use the pills. That wouldn't be hard, but he also had to convince him to trust a strange boy with his son's life. Tomorrow Charles would try to figure that out. Tonight he needed to make sure the pills were safe for a human. There was only one way to do that.

He had to take one of the pills himself. Logic and statistics told him there was little chance it would hurt him. People had been taking this medicine for over a decade with very few problems. It was safe even for guppies, each one the size of his pinky finger.

But no matter how firmly a person believes in science, his brain is never quite sure. A skittering mouse of doubt hides in the cabinet of every mind, scratching and furtive. Not enough to destroy the entire structure of belief but enough to make a person nervous and uncomfortable. What if Martin was allergic to penicillin? What if Charles was? Should he ask his mother first?

No, was the quick answer. His mother would forbid it unless he explained in great detail. If she understood the explanation, they would decide he was crazy. But if the pill were deadly to him and he did not survive, it would be mean to make them spend the rest of their own lives wondering what happened to him. As a compromise, he wrote a note to them explaining just a bit. That he was curious if fish medicine was safe for humans, so he'd taken one pill. That his "research" suggested it was, and it cost a lot less than prescription drugs. So he was taking one pill before he went to sleep.

If he woke in the morning, he would tear up the note. If not, and the experiment was a failure, he wrote that he loved them. After thinking about it, he added a note about how much to feed his guppies and to clean the sand in the tank every two weeks. He signed his name and set the note on the table by his bed. He stared at the pill in his hand, then had one more thought. He wrote: "P.S.— our ghost's name is Martin. He's just a kid."

His stomach twisted and tightened as if he was staring over the edge of a cliff with jagged rocks far below hoping to smash his body into oatmeal. Then, before he could change his mind, he took the pill and gulped down some water from the glass. He lay down on the bed, covers pulled up tight, and waited to see if he noticed any side effects. He especially watched for convulsions, muscle pain, shortness of breath, cramps, or general insanity.

A tiny part of him thought it would be more interesting if he experienced side effects. As the minutes ticked by and nothing happened, he gradually decided the medicine was safe. Still, it took a while to fall asleep.

Chapter 44

It was an unusual dream in one way: Charles knew he was dreaming and knew that, in his dream, he was near the ocean. It was a vivid dream; he could smell things precisely, hear acutely, and see the entire spectrum of colors. With his eyes closed he heard waves roll and rumble and splash not too far away. A sea gull called, sharp and distinct, as it flew past. A cool breeze touched his face, smelling like rotting kelp and decomposing driftwood. He opened his eyes.

He sat on a hill of dirt and dull rocks overlooking huge sand dunes with the gray ocean visible beyond them. Scraggly bushes and stubborn grass clung to the hill beneath him, but nothing grew on those grand waves of sand in the near distance. Ten feet below him on the hill a young man and woman sat on the ground. They were both thin and very good-looking. They sat two or three feet apart, gazing out at the dunes and the mist that lingered above the water. They looked comfortable with the place and with each other.

The woman looked vaguely familiar. Maybe she was someone who attended Charles's church, or a teacher at his school. It doesn't matter, Charles thought. The sun found an opening between clouds and the sudden warmth felt good on his arms. The man pointed out at the hills of sand.

"Sarah, so much of the world looks just like that," he said. "Barren, lifeless, dirt and sand blown about by tireless winds, jagged grains of granite polishing each other until the sharp edges are gone and they resemble little spheres. Time grinds the hardest, fiercest stone into faceless anonymity."

"I don't know anyone who talks like you," Sarah said. She watched the sand and the clouds, changed in an instant by the burst of sunlight. "It's lovely, in its way."

"Yes, but lifeless," he said. "If you could bind the sand together, irrigate it, manage it. Imagine the crops one could grow! There is more desert in the world than cropland back in Iowa."

"Don't tease me about Iowa, Frank," she said. "Anyway, you only see the surface of the sand. Maybe great creatures live beneath it. Maybe they churn out their own kinds of crops, like bees manufacturing honey inside their secret hives."

Frank smiled and nodded.

"I would not discount any possibility," he said.

"It would be hard to harvest corn on such hilly fields," she said.

"You are a very practical woman, Sarah."

"And you are a man from the future, aren't you, Frank?"

"I have never said that."

"You didn't have to. This whole summer you've been careful not to describe some things too completely. And your ideas— they are not of this time."

"Now who's teasing?" he said.

"I'm not so sure." She paused. "At any rate, you've come a long way to sit on this lonely Oregon coast. Longer than you tell."

"I came from Tacoma, Washington," he said. "It's not that far from Florence, Oregon.

She smiled.

"Yes, so you say. Washington is is much closer to this beach than is my beloved Iowa. And yet your clothing reeks of a great distance."

"Are you impugning my smell?

She giggled.

"I love the way you smell. I'm only saying that when the conversation drifts to specific origins, your clever words become vague. Your stories contain mysteries. Sometimes I wonder if you are secretly married."

"The most complicated man collects fewer secrets than the simplest woman," he said. "And you are no simple woman."

"I've become convinced that either you have traveled through time to be with me, or that you come from one of the planets. Mars, I should think."

319

"You've come a long way yourself. Across a country, on trains and boats. And for what reason?"

"Perhaps just to sit here with you; to watch the wind rearrange the landscape; to watch your little dog chase seagulls."

"It's reason enough for me," he said.

"But you will be leaving soon, won't you." She did not say it like a question. She knew the answer.

"The time we've had together, it is not a temporary thing. I'm sure of that, though I can't explain it. But, as I have said before, I only follow where little Bub leads"

"The dog gave you that scar above your eye. Yet you follow him wherever he leads."

"That was an entirely different dog. A savage malamute that attacked when I was an infant. No, Bub is a special dog in ways I cannot explain."

"So you will leave me when your dog tells you to leave? That is not the priority a woman prefers to hear." The woman made a pouting face, but she was obviously teasing.

"Miss Sarah McCall, you cut me to the quick. I am an indentured servant to a canine and he is a demanding overlord. Perhaps one day man will be master of planets, perhaps even galaxies. But he will never be master of the things he loves."

"Mr. Herbert, I think you love nothing so much as your own clever words."

"There you are wrong, lassie. There you are wrong."

"I have tried to make this wild coast appealing to your little employer," she said. "He has not lacked for succulent treats or sticks to chase."

"Indeed you have. And I have as well. I must tell you this much: my fondness for you is no fiction. If I could paint sorcery, I would wave my wand and paint this scene with those waves in the background and the wind playing on your hair; I would paint a scene to step into at will. But yes, I must leave, and soon, I fear. There may be no warning. But though you may not see me, I remain with you and you with me. We have planted seeds within each other that no one else will ever know. Who can imagine the garden that may grow?"

"I will remember you, Frank Herbert," she said. "and maybe someday you'll return and explain…"

The little dog ran up to them and sat at the man's feet. It looked up pleadingly, as if wanting to be fed. The man reached down and scratched it behind the ears. Then he suddenly looked up at the woman, a startled, pained look on his face. He opened his mouth to speak…

And Charles woke up.

Chapter 45

Charles remembered many details clearly after he woke: the smell of the kelp, the tall grass on the hillside moving in waves with the breeze like a green lake. Vivid dreams weren't listed as a side effect of the pill he'd taken. Even if they were, the fish pills were probably safe to give Martin. Dreams are an acceptable side-effect.

Unless all this had already happened. What if he had already traveled back in time, given Martin the pills and the little boy died because of the pills, not the fever? Charles tore up the note to his parents. He went to his piano lesson. He fed his guppies, sat on the porch, and read old books.

But he couldn't forget his plan. He wrote another note, this one to Mr. Whiting. If he got to the correct place and time but couldn't talk to Martin's father he'd leave the note and return home as quickly as possible. He explained the dosage. He removed all the pills from their packaging and put them in a paper envelope. Even if the envelope had modern glue or paper, it would all degrade before science developed the tools to analyze it.

Finally, he finished his note: "This is a very modern medicine, discovered by a French doctor, Ernest Duchesne, but not yet available to the public. (That was true, but not many people knew it because no one followed up on Duchesne's discovery for decades.) It has been tested extensively with excellent results against fever. (This was also true, it just hadn't happened in the 1800s.) Your son Martin has been selected to receive this new medicine. We trust you to keep the matter in strictest confidence. We hope that it will prove efficacious."

He put the note in the envelope with the pills.

Now all he had to do was travel back in time to 1897, then convince Whiting to trust his son's life to an eleven-year-old stranger. What could possibly go wrong? Only the possibility of getting stranded in a strange time with no friends, no money or home, in order to give a child a potentially fatal dose of something that would seem like witchcraft to the police of the time.

He looked at his copy of the book Ivanhoe, studying the cover's ancient tea stain. FH Whiting was neatly written in the top right corner of the title page. He ran his fingers over those words. So little remained of the man or his son, just fading ink in an old book and eerie noises in the night.

The haunting sounds had grown more persistent and it now bothered the rest of his family. The pitiful crying of a wounded animal; scratching sounds in the wall, too loud for any rodent; thudding footsteps and things being dragged across the attic floor. Perhaps murderers dragging the bodies of their victims, Raymond suggested, helpfully.

Maybe ghosts experience a form of sleep themselves, a time of reliving memories and dreaming things that never were. Maybe they sleepwalk. A lonely boy, long dead but unaware, dreaming of bright days and bold adventures— surely one could forgive his restlessness.

On Monday morning as soon as his mother left for work and Raymond left to visit a friend Charles went into the dog pen.

"That's a good boy, Fritz," he said, scratching the dog's ears. "I'm going to be gone a while. I hope I can return here." The dog stuck a wet nose in his face. For some reason, that made him feel like crying. "It's OK, boy. I won't be gone long."

Charles went under the porch and sat on a bale of straw. There was no sign of Martin or Pan, nor had he expected any. They didn't just show up randomly—they materialized when he tried to do magic. That pattern was now clear. When Charles was asleep, Martin often wandered the house, crying, looking for his parents, lonely. But when Charles was with him, Martin's form was very real. He could take bites out of apples and pull a rifle away from its aim. When Charles tried to influence a fly or coin flip, the attempted magic summoned those who sleep, as he thought of them, but in an arbitrary way. He might get a visit from Jim Baker or one of Smith's gang. Or maybe even the Arapaho woman. He did not want that.

Charles pictured Martin sitting beside him on the bale of straw. He focussed all his attention. Then he tried to make one particular straw on the bale move, using his most magical thoughts.

"I didn't think you were ever coming back." Martin stood out in the sunshine with Pan beside him. Charles went out to stand next to him. The dogs sniffed the goat like old friends. "You can't make my family remember me, can you?" Martin sounded sullen.

323

"I have one more idea," Charles said. "I want to try to talk to your father again. Before he went to Alaska. When you had the fever."

"What good will that do?"

"Maybe I can make him see you."

"How?"

"If you're invisible because of the fever, I might have some medicine that could fix it."

"He won't believe you," Martin said.

"I know. I'm trying to figure that out now. Do you know how your father got his middle name?"

"No. I think it was grandma's idea."

"Do you and your father have any secrets? Something nobody else would know?"

"I don't think so. The Bible doesn't like secrets. Grandfather Timothy was president of the Bible society for twenty years. But I think everybody knows that."

"OK, well then, I'm just going to have to convince him by using logic."

"Grandpa said people don't get convinced by logic. He said people use logic to explain what they already decided. Anyway, I don't like the time when I had fever. I had bad dreams."

"If this works, maybe all the bad dreams will be over."

"OK," he said. "But I don't want to stay there very long."

"I don't either. It shouldn't take long."

They both put their hands on the goat's head.

"Think about your father," Charles said. "And I will too."

Only a moment passed before things were different. He still stood in front of his house, the mountains in the distance looked the same. But the house had transformed. The top floor was no longer painted white, but was a dark brown color. The steps leading up to the porch revived until they looked made of newly-cut lumber. The two hackberry trees shrank to saplings. The few houses that had grown up below the hill in the 1940s simply vanished.

And neither Martin nor Pan stood beside him. For a moment he panicked. Had he made this journey alone, with no manitou to ease his return trip? Was he stranded forever in 1897? Would he become the ghost haunting his own house, an invisible presence groaning in his sleep, frightening the current residents?

Then he had a disturbing thought: What if the ghostly sounds his family heard were actually him?

Be calm, he told himself. Collect data, use logic. Do not jump to conclusions. Especially refrain from believing things only because you fear them.

Someone was whistling a sad, familiar tune from some symphony. The sound came from the front porch of the house. OK, Charles thought. Martin usually wound up asleep in his own bed when he came here. That's probably where he was now. Charles should just try to complete his mission and then worry about the future.

He walked up the wooden steps and nearly opened the door from force of habit but stopped himself. This was not his house, not right now. He knocked on the door. In a moment Mr. Whiting opened the door, obviously surprised to see anyone at all at his doorstep on this sparsely populated hilltop, let alone a boy. He quickly recovered his composure.

"How may I help you young man?"

"I'd like to speak to you, Mr. Whiting," Charles said. Martin's father was an educated man and he spoke in the cadence of the old books Charles read. Charles wanted to sound smart, too. "It is a matter of some urgency."

Mr. Whiting smiled in a cautious way but did not invite the boy in. He looked behind Charles, wondering if some grown up was behind the intrusion and had sent the child up first as a decoy or scout.

Charles had spoken with him in the following year so Mr. Whiting would have no memory of him or their conversation. Next year, in Alaska, if that exchange happened again, Charles wondered if it would seem to him like he'd already lived it? Or if the exchange itself would not happen because Charles had altered history just a tiny bit. He remembered the old Huron saying: "Yes, Teardrop, every stone beneath the surface affects the river's flow. But not as much as it thinks it does."

"Are you alone?" Mr. Whiting asked.

"Yes sir."

"I did not notice you walking up the driveway," the man said casually. There was an implication in his comment. Had Charles snuck up the hill like a thief, keeping himself hidden? Had he come up from some other direction? What was the story behind his sudden appearance?

"No sir, I did not walk from that direction. I harbor no felonious intent, I assure you. I'm quite alone and unarmed. It's about Martin"

Mr. Whiting stared at Charles for a moment.

"Martin is quite indisposed at the moment. Perhaps you should return at a more auspicious time." He began to close the door.

"Please sir," Charles said. "I've come to talk with you, not him. It will only take a moment."

Mr. Whiting looked down at Charles's sneakers, which surely seemed out of place. Once he noticed that oddity, his eyes moved upward to the boy's jeans and finally his black T shirt. None of them belonged in that time and place.

"You're not from around here, are you son?" the man said softly.

"My situation does not lend itself to quick summation," Charles said.

"Very well then." Mr. Whiting opened the door and Charles stepped onto his own family's screened-in porch, only now there was no screen. It felt much more open and simple. Charles wondered if the flies and mosquitoes tormented the Whiting family, or if back in this time maybe there just weren't as many and the screen was less necessary? Or maybe screens hadn't been invented yet. The porch smelled of fresh-cut wood and peppermint tea. Two rocking chairs sat at the far end. That spot had the best view of both the mountains to the west and Denver to the south, so it was one of Charles' favorite places. Only now the view was mostly prairie with very few buildings and trees. In the distance, smoke rose from scattered chimneys in Denver City.

Mr. Whiting motioned to the chairs and Charles sat in one.

"Tea?" the man asked. Despite Charles's sudden appearance at his door, he treated the boy with the dignity and politeness he would bestow on a traveling priest.

"Thank you, sir," Charles said.

Mr. Whiting poured two cups of tea from a ceramic tea pot, handed one to Charles, then sat in the other rocking chair.

"You have me at a disadvantage," Mr. Whiting said. It took Charles a moment to figure out what he meant.

"I'm sorry, Mr. Whiting. My name is Charles."

"Not Charlie?"

"No sir. I'm not ashamed of my given name."

"A sentiment I applaud. You say that your situation does not lend itself to brief summation?"

"That's correct. More than that, there may be some peril to divulging too many details."

"Telling me your precise story would put you in peril?"

"No sir. Well, maybe, I'm not sure. But more importantly, perhaps you."

The man nodded, his face firm, looking far into the distance, listening but reserving judgement.

"Honest men have no fear of the truth," he said.

Charles reminded himself to think in terms of the 1890s, things people knew, what they believed. He wanted the man to trust him, not think he had been sent by the Devil.

"Yes," Charles answered slowly. "And I shall be truthful with you. But sometimes the truth speaks in metaphor and story. We no longer fear becoming 'fiction fiends' do we?"

"Of course not. Those were ideas from my childhood. We have progressed. Reading stories causes no harm."

"And we shall continue to progress," Charles said. "In ways no man could predict."

"But perhaps a boy could?"

Charles smiled at his obvious trap.

"No sir. I do not pretend that. I am no Edison nor am I an angel. And I'm no visitor from the Moon. But imagine for a moment that one of those came to you, as if Mr. Wells wrote truth and not fiction, with something that might help Martin. And yet divulging too much carried great risk."

"Then that messenger would face a daunting challenge."

"Yes, sir. And that is my predicament."

Whiting sipped his tea and gazed at the mountains thoughtfully. Charles waited.

"Any father would be tempted by an offer to help his child."

"Yes," Charles said. "I understand that. And he would be wise to fear false hopes. But he would also want to gather information before precluding any offer."

Whiting looked at him more sharply. "You seem sincere," he said. "And your argument is logical. May I inspect your shoes?" he asked.

"Excuse me?"

"I am unfamiliar with your footwear. Would you allow me a closer view?"

Charles took off one of his sneakers and handed it to him. It had been a week or so since Charles' mother ran them through the washing machine and hung them on the clothes line to dry, so he hoped they didn't smell too bad. Whiting held it close to his face, turning it over in his hands.

"Canvas shoes. Interesting. The material on the soles," he said. "It looks patterned after the suction cups on an octopus tentacle. Is that for traction? Can you explain it?"

"Not really," Charles said. "They're Keds. I think it's just plain rubber."

"Plain rubber," he said. "Charles Goodyear's invention, a material of great value molded on the sole of a child's shoe made of canvas? Remarkable."

He returned the shoe.

"You are indeed not from around here," Mr. Whiting said. "Excuse my bluntness. Where do you come from?"

"I was born right here in Colorado," Charles said. "But the complete story of my journey to this moment would take so long and seem so fantastical as to make you doubt the important part of my story."

"Which is…?"

Charles pulled the envelope with the penicillin pills out of his pocket.

"I have medicine that may help Martin. It may keep him alive."

"So you won't tell me who you are or how you arrived here and yet you expect me to believe you can do more than the finest doctors in Colorado?"

"Yes. That's exactly what I hope you'll believe."

"And why should I?"

"First, because you have no alternative. His fever is high; I'm sure the doctors have told you he won't survive much longer."

"We continue to pray. All things are possible with the Lord."

"Even a messenger with medicine you don't understand? Would that be possible with the Lord?"

"Son, you tread perilously close to blasphemy!"

"I'm not asking you for money or anything else. I have no motive for deceit. Let me tell you a few things I do know so you don't think I wandered in from a gang of confidence men. I know your father Timothy was president of the Bible Society."

"That has been in newspapers."

"I know Martin found a priest's bell in some sunflowers."

"He could have told his friends about that."

"I know you read Ivanhoe to him and other books. I know he likes the funny parts."

"Every eight-year-old boy likes the funny parts. Wearing strange shoes and knowing a few random facts qualifies you only to be in Mr. Smith's gang of confidence men and scoundrels. Even those ruffians employ bits of fact to give their false criminal stories a touch of verisimilitude. Do you know the word?"

"Only by context in the books I've read. I believe it means 'elements of truth inserted into a fiction.'"

"That's a close definition," Mr. Whiting said. "Bits of truth lend credence to a scheme. Among the educated, an extensive vocabulary has a similar effect. But neither verisimilitude nor its definition are proof of anything. Nor are they sufficient evidence for me to conduct experiments on my son." He took a breath. "They certainly do not justify the risk of giving my son medicine delivered by a stranger, a boy at that."

Charles searched his brain desperately. Surely he must know something that would convince Mr. Whiting.

"He loved a horned toad that he lost. It was named Noceratops. He thought its ancestors might have sat on your hill, watching the mountains just like him."

"He could have told others at Sunday school of his pet. These are not great secrets, just grains of sand on a desert. I think you'd better leave now."

"Nor would they be for me, sir," Charles said. "Bits of truth are, as you say, only grains of sand…"

Suddenly Charles had a thought. Not grains of sand on a desert. Sand on a beach. The woman in his dream had seemed familiar and now he realized where he'd seen her. She was the woman in the old photo on Mr. Whiting's desk.

What had Martin said about her? Or was it something Mr. Whiting said, something his own mother told him but no one else? That was it. Frantically, Charles tried to remember the incident. They had been in

Alaska. Whiting started to tell him something but hadn't gotten to finish the story and now Charles couldn't recall what it was going to be about.

He put his sneaker back on, stalling. Something about Whiting's name? Maybe his middle name? That was no help. He didn't know what Whiting's middle name was.

"Listen," he said. "I don't know for sure if this medicine will help him. I know it's helped many other people who had different kinds of fever. I'm no scientist and I'm surely no great magician. It's a long shot gamble by any calculation. I took one of the pills to make sure it was safe and the only side effect was a vivid dream."

"I'm not going to gamble with my son's life." Whiting stood up from the rocking chair. Clearly, the interview was over.

Charles had an idea. Maybe some vivid dreams have a bit of truth hidden within them. He stood up too.

"Sarah met a man," Charles said. If phony magicians could use tricks, maybe this once he should too. Fake magicians provide little clues in hopes their victim will volunteer more information…

"Excuse me?"

"Sarah met a man who had a beagle. The dog's name was Bub."

"How do you know of Sarah?"

Charles didn't know if Whiting's mother's name was Sarah, or if the man knew someone else by that name but clearly he'd touched some nerve.

"They met near sand dunes in Oregon. There was something unexplainable about him. Perhaps some kind of verisimilitude she could not describe. I'm probably not using the word correctly. Do you know what I'm talking about?"

"I will not play along with the swindler's trick of careful questions."

So he did know, Charles thought.

"Sarah and this man became fond of each other. It was before you were born. He had big dreams that involved science, but also something more mysterious than science. They knew their lives would separate and

331

move on different tracks. But they swore to remember each other. His name was Frank. Just like yours. And his initial was H…"

"Just like mine," Whiting whispered.

Suddenly it became clear to Charles. He nodded and closed his eyes.

"But few know the story of how she chose the name Herbert."

"Only Martin," Whiting said. "She told me that story but no one else. I told Martin and no one else. We swore secrecy to avoid… hurt feelings." He shook his head. "How can you possibly know the story?"

"Perhaps via the mysterious ways you do acknowledge."

Whiting turned his head slowly, surveying the distant mountains, then the prairie and fields below, then the blue sky smudged with white clouds. Then he shook his head again, vigorously, as if to shake leaves out of his hair.

"I remain unconvinced," he said at last. "But tell me what you wish of me."

Charles opened the envelope, took out one pill, and set the envelope on the porch ledge.

"This is a new kind of medicine," Charles said. "There can be no guarantee, of course. But I believe it may defeat Martin's fever. Here, you may inspect it."

Charles handed him the pill.

"Interesting," Mr. Whiting said, frowning. "You claim it is new medicine. And yet it is obviously not made like one of Doctor Upjohn's friable pills."

"Friable? I don't know the word."

"Crushable. More easily digestible. It is a recent development, but surely any legitimate new medicine would use his technology. This pill feels hard."

"You are the engineer," Charles said. "I can't explain the science. I'm just the person who could… who could make the delivery."

"Yet you believe it to be safe?"

"I took one myself to be sure. And I will take another right now to convince you, if you wish."

"How many would be prescribed?"

"I've written specific instructions. I wasn't sure I could have a conversation with you."

"I see."

"I included more pills than you should need. "

Charles handed him the note. Whiting read it and smiled.

"I've never heard of Ernest Duchesne."

"No sir. But as others duplicate his success, the medicine's fame will grow. I would bet money on that. I may not be able to stay much longer. I don't seem to have much control over that."

"Sort of like the man my mother met on the sand dunes?"

"Exactly like that, I suspect. If you would choose any one of these pills, I will swallow it right now. Then you may make your own decision."

"You will either grow up to be a scientist or a story teller," he said, his mouth twisting upward in the hint of a smile. "Or at least a politician. You may leave your pills and I will decide. But I will ingest the sample myself." He held out his hand and Charles dropped a pill into it.

Mr. Whiting's eyes opened wider with apprehension at what he was about to do. He looked out at the view of the mountains and plains with obvious fondness tinged with hope and with sadness. Perhaps he was about to swallow poison. If so, this might be the last time he saw that view. He put the pill in his mouth, lifted his tea cup to his mouth and swallowed.

"It's a lovely view, isn't it?" Whiting said.

"Indeed it is," Charles answered, and they both stared out at the world before them.

The vast dry prairie stretched for miles. In the distance, Pike's Peak was a faint shadow on the horizon. Then the prairie changed. As Charles watched, buildings seemed to rise out of the ground, a smoky haze settled over them. Within a few seconds the modern 1950s version of Denver was complete, with noise and smog and traffic. It was like the transformation of the gelatinous horned toad egg melting away to reveal the tiny reptile inside

Charles was on the porch, but Mr. Whiting was no longer there. Charles' cat Lucy rubbed up against his leg, purring for attention.

"Did it work?" he asked the cat. It was the only living creature within the sound of his voice. From the angle of the sun above the mountains, it was late afternoon. He was almost certainly alone for another hour or so.

Quickly he went down the porch steps and entered the dog pen.

"Martin!" he shouted. "I think my idea worked!"

But Martin did not answer, Charles called again. From beneath the porch, Pan bleated sadly Charles crawled under the porch. "Martin, are you here?"

Then he saw the boy, curled up by the straw and motionless.

"Martin, are you OK? Martin answer me!" He had a terrible thought. "Martin! Didn't he give you the pills? I thought for sure…" He stopped. Maybe Martin wasn't in his bed when his father went up there to give him the medicine. Maybe he was already here, with Pan beneath the porch fifty years into the future.

His idea hadn't worked and now Martin was obviously very sick and stuck in the wrong century. His nightmares would continue. The haunting would get worse. Charles crawled out from beneath the porch. His dogs jumped around him, tails wagging furiously, wanting to play.

"Not now, Fritz,' Charles said. "Down Keisha. I need to think"

The sky was a deep perfect blue. A jet crawled across it leaving a bright white contrail behind it. The contrail gradually spread and became faint until it dispersed into invisibility.

Standing outside in the bright sunlight, the area under the porch looked black as a cave, Charles couldn't see Marin, or Pan, or the bales of straw.

"I'd like to help," he said out lout. But the only thing he could think to try was transporting with Martin and Pan back to 1897 once again. But what if he couldn't get back home? What if Martin died while he was there? Would Pan even recognize him again?

He remembered what his mother told him: "You should always try to help people," she had said.

"Even if it's hard?" he answered "Even if it costs me something? Even if it involves a sacrifice?

"Especially if it involves a sacrifice," she said.

He went back under the porch. Pan was lying on the ground close to Marin as if they were litter mates cuddling together for warmth. Charles sat beside them.

"OK, buddy," Charles said to the goat. "I don't know how this is going to work. We need to get Martin back to his time and before he got this sick…"

He stopped. He had never been able to aim at a specific time very well. Sometimes he missed by hours or days, but he'd also missed by centuries. Whet if he got Martin back to his own time but before Charles had given Mr. Whiting the penicillin?

"Wait here," he said. He ran inside and up to his room. He still had three penicillin tablets left. He put them into his shirt pocket and raced back downstairs and outside. Three pills was much less than a doctor would prescribe. A doctor would say take three or four a day for ten days. But it was better than nothing, and it was all he had.

Martin and Pan remained cuddled together, not moving. Charles couldn't tell if either one was breathing but he didn't want to get closer and check.

"Ghosts probably don't breathe, anyway," he said to himself. "It doesn't mean anything." He took a deep breath, put his hand on Pan's neck, and closed his eyes. He pictured Mr. Whiting on his porch, the way he'd seen him five minutes ago.

Nothing happened.

He pictured the view from the porch before the buildings sprouted up. He repeated the things he'd said to Martin's father and remembered the man's responses.

Nothing happened.

"You mentioned his horned toad and I said he called it Noceratops," Charles said softly.

"Reading to the dogs again?" Raymond's voice interrupted him "Or just taking a nap?" Charles's brother stood just outside the dog's pen with a mocking look on his face.

"I'm busy," Charles said, irritated. He opened his eyes. "Can't you go bother someone else…"

Charles stopped.

He was no longer under the porch. Raymond was nowhere to be seen. Charles was in the sunflower patch. Martin and Pan lay right beside him, still curled up together, still unconscious.

"OK," Charles said out loud, hoping they could hear him. "Maybe we got to the right time but missed the location by fifty yards or so." Leaving Martin and Pan sleeping, he crawled out of the sunflower patch and stood up.

The big hackberry trees were saplings once more. There were no highways in the distance and no traffic sounds. But the house itself had also changed. Someone had nailed wooden boards across all the doors and windows.

"I don't understand," he said to himself as he walked toward the house. Tumbleweeds grew where the Whiting garden had been. He ran up to the house and pounded on the boards over the porch door but no one responded. He walked around the house, pounding on the doors covering each of the windows he could reach. There was no sign of activity. He tried the front door again.

"Mr. Whiting!" he yelled. "Mr. Whiting can you hear me? We need to talk again! It's important!"

A late summer breeze whisked scraps of dead weeds around his feet. A crow called in the distance, but no other bird responded to it. Charles stared at his own house, so different now. No one lived there any more. At at this time, there were no neighbors. He walked back toward the sunflower patch and crawled into the little thicket.

"We've got to try again," he said. But Martin said nothing. Charles didn't wait for him. "OK, Pan," he said, nudging the goat. "It's up to you and me…"

Pan did not move. The goats's eyes stared blankly.

"Pan!" Charles shouted. "Wake up Pan!"

The goat did not respond. Charles put his hand on the goat's forehead. "No, Pan," he said and gently moved his hand until it touched the goat's eyelid. Veterinarians used this trick to see if an animal was still alive. The animal's rectangular pupils did not move; the animal did not flinch or blink.

"Martin," he said sadly. "Looks like we're going to have to try this without your manitou." He nudged the boy's leg.

But Martin did not move.

"Martin!" Charles shouted "Wake up Martin!" Charles nudged him harder but whatever life had inhabited him had flown away.

Charles sat back and panic surged through him. He was absolutely alone, marooned on a deserted hilltop that had once been familiar. The sun was beginning to sink over the mountains tinging the clouds with pink and yellow pastels. He had no family, no friends, no tools or weapon. He had failed and now Martin was truly dead.

But how could that be? How could a ghost die? Except for the boards on windows and doors, the house had not changed. The trees he knew were still saplings. Surely he had traveled back to when Martin was alive.

No, he realized with a start. He had traveled back to slightly later date, a date after Martin died. The ghost and the body were reunited and then extinguished along with the goat that allowed him to travel through space and time.

What should he do? Think, Charles, he told himself over and over. Should he try to hike to the nearest house, wherever that was? Should he try to tell someone a little boy was dead in the sunflower patch? But if he left, coyotes would find Martin and Pan. He shuddered at that image.

Maybe Pan's magic had not left his body yet. The only chance he had was to try to transport them all back to an afternoon in 1897 with Mr.

Whiting on the front porch. Maybe if he kept one hand on the dead goat's neck…

Charles could not concentrate. The image of a snarling coyote kept imposing itself on his brain. That was followed by the image of Sapania killing the jackrabbit. Maybe if he had a weapon he'd feel safe enough to concentrate. Any weapon.

As the sun sank and the light began to fade, he searched the ground around him. He'd settle for a rock, something like the rock he'd thrown that startled the jackrabbit.

He crawled to the spot the thought the hare had been hiding but there was no stone. He sat back, dejected. Not even a rock, he though. He fought back tears.

Then he admonished himself. "Snap out of it. Edison would not have given up so easily. Use your brain."

He was looking for the rock in the wrong spot. Startling the jackrabbit hadn't happened yet. It wouldn't happen for fifty years.

No good landmarks defined the weed patch. Even the sunflowers themselves were different from year to year as new seedlings annually replaced their dead ancestors. Finally he found the big rock, only a few feet beyond the bodies of Martin and Pan.

He sat with his left hand on Pan, and clutched the rock in his right. He tried hard not to picture his own bedroom, his parents, his own time. No, he probably only had one jump if he was very lucky. If he could get Martin and the goat back to the right time, there was a chance that, with a healthy manitou, he could make another leap into his own life. But if he tried to go there directly, Martin would still be dead and separated from his own family.

He pictured Mr. Whiting on the porch drinking peppermint tea with Pikes Peak rising faintly in the distance

But nothing happened. He tried over and over again. He repeated all the Latin words from his list. He made up new words that sounded magical. The western sky glowed red now between clusters of sunflower leaves and stalks.

There was nothing else to try. He sat back.

This was too big. He would never see his mother or father again. Never see Raymond, or Mrs. Klein or his dogs or cat. None of his school friends. None of them were alive right now, not while he was.

Is this what old people feel as their parents and friends die around them? You lose them one after another until finally you know more dead people than living ones. Then suddenly you realize you're all alone, a ghost in your own life.

"Well, I'll probably be fine in 1897," he said, trying to sound optimistic. "Hey, I've already read many of the books."

He would stay alert tonight, then in the daylight he'd walk south toward Denver ("Denver City" in 1897 he corrected himself). Or maybe he'd walk over to the Pillar of Fire. He corrected himself: Westminster College. If he'd landed in a time where it was used as a university, someone would take him in. His knowledge of science (most of which had not happened yet) would make him valuable. He'd do fine.

He stared at Martin. He couldn't even dig a hole in the hard prairie dirt to bury him. The boy deserved something to mark his sad, short life. At the very least, a ceremony of some sort. Charles needed a ritual of as much as Martin did.

Some science experiments seem ceremonial, with exact procedures to repeat, but that didn't feel appropriate. His attempts at magical ceremonies all failed, so that didn't seem right either. He hadn't attended church regularly enough to remember the various rituals. Church-service words probably made sense to someone, just not to him. They often included music.

A sacrifice! Ancient ceremonies all involved a sacrifice. For the Mayans and others, it was a human death. In more modern religions a symbolic sacrifice, like a cash donation to the church into a plate that was passed around. Ceremonies involve giving up something that matters to you. A sacrifice.

He touched his shirt and felt the old bell beneath it. Except for his clothes, it was all he had left of his life. But the bell was of no use to him now, not really. People had seemed eager to get their hands on it, but that never made much sense to Charles. It was just a crusty bell and ugly as an old radiator cap. Completely useless, but it represented his entire life up to now.

He knew what he had to do. He would live out his life in the 1800s—he couldn't change that. But this night, this sunset, belonged to Martin.

He used a stick to dig a little hole. He removed the bell from his neck and untied the shoelace he'd used as a necklace. Then he spoke to the lifeless forms on the ground beside him, the boy and the goat.

"Martin, it's been a pleasure to know you. Pan, you too. You've shown me adventures I never would have known. So thank you both. If there is an existence after death, I hope yours is wonderful. Maybe we'll meet again. Goodbye."

Charles held the bell by its little handle and struck it three times with the stick, very slowly. The sound was pure and clear and sad.

Then he buried the bell and set the rock on the dirt beside it. The little mound of dirt capped with a cold stone looked a little like a grave. Charles felt inside his shirt pocket and took out his last blue feather. "To make it a bit cheerier," he said, and he shoved the feather into the dirt so it stood up like a little flag.

He sat cross-legged on the ground, his hands on his knees. Tonight he would keep watch over his friend and the goat. He would protect their bodies. Any coyotes or raccoons or con men or witches would have to get past him before they messed with this place or those bodies. And this time, even if he was no longer in his own time, he knew he could conjure enough magic to discourage even the most evil and bloodthirsty opponent.

Something touched his hand and he looked down. A dragonfly had perched on his knuckle, its tiny strong claws gently clutching his skin. Charles smiled.

"So, my guardian angel has returned. Nice to see a friendly face, buddy, even one with multifaceted eyes and a segmented body." Very slowly he lifted his arm until he and the insect stared at each other from the same height. "So, after all this, what we've proved is that dragonflies like bell music. Seems like there could have been a simpler experiment."

The dragonlfy closed its wings once, then opened them again. Just then, Charles felt a familiar tickling in his nose.

"I'm sorry, little guy. Sunflower pollen always gets to me sooner or later." He slowly moved his hand close to a plant. With his other hand, he squeezed his nose, trying to hold in the inevitable sneeze that would certainly frighten the insect away. If the dragonfly was on a plant, maybe Charles could turn away, muffle the sound with his elbow. It was silly, he knew, to try to keep an insect companion for a few more seconds. "Go on, little guy. Step onto the leaf."

But the dragonfly refused to leave his hand and finally Charles couldn't hold the sneeze any longer. It exploded from him. He tried to hold still, he tried to muffle. He squeezed his eyes tightly shut and felt certain the insect would be gone when he reopened them. The thought saddened him even further.

"How did you do that?"

The voice startled Charles. It sounded just like his brother Raymond, but that wasn't possible.

"I said how did you do that?"

Charles opened his eyes. He was sitting beneath the porch, leaning against a bale of straw and Raymond stood outside in the sunshine, pointing an accusing finger at him.

"Did you use mirrors? I know there's a trick. You tell me right now!"

Charles was as stunned at being at his own home, in his own time, as he would have been had he woke up on the moon. There was no sign of Martin or Pan. There was no bell beneath his shirt. But a big black dragonfly clung to his index finger with its hard miniature fingernails. Charles stared at the insect.

"You speak up right now," Raymond insisted. "I was looking right at you and then you vanished. I don't think Mom will be happy to learn you've been practicing magic again!"

Charles thought fast. From out in the sunlight, Raymond probably couldn't see him very well anyway. A tear formed in the corner of Charles eye and he wiped it away. He hadn't been able to save Martin, but he had done his best. And now he was back in his own very ordinary life, but with a dragonfly perched on his hand.

"How long was I gone?" Charles asked, trying to keep his voice calm. His voice startled the dragonfly and it flew out into the bright sunshine, flying fast and swerving as if evading a pursuer. Within two seconds it had joined a new century.

"Ten seconds! Maybe fifteen! You teach me the trick and maybe I won't turn you in!"

"Let me get this straight. You think I simply vanished for fifteen seconds without using any mirrors or other equipment?" Charles continued to stare out at the bright new world the dragonfly had disappeared into.

"Don't be ridiculous. Of course you used mirrors, or a hidden wall or something. You show me right now or I'm telling!"

"I see." Charles shook his head thoughtfully. He crawled out from beneath the porch and stood beside his brother. He brushed straw and dirt from his jeans. "So, Raymond, have you been feeling alright? Getting enough sleep?"

"What?"

"It's OK, Raymond, I won't tell anyone you've been hallucinating. No need for Mrs. Klein to know. I'm sure you don't want them to send you to the sanitarium. You know, the one with snakes."

"You used mirrors!"

"Whatever you say, Raymond. It's probably not good for you to get excited. Crawl on under the porch and look for yourself. No mirrors, no wires, no secret compartment. You're probably just not getting enough sleep."

Raymond scowled. Then he crawled under the porch.

"Where did you hide them?" he said. He didn't sound so sure anymore.

Outside in the sunlight, Charles looked at the clear blue sky and shook his head.

"I'm sorry, Raymond. You've got it worse than I thought, I'm afraid I really need to tell Mom and Dad."

Raymond came out and stood beside him sheepishly.

"Well, maybe I just looked away for a minute," Raymond said quietly. "There's no such thing as magic."

"Of course not," Charles agreed, "There's no such thing as magic."

Chapter 46

The haunting stopped. There were no more scratching sounds, no more phantom footsteps. The house creaked and moaned with the wind, but his family slept through it. The summer passed in a very ordinary way. Charles went to piano lessons but, to no one's surprise, he did not improve. His guppies multiplied and he set up a second tank. The patch of sunflowers froze in the autumn and their leaves dried to dust. His father recovered and came home from the hospital.

Now that he knew he could control magic, Charles no longer felt the urge to do so. He could stop arrows in mid flight, and defeat an evil witch/ warrior from a distant time. He didn't need to do card tricks.

In September, the school year began again. His new teacher was a man. He'd never heard of a man teacher before. The class was cautiously orderly because no one knew how a man might react to kids who misbehaved. Charles still refrained from using big words. Sometimes he forgot, but by now everyone had matured about one year's worth and no one paid much attention.

Halloween came and went. A couple from church bought a color TV, and invited Charles's family to watch "Cyrano de Bergerac." The color made the show seem miraculously lifelike; none of them had realized what they were missing. Driving home, Charles's father sadly said they'd probably never be rich enough to own a color TV.

Thanksgiving passed, with its warm smells and hot ovens.

Charles loved the day after Thanksgiving because it was predictable. He knew he'd make a turkey and cranberry-sauce sandwich. He'd eat cold mashed potatoes and gravy because it's hard to re-heat mashed potatoes on the stove. The day after Thanksgiving Charles started to think about Christmas. He liked the whole event: the tree, the food, even the church services because they sang songs he knew.

After eating his sandwich, Charles went down into the basement, a cool dark place that wasn't usable by most people's standards. The house's foundation of sandstone blocks served as walls. The floor was uneven concrete and dirt. Ceiling joists were exposed; between them ancient wires and pipes sagged unevenly. Piles of boxes containing tools and hardware and electrical parts his father bought at surplus stores collected in groups. Cobwebs gathered dust in every corner and dangled from the ceiling. It smelled musty and oily.

Charles felt very comfortable down there.

One spot was sort of a secret. A circular hole in the concrete floor, five feet across and two feet deep was covered with boards. The original coal furnace had stood above that depression, years earlier, and a tunnel extended under the floor to provide air for combustion. Charles's parents moved the old furnace outside to use as an incinerator when they installed a new gas furnace in a different location. That left the hole in the floor where the old furnace had been. They never bothered to fill in the hole or its air tunnel. They just covered it with boards so no one would fall two feet and twist an ankle.

The tunnel was large enough that a boy his size could imagine squeezing through it, braving spiders and monsters to solve its mysteries. But Charles never did. He pictured himself getting trapped in there, facing unimaginable creatures where no one could hear him or rescue him before he ultimately starved to death. The joy of discovering a possible outside opening did not move his soul quite enough. And now that his body was growing faster, soon he wouldn't fit. The passage of time would remove his options.

Sometimes he took a flashlight down there, removed a board, and stuck his head down a few inches. Maybe this time he'd see something.

And this time he did.

Right below his head stood a big land turtle (a tortoise, he corrected himself) eight inches across. It wasn't at all concerned that a human head intruded into its territory. The beast stood with legs firmly planted on the dirt floor, its head extended from the shell, staring up inquisitively.

Charles set down the flashlight, reached in with both hands, and gently picked it up. The tortoise was completely unfazed. Charles held it up in front of his face, amused by its courage.

"So, little guy, how do you survive down there? What do you eat?"

345

It cocked its head to one side as if listening. Charles smiled.

"Well," he said. "Probably earthworms, right? And if the tunnel really does open up outside somewhere, maybe some weed roots and mushrooms. I bet some bugs fly down there, too. Am I close?"

The tortoise did not answer but it didn't withdraw either. It just stared at Charles who held him even closer to his face, smiling. A moldy dirt smell clung to the subterranean reptile, but not in an unpleasant way. It reminded Charles of petrichor, the smell the earth makes after a rain. There was also another smell, much fainter and almost sweet. He recognized the incongruous scent of vanilla, and it triggered happy memories.

"You're pretty trusting, aren't you?" Charles said. "You sort of remind me of my old friend Martin. He was trusting like that. Maybe I'll call you Martin after him. If he's still alive he'd be as old as my grandfather by now. I guess you could be that old too."

It felt weird to think of little Martin as an old man. And weird to think the creature in his hands could also be that old. In fact, maybe this turtle had lived in this tunnel since Martin was little. Since the time Charles visited him in his bedroom, if he really had. He smiled at the thought.

Charles looked up from the turtle. The basement was suddenly much darker. The hole in the floor had filled in and was now covered by neat hardwood boards, all polished and lovely. There was a light over to his right. Still holding the tortoise he forced his eyes to focus, as if he was waking from a hard sleep. Everything looked blurry... and then it cleared.

He was no longer in the basement, he was in his bedroom. But it was no longer his bedroom, it was Martin's bedroom. Martin was sitting up in bed, covers pulled up to his shoulders. His face was tan and healthy and he was no longer so skinny. His father, Frank Herbert Whiting, sat in the chair bedside him. A small electric lamp lit both father and son in a pale yellow glow. The air smelled like pine trees and cinnamon and vanilla and hot chocolate. It smelled like Christmas. Charles looked at the reptile in his hands. "Did you do this?" he whispered to it. "Are you...?"

Mr. Whiting had a newspaper in his lap and a big smile on his face. "Martin, you ask an excellent question," he said. "One that others have asked..." He stopped, obviously startled, and looked at Charles.

"I did not expect to see you again," he said.

"So you can see me?"

"Indeed I see you," he said. "and your tortoise. You are most welcome to join us."

"Who are you talking to father?

Mr. Whiting looked at Martin, then back at Charles.

"I begin to understand," he said. "Your medicine worked, as you can see. I visited our bee hives, but didn't have to tell the bees anything except thank your for the honey. And thank you as well." He picked up the copy of Ivanhoe, opened it and wrote something inside it. He nodded at Charles and put the book down.

"Understand what, father? And thank you for what? But don't change the subject: is there a Santa Claus or not?"

Charles smiled and nodded at Mr. Whiting., who nodded back then turned to Martin.

"In an interesting coincidence, Martin, a girl in New York recently asked the same question. The response was in The Sun, which the Denver Evening News reprinted. I'd like to read it to you. And to whoever else might be listening." He began to read from the newspaper. He read a little extra loud just to make sure Charles could hear.

"Nobody sees Santa Claus but that is no sign that there is no Santa Claus. The most real things in the world are those that neither children nor men can see. Did you ever see fairies dancing on the lawn? Of course not, but that's no proof that they are not there. Nobody can conceive or imagine all the wonders there are unseen and unseeable in the world.

"You may tear apart the baby's rattle and see what makes the noise inside, but there is a veil covering the unseen world which not the strongest man, nor even the united strength of all the strongest men that ever lived, could tear apart. Only faith, fancy, poetry, love, romance, can push aside that curtain and view and picture the supernal beauty and glory beyond. Is it all real? Ah, Virginia! In all this world there is nothing else real and abiding."

And then both Martin and his father faded to invisibility. The room shuddered, the light shifted, and Charles stood alone in his own bedroom, with his bunk bed and his own posters on the wall. Bumps the horned toad scratched at his box. Charles still held the tortoise with both hands. From downstairs, his mother's voice called up, "Charles, it's time for dinner. Remember to wash your hands."

"I'll be right there," he called back. He smiled to see Ivanhoe on the little table beside his bed, a book of words that had not traveled back and forth through time but simply existed as time swirled around it. He opened it. It did not fall open to page one, as it usually did. Instead, it opened to the title page. On the title page, someone had written in faded ink: "To Charles, who made the rest of the story possible."

THE END

Photo of Westminster University, later called Bellevue College, then Pillar of Fire. Westminster, Colorado.

Photo taken sometime in the 1890s

AFTERWORD:

About This Book
by Kenn

Much of this book is autobiographical; it is possible some things in it are also true. Many of the characters are drawn from historical figures. In some (but not all) cases, I've given them bits of dialog that we know they actually spoke. But the book is total fiction and, despite my appropriation of names and bits of history, don't believe any of it. Certainly don't sue me for defaming your grandfather or whatever. I've also used some actual places and fictionalized them.

I grew up in an old, spooky house on top of a hill north of Denver in the 1950s. People claimed it was haunted. I thought the house would make a cool setting for a novel. That's how this project started.

Frank Herbert Whiting house, Westminster, Colorado photo from 1890s Used by permission of the Westminster Historical Society and the Whiting family.

The original working title was "Small Magic." I wanted to explore what might happen if someone had just a very small amount of magical power — they could make an insect land one place rather than another, for example. What would a person do with a tiny amount of mysterious power? Could one person with a tiny gift have a large effect? I hoped they could. The book evolved away from that idea but that's where it started. I also wanted to include little bits of history, not just because the house itself had some interesting history, but also to connect the story to real people and events.

I started to write it in about 2008, while living in Colorado. As I wrote, a few small and mildly weird coincidences occurred. That's not unusual; I often notice tiny coincidences when I'm in the midst of a writing project. I've come to expect them, notice them, and be grateful for them because they imply, at least to me, that I'm connecting with something larger than myself.

Then I got distracted by writing three other books, and with sorting through various family and business emergencies, and moving to Oregon. Once I returned to this project, the weird coincidences began piling up again. I noted them in casual journal entries, mentioned them in various emails to family and friends, and in the occasional Facebook post. One of my sons suggested that the collection of anecdotes might make an interesting introduction to the book. I wish I had kept them all.

I finished the first draft of the book in 2019, but decided I could not put these little stories at the beginning of the book because they might spoil the story for readers, and also because they could chase away people before they'd read a single page of the book itself. So I'm putting them here, at the end. I've added a few since then. You don't need to read them; there will not be a test. They probably won't be included in the published book, if there ever is one. I'm not going to try to organize them much, but just copy the notes I made at the time (or that I sent to various friends via email) with only gentle editing. They aren't strictly chronological and there will be a bit of repetition. But then, life involves repetition. Consider them echos.

July 2009

This morning I went jogging my usual route. I typically leave my house and jog for about a mile and half, then alternate bursts of jogging and walking back. On today's return route, a big predatory bird circled in the sky — an eagle or hawk, I don't know my birds that well. This one was big with a white chest, a tan head, and black feathers on the sky-side of his wings. He landed atop a light pole looking down on the path ahead of me. I walked toward him slowly and got close enough to see him well before he casually pushed off and flew down the path to land on the next light pole. He didn't seem frightened, just exercising prudent common sense. We had looked in each other's eyes and seen nothing much to worry about.

By now it was time for me to jog a section, so I ran toward him as fast as my withered old legs would take me. This time, he didn't fly away at all and I ran right beneath him. I didn't look back but jogged, then walked, then jogged the remaining half mile or so home. Once there, I collapsed on a chair, sweat pouring off me.

Cheryl came into the living room and stood nearby to ask about some book order. She looked out the window and said that there was some big bird, maybe an eagle, perched on the roof of the house across the street. She'd never seen a bird like that in our neighborhood. It was my new jogging companion.

"I guess he followed me home," I said.

When you write about communing with butterflies and then a day or two later an eagle follows you home, you remember that there's a funny kind of magic involved with this writing business.

    xxx

Small Magic is becoming interesting. You know I don't talk much about books while they are writing themselves, but some of this seems interesting and not harmful to my notorious "process." I don't remember how much I've told you, so some of this will be a repeat. It will probably be way too long, so sorry about that.

I'm using bits of historical fact to lend some verisimilitude to "Small Magic." The book is set in the 1950s in the old haunted house I grew up in in Westminster, Colorado, coincidentally in the 1950s. The protagonist

(Charles) is a kid who lives there. He reads old books, believes in both magic and science, and has a large vocabulary for which he gets teased. Don't know where THAT character comes from, but I digress. He encounters the ghost of a kid (Martin) who died in that house in the late 1890s (a kid named Martin did die there back then) and also some more sinister ghosts. I googled deaths in the area in the late 1890s hoping to find an obituary from 1897 of someone buried in the cemetery at the Pillar of Fire campus. No luck. So I tried to find someone at least in that area who died that year. I was sort of auditioning ghosts and came up with Jim Baker, trapper, marksman, and scout. I liked the way he looked, so I chose him. (https://www.wyohistory.org/encyclopedia/jim-baker-frontier-scout)

I checked out a book about Baker from Oregon State U, read it and took notes. I was stunned to learn that he lived either on the site of the Berkeley School at 50th and Lowell in Denver (which I bought from the City of Denver and remodeled in the 1970s) or very near it. He owned it in the 1850s. What are the odds?

Martin's father (Frank Herbert Whiting, who built the house my family later owned) was a civil engineer for the railroad, worked for Buffalo Bill Cody for a while, and was present in Alaska when Soapy Smith got killed in a gunfight. All that's historical.

Obviously, I had to include Soapy and bought a book ("Alias Soapy Smith" by Jeff Smith) about his life.

Jim Baker

Soapy Smith's grandson Jeff Smith impersonates his notorious grandfather. This is Jeff Smith in 2021

Alias Soapy Smith had an index, so I tried to see if maybe Jim Baker had any intersection with Soapy, but no. Reading about Soapy's demise, a mysterious guy named Jess Murphy showed up at the event, played a critical role (by some accounts, he fired the fatal shot) and soon disappeared forever. Nobody seemed to know much about him — prime ghost material. Alas, there was no one named Murphy in Baker's life, or Soapy's or Whiting's as far as I could tell. So I thought, hey, maybe there was a "Murphy" rifle brand and I'd give Baker a buddy who owned one and acquired the nickname. Turns out, no there was not. But that google search did come up with a Timothy Murphy, a fabled marksman and remarkable character in his own right during the Revolutionary War. He died the year Baker was born. This earned him the status of "Kenn's new ghost," and provided a whole new twist in the plot. You won't be surprised to learn that someone wrote a novel about his life in 1953 called "The Rifleman." Or that the University of Oregon has one of the few remaining copies. Or that I checked it out and read it. He was raised by several different tribes and families, so was known by several different names over his life. Being a little silly, I decided to name him "Just Murphy" because a witness to Soapy's demise might hear "Just Murphy" and think the speaker said "Jess Murphy" and thereafter that's how he'd be listed.

Right: Timothy Murphy, sharpshooter in the Revolutionary War. Photo: Artist's conception in oil in Town of Fulton History Local History Sec. IX History Room. Middleburg Library, Mohawk Valley Library System, NY

xxxx

Alias Soapy Smith had an index, so I tried to see if maybe Jim Baker had any intersection with Soapy, but no. Reading about Soapy's demise, a mysterious guy named Jess Murphy showed up at the event, played a critical role (by some accounts, he fired the fatal shot) and soon disappeared forever. Nobody seemed to know much about him — prime ghost material. Alas, there was no one named Murphy in Baker's life, or Soapy's or Whiting's as far as I could tell. So I thought, hey, maybe there was a "Murphy" rifle brand and I'd give Baker a buddy who owned one and acquired the nickname. Turns out, no there

Right: Timothy Murphy, sharpshooter in the Revolutionary War.
Photo: Artist's conception in oil in Town of Fulton History Local History Sec. IX History Room.
Middleburg Library,
Mohawk Valley Library System, NY

was not. But that google search did come up with a Timothy Murphy, a fabled marksman and remarkable character in his own right during the Revolutionary War. He died the year Baker was born. This earned him the status of "Kenn's new ghost," and provided a whole new twist in the plot. You won't be surprised to learn that someone wrote a novel about his life in 1953 called "The Rifleman." Or that the University of Oregon has one of the few remaining copies. Or that I checked it out and read it. He was raised by several different tribes and families, so was known by several different names over his life. Being a little silly, I decided to name him "Just Murphy" because a witness to Soapy's demise might hear "Just Murphy" and think the speaker said "Jess Murphy" and thereafter that's how he'd be listed.

xxxx

Monday morning I went down to the New Day Bakery, which has become my favorite writing haunt, to scribble down the scenes that arrived in my brain over the weekend. But no. A writer friend who does improv under the name "Gabriella" stopped at my table and we chatted at length. That was fun but I did not complete all the writing I intended to. When I got home, household maintenance demanded attention and then the day was gone. I remained eager to spend some uninterrupted moments with all the characters who were clamoring for quality time with my pen.

While I was chatting with Gabriella on Monday, she mentioned that she was on a "news fast." It's all just too upsetting to her, but she thinks maybe she has a duty to stay informed so she's conflicted. I said, you know, everyone plays a different role. That guy over there at that table wearing the hat? Maybe you do something nice for him, something insignificant — maybe you give him a nice blue feather for his hat — and it cheers him up and he doesn't mail out the pipe bombs he's been building. Your little act of kindness could be more important than arguing politics with someone you'll never convince. I think that gave her permission to avoid some of the contagious insanity to which I suspect she has very little immunity.

Tuesday, I went back to New Day Bakery and had fun writing about all my ghosts. I sat at one of the long community tables in the center of the room. They're like picnic tables. At the next table sat two women with an adorable little girl maybe three years old. She had wild blonde hair sticking up in every direction and reminded me of the kids hippies had in the sixties named Moonbeam or Unicorn. A feral child. She was mostly very calm, but at one point she stood up on the bench and began yelling and pointing at a small print of a painting, maybe 12 inches square on the wall at least a doze feet away from her. She was very insistent. Nothing interesting was happening over there, and we were both too far from the print to see it very well, so I thought it was odd. The guy sitting at the booth beneath the art became nervous for her and admonished the kid to sit down, she could fall. Finally her mother settled her down. After a while they left.

Being a guy who's interested in the weird, in a few minutes I went over to that booth and told the two guys who were now there not to panic, I just wanted to see the art on the wall. It was a print of a painting done in an old style and depicted a tired bagpipe player sitting down while rustic village folk danced around. Nothing remarkable about the painting at all, or the wall near it; the little girl had clearly been imagining something. I sat down again and continued writing. When I finally was ready to leave, no one occupied that booth so I went over one more time and got my face right next to the picture. Still nothing interesting. Just before I turned to walk away, I noticed one little detail: the guy in the center of the painting, the main dancer, wears a dark hat.

In the band of his hat there's a tiny blue feather.

If a guy is looking for odd coincidences, he can find dozens every day. If he's looking for clues that the universe thinks his writing project is on the right path, he can probably find those too. That's a more fun choice. I added some blue feathers to my book.

On Wednesday I went down there again and wrote several pages. I sat in the exact same spot, so I could keep my eye on that little painting. After about an hour, I got up to stretch my legs. No one was in the booth below the painting so I was inspired to think hey, I've got a cell phone, I can probably take a picture of it to remember the incident. I got close just as another guy arrived, coffee cup in hand. I assured him I didn't want the booth, I just wanted to take a picture of the painting because something weird happened earlier in the week involving it. He was totally cool with it and said, "It looks like a Bruegel." I said what? He said he didn't know the painting but the style was like Bruegel. He claimed he wasn't really into art, but he remembered some bits from college decades earlier. I took my picture and went back to write.

After another half hour or so, the guy came over to me. More curious than me, he'd used his phone to track down the painting. Sure enough, it was a copy of a Bruegel called "Peasant Dance" painted in 1569. It seemed cool of him to search that out, so I shook his hand and introduced myself. His name was Martin.

OF COURSE his name was Martin.

Bruegel did a strange thing: he inserted pictograms depicting various wise contemporary proverbs into his paintings. One painting had over a hundred of these representations. That seemed like an odd thing to do, so I tried to find proverbs that he actually used. They did not translate well at all, but that's where I came up with all the nearly nonsensical phrases in the section with the painter. Those are all things he said, or at least represented in his paintings. I liked that it made the journey back in time to another culture and language feel more foreign, as it surely would.

Bruegel the Elder, self portrait

Left: a young Frank Herbert Whiting in Alaska
This was taken in Alaska and it's the image I used while imagining him. But there were two Frank Whitings involved in building the railroad, the other one was a doctor. It's possible that's who this is. Or that people only *thought* there were two of them…

Thanks to:

Sandra Johnston / Library Asst. II

Alaska State Library Historical Collections

PO Box 110571

Juneau, AK   99811-0571

I was an old man before I learned anything at all about the guy who built the house of my childhood. Once I did, It seemed weird to me that he was named "Frank Herbert Whiting" because I love the Dune books written by Frank Herbert and it's not a common name. Especially not years before the author was born. I wondered if there was any connection between the two men, but I didn't see anyone in Whiting's immediate family named Herbert. That left only one possibility: Frank Herbert the author had his own manitou and traveled back in time and had some sort of friendship with Whiting's mother and she named her kid after him. They probably met on the coast of Oregon, which is where he got the idea to write Dune. Apparently, his beagle "Bub" was his manitou. I can't really think of any viable alternative theory.

A young Frank Herbert, author of *Dune.*

We recently attended the play "Dracula"and discovered that the book Dracula was published in 1897. That sound you hear is the Universe honking its horn at me. Now, to honor that coincidence, I let my main ghost's father read it as a brand new book. I didn't know how he got it, because it was published in London and he's in Colorado, but I invented a story. Dracula plays only a tiny role in my book: Martin's father quotes it a couple of times. It makes perfect sense and adds a little flavor. He gets his copy from a guy named Delius. Bram Stoker (author of Dracula) was a sickly kid whose mother told him scary bedtime stories. I looked up some Irish tales that were popular at the time and let Mrs. Stoker tell one I thought young Bram might have enjoyed.

A young Bram Stoker

xxx

I may have told you that the main ghost in my book owns a magical goat which I named, with a stunning lack of originality, "Pan" after the goat-like critter from mythology. Now that I invented him and gave him a name, he keeps turning up everywhere.

We recently attended a concert featuring the music of Brahms. It did not surprise me much when the conductor told us that Brahms died in 1897, same as Martin. So why not let my main character accidentally visit Brahms? I read a little about Brahms just to add a bit of color to whatever mention I gave him, thinking it would be one paragraph. I thought it would be cool if if Brahms had a pet, perhaps a dog, who might (or might not...) also have powers. By googling "Brahms" and "dog," I discovered an incident when a big dog named Marco rushed into a rehearsal, knocking stuff over. That became the scene I used so I looked up the dog's owner, Ethel Smyth, to describe her. Based on the tiny fragments I found, she was a fascinating character herself, a composer, suffragette, athlete, and writer.

After I finished writing the first draft and was editing, rewriting, and adding tidbits, I found a blog about her (https://blog.oup.com/2014/05/facts-dame-ethel) written by Christopher Wiley that includes this:

"Smyth kept a series of dogs for over fifty years. Her first dog, given to her in 1888, was a St Bernard cross called Marco, who travelled everywhere with her. In 1901, a friend presented her with an Old English sheepdog puppy she named Pan, who became the first in the line of sheepdogs she successively numbered Pan II, Pan III, up to Pan VII. Her lesser-known book Inordinate (?) Affection: A Story for Dog Lovers (1936), a collected biography of some of her canine companions, stands alongside such classics as Virginia Woolf's Flush and Jack London's The Call of the Wild as famous examples of dogs in literature."

That seems weird to me. In real life, Marco knocked over a cello stand at a rehearsal with Brahms. In my book, that's because he's chasing over to visit Pan, my fictional goat. Then in real life, Ethel names her next seven dogs after my imaginary goat. Doesn't that seem just a tad... unusual??

I followed a link from that blog to a recording of her speaking. She was interviewed briefly on BBC in 1937 about an incident that happened to her in 1906. The host speaks for a bit, then Smyth starts speaking about two minutes in. You can hear a hint of her feistiness, although the incident hasn't much to do with my book. Still, hearing her voice was like listening to an actual ghost.

http://www.bbc.co.uk/archive/suffragettes/8314.shtml

All this might not add one line to the scene where she appears, but it feels interesting to me.

xxx

Ethel Smyth wrote several memoirs. I bought a book that claimed to be the best excerpts of those, just to get some tidbits about Brahms. The few paragraphs I've read so far surprised me: Smyth was a wonderful, engaging writer and a total character. If she doesn't have her own series on British TV, she should. I opened her book at random and learned of her pretty housekeeper named "Ford" who died very young and who loved Marco and probably Ethel as well. So I added a paragraph today in which Ford's ghost makes a brief appearance and speaks a line she actually said while alive. Marco was already the star of the scene, so it all felt very lucky.

FEB 2019

As I was writing the last pages of my novel, I wanted to add a long-lived critter that could be alive in 1897 as well as 1955, so my hero discovered a land tortoise. A couple of days later, scientists discovered a tortoise in the Galapagos last seen in 1906 and believed extinct. My family insists I can take no credit for the discovery, so I won't. But it's still cool.

INORDINATE (?) AFFECTION

A Story for Dog Lovers

by

ETHEL SMYTH, D.B.E.

FEB 24 2019

When I discovered that Ethel Smyth named a series of dogs "Pan I, Pan II, etc" after I'd written about her meeting the goat Pan in my book, I checked into her experience with dogs. Turns out, she wrote a whole book about her love of dogs, called Inordinate (?) Affection. The question mark is hers. So I added a line to my own book as a bit of an inside joke for her fans, using the word inordinate. Went online to see if I could buy the book (I'm curious why she named all her dogs Pan) and there were several copies for sale, but they seemed expensive so I waited. The next day, they had all disappeared except for one copy in England for a hundred bucks. I was not that curious. I decided to check periodically, see if any came up. This morning, searching her name and "books" I found some books that mentioned her. One told about what a skillful singer she was and mentioned three or four songs she sang, only one of which she sang in English, Come O'er the Sea. I googled it and it was a Thomas Moore song, still sung today. Well, Moore put out a book in 1808 where he swiped old Irish melodies and wrote his own poetry to them in English. His book became very popular and shaped Irish music since then. It also doomed the versions of songs in the book I own, The Irish Musical Repository also published in 1808. So I hate him for that, and have for several years. As you know, I've arranged several songs from my old book and may well be the only person in the world that sings any of them. (my versions of those songs are on my music website (kennamdahl.com)

I managed to find several YouTube versions of Come O'er the Sea and tracked down the lyrics. I inserted a couple of lines from the lyrics into my own book, letting her sing them. I did not recognize the melody but wondered if Moore swiped the tune from some song in my book, as he did with many others. I looked through my book, but no. I finally found the sheet music and played the melody, but it wasn't familiar. Then I searched to see if I could find a "to the tune of" or "to the air of" (many old Irish songs shared the same tune). Amazingly, in a book published in 1892 it says Come o'er the Sea was sung to the tune of Cushlamachree, a song from my songbook which I learned and like. Alas, this melody is not that melody. Perhaps it was originally to that tune and in the 80-some years after that the tune changed. Perhaps there was more than one Cushlamachree. Perhaps he just blundered swiping the tune, or perhaps the guy who wrote the book in 1892 was wrong about which air it used. Ethel might have sung the melody I know, but more likely the later one. Whatever the case, it surprised the heck out of me to see the name of that song, a song that is sung by only me in the whole world as far as I can tell, in connection with the only song I know Ethel Smyth sang in English.

Since I wrote the book, Smyth's music has seen a bit of a reincarnation. In 2021 she won a Grammy.

xxxx

I wanted a quiet place to write about an odd ghost that showed up and baffled me in the book I'm writing. So I hiked into a lonely cemetery I'd never visited (most graves from the Civil War). After I'd written what I wanted to write, my fountain pen started bleeding ink all over the page. Huge mess. In all the decades I've written with a fountain pen, that's never happened. Probably a coincidence.

xxxx

We attended a Christmas concert by the Emerald City Jazz Kings. In the introduction to one Christmas song, they mentioned how its origins involved the year 1897. After some research on their reference, I think I have the image that will end the book. If you just pay attention, these books will write themselves. Or maybe haunt you forever.

xxxx

The blog that informed me of Ethel Smyth's dog book also mentioned Flush a book Virginia Woolf wrote from the perspective of Elizabeth Barrett (Browning)'s dog of that name. Smyth and Woolf were friends. I am ashamed to confess I've never read anything by Ms. Woolf, so I bought a cheap used copy. I've been reading it very casually, a random page now and then. Those few random samples demonstrated that Woolf was a very lush, elegant writer, so that's been fun.

I picked it up this morning and read a page, and was startled when she mentioned "Pan." I know I look for weirdness where there actually is none. For example, just because someone cooks an egg in a frying pan does not mean they have a mystical connection with the goat Pan in my book. But I was still groggy and it really startled me. Anyway, it's a nice passage :

From *Flush* by Virginia Woolf:

"Writing…" Miss Barrett once exclaimed after a morning's toil. "Writing, writing…" After all, she may have thought, do words say everything? Can words say anything? Do not words destroy the symbol that lies beyond the reach of words? Once at least Miss Barrett seems to have found it so. She was lying, thinking; she had forgotten Flush altogether and her thoughts were so sad that the tears fell upon the pillow. Then suddenly a hairy head was pressed against her; large bright eyes shone in hers; and she started. Was it Flush, or was it Pan? Was she no longer an invalid in Wimpole Street, but a Greek nymph in some dim grove in Arcady? And did the bearded god himself press his lips to hers? For a moment she was transformed; she was a nymph and Flush was Pan. The sun burnt and love blazed. But suppose Flush had been able to speak — would he not have said something sensible about the potato disease in Ireland?"

Photo of Virginia Woolf above.

John Burns   In his 70s, he gained fame as a marksman in the Civil War. He once met Abraham Lincoln, his hero.

If you look closely at the photo of the Whiting House (on page 2 of this "about the book" section) near the house to the left of the porch stands a child. For some reason, I got it in my head that that was Martin. Using Affinity Photo, I zoomed in on just that one figure and this is what I got:

18

Kenn Amdahl on the porch of "the Whiting house" (by then known as "the Amdahl house"). Photo taken early 1950s.

Picture of a young white goat with one brown ear I found on the Internet, Jan 13, 2022. Apparently, it's possible https://www.centreaudiovocal.com/

Keisha and Fritz

behind them, the "under the porch" area

This is Gertrude Simmons Bonnin, born in 1876 to a Yankton Sioux mother and white father. I'd never heard of her or seen her picture until after I finished writing this book, but when I saw this photo I immediately thought, geez, this could be Sapania's more-enlightened sister.

Gertrude attended a Quaker school and later changed her name to Zitkala-Sa, which translates as "Red Bird." She became an influential writer and musician in the early 1900s. A fierce advocate for Native Americans, in 1926, she founded the National Council of American Indians hoping to redress Native American grievances. Her own writing is still available, and so is a 2019 biography called "Red Bird, Red Power."

I've always been uneasy that my "bad guy" is a woman, and a Native American woman at that. I hate to perpetuate stereotypes and apologize if my book tended to do that. It was not intentional. Good people and bad people come in all flavors, all shapes and sizes. Sooner or later we realize that many bad folks look just like that guy in the mirror.

I hope to learn more about powerful, positive, and interesting Native Americans as well as other forgotten women (including Zitkala-Sa and Ethel Smyth) of all nationalities.

On the table next to young Martin's bed, along with Ivanhoe and Dracula, Charles notices a book called Spun Yarn by Morgan Robertson. Robertson later got briefly famous for his book about a huge ocean liner called the Titan that sank after it hit an iceberg. Many details were weirdly similar to the Titanic tragedy, but he published it fourteen years before the Titanic sank. He wrote other books that also seem prescient, including Spun Yarn, a collection of short stories. I haven't read anything the man wrote, and by the time I discovered him I'd already chased down

way too many rabbit holes so I just walked away. But I could not resist mentioning his 1898 story "Slumbers of a Soul." even though it was published a year after Martin's "death." Surely one can take such liberties in a work of fiction.

Late 1950s. Two old friends who both lived on the same hill in Westminster, Colorado

21

Prairie Dog O'Byrne and his team of elk, "Thunder and Buttons" in Colorado, in the 1890s.

March 14, 2022

From my son Paul:

hey dad, I started reading your latest book today. I don't remember what year you kept getting your inspirations from but this photo appeared on my Facebook feed today from 1895 and it seemed oddly relevant.-Paul

BIG HORN BASIN BUILDER IS DEAD

Whiting Constructed Wyoming Irrigation System.

Denver, Jan. 7.—(P)—Frank Herbert Whiting, 78, who built the first electrical car in Denver, died last Friday in Seattle, friends learned Tuesday.

He was born in Mount Pleasant, Ia., and came to Denver in 1889. He constructed the Colfax avenue electric railroad which replaced a horse car route in Denver. Later he planned the Denver-Interurban. Construction was halted by the panic of 1893.

In 1898 Mr. Whiting built a railroad connecting French and Dawson in Alaska. Later he built a railroad from El Paso, Texas, into Mexico. His greatest engineering achievement was construction of the Big Horn Basin irrigation system in Wyoming.

Mr. Whiting married Millah Cherrie of Mount Pleasant. Her daughter accompanied Theodore Roosevelt on the River of Doubt trip. Mrs. Whiting died 12 years ago.

Funeral services will be held here Wednesday. Three daughters and three sons survive Mr. Whiting, among them H. C. Whiting of Yakima, Wash., and R. T. Whiting, of Seattle, Wash.

Frank Herbert Whiting, as an older man

Thanks to:

Sandra Johnston / Library Asst. II

Alaska State Library Historical Collections

PO Box 110571

Juneau, AK 99811-0571

Billings Gazette

Billings, Montana

08 Jan 1936, Wed • Page 12

After reading this obit, in Jan, 2022, I googled *River of Doubt*. Candice Millard's 2005 book of that title documents Roosevelt's adventure. The book won awards and sold many copies, and sounds great, I've ordered a copy and look forward to reading it. -- kenn

Update, March 12, 2022: I bought River of Doubt but haven't read it yet. Its index doesn't list anyone named Whiting. But the chief naturalist on the expedition was George Kruck Cherrie (photo to the right). My ghost Martin's mother's maiden name was Cherrie. The obit writer made a mistake: Millah's brother George, not her daughter, went with Roosevelt. In fact, he was the main naturalist on Teddy Roosevelt's "River of Doubt" expedition. George was a famous explorer and scientist and I immediately felt a bit of kinship

with him. He often worked for natural history museums, enjoyed taxidermy and birds (just like I did as a kid. My father printed business cards for my "Westminster Museum of Natural History" that I maintained on the front porch); several species are named after him including "Cherrie's Tanager." His schedule of jobs and expeditions suggest he could very easily have visited Martin while he was alive, maybe spent a summer there. He might have slept in my old bedroom, the one I imagine Martin also occupied. George died at age 82 about a year before I was born. In 1927 the Boy Scouts of America created the title Honorary Scout and named Cherrie as one of the 19 people awarded the title that first year. Others included Charles Lindberg, Kermit Roosevelt, and Orville Wright. Obviously, it's tempting to add another teensy little scene or two, but I am resisting. I did let Martin call him "Uncle Kruck." George wrote several books, including Dark Trails about his adventures. Worldcat.org says the U. of Oregon library has a copy…

The "River of Doubt" team.
Far left, George Cherrie; center Teddy Roosevelt; far right Kermit Roosevelt

Update: I read *River of Doubt*. Lovely book, well written, very dramatic and dangerous expedition.

June 26, 2022

Friday I woke in the middle of the night. When that happens, sometimes I recall a random scene from my current writing project and play it out in my brain. Friday night I chose the one where the teenagers accost young Charles at the Pillar of Fire and he summons an owl to attack the kid from above. I enjoyed the scene, then fell asleep. I don't dwell on the soporific effects of my writing.

The next morning, I took Cheryl to Lowe's. I had to get some two by three boards, she wanted to get some plants. Lowe's has a huge atrium-type room with a very tall glass ceiling and a big opening to the outside. It's a cool room; there are rows and rows of flowers, plus other garden items. Sometimes birds wander in and flit about until they remember how to get out. I easily found Cheryl in there when my own shopping was done. She said she'd had the weirdest experience. A black bird that looked like a small crow had dive bombed her and whacked her on the head. She could feel its little talons trying to grab her hair. It did that three times. Remarkably, it didn't frighten her, just surprised her.

So now I'm under orders to only visualize pleasant parts of the book.

As I write this, I notice an actual crow is cawing out in my yard…

Just wanted to share that with you.

kenn

December 11, 2022

I've been reading the book from cover to cover, trying to trim extra sentences and correct small flaws. I've given up on fixing the large flaws but I want to be done with the project.

Near the end, Charles wants to write a note to Martin's father about the pills he hopes to give him. To give himself credibility, Charles implies that Edison is involved. This morning I thought, hey, I wonder if there was a famous biologist in 1896 or 97 that would make more sense? After five minutes with Mr. Google, I discovered a guy named Ernest Duchesne. Turns out, he discovered penicillin in 1896 and published his findings but nobody paid much attention to it at the time. So Edison is out, Duchesne is in. Sorry, Tom.

Regarding the title, January 25, 2023

When I started writing this book in 2008, its working title was "Small Magic." As the book neared completion, I discovered Terry Brooks named a collection of short stories Small Magic in 2021. I also learned there's a "Small Magic" about micro-dosing, and another about quilting, plus a novel by Billy Coffey. To further discourage using the name, in 2018 Elizabeth

Gilbert released "Big Magic." Brooks and Gilbert probably have different readers, but either set would assume I swiped the idea to ride their impressive coat-tails. My new working title became "Echoes of a Distant Bell." That seemed pleasantly mysterious and no one else had snagged it. In 2022 I shortened it to "A Distant Bell." I used that until last week. After I got a proof copy of this book using that title, one last online search revealed that someone else used that title a few months ago. As of this moment, I can't find another book named "The Manitou Bell," so that's what the book is now called. I should probably hurry to release it while the title is available.

Kenn Amdahl has been a businessman, musician, and author. He spent most of his adult life in Colorado and now lives in Eugene, Oregon with his wife Cheryl.

Clearwater Publishing Company, Inc. has published the following books written by Kenn Amdahl:

There Are No Electrons: Electronics for Earthlings

Algebra Unplugged (with Jim Loats, Ph.D.)

The Land of Debris and the Home of Alfredo

Calculus for Cats (with Jim Loats, Ph.D.)

Jumper and the Bones

Stones in the Water (poetry)

Revenge of the Pond Scum: Searching for the Causes of ALS and Alzheimer's Disease

Joy Writing: Discover and Develop Your Creative Voice

The Wordguise Alembic (collection of blog posts, e-book only)

Jumper and the Apple Crate

The Manitou Bell

Most of these titles remain in print and available from bookstores everywhere (although the store may need to place a special order from Ingram, a huge wholesaler that bookstores routinely use). They are also available from online stores like Amazon.com.

Website: ClearwaterPublishing.com

Kenn's songs: KennAmdahl.com

www.ingramcontent.com/pod-product-compliance
Lightning Source LLC
Chambersburg PA
CBHW022244020726
47496CB00004B/1049